The German Numbers Woman

BY THE SAME AUTHOR

Fiction
*Saturday Night and Sunday
  Morning*
*The Loneliness of the Long Distance
  Runner*
The General
Key to the Door
The Ragman's Daughter
The Death of William Posters
A Tree on Fire
Guzman, Go Home
A Start in Life
Travels in Nihilon
Raw Material
Men, Women and Children
The Flame of Life
The Widower's Son
The Storyteller
The Second Chance and Other Stories
Her Victory
The Lost Flying Boat
Down From the Hill
Life Goes On
Out of the Whirlpool
The Open Door
Last Loves
Leonard's War
Snowstop
Collected Stories
Alligator Playground
The Broken Chariot

Non-fiction
Life Without Armour
  (autobiography)

Poetry
The Rats and Other Poems
*A Falling Out of Love
  and Other Poems*
*Love in the Environs of Voronezh and
  Other Poems*
Storm and Other Poems
Snow on the North Side of Lucifer
Sun Before Departure
Tides and Stone Walls
Collected Poems

Plays
All Citizens are Soldiers
  (with Ruth Fainlight)
Three Plays

Essays
Mountains and Caverns

For Children
*The City Adventures of Marmalade
  Jim*
Big John and the Stars
The Incredible Fencing Fleas
Marmalade Jim on the Farm
Marmalade Jim and the Fox

ALAN SILLITOE

The German Numbers Woman

Flamingo
An Imprint of HarperCollins*Publishers*

Flamingo
An Imprint of HarperCollins*Publishers*
77–85 Fulham Palace Road,
Hammersmith, London W6 8JB

www.**fire**and**water**.com

Published by Flamingo 1999
1 3 5 7 9 8 6 4 2

A catalogue record for this book
is available from the British Library

ISBN 0 00 225960 5

Set in Galliard by Palimpsest Book Production Limited,
Polmont, Stirlingshire
Printed and bound in Great Britain by
Caledonian International Book Manufacturing Ltd, Glasgow

To Ronald Schlachter

'What then, if there were no Capacity existing in the Universe? – Impossible – But if these are all the Species of Physical Motion, it follows, that WITHOUT CAPACITY there can be no such Motions.'

James Harris *Philosophical Arrangements*, 1775.

Part One

Observations from the Heaviside Layer

ONE

Gulls skirmished the sloping roofs and chimney pots, squabbled and reconnoitred, a noise like nothing on earth, or in heaven either. They'd been fractiously squealing before his birth, and would do so for ever after, Howard grinning that even the rank breath of Chernobyl hadn't pulled the buggers down. Such sounds lifted the heart whenever he came out of doors, though sometimes they were heard inside as well.

He paused, envying their freedom – what luck! what style! – head back as if to find the cause of such worried belligerence. Disputing for air at the ends of their wing tips, they mistrusted each other with almost human cries, while performing exquisite aerobatics.

He closed the garden gate before going downhill, aware of how many paces were needed between each step, arcing the white stick before him. The news had said it was 15 August. They always told you the date, an item worth knowing because it meant that although there was one day less to live a new one had even so arrived, and as long as that process went on he would see no reason for complaint: To be halfway happy was to be among the happy of the world.

Someone coming up edged aside to let him freeway by. A woman, because of the perfume. She was youngish, but her breath was hard at the ascent, and two plastic bags of shopping rustled against her legs, someone who didn't know him, and too puffed on her short cut over the hill to say a word.

Pottering his slow way down, the tall greystoned houses made gaps to let the wind through. His cheeks were wind vanes, he a perambulating anomemeter – a long-remembered word which caused a smile. It always did. He used it every day on his way into town, carefully noting the serpentine route towards the beach.

3

No need to beware of traffic, since only pedestrians came up and down. The breeze touching his cheeks was southwesterly, to a degree or so, and more than welcome for its balm. Such days couldn't come too often, but they soon enough wouldn't until next year. He'd expected tonic weather but had cheated a bit on the wind, having taken all details yesterday on his typewriter, straight from Portishead, words tinkling through at top strength on the new radio Laura had bought when her National Savings Certificates fell due.

'Morning, Howard.'

That's me, but no need to stop. 'Morning, Arthur. Your bag's heavy today.'

A laugh. 'Not for long. Nothing for you, though.'

'I can live without it,' which, sounding harsh, called for another word or two: 'It's welcome when it drops onto the mat, except for the bills.'

Arthur opened a gate, the latch stiff from corrosion. 'They all say that.'

No mail was good mail, as far as Howard was concerned, and he could take whatever news he wanted from the wireless, though even that was a case of here today and stale tomorrow. A man went by, in a hurry to go down, giving a whiff of sweat. Off to cash his giro, so he would be slower on the way up, especially with a pint or two inside him. That's how a lot live these days, too many in a town like this, though there's work in summer when the holidays get going.

Good when the sky and your wife look kindly on you, allied to sunshine which gave zest. Laura liked to read his weather printouts, never ceasing to wonder at his ability. Magic, he told her, to keep the priceless spirit going. And magic it was that bound them after so many years, for what man would grumble against Fate when someone like Laura had taken over his existence, and he'd let her do so because there had been no option?

The massive presence of the church was felt to the left, a bulwark flanking his darkness, the picture accurately grey. A door opened, and someone passed in, as Laura now and again did for Evensong on Sunday. She needed such musical platitudes to reassure and warm her soul, a satisfying dimension beyond dull life in the house, and continually looking after him. Last time in such a place was on church parade the day before his crash landing, and he'd felt no pull to go into one since.

The small Peugeot was parked at the bottom of the steps, and he touched the wing mirror, stooped at the door hinge and imagined he caught a whiff of Laura's hair. Damned sure he did, on straightening his back and walking with more vigour.

He yearned to spring along with speed, swing his stick and cry them out of the way, but knew he couldn't, must not, too many excursionist bodies dogging the way. All the same, nothing gives a straighter back than misfortune. The one-way High Street was all obstacles and pitfalls, so concentrate on the map o' the mind and keep the dopplers going. Swing the direction-finding stick along the shop fronts, with smells of meat, bread, furniture, maggots and fishing tackle, hoping not to put his boots in any dogshit, such peril the shame and bane of his life, because Laura (forgive me, Lord, for I can't know what I do) had to make good. Rare was the day in this dog-loving town when he didn't feel that sinking and sliding sensation underfoot, and know she would have the job of wiping the mess away with newspaper, and scrubbing out the stink with Dettol. Sometimes on fine days he would sit in the garden and call for the cleaning kit to do it himself, before coming into the house.

Thinking on better things than churches and dogshit now that he was in traffic, he let the stick go in front, a left and right weave, rhythming a morse letter on the ground, tap-tap-tap-tapping at the kerb, a regular Gene Kelly but never, he hoped, an SOS. All the same, cars go too fast, often not stopping at [Hore] Belisha's beacons. A shade of warmth from the sun, he unbuttoned his jacket, brown she had said though he knew already by the pockets, and a neat diamond darn after catching it on a twig while digging in the garden.

He laughed inwardly at life's challenges. That lorry ought to get its carburettor seen to. The escarpment into the gutter was measured by his stick, a precipice out of *The Lost World*. Or he was a land surveyor in Lilliput, but it was there right enough, and he could only wait.

'Come on, I'll see you across.' A stranger from the world of the seeing usually helped, but now and again he relished the life-and-death gamble of doing it alone, a trip as lethal as that last raid over Germany, should a rogue vehicle strike. He would count steps to the middle of the motor torrent and stand a few seconds testing his luck, or as if to get breath (hating people to think he was afraid, or didn't know where he was going) but really to taunt God or Fate, and find out whether his number was on a ferocious little ginger-pink hatchback given by a thirteen-year-old who had just stolen it – though by that time the colour wouldn't matter – swivelling like Ben Hur from the sea front and going mindlessly inland. In which case someone would pull the card from his inside pocket, find the home number inscribed by Laura, and phone for her to collect his remains in the biggest plastic bag she could sort out from under the stairs. Macabre, but tempting to think about in such a dull life. They had always brought their thoughts into the open, though this picture was a fantasy to be kept on the secret list.

'That's kind of you.'

She held his arm. 'You'll be safe with me.'

'I'm sure I shall.' Mostly women did this sort of thing, and he wondered what he would do if – on reaching the side closer to the sea and, talking in her angel's voice, the small warm hand still firmly in his – she led him along meandering flower paths to a paradise only she knew about, to an utterly different life wherein he would be able to see.

No matter how well arranged a man's existence he still must dream, secret dreams and unexpressed thoughts forming the necessary backbone for survival in a sometimes meaningless world. Noise hit the senses like blades as cars came and went. 'You're being very kind,' he said to her.

'I like to help. I would want to be, if I was like you, wouldn't I?'

'I hope you never are,' he smiled.

'Yes, but you don't know, do you?'

'I don't think you do. What's your name?'

'Janet.'

He almost smelt the fact when people were embarrassed at doing a good deed, not seeing why they should be. Sensibility to another's needs had many reasons, one being guilt at knowing they were so much better off – as indeed they were. Or did they sense his extra power because he had adapted to living in darkness? Inner light at least was more vivid, though power beyond his understanding wasn't always what he wanted, and he would willingly have traded it for an occasional glimpse of street or seashore. Maybe people thought he had an ideal life in that his affliction would allow no other cares to gall him but, whatever mixture of guilt, fear or envy it might be, how could such deadly sins matter if a kindly action resulted?

She released her hand. 'Will you be all right?'

'You've been very kind.' To sit over a cup of coffee with her would make a memorable day. 'Off to do your shopping are you, Janet?'

'No, I'm going to meet my boyfriend. He works in the arcades, mending the machines.'

'Thank you, then, and I hope you have a nice day' – for putting such notions into my head, though better not think so much, unless I want to get run over. Her light and quick footsteps were lost among others, crowding into the High Street, holidaymakers, mostly, out from boarding houses and hotels, or walking down from the station.

A poor kid got smacked for craving an ice-cream. There was a double stretch to cross where two streets merged. A dog barked, at what he would never know, but its throat grated, so it was on a lead, giving a shriek of despair at some minor loss, dragged from a rancid smell perhaps, or begrudged a tailwag with a possible companion. He stood, and laughed, dryly and alone, in tune with the animal's moans of commiseration as it passed the pet shop.

The studs of the crossing made a wide enough runway, and the baker's smell on the other side was a beam to draw him over. Ten times more traffic than forty years ago. A car stopped at seeing him, a big one this, station wagon maybe, certainly not a Mini. Here goes, and he went, a lift of his stick to the motorist, who pipped his horn – a vocal handshake. Another car stopped, this time small, all considerations shown, though he was glad to tap the lip of the kerb: the one-engined blind old kite had landed, the beam approach of studs and smell had worked, flying control had rolled out its expertise, just how he liked it.

Ozone caressed his nostrils from the one unmistakable direction, an endless horizon of green and blue, duck-egg blue maybe, a touch of turquoise, and the odd high cumulus above the line. A sail now and again might speck the water, anything from white to orange, though the fishing boats were already long back from their night's work. He could smell that, too, another odour of eternal life, healthy as well, as he crunched over shingle and picked up the tang of tar from the tall huts called tackle boxes in which nets were hung to dry.

So it was easy, as always, to know where he was among the radar of aromas, familiar from years of living in the same place, gratifying that in nil visibility he could make his way at a sure pace to where he wanted to go. From rightwards came the shrill calls of children living out their lives on the boating lake and in the paddling pool, and the muted clank of the miniature railway making its slow way up and down, all sounds providing cross bearings to his navigation system, perfect cocked hats to fix his location from the constant rush of traffic behind.

At this point, between the huts and the broken concrete pier, he always thought of when Laura had led him here for the first time. Every day it came to him, as if there had been little progress in their lives since. Hands firmly held, he had smelled the tears before they came to her eyes, on him remarking that he could taste the salt water turning into spray from the sullen waves falling line by line onto the stones. A common observation, not one to make her cry, he would have thought, but she hurried him back up to the house, as if she found it too painful to be seen walking out with him, husband and wife at twenty-two, not a word from her on the ascent. Halfway, he assumed it was because of the summer rain that fell in plates and drenched them after a few yards.

Once in the door she put his stick away. He saw her as the young girl she was, how she threw the stick rather, though in those days people weren't counted as young at such an age. The stick flew at the wall and bounced. She took off his saturated jacket and waistcoat, and sat him down, breathless from the climb though he was not, but he felt a light before his eyes as if about to get his sight back. She played Elgar's *Enigma Variations* on the radiogram. He'd often told her how much he liked it, so she'd gone out the day before to get the records for his birthday, not for another month.

He heard the angry crash of the curtains sliding to, then – silence but for the duet of their breathing. She put on one of the records to hide whatever devastating emotion still blighted from the beach. 'This is for you, darling' pulling him roughly to his feet. 'Only for you.' Salt tears again, as they listened and held each other, mixing with his to run down both faces, an amalgam of happiness as much as despair for a plight that would lock more firmly than any marriage.

He couldn't talk, blocked at the throat, a dumb tongue adding to his blindness. She had brought the records as a surprise, and the colours of music flared and expanded across white space, lighting every dark corner, his heart buffeted by the sweet strong music. Neither could she talk, didn't want to, pulled and pushed, kisses of possessive disregard for that one time which her love had to go through, noises meeting with his, no words possible, a dull erotic burning conquering them both, taking them away from house and seascape and the downs behind. Each other's clothes were clawed off, too hot in their passion to wait, that must have been it, they fell onto the carpet wailing and lost in a maelstrom of despair and pleasure that even now they hadn't fully learned to separate, while knowing they had been made for each other even before birth.

More than thirty years ago. Kids, they might be called. He tapped a bigger stone than most, pushed a hump of seawrack out of the way. That's what we were, yet it was all so dammed lucid still, and why did it come back every time he stood on this spot, the anchor stone of his life, and hers as well? Little more than twenty, how grown up we felt, and were, as if we'd lived a whole life already; and had, because there'd been no more since, not knowing we were set for an eternity of same days.

A gull came close, painted him with a rush of air from wing tips, slicing away the mark of Cain perhaps, or to stick two good eyes back beneath his lids as a gift from the gods, though even one would do. He envied Polyphemus at times and, hearing Laura's divine and measured voice as evening by evening she read through the *Odyssey* from the other side of the fireplace, cursed the brutal Odysseus for taking a burning fire brand to gouge out that one sensitive solitary eye, while supposing he would have done the same to save his friends.

He swung his stick in case another curious gull thought him a piece of rock. Memories had ossified in him, since he'd stopped having them from the age of twenty. Cloud hid the sun, cooling the air,

senses sharp enough to pick out the arrowing sloosh of incoming tide
driving between the two halves of the broken harbour pier. The past
was nagging even more than usual today. When he first met Laura at
the station dance he'd seen her as a young rather severe girl, white
blouse fastened to the neck, brown cardigan open to show her shape.
She smelled sweet, hair freshened by shampoo. His aircrew insignia and
sergeant's stripes were newly sewn on, and he felt second to none,
though slightly drunk from the cider.

They went around in the quickstep, and he knew it was polite to talk:
'Would you like me to be your cavalier?' Before she could answer he
went on, pell mell to obliterate such a daft beginning: 'Now there's a
remark to strike you, or it will when you wonder in the future how we
first met.'

Nor had he ever needed to wonder, but why had he blathered such
triteness when not really believing there could be any hope?

He had been blessedly wrong. She didn't laugh or scorn. 'Yes, you
can be my cavalier.'

She had waited for him night after night to come back from raids,
and then he returned a different person to the one who had set out,
but in the hospital she took his hand and, through the confusion of
his darkness, said once more that he would be her cavalier, forever.

There were days when he felt the bow was taut, as taut as before
the arrow flies. No explanation, but a tightening of anguish which was
there when it shouldn't have been, making this day different though
in what way from others he couldn't know. A clock began striking,
later beats muffled by car noise. Ten o'clock, in any case. His heart
missed a turn, marked time, carried on. As always he would recross the
satisfyingly perilous roads, trawl along the High Street to get Laura's
Guardian, and reach home in time for their morning coffee.

TWO

One day he'll fall. Blind men do. He would fall a long way. Or would he hit the ground like a baby and not hurt himself? On the other hand, why should he fall? If he did maybe she would be there to see. If not she would hear about it. You could turn off a tap but not stop the invasion of your thoughts. One day either he or she would die, but who would go first was impossible to say. The time could be a long way off, but the problem was a cruel one to ponder, so she preferred not to, because wanting him to live long could mean she would drop dead first. There'd be no one to guard him then. Best not to think, since the future belonged to nobody. She watched from the front room window, as always when he set out. He would know what was in her mind. 'And my life will be finished,' she said.

'Oh no it won't' – his tone a balance between humour and annoyance, the closest he would allow. 'In any case, that's as maybe, and good old maybe is always unpredictable.'

Why do I let such idiocies through my head? No one was steadier on his feet, and his health was robust. He seemed forty rather than sixty. 'And so do you,' he said when she told him.

He had climbed more steps and hills than she could remember. Choosing holidays, he opted always for inland, as far from the coast as they could get, somewhere in the Derbyshire hills, the Malverns, or Scotland. He was never happier than when they set out after breakfast from the hotel, walking a path between trees and bushes, into the open of higher land.

'It's like being in the clouds,' he said. 'It's like flying in an open cockpit.' Then his talk would stop, and he would go on, locked in for a while until: 'At least I can feel the wind, and that's worth a lot.

11

There's heather in it. Flowers and trees as well. The flowers are over there. Let's look at them.' He stroked the stalks, stamens and petals, bending down for a closer look, touching without damage.

The bed hardly needed making, they slept so deeply in their separate dreams, but she pulled it apart for freshness. The room was large and gloomy, backing against the cliff. She shook the sheets smooth, pulled blankets straight and folded them in, banged both pillows into shape. At least the little iron fireplace when filled and glowing took out the damp of winter, the room a delight to be in then, shadows on the walls at dusk. Howard couldn't see them, though said he could, at the sparking of the flames, lying in bed with a three-day flu last winter. 'The first days out of action,' he said, 'since the crash.'

Two people couldn't be ill in the same house, so no debilitating flu or colds for her. Howard knew this only too well, and swore he would keep fit till his dying day.

After bumping the Electrolux around the living room she noted its bag was full. Hadn't emptied it for months, so unclipped the top, lifted out the paper container bulging with dust, and walked through to thump it into the kitchen bin. Fitted with another, the nozzle sucked perfectly, though there was little enough to feed on.

She cleaned the house while he was out, easier than when weather kept him in, even though he sat in the wireless room, as he called it, listening to his eternal and mysterious morse. She liked him to go out because he was always more cheerful when he got back. He was like a baby to look after, but would die of shame if she told him. Which he might have assumed was why she hadn't had any, not knowing the reason had been hers more than his.

She fought against tolerating vain regrets. Regrets poisoned the soul, and the soul seemed frail enough at times, Howard knowing he can't – she thought – tell me how nice I look, though he was able to at the beginning and did so in such a way as to last me for life. But I always dress for him and look smart, so that people will think the same when I walk out with him. And I dress as well as I can when in the house because it makes me feel good, and there's always the thought that if there was a sudden miraculous peeling back of his blindness, I would want him to see me at my best.

It was essential to tidy up so that he would know where everything was. If an ashtray or chair, or one of his three pipes was out of place, his system for getting about without knocking anything over would, he said, go for a burton, so she took care that nothing did. If he asked where something was it would be that even she couldn't find it. The house was his universe, every object one of the innumerable stars that lit up in his darkness for guidance. As long as he could find the domestic radio, however, and the record player to put on a piece by Elgar or Gustav Holst, all was right in the world.

She cleared the plates, all shining and stacked. He would be back for coffee, the newspaper under his arm. 'Read me whatever you think I might find interesting.' There was usually one item or another, to be marked with a pencil and reserved for tea time or after supper.

She kept two pencils by the telephone, in case the point of one snapped off while writing a message. Sharpening both, though they had hardly been used, she threw the shavings into the bin. If she went out Howard could just legibly write the number of anyone who called and wanted to hear from her. Sometimes they descended the hill together, but mostly she let him go. He wandered everywhere, and came back happy, though occasionally exhausted. Or so it seemed. He always denied it. When she went with him he became irritated by the smallest thing, such as imagining she resented going slow for him. It galled him, but not her. When they got home he was burning with inadequacy, even after all these years, as if thinking he had failed to lead her to somewhere wonderful, or hadn't brought her home to a heaven more alluring than the one they had left.

They talked about it. She never asked, but he volunteered. 'The secrets of my blasted heart,' he said, 'are all I have to give you. I want to be more than your ball and chain of flesh. I want to lead you to I don't know where. But it's a yearning, you see, and it gets me at the heart every so often. I can't think why.'

'That's silly,' she said. 'You've brought me there already.' She proved it with a kiss, for it was true enough, had to be, after living so long in stasis, never moving beyond the vivid days of their youth. For his sake there was much loving she had to feel, yet did so with neither thought nor effort.

On one level they lived beyond hope, but what loss was that? There never had been any after his crash, and being without hope was the unspoken compact, the firmest base there was, reassuring and reinforcing. To live without hope was less of a sin, and less cruel, because the peace it gave was the bedrock of an understanding which made them feel ageless to each other.

In the small room side on to the house she dusted his heavy black-cased wireless with its curving multicoloured window and thick control wheel for changing stations. The new radio she had sent for from Derbyshire lay by its side, a key pad in front, and the brass morse key which he played from time to time. 'My therapy,' he said, 'for when I want to shift the black dog from my shoulders. The black dog hates the sound of morse. It terrifies him. He runs back to his hidey-hole and leaves me alone.'

When he sat with the door closed, earphones clamped on, he was in a world which nobody could share, a world in which ears were everything and lack of sight not an issue. Only his rounded back was visible through the glass panel, animally moving as he put what he was hearing onto the heavy sit-up-and-beg old capital-letter typewriter. The electricity of a modern one would, he said, distort the reception, and make it no easier to use.

Nothing needed to be touched, a stack of paper in its usual position, a silver propelling pencil by its side which he'd kept from his schooldays, maybe as a symbol of hope (no one could be entirely without it) that one day enough sight would come back for him to handwrite what he heard.

Once when he was out she'd polished the brass parts of his morse key to a brilliant shine, wondering if he would notice. He did: 'I can see it glowing. Looks wonderful, I'm sure. Thank you, my love.' But of course, he had picked up the Duraglit smell.

The ashtray needed emptying, dottle and match sticks overspilling. He often did the job himself, anything to help, but she took it to the sink for a scouring and brought it back. The wastepaper basket was usually full of discarded transcripts, mere formulae to her, ciphers and letter codes she would never ask him to explain, even if he could, but the last few days he had hardly been in his wireless room, a worrying

14

loss of interest, as if no longer drawn by his alternative world, without which he could neither fuel nor sustain his own. Yet after such periods he always went back to it, and she wondered which was more real to him.

When the wireless didn't hold him he brooded, though he would use a different word. Lassitude was obvious in every bone. He sat for hours, unable to move and then, not knowing how or why, he got up, took cap and stick, and set off down the steps, to walk for miles along the beach and about the town. When he came cheerfully into the house he said he hadn't felt at all tired on his expedition, which at least proved that such lack of energy hadn't been due to illness. 'But then, it never would be,' she said aloud, her palm pressing the grinder whose noise for a moment crushed out her thoughts.

It was as if a shadow had slid across the window and come into the room. She knew what it was. The heart was as fluctuating as the weather. Only a looking glass fixed its effects on the face, as much as anything could, just as the weather was still, only a moment before altering for better or worse. If you accepted such rhythms, as of course you had to, existence was tolerable, hardly ever unpleasant for long.

On first hearing the news of his blindness she said she would never look in a mirror again, because Howard could not, but there had to be one in the house otherwise he would wonder why, and she would have to tell him the reason.

The mirror showed everything she didn't want to know about herself, so she avoided it as far as possible, only able to look by persuading herself that the image was of somebody else: easy with the small make-up used to treat a glass off-handedly, as if it had no ability to destroy her equanimity, as nothing must be allowed to since recovering from her abortion.

Her whole past with Howard, their entire life in fact, was connected to an event he was never to know about. The episode, forgotten for months at a time, had lately corroded her with haunting affect, the shadow almost meteorological – to use one of Howard's words – in its unpleasantness. She didn't see any justice in it, felt she had paid the price in dealing with the event all those years ago. Sensing the threat now, she let the murky pictures run through her mind so as to get

15

rid of them sooner, though knowing they wouldn't pass so willingly, having a power greater than her own.

The sciatic pain was as if a scalpel had gone through the nerves of her lower back. She sat by the Formica-topped table to reinforce herself, to stiffen her body like a box hedge against the wind. The colours were always dark from that time, but the day it happened had been sunny. She had called on him at his large gewgaw-strewn flat on Baker Street, passing while in town to say hello.

Dear Uncle Charles, she had known him from birth. 'Let me show you around this rambling old place,' he said. There was no reason to say no but if she had would it have been different? He had been watching her, and waiting. She was happy, and unknowing. In the bedroom she had no chance. He was a tall lumbering man, and she was too shocked to shout or scream. The bang across the head, and his cry – almost a shriek – that she should be 'sensible', made it impossible except to let him do what he wanted.

He babbled, while holding her in a maniacal grip, that he had needed her (his words) for as long as he could remember. He was incomprehensible. She had loved him as an uncle for his eternal kindness, though not in this way, if this was love, which he swore it was.

He said afterwards that she had encouraged him. The violence that was done to her was meaningless but meant everything. He had made her, and the blood proved it. Everything must be kept quiet, he said afterwards, a secret between them alone. He paid for the abortion, arranged it all, but only ever touched her that one time, terrified at what he had done. A prostitute would have been cheaper, but it was her he wanted. The operation (hard to say the real word) was so botched that she couldn't have children even if she had wanted.

She ran the whole thing through, hoping it would be goodbye, at least for a while. Charles had died of cancer, brought on, she liked to think, by his guilt, and grief which often at the time seemed genuine enough, and reinforced by his suffering which she could hardly bear to watch when her unknowing parents took her to see him in the hospital, though nowadays she burned with shame at having felt such sorrow. How could it have happened so that no one in the family knew? He was so skilled, or frightened, and she so compliant at evading and avoiding all signs of distress. If there had been more than one side to her then, there was only one now.

She went to church occasionally, hoping to retrieve her faith, but none had come back as yet. Howard thought it was for spiritual comfort due to the isolation of their lives, and to vary her days. They had no secrets above the level at which she chose to live, and at which she had decided he must live. The shame and disgrace would never be told.

In his will Charles had made over the house for her to live in with Howard after they were married. 'It's a fit place for a hero,' he said, laughing slyly as he sliced the seed cake on the tea tray when he told her. 'And besides that, you might call it just one more bit for the war effort on my part. After all, I have this flat in town, and nobody needs more than one place.' He had been in Whitehall throughout the war, so she didn't see how he could feel guilty about that as well.

They stood in the rain by his grave side, and heard the panegyrics at the memorial service, Howard squeezing her hand at each remark about the dead man's generosity and manliness. Even before death Charles had sent money to augment Howard's pension, and then in his will left an income for them as well.

Not to accept anything would have led Howard to ask why. He reacted sensibly to their prosperity, and was grateful. 'We must keep Charles' photograph always on a table in the living room. He's been marvellous, and deserves as much.' And so they did, but she bought an identical frame for the blank side of the picture, a white sheet instead of a face, not wanting to see his staring grey eyes and bushy moustache (sheer black, though it must have been dyed) whenever she turned her head, a reminder too hard to bear. If visitors or any of the family called – rare events – she made sure to replace the real thing, in case comment was made. Not having a frame at all was impossible, because Howard could feel his way to every object in the room.

They lived just that much better by having the house and what Charles had given but, all the same, she was never free of the feeling that she had sold her soul to the devil by not having told Howard about the abortion before her marriage – there, she had said the word now – though if she had there might have been no Howard, such an event impossible for him to live with.

The recall passed at its usual slow rate, but her hands shook and she felt unsafe on her legs while flicking the kettle switch and pouring coffee grains into the pot.

THREE

Ebony the cat came into the wireless room, attracted as usual by squeals of morse, as if a flight of colourful and unheeding small birds had broken loose from their cage. Howard kept the door a few inches open so that he wouldn't feel entirely cut off from Laura and the rest of the house. She liked it that way, though with earphones clamped on he was deaf to whatever might happen beyond his aetherised world.

Sometimes he took the phones off and pulled out the plug, let morse ring from the speaker and ripple through the house, telling the walls he was alive to their constrictions, though hoping such self-indulgent noise didn't worry Laura.

He dropped an arm to compensate the disappointed cat, fingers riffling through fur, thinking he could tell the difference in texture while crossing from black to the small white patch near its nose, as the whorls of milk mixing with the coffee might, he imagined, be felt by a slowly stirring spoon. He could trace flowers on the wallpaper and notice where colours changed. No, it was all in the mind, except that sometimes his fingers had eyes.

She picked up the coffee cup. 'Anything interesting this morning?'

He touched her hand. 'I'm just trawling. There's a liner called the *Gracchi*, calling Rome International Radio, and getting no reply. Then again there's a Russian ship leaving England and heading for Lithuania with a hundred used cars on board. Wouldn't like to say where *they* came from.'

She took the cat for company. 'Come on, Ebony.'

His wireless room was at the weather end of the house, the wind a fine old comb-and-paper tune today. A slit of the window left open took his pipe smoke away. That's how the music was made, a howling and forlorn oratorio playing from wall to wall. So much noise gusting would disorientate his senses if he went for a walk, so it was as well to be sheltered.

Headphones back in place, he tuned in to the German Numbers Woman, who spoke continuous numbers in a tone suggesting she was the last woman on earth, enunciating from a bunker in the middle of some Eastern European forest, her voice on the edge of breathlessness, as if fearful of an assassin breaking in: 'SIEBEN – ACHT – EINS – NEUN – DREI – FUNF – VIER – ZWEI – SECHS – ACHT – EINS – SECHS – EINS – NEUN.'

On and on. She spoke in the ghostly tone of a person who might have a gun by the microphone, and Howard had listened so often to the deliberately mesmerising recitation of figures that he felt he knew much about her. The question was whether anyone else was listening, and taking down her endless numbers, and if so not only who, but what use they were making of them.

On this earth everything was for a purpose, but what hers was he could never know. Or could he? He could but go on intercepting, though he only did so now and again to check that she was still there, and she always was. She spoke on several frequencies simultaneously (he'd found her on eleven different ones already. Others he hadn't bothered to log) so her equipment was not simple. She was no pirate of the airwaves prating for the fun of it, though if she had been a classical pirate he could imagine her making people walk the plank, counting them one by one down to the sharks in her deliberate, impersonal, cold-hearted voice.

And yet, and yet, perhaps she was misjudged. By eternally speaking numbers she was merely doing her job, and not for much money, either. Occasionally the frequencies were closed down, and she was off the air for a time. Then it could be she had caught the bus like any ordinary person, and gone home to feed her children – after shopping on the way to find what treats she could buy for their supper.

She bathed them and put them to bed and sang them songs and told them stories in a voice utterly unlike that with which she shelled out numbers on the air. Her husband had left her years ago because he couldn't stand the numbers voice being used in their quarrels, the ruthlessly catalogued recriminations of his misdeeds. Life on her own was hard. With the children in bed she cleaned her tiny flat, darned and washed their clothes and, if there was half an hour to spare before sleep time, and she wasn't too done-for (she never was) she would play some Mozart or Beethoven on the record player.

Family who would have helped in her lonely life had been killed, or sent off to camps by the Russians at the end of the war, or were maybe lost in one of those air raids Howard had taken part in, sitting hour after hour at his TR1154/55 Marconi on those cold and terrifying nights during the last winter of the war, the happiest moment when, driving through the flak, the tonnage went down and the bomber lifted, and they could turn for home.

And now someone called Ingrid von Brocken came on the air to taunt him with his guilt at having, albeit at some risk, unloaded the wrath of God on her family, though she would have been only a baby at the time.

The headset brought her clearly into mind, queen of the shortwave spectrum naked under a red plastic mac reading off numbers from a pile of sheets by her left hand, the voice as always loud and precise. Maybe there was no woman at all, only an endless leftover tape playing in a forgotten East German bunker transmitting instructions to various agents. No one had thought to switch it off, current still pumped so that it would go on forever, even when all the spies were dead.

The German Numbers Woman made him sweat, so he couldn't listen for long; but she filled his darkness with Brünnhilde eyes, and a gleam of red hair which she tied back at work, though made into braids on Sunday. He couldn't think she was all that fearful because she made him see, thought no ill of her because in his world she was real and he knew her well, his only fear being that she might become bigger and more immediate than Laura. But that's another matter, he soothed himself, one between me and my conscience, letting me enjoy whatever secret compensations are available.

Somewhere she must exist, and could be utterly different to the way he imagined her, but that did not matter, because whatever he made out of the voice was solidifying grist to him. He switched on the tape recorder so that he could play the voice to Laura and ask what she thought of it.

She was knitting a beige cardigan for the winter, had been on it for weeks, the body and one arm done, halfway through the other. The work settled on her lap. 'German, isn't it? Numbers?'

'Yes, but what does it suggest?'

'I can't say. She's counting, by the sound of it. I've no idea what it can be.'

Ingrid would smile if she could hear this. 'You don't wonder what she looks like?'

'Well, I can't imagine. Ordinary, I suppose. Plain. Could be middle aged, but you can't always tell from a voice, can you?'

He switched the machine off. 'No, I don't suppose you can.' He had done his duty: no secrets between them. No secrets on the airwaves, either, even when items came through in morse. Someone was always listening, so who was the person, or people, writing down the text from the German Numbers Woman? What did her figures mean? Were they weather codes, or spy instructions? 'There's no way of finding out,' he said when she asked.

'Does it bother you?'

'No, but I'd like to know. Two receiving stations can get a cross bearing on the transmitter to find out roughly where it is, but I don't have the equipment to be one of them. If I knew another shortwave listener we could talk about it, and maybe rig something up.'

She held the knitting to her chest, and fetched a pattern from the other side of the room, thinking how often an advertisement for the local paper had gone through her mind: 'Wireless operator, ex-RAF, blind, would like to meet similar with sight to send morse code and talk radio matters. Two hours a week. Terms, if necessary, can be arranged.'

A hint to Howard that she would put it in showed that he needed all his self control not to be angry. And she couldn't think why, except that he saw it as a blow to his pride, an assault on his privacy which he prized above all else. She regretted not having strength enough to force the issue, put the ad in anyway, make up a story so that the meeting could take place – not having acted courageously and broken the barrier. Howard talked sociably enough to people in the pub whenever there for a pint – his maximum intake on a walk – because she had once met him as arranged, and even before pushing open the door heard his laughter and easy responses among the loud chatter.

Alone, he was king of his world, no territory of greater expanse than in his mind when assisted by varying and multiplying noises coming into the earphones. Aether sings, is never silent, indecipherable morse lost in vague ringing tones or a low roar as of the sea suddenly punctuated by a rogue whistle coming and going, the momentary growl of a button-message, arrowing from where to where? With such noises he could see, and the universe surrendered to him, at least that part between the earth's crust and the heaviside layer, where no part of him was tied to the yoke of his blindness.

Mysterious morse signals, in plain language or in code, ragged beyond comprehension and impossible to grasp, suggested a ghost wireless operator somewhere, wild eyed and stricken with eternal panic, the shirt half flayed off his back by the wind, the only other man besides the captain still on the *Flying Dutchman*, sending messages on an ancient spark transmitter, the ship forever caught in savage gales south of the Cape of Good Hope.

Distress signals from the ship came and went into Howard's earphones, mercilessly chopped by interference or atmospherics, weakened by distance, containing harrowing accounts of the *Flying Dutchman*'s plight but impossible to make sense of. Maybe lightning had shattered their eyes, but both captain and wireless operator thought they could see perfectly well, yet were unable to distinguish between dark and day in the howling torment of the waves. Signals from the ship turned up all over the spectrum, vague, hardly recognisable, trying to break through and make sense to someone with the superior knowledge, intuitive skill and power to release them from their spellbound circuits around the waters. Maybe they prayed for a Nimrod aircraft or a fast destroyer to rescue them from their plight. Masts gone, at times waterlogged, the ship struggled to stay afloat, and they couldn't know that nothing would make it sink because the eternal powers of the universe would not allow it.

The captain in his travail had gone insane and, roped to the wheel, drove the ship on automatically with declining yet always-renewable strength, while the wireless operator in his cabin sat hour after hour

23

tapping out his unreceivable messages of distress, hope and no hope fusing an addled brain that gave no rest.

At times Howard knew he was close to the wireless operator of the *Flying Dutchman* because nothing could be done for him either. His fate was settled. The vessel was adrift and could not make port, but the man persisted in his task, no thought of saving himself, because staying on was the only chance of survival, making life ordered even in damnation.

He never stayed long on one frequency, and in any case the *Flying Dutchman*'s signals always drifted away, impossible to follow, too painful to chase. Shrieks of static and dying whistles ate into the eardrums and conjured bad pictures, so he settled on the clear top-strength machine morse of the station giving the Mediterranean weather forecast, pulled over the typewriter and touch typed on his beloved elderly machine that, having only capital letters, made it easy to use for transcripts.

A seasonal low pressure area was what he noted, gales and thunderstorms at the beginning of September, southwesterly wind force four increasing locally, mainly clear but with increasing cloudiness, moderate visibility, generally changeable. The Adriatic was no better, or worse, the same with the Aegean and the Levantine Basin.

He took two pages, then changed band and swivelled the wheel onto a typhoon warning from Taiwan, said to be moving west at ten kilometres a minute, with sustained winds near the centre at 155 kilometres an hour. At least the *Flying Dutchman* wasn't involved in that one, and nor was he, snug in his familiar listening post at what he could only think of as the hub of the world.

A change from the tinkling of morse, he went on to a telephone frequency, spun the wheel and heard a Donald Duck squawk, hard to know whether it would turn out male or female, till he tuned in sharply and with delicate fingers pulled a recognisable male voice out by the tail:

'You're not supposed to drink when you take that stuff, are you, Beryl?'

What stuff? Howard removed the earphones, plugged in the speaker, and flicked on the tape recorder, perhaps to amuse Laura later, an action utterly against the law, though he would obliterate such private

24

talk afterwards. The Post Office regulations were severe: 'Interception of communications is forbidden. If such communications are received involuntarily they must not be produced in writing, communicated to other persons, or used for any purpose whatever.'

Plain enough, but too much of a sacrifice to his existence to obey such rules. In any case his transcripts were used to make the morning fire, and all tapes rubbed out to leave space for other items. If he played them occasionally to Laura what matter? Weren't man and wife supposed to be one person? He was sure there were villainous London thieves who used VHF scanners to keep track of police movements before doing a robbery, but he wasn't in that league, and wouldn't have been, even with normal sight.

He felt himself a snooper nevertheless when listening to personal telephone talk, though surely those who made calls from ship to shore must know someone might well be listening, no great feat these days, with technology coming on the market cheap, even for ordinary telephones to be tapped. Often he amused himself at midnight listening to two or three trawler skippers chatting at the fishing grounds, which he wouldn't record for Laura because the dexterity of their bad language was astonishing to hear.

Poor husband, or boyfriend, stuck on shore. 'You're not going to remember this, are you?'

Howard could hear him but not the woman.

'You all right?'

He was an American.

'See you on Friday? Look, I think you're loaded. Why are you crying? Phone you Thursday, at three o'clock.'

Perhaps he had sent her on a Caribbean cruise, when the last place she needed to be in was a vast floating boozer.

'Honey, please don't drink too much. I got a meeting at five o'clock. Listen, please don't drink too much tonight. Damn, you're really drunk.'

Howard wanted to hear the response, instead of filling in the details from his own heart.

'What does that mean?' the man said, a mixture of concern and exasperation.

25

How else to learn about life if you were blind?

'All right, I'll call you at five-thirty on Thursday. Can you write it down so you won't forget? Why not? You're drunk. It's that stuff affecting you maybe. Please don't drink anymore tonight. So you want to go, eh? OK. Love you. Bye.'

Operator's voice: 'It was twenty five minutes there.'

Such a long time for the poor chap to have been locked in a dead end debate with his wife or girlfriend. The catalogue of miseries was endless. Disasters also. A whistle went parabola through a blank frequency like an uncontrolled star across space – or a bomb making its way from a plane onto helpless people below. No knowing where it was coming from or heading for. Then the mixing warble of two oscillators made a noise like an angel drinking water.

The aerial blues were on him, which even the tom-tom telegraphist blasting through from a Soviet Black Sea tanker couldn't penetrate. But you must never despair, he told himself, ever, and if he didn't, no one should.

The man pleading with his wife wouldn't leave him alone. Witnesses were as much in danger of despair as those involved, who at least had the umbrella of each other's misery, as well as their own. The basic theory of magnetism instilled in the classroom was that 'like poles repel and unlike poles attract', but in human relationships if it went on too long the opposite would happen and both poles begin to repel. Iron filings as the uncontrollable grit of the human spirit are unpredictable in their behaviour, and nothing can save people from the unknown in themselves except endurance and understanding. Call it observations from the heaviside layer, for what they are worth.

To take the weight from his heart – that was one way he didn't want to go – he reached for the morse key which Laura had found in the ex-service junk store at the bottom of the steps, and tapped out a condoling message to the man who would not hear it because no transmitter was attached, though maybe Someone in the sky would take heed and filter the comfort through:

'I know more about you than you can know about me, though if you could read what I am sending you might know more about me than I am allowed to know about you. You are the hero of my evening, and your wife is the heroine, perhaps even the highlight of my week, and I am your only listener, who can know more about you in the beginning than you can know about me because I can hear you while you cannot hear me. You don't even know I am listening to your voice coming clear enough through the aether by electrical impulses, but all I want is to wish you well.'

Four minutes at the key made his own arm ache. The vagaries of human contact were forever mysterious. Electrical impulses jump between terminals, make contact, but when communication goes on too long the power fades, and must either be renewed or stay dead. Current was low and frequency likewise between him and Laura, but the equilibrium was continuous and could never be damped. As social worker jargon might have it, they took each other for granted, but did so because they loved each other, and it was the only way to get by.

She had gone shopping in the car, and promised his favourite pizza for supper. Elaborate cooked meals came only a couple of times a week, and who could blame her? He mused on whether the man whose wife was an alcoholic would like to meet the German Numbers Woman, thought he ought to be glad to make the acquaintance of someone with a rigidly ordered life. He would see her, neat, clean, tall and dressed in a colourful frock, proudly leading her two children for a walk on Sunday morning. They would sit at a small table by the pavement in summer, coffee for her and cake and ices for the children. Our man at the next table would be captivated by their intimacy, which he did not like to break into. But a smile cost nothing, either for him or her, and after several weeks a word or two passed between them. Both came to look forward to their brief talk, and one morning he handed the children a plastic bag filled with empty tobacco tins (or perhaps cigar boxes) which he couldn't bear to throw away, they were so neat and useful. The children accepted with alacrity, because no one but their mother had given them a present before, and played on a spare table as if they were precious toys given out at Christmas. The German Numbers Woman smiled with pleasure, and he knew what he had always known, that the way to a woman's love was through her children.

More weeks went by before he asked this blue-eyed rawboned, though attractive, woman if she would come out for a drink one

27

evening. Or did he invite her and the children to a show at the cinema? Hard to know what she would say, though Howard liked to think yes, but her previously open and youthful nature had made her a victim of predatory men, and she was wary. Yet she was also lonely, hungry almost, given her isolation with the children, and the secrecy of her work.

Howard worried about the matter for weeks, saw the relationship in all its detail. Her dedication at transmitting numbers was indefatigable. She was conscientious because her work was of life-saving importance. Without her numbers, someone would perish, lose all hope, face peril if not destruction and, as the analog of his receiver rested on a frequency unused except by caustic atmospherics, the answer came to him that her numbers were meant for the wireless operator of the *Flying Dutchman* who, when he wasn't sending his melancholy and distressful messages, was tuned in to receive her strings of numbers.

There was no other solution, no answer, it made sense, fitted into Howard's god-like manipulations. Her numbers were transmitted to give the *Flying Dutchman* hope, to keep the wireless operator and his captain from going finally into the deep, to warn them of the approach of the wildest typhoon weather, a life line to their ultimate survival. The tone of her voice, so hard to Howard, was like honey because the shade of absolute command and confidence kept them going, saying they were not alone, that they were not forgotten, that they had some link, however slender and uncertain, with the rest of the world.

Yet there was something else, a thought so outlandish, and for that reason absolutely convincing, as to chill the bones. He played with it awhile, doing shuttlecock and battledore with disjointed words, going into dreamland on Air Uterine and absent-mindedly flicking the tuning wheel to hear something which would divert him from a notion slowly forming, which was (for it could not be held back) that the German Numbers Woman's outgoing peroration fed into a mechanism of the *Flying Dutchman* which prevented them ever seeing land, kept them at sea, going round in great circles, and helpless to escape any of the storms. The wireless operator spent all his time when not sending or receiving vainly trying to break the code of her numbers, lost in a cryptographic maze incapable of solution, but under the impression that if he did reduce it to sense their tribulations would be over and a calm tropical landfall come in sight.

While the wireless operator became demented in grappling with the codes, not knowing that the greatest brain of the universe would be unable to break them, Ingrid the German Numbers Woman sat with her children talking happily to the man at the café on Sunday morning. The benighted sparks of the *Flying Dutchman* sweated and swore as huge waves lifted and spray battered his cabin, while Ingrid put a chocolate into her mouth, and her new-found boyfriend lit a cigar, and the eternal trio stayed locked into the triangular and mysterious fix, held there by Howard – the only way he could disentangle himself of the German Numbers Woman and her codes and give himself peace.

Laura removed one of the earphones: 'I got a video from town. Thought some entertainment together might do us good. It's called *Zulu*. We can watch it after supper. I'll tell you the landscape and what's going on.'

He wanted to stay in the wireless room, but the treat was impossible to resist. To do so would be churlish. She had grown so perfect at describing scenery and action in films that he might as well not have been blind.

She called that the meal was ready. For the first course there was grilled herring fresh from the boats, and a bottle of cold white wine – straight out of the refrigerator. 'You feed me too well,' he said.

She took the headset off. 'You need it, burning your energy at that wireless.'

'I'll get fat. I'm putting on weight as it is.'

'You are,' she laughed. 'So much the better for me. Come on, silly.'

He clattered back the chair, stood to hold her for a moment, then let her lead him into the dining room.

FOUR

The field sloping up from the broad canalised river was opaque and dark compared to the luminous streak of water which looked set to run over the banks at the next visitation of rain. Little more than the roof tiles showed, until Richard got to the crest of the opposite rise, white overlapping planks of its walls standing out in the dusk.

Thick grass, rich food to fatten sheep and cattle, bent under his boots, and he wondered when the rabbits would feel the sting of hot shot from the twelve-bore carried by Ken who walked at his own pace behind. Clean Sussex air gusted over the wooded ridge and, closing the gate carefully, Richard paused as the last daylight melted in the meadows to either side of the river.

Ken drew level. 'It ain't dark enough.' They walked along the lane to a position downwind, Ken's wellingtons squeaking on the saturated grass. 'Won't get no darker, though.'

'I don't suppose it will.' Richard's leather Trickers squelched into ruts and potholes which couldn't be dodged. He was glad, without knowing why, when a rabbit went shot-free in crossing the track. Last night one ran almost the whole length of the lane before the house, caught in his car beams, as if a jump to safety meant the drop of a thousand-foot cliff. Lit up by the chase, Richard wanted to run the bunny down, but it took the risk rather than be crushed under his tyres, and must have been relieved to find itself alive.

'Flash a light,' Ken said softly.

He steadied the eight-volt lamp, till a rabbit lifted its head in the beam, ears flattened. Water in his eyes distorted the image. Hard to make out what it was.

'It's something,' Ken said. 'Keep the torch on.' His double-barrelled twelve-bore had been left to him by Group Captain Willis, for looking after his estate, a light and efficient killer of wildlife at seventy yards. Richard had looked at it, a new toy to handle. Daedalus the ancient artificer couldn't have made one better – if it had been possible in those days.

Ken slid two plastic-coated cartridges primed with black shot into the breeches. In his sixties, he still had the best of eyesight, certainly better than mine, Richard thought. 'What are you waiting for?'

'It ain't a rabbit, but blessed if I know what it is.'

Richard's eyes were still blurred by the wind, and he focused them on Orion's Buckle and Belt rearing over the wood like buttons on the cloak of an otherwise-invisible man. 'So what can it be?'

Ken stepped forward and looked across the greying fields. 'Darned if I know. I'm flummoxed.' He had whispered in Richard's kitchen one night over a glass of whisky about having grown up poorer than the poor. In the thirties his parents and four kids had been turned out of their tied cottage, to live in a tent most of one winter in Cotton's Wood, till the father found another place. 'I used to look at the stars, and say I'd never live like this again. And I was only ten. People don't know what poor is these days.' Which was a preliminary bit of hype for the cunning old rogue to suggest, a few days later, that Richard pay a higher rate for having his garden looked after. Hard to refuse after hearing such a hard luck story. He should try being at sea on a small boat with nothing but a wild gale as an overcoat. Still, he didn't want to deny Ken's truth about his appalling childhood.

A phosphorescent glow by a clump of reed grass might be the tail of a rabbit and, if so, Ken was sure to score. Sharp sight and country know-how had put him in charge of a Bren gun section in Normandy during the war, and he had been in some of the worst fighting. After five years in the army he rarely moved beyond a few miles from where he was born, as if the luck of surviving had unnerved him. The only mechanical transport he allowed himself was a bike, though he would go on a bus if his wife was with him. He didn't smoke, and drank little more than homemade parsnip wine in his cluttered parlour.

A grunt as he fired. The flash and noise sent pigeons rattling in the trees, and Richard felt Ken's reluctance to dash along the torch's beam.

He must have known there was no rabbit at the end of the light, but Richard's presence had distorted his judgment. The wasted bullet had gone through a rectangular cake of cattle salt. Luminous in the dazzling light, it lay as if it had been manufactured with a hole in the middle.

Richard brought the gun to his shoulder, and Ken wondered what the silly so-and-so was up to. On his own, he'd have had a couple of bunnies for the pot by now. Not wanting to go home without having fired a shot, Richard squeezed the trigger, and the cake of salt disappeared.

An owl hooted from inside the wood, the letter R in morse. 'Sounds a bit like them noises I sometimes hear coming from your attic,' Ken said. 'All them squeaks.'

Richard broke the gun, stooped to put the empty case into his pocket. 'That's just my hobby.'

Mud at the gate had been churned by cattle and tractors. 'I often wondered,' Ken said. 'They used to be spies as did that, didn't they?'

The wind was fresh, though not cold for October. Weeks of rain had left the fields spongy. 'In war, they did.' Richard decided to use earphones all the time from now on, in case the police sent a specialist to snoop in the bushes and listen to what he was taking down. 'I don't suppose there were any spies around here. They were caught early, so I read. They hanged them. Or maybe they were shot.'

He hadn't noted such a vindictive tone from Ken before: 'Serve 'em right, as well.'

Out of Richard's unease rose the question as to why he had decided to come out for a night's shooting with his bumpkin of a gardener. Even harder to say why he was on earth, as if looking at the stars might bring back a long-dead sense of right and wrong.

'No rabbits'll be seen on such a night,' Ken said, on the way up the gravel path to Richard's house. 'I'll be off now, to see what the wife's got for supper.'

'I'll drive you.'

Ken sensed that Richard didn't care to. 'It's only a mile. A walk'll do me good.'

He locked the garage, and saw him out of the gate, on the way to the back door noting his aerial slung between two willow trees, branches shaking in the wind. Must stop it going up and down like a yo-yo –

though he was satisfied with the circular plate-like satellite dish clamped to the roof and beamed into planetary realms. In that respect it was a suitable house, up on a hill and giving good all-round reception.

He would have liked a smell of supper when he got in. Was it from spite, or indolence? She thought of everything, so it must be spite. He shook off his boots by the cloakroom door, set the guns in their cabinet, and put on slippers, unable to say what room she would be in. Couldn't much care. Probably in the sitting room.

Roaming the fields made you hungry. Ken would sit down to his roast or hotpot, with jam roll and custard to follow, his fat wife slapping it down yet glad to see him eat; but Richard put a slice of smoked bacon in the pan and when it was halfway brown cracked in an egg, and two hemispheres of ripe tomato. A breakfast at night was enough to go to bed on, though he wouldn't get there for some time. No need to watch his weight, being slim enough at forty. Pale hair, which Amanda always said resembled a toupee, was short enough to never need combing.

He ate quickly, a blob of yolk splashing the knee of his jeans, wiped with a paper towel. Smoke from the toaster came up, so he banged the side and trowelled butter on burnt bread. Amanda stood in the doorway: 'You're stinking up my kitchen with your fry-ups again.' She pressed the switch: 'Try using the extractor fan.'

The noise was like that of a plane taking off, and he relished silence now and again. 'I forgot.'

Relaxed, or so you might assume, he was ready to spring, like a panther and as unpredictable, blue eyes turned on her, looking slightly mad, as always, and fully knowing the power of his expression. He was about middle height, less tall than she, but tight with violence, always to be feared, except when he was feeling northwest passage and midnight sugar rolled into one. Then she was as mad as he, but with love, so that was all right. 'You always do forget. It's there for keeping the smells of cooking down.'

'Is that right?'

'Well, you paid for it.'

The only way to let her have the last word was to keep quiet. He needed to mark the cessation of the day by a sanitary cordon of tranquillity, but she had often said that if she didn't talk she felt like a waxwork and, he admitted with a smile (which could only annoy her) she certainly looked a pretty one, beautiful even. 'Have you eaten?'

'I had a salad earlier. Where were you?'

'After rabbits, with Ken.'

'All boys together, eh? Why didn't you let me know you were going out?'

'You were nowhere to be seen.'

'I was at Doris's. She did my hair.'

'So I see.' The treatment of her short fair hair had kept the aureole of curls tight to her head, and he liked that, but blue-grey eyes and smallish mouth gave her a desultory, hungry look, as if never getting enough of what she wanted out of life, whatever that might be. She wore a high-necked white blouse with a broad tie of equally white bands hanging between the folds of her small bosom. In her late thirties, she could at times look blowsy and haggard, but the glow of dissatisfaction had restored her to the younger woman he had first seen sitting in a park bench reading a book, and fallen in love with. 'Your hair looks wonderful,' he told her.

'It's always best if somebody else does it. When I help Doris in the salon though she pays me well. Says I'm one of the best hairdressers she's ever had.'

'I'm sure that's true.'

She liked his compliment but wouldn't show it, lit a cigarette and said: 'You could have left a note when you went out.'

'It didn't occur to me.'

'It never does.'

Being married, who needs enemies? He wanted to smack her around the chops, but what was the use? He once did so, and she'd walked out. Then she came back, by which time he had got used to living alone. Now he'd got used to living with her again, and didn't want her to go. Maybe that meant she would. She was more of a mystery to him than he could be to her, whatever she thought. Perhaps he had been neglectful. All she'd wanted was for him to leave a note so that she would know he would be coming back. Whenever he went out she feared he might not (though that could be because she didn't want him to) unless he let her know exactly where he was going, and that wasn't always possible. So now and again he made up fancy little itineraries out of kindness, though he didn't like having to tell lies, which they really weren't, since no other woman was involved. He supposed their ten-year marriage had gone on too long, more and more memories neither of them could mention without spiralling into dangerous arguments, topics well recognised so that whoever brought one up knew very well what they were doing, thus breaking the rules, which happened when a seeming indifference on one side or the other caused boredom too painful to be endured.

She was bored now, with him, with life, above all with herself, and the glow of argument was in her.

'The thing is,' she said, 'you're too selfish. You're too mean to share your thoughts with anyone.'

And that's how it should be, yet to be called selfish riled him above all else, too proud to go through the list of what he had done for her, and though to be honest assumed she had done as much for him, he couldn't think for the moment what it was. He only knew he'd helped other people, often, but such unthinking bastards hadn't thanked him because they considered his money had come too easy.

'I haven't known you to do a good deed in your life,' she said. 'It just isn't in you.'

He'd never told her, because if he did she'd say what a fool he had been to help such people. And so he was. But a pure good deed from the goodness of his heart to someone who would appreciate it out of the goodness of his? No, she was right. 'Oh, pack it in, for Christ's sake.'

His menacing tone didn't scare her, though she knew it should have. 'Of course, it could be there's nothing there. I should have realised it from the first. The trouble with me is that I take so long to learn.'

Such painful denigration in her laugh he knew to be a sham. Silence was the only way to calm matters, though she would consider it a weapon. After pouring tea he sat without moving, though smoke from his cigarette signalled that at least *he* wasn't a waxwork. The food boiled in his stomach, for there was nothing he could safely tell her. If he really told her what he did to get money, and described the state of his mind, she would scream herself to death, or bury him with scorn. No, she was as hard as nails. They both were, two worlds incapable of meeting

35

on a human and tolerant level. She already suspected he did something crooked to get money, for how else could he have paid for the house from a suitcase of cash? He wasn't the mortgage type.

She fished for the truth with barbed hooks, the last way to get anything. If one day they decided to kill him because he knew too much they might do away with her as well, and should the police pull him in he wouldn't want them to think she had been involved. He lived such a life that the luxury of easy conversation couldn't be for him, and so not for them. Everything cost something.

She sat and faced him. 'Why did we have to buy a house like this?'

The same old question: a hilltop house with every comfort, only ten miles from the coast, and within a couple of hours of London. 'It's convenient. It has a good view.'

'You mean for your aerials?' She'd heard it before. Often was too often. She nearly died with worry when he went to crew a yacht back from Gibraltar, and listened to the dreadful weather forecast every day. He took off in the car one morning and said he was going to London, then no word for three weeks. 'If I'd told you, the worry would have been far worse. If things had gone wrong you might have ended in the drek.'

He was, at best, lavish and fun to be with, so could you wish a man dead for habits which were as much part of his act as falling in love with you had been, though so long ago? One way or another he had made ten years seem like forever, which in a way she supposed she couldn't fault him for, if she wanted to live that long, which she could never be sure about, with someone like him.

'There's nothing wrong with the house,' he said.

She lit another cigarette, and puffed smoke at his face. 'Nothing a bulldozer couldn't set right.'

He blew smoke back. 'What do you want?'

'If I knew I wouldn't be here.'

'Where would you be? More tea?'

'How the hell would I know? Please.'

The agreeable feeling of mindlessness he'd had while out with Ken had gone. Freedom and the spacious fields had taken away all worries

– the sort of mood she couldn't know about, or envied him for having. 'I do what I can for you.'

Like pouring tea. Thank you very much. You know how I live for it. So much preoccupied him, and he wouldn't or couldn't tell her about it. He was indifferent to her, didn't have the resilience to argue and break her boredom. All these years she had sat in the house trying to unravel what routes his blood ran on, but with so little evidence it was useless. He seemed not to care, and only reacted when she goaded him beyond endurance, not even then giving anything away. He would swear and bang his fist against the wall, and go off to sulk in the attic room, where he would either stare despairingly out of the window, or at the curtains when they were drawn. If it was daylight he would glare at the green hell of the countryside. Or he'd sit hunched up at his special wireless taking messages which he said were no business of hers. She might as well be living in a gorilla cage.

He stood, and came to her. 'Let's not have a bust-up. I know life's not easy for either of us.' A warm tight hand on the back of her neck usually worked in bringing her to what they both wanted. He'd read in a book that the neck was one of the erogenous zones, and he supposed that was because the main cables from the brain ran through such constricted space to get to the sexual regions lower down. Also there was hair close to the neck, as in the other place. 'You know there's nobody else I love like you, nobody I care about, almost nobody else I know, in fact, except the people I have to work with, and I'd rather not know them most of the time.'

He was talking, not exactly motormouth, but it would have to do. She stood, and who kissed first was hard to say. His body was a stove. She was always amazed at the heat it gave off, how it warmed her into wanting him, or not being able to resist what he had to give, or thinking that to make love was the only way of quietening him, and herself, come to that. She wanted something, anyway, and at the moment it seemed to be a bit of all three, as long as neither said anything more but just got on with what she must have wanted all day, and what he needed as well by the feel of it.

Green hillside spread up the other slope of the valley, a panorama to calm him. A black and white cow was painted halfway, always the same though sometimes it moved, always when he wasn't looking. Whenever he opened the curtain there it was, and who carried the animal to another position in the night he never knew. Maybe it wasn't the same cow, a different one taking its place when the present cow had gorged itself sufficiently on succulent grass it didn't even have to stand up and search for. Perhaps the cattle had a pow-wow as to who should have the hallowed spot the following day. Being so prized it had to be shared, the riches of the world passed from mouth to mouth. No one cow could be allowed to scoff too greedily at the trough. Well, he'd had more than a good patch in the last few years, and nobody had come to push him aside.

He put on the radio, a flip of the dial, and the only true music came from the stratosphere, a contemporary rendering of the heaviside quartets tinkling through clear sky and hitting cloud which sorted out the various rhythms. Every note he could get sense out of meant money in the mattress.

He'd made enough from a couple of Gibraltar trips to buy the house, and put something by. On the way he had taken down the weather in morse from Portishead Radio, and steered them from a storm that might have swamped the boat overloaded with the most head-banging powders on earth. He fiddled with a receiver which a crew member had bought for a tenner in a pub thinking it was an ordinary wireless. Near to home on the return trip Richard had heard jabber from the coast guards, so they knew what coves to steer clear of, which so impressed the Big Man (they called him Waistcoat) that he was promised money whenever he sent in a transcript from Interpol.

No problem, so it turned out. He was able to let them know when the police would be waiting at Frankfurt for a consignment from Colombia, so the bods on board were advised to come down in a different place, and all was well. The police waiting at Frankfurt had their names, dates of birth, what luggage they had, and how they were carrying the stuff. False bottoms of suitcases was the least of their ingenuity. Somebody must have put in a word for whatever reason, and Richard's intelligence might indicate who and why, so he didn't doubt that a few had been snuffed out for their try that went wrong.

After eight years as a radio officer in the Merchant Service he could get anything that was floating in the aether out of a radio. He was good at it and could do no wrong. Whenever anything useful came up he phoned it through, and they paid him well, money for old rope, just for sitting on his arse and trawling the short waves all day between looking at that picture-book cow noshing the best of green grass on the hillside – a gilded calf if ever there was one. He couldn't understand why the Mafia and all big outfits of the criminal world didn't recruit personnel to scour the communication systems of their law-enforcing enemies. It would have made sense and cost little.

Money unblocked the log-jam of one's dreams, brightened the nights and days. All the sharp and clever people wanted their share, made a beacon out of themselves hoping money would home in and stick. He'd picked up a long signal from Africa, concerning Sambo Jean-Jacques who was a chauffeur and guard of the secretary of state for defence in Zaire – or some such place – and purloined a hundred million francs by forging his boss's signature at the local bank when he was away on leave. Jean-Jacques was last seen heading towards Uganda with his girlfriend, false passports in their pockets. Richard hoped he had got clean away, after such ingenuity, and even worked out all possible routes on a Michelin map to see what his chances were, deciding they must be good, despite wireless signals going all over the place trying to stop him.

He was aware of such power, though often afraid to use it, except for prompt and spot cash. His French was good enough to pick up plain language in morse from the police network in France. It was interesting to hear vital statistics of criminals and their whereabouts. Some villain, he learned, had stolen a car in Nice (a good Mercedes, licence number given) and was on his way to his sister's in Lille. Her name, address and telephone number were given, so Richard had the power to pick up the phone and in two minutes warn her that trouble was on its way. Schoolboy French would just about run to it. He would whisper that she should try to save her errant brother, except that to do so might be too risky. He was putting himself enough on the line as it was. How could he tell Amanda what he was doing? All she needed to know was that wireless listening was his hobby. A high-tension shock had gone through him only this morning, after a wonderful night of making love. She had even got his breakfast of coffee and rolls, butter and jam, and no one could have done it better.

'The police called yesterday,' she said.

The jam turned sour. 'What the fuck for?'

'Don't swear, darling.'

Why not? It was too early for fear not to hit him. 'Sorry. What did they want?'

'It was about the football field at the end of the lane. Some vandals had sawn through the goalposts with an electric saw, and they wondered whether we'd heard or seen any of them driving away.'

'I didn't.' His head had been down on more important matters. The jam tasted halfway good again. 'Didn't hear a thing.'

'Neither did I.'

'If I had, I'd have killed the bastards. They should be shot on sight.'

She poured coffee for them both. He wished she could be like this all the time, but knew he had to earn such brief interludes of care and attention. 'I do wish you wouldn't use violent language, though,' she said.

'I know. Sorry about it. But vandalism like that gets my goat. I hate it. The kids in the village play there a lot. I really would have liked to have caught them.' He would, except they might have been the ones who did it. They'd have thought lightning had struck. His fists itched. They always itched, from knuckles to wrists, but the knuckles especially, though he resisted scratching. They had got at him personally, whoever had done it. Such destruction was purposeless, sheer spite, enjoyment of the lowest sort, done out of hatred against everyone and everything.

Apart from that, it put the shits up him to know that the police had called at the house. Maybe they had another reason altogether. 'What else did they say?'

'Nothing. They were very nice and polite. I almost fancied one of them.'

'You bitch.'

She was in his arms. 'But I fancy you most of all.'

He tuned in, and the signals came through loud and clear, right on cue. Sometimes you had to wait, or search endlessly through the megacycles, because they changed frequency often, maybe to catch you out. It was like watching for fish, but this morning the messages smiled through, every bright sing-song of morse a pound coin dropping into his greedy palm.

FIVE

Laura knew when the east wind cometh, when it was close, when it was blathering and grating in the here and now. It meant torment for Howard, but he tried to laugh off its advent, regarding it as inexorable, though devilish while it lasted.

'When the wind is in the east a blind man dances with the beast,' he said, and probably everyone else did as well, though in a minor key because they could see it coming by the writhing of leaves, as well as dust and rubbish peppering along the streets, while he only got advanced warning from Portishead.

'The beast is on its way,' he'd say, switching off the wireless, 'but I'll try not to let it get at me.' Sometimes he lost all sense of equilibrium, felt that because he couldn't see anyone no one else could see him. A gremlin turned the town plan around, making his morning walk as if through treacle, so he stayed at home. 'Navigation all to cock,' he would say. At the worst of times she heard him knocking his head against the wall. He thought she couldn't hear, his door being closed and the morse loud, or everything drowned by the worst of static. But sound carried. There were vibrations, and they passed right through her. He wandered around like old blind Pugh in *Treasure Island*.

In one of his worst bouts she had driven him over a hundred miles to an air show at Duxford near Cambridge. He forgot the nagging wind on climbing into a bomber sat in during the war, and hearing a Wellington and a Harvard. She felt a shiver from his hand at the throaty roar of their engines. He looked up, no doubt saw the picture clear in every detail. Good to know there were things no wind could spoil. By the time they got back the dreaded easterly had veered or dropped.

Well, she couldn't do such a trip every month, nor would he let her, half ashamed at having put her to the trouble, the other part consumed by his pleasure at exorcising two devils at the same time. Walking up the steps of home he said: 'There are times when I can't get under the make-up of the blind man to the real me underneath. It's a horrible feeling. But today I could, and it'll last a long while, thanks to you, my love.'

'We must go again, in a year or two,' she said. 'I quite enjoyed it, as well.'

But this morning he had knocked two of her precious Yuan breakfast cups off the table. Such crockery came in sets, and a gap had to be made good, otherwise it was not only a slight to the eyes as they lay in the cupboard, but a disturbance was felt, as if a splinter of herself was missing, an opening for unwelcome thoughts to come through.

After coffee she made sandwiches for him to eat at lunch, set him at the wireless to get what solace he could, and walked down the steps to the car. At the China Parade shop near the edge of town she could buy replacements for the cups. She wondered why he had stumbled. Always careful, he must be even more upset than an east wind warranted. Was he getting worse? Losing his sharpness and care now that he was sixty? After the cups were wrapped and boxed she drove ten miles to Bracebridge and collected a replacement for the parlour stove. Her nerves weren't at their best, either, from the buffeting wind, because she hit the kerb in the village and, hearing bumps under a front tyre, knew it was a puncture, the first since buying the car five years ago. A lay-by was close, and she trundled in to change the wheel.

A twin-tailed squarish combat plane in camouflage colours came low along the river. Two jet engines were centred on the fuselage between the greenhouse cockpit, either low flying practice or had they rumbled him and were trying to find out what stations he listened to? He didn't think they had the technology, in spite of what Peter Wright claimed in *Spycatcher*.

Rain splashed the windscreen but the pint had been good, safe inside, and not to be got at. Two would have been better, three even more, but to be pulled up and breath tested would draw the eyes of the law on him, and should he be over the level, the misdemeanour might lead towards something bigger. Take care of the small, and no one would rumble anything worse. Anonymity was the rule, to be a fish in water.

He managed a cigarette without taking both hands from the wheel. An east wind was usually dry but this one had turned the trees jungle green, drizzle from Russia with love. Halfway along the straight he slowed on seeing a car in a lay-by, where a woman was trying to fix a wheel. Well, she had the jack in her hands, turned away, wondering what to do next, not imagining golden boy was homing in.

She would be alarmed, fear he was a predator with a rape-knife and unbreakable stranglehold. A hundred yards to walk, the view from behind was good, shapely legs, dark brown hair down to her neck, signs promising well for looks and, if not, certainly a presence. He had sometimes followed a woman with the most gorgeous hair, walking rapidly ahead then turning back as if he'd forgotten something, only to find a face like the back end of a tram smash, which phrase his father had often used. An article in the paper said that if you saw a woman walking down the street at dusk or in the dark you should reassure her by crossing to the other side. Give her a wide berth. He wasn't that much of a gentleman, though neither did he feel himself a villain. He would talk his way in, and put her at ease.

'I'm sorry to intrude. You seem to be in trouble with that wheel.' Not many marks from Amanda for that, but she had gone to London, and he was his own man today. 'It won't take five minutes to change, and then we can both be on our way.'

This tall woman, seemingly in her forties, turned, put the carjack on the bonnet, a wheel hub by her feet. 'I'm quite capable. I just can't quite find the place to put the jack under the body.'

'My wife used to have one of these cars, so I can show you.' Amanda didn't, but he felt around and found the place, glad to be helping this cool stately woman who gave him the most calculated weighing-up he could remember. Not much more behind her grey eyes than that, so he immediately felt calm at being near, especially since, in handing over the jack, she seemed to trust him. She needed the expertise, after all.

The nuts were so tight he had to stamp his shoes down on the spanner, kicking at each till they loosened and could be taken off, which brought on a bit of a sweat. She would never have done it on her own, but for him it was easy, and he slowed down because he wanted to stay a few more minutes near her. 'Do you have far to go?'

She told him. 'I've just been to that stove place near Bracebridge. I've never had a blow-out before.'

'There's always a first time.' A touch of grey on darkish hair added to her dignity, and he could only wonder where it came from. Straight backed, nothing ambivalent about her, English to the bone, she was the type he had never been so close to before. Her sort were usually too knowing to clinch with him, so good behaviour was the order of the day.

She felt a fool but thought never mind, it would have been awkward struggling with the bolts, and he seemed familiar with such things, not put out either by drizzle and muddy pools around their cars. She considered herself lucky, and smiled, trying not to hover at each phase of the operation.

'I live out near Benefield,' he said. 'My wife and I bought a house there two years ago.'

'A nice village.'

He told her about the goalposts, and the police visit, surprised at rattling on in a way he rarely did with Amanda.

'You seem very efficient at this type of thing,' she said. 'It would have taken me twice as long.'

At least, he smiled. 'Part of my trade is messing about in boats, and a sailor can turn his hand to anything. Six months ago I went on a thirty-two-footer to Boulogne and back, and we had sails, but the engine broke down, and getting out of the harbour without it would have been tricky, so I set to, and got it going.' He certainly had, driven by what they had on board, but he couldn't mention that. He had made a special Consol lattice on the chart so they would know their exact position in poor visibility with regard to the coastguards. He didn't think it worked, but at least the trip had gone off all right, and paid for a good bit of his BMW.

'You were in the Navy, then?'

'Merchant Service. Radio officer. But I came out. They didn't pay enough for my liking.'

'Oh!'

Her façade was broken. Maybe she'd had a brother in the Navy who had been drowned, and he'd touched a chord. She flushed as if he had come out with something embarrassing, so plain was she to read. Or had he shown himself as too mercenary and common? 'You seem surprised.'

He had done her one favour, so she could hardly ask him for another, though perhaps that was all the more reason to. 'No, it's just that, well, if you were a radio officer, you must know the morse code.'

Now he was surprised. 'Read it like a book.'

'Of course,' she said.

A funny question. Maybe she would ask him to teach her Brownie group or Girl Guide class. Or perhaps she was an off-duty policewoman, and wanted him to teach signals twice a week to the force – which would lead him quicker to his doom than being breathalysed. He'd often fancied himself as a teacher, but not that sort. No, she couldn't be in the police, because she would at least be able to change a wheel, unless they had planted her as a decoy for swine who preyed on women in difficulty on the roadside. He looked at the trees, towards the hedge decorated with a plastic bag, at the ditch strewn with tins. 'But why do you ask?'

She liked his trim efficiency, medium height, slim build, face with no fat on it, showing features clean and – well – hard in a way, tough you might say, certainly a sailor, now that he had told her. 'My husband was a wireless operator, in the Air Force.'

No coincidence. There must have been tens of thousands trained in the old dit-dah. 'Is that so?'

'He got shot up, at the end of the war.'

'Oh, I'm sorry.' He put the hubcap back in place, tapped it with the muddy toe of his shoe. 'So he's one of the fraternity.'

She liked the word. A fraternity. 'He's blind, but he gets around all right.'

'I'm sorry to hear he's blind.' He was. Who wouldn't be? 'It happened to many, always the best people.' That's what she would like him to say. He wanted to keep her talking, hoped she wouldn't leave, though they couldn't stand forever in the mud and grit. 'There's a pub down the road. Would you join me for a drink.'

That damnable east wind blew against her coat. Howard might be taking a nap now, dreaming his dreams, which could never be remembered. No man had invited her for a drink since before her marriage, but it would be impolite to hesitate. 'Are you sure?'

He held up his blackened hands. 'Then I could wash these.'

Rain, unaccountably, made her thirsty. Strange, that. 'Yes, all right.'

Another pint would go down well. Not too much to drive home on. He didn't know what the attraction was, but he tried not to look at her too intently. Not entirely sexual, either. 'I can't go home like this. My wife might wonder what I'd been up to.'

She had said it, and felt the joy of being young again. 'I can have a fruit juice, or something.'

He fastened his blue duffel coat and adjusted the naval-style cap to a sharper angle. 'I'll meet you in the parking place. You won't miss it.'

In any case, she wanted to use the toilet, the effect of the rain, no doubt. 'I think it's only right that I should buy the drinks.'

He paused at opening the car door. 'No, that won't do at all. I'm inviting you.'

Perhaps she had offended him, difficult to recall the procedures from so long ago. It was too late to rectify, so a smile was called for. 'Just as you say.'

She used language precisely, diffidently, as if not sure she would be understood, or maybe as if she had never been in a similar situation before, and in any case met very few people.

The car stayed in his rearward window, and he went slowly so as not to lose sight, or cause her to go at a higher speed than usual. They parked side by side, at more or less the same time, as if one car was then to take on board packets of drugs from the other. He laughed at such an idea while with her, and led a way to the lounge.

You had to be careful even what you thought with such a person, though he knew he could manage her, easy after the long hard school with Amanda. Oh, how she'd occasionally dug her own grave! Setting the drinks down, he saw himself in a mirror, a glance, glad to be wearing a jacket and tie under his coat instead of the normal shirt and jeans. 'You must have married young, to be with a man wounded in the war.'

'Well!' Undoing her coat showed a nice rounded bosom under a grey

47

sweater. Lines by her mouth, but the skin was otherwise pale and clear. Shapely hands with long fingers reached for her drink, to sip. 'Why do you say that?'

'I mean, for a woman in her forties.'

He liked her laugh also. 'A tiny bit more than that, I'm afraid.'

This silenced him, for a moment. Better get back onto the topic of morse code – as she had hoped he would. 'So your husband still listens to the music of the spheres?'

'It's good for him.'

She wasn't the sort of person you should lie to, but he had no option. 'I haven't heard it for years.'

That wasn't so good. 'According to Howard you can never forget it.'

'True enough. But you do get a bit rusty.'

'He says listening to the wireless keeps lack of moral fibre at bay. His words, but I suppose it does. He listens happily for hours.'

'He must be good at it.'

'Oh, the things he gets!'

He would like to know. 'Really?'

'He sends morse to himself sometimes. He has one of those tapper things, a key, and says it keeps his hand in, though what for, I can't imagine. But you can see what a good hobby it would be for a blind man.'

The pint was almost gone and he wanted more. Why was it ideal, even heavenly, to drink while talking to a woman? Actually, it was good to drink whatever you were doing, but he would hold back in quantity because a woman like her would think little of him if he took too much. 'Sounds like a sort of therapy.'

'That's exactly what it is.' She took another sip of her fruit drink. 'Did you like doing it when it was your work?'

'It was a good job, as jobs go. I'm Richard, by the way.'

'Mine's Laura.'

He wondered whether she'd been quite ready to give it, or as if she didn't find his unusual enough. 'It got me about the world.'

'But you liked your work?'

'Sure. It was enjoyable being at sea, but better still on land, eventually.' So she was a lonely woman, full of unshed liveliness, looking after

48

her disabled husband, a fate as dull as death. 'But I've never had any reason to complain about my existence.'

'Neither have I.' She was a little too definite about that. 'And neither does my husband.' Talking so openly surprised and pleased her. Even with the vicar at church her conversation had been distant. It was hard enough with Howard at times, to unravel words from the stone within. What would he say when he knew she'd met such a pleasant man?

'All the same, he sounds something of a hero for not complaining. People whine too much these days. They don't know they're born. I only hope I'd be the same as your husband.'

'People have to be, when it comes down to it. He has his black moments, usually when there's an east wind like today. He tries hard to keep it to himself, but of course, I'd know, wouldn't I?'

You poor woman, married to a wind vane and barometer rolled into one, sometimes the same with him, though nothing a few pints wouldn't cure. He supposed they lived on a pension, and couldn't afford to drink. She was modestly dressed, but attractive all the same. For a few bob these days you could get rigged out from an Oxfam shop. Amanda was wearing such stuff when he first met her, and she looked stunning. The handbag might have come from a charity shop, unless she loved the style because it reminded her of better days. 'It's certainly not the time to be at sea. Can I get you another?'

'I ought to be going. Thank you again for fixing my wheel.'

'I enjoyed a bit of work. You made my day.' To touch her hand was definitely not on. He drew her chair back so that she could stand.

If I were married to a man who could see, this is what it would be like, she thought. 'There's just one thing I would like to ask you.'

He opened the door. 'What's that?'

They stood in the porch, looking at the rain, and wondering about each other. 'I really don't know how to put it. I'm not used to asking favours, not of a person I've just met.'

Such punctiliousness would have been irritating in someone else. He wondered what she wanted him to do, but decided he would do it anyway, though would it be obscene or obsequious? She obviously expected him to run a mile. He detected a layer of ice over the turbulent sea inside, but if he walked on it he would fall through. Did she know

49

how icily charming she was, how flagrantly attractive? Married or not, he wanted her telephone number, but it would be stupid to ask. 'All you have to do is speak.'

'I know.' She felt seventeen again, gauche, uncertain, too proud perhaps. 'If it's completely outrageous, just say so, and I'll understand.'

He took time to light a cigarette. 'What, then?'

'You can imagine my husband is a desperately lonely man at times, though he wouldn't agree. He wouldn't like to hear me say so, either. But I wondered if you would call some time, and talk to him about wireless. Even send something on his little apparatus.'

He'd sensed what was coming. 'I see.'

'I told you it was a mad idea.' She trawled the car keys from her handbag, knowing that indeed it was, though she felt no shame, rather glad at not having been too stiff-necked to ask, all part of the ease of meeting him. 'Don't worry about it. I'll be going now. It really has been nice talking to you. And you were so very good to help me with the wheel.'

He would, in the classic phrase, blow his cover. Or he might not, with so much experience in telling untruths. Amanda knew him as the epitome of slyness. 'There's no real you,' she said. 'What bit there might be you keep for other people. I don't get a look in.' No more you will, he had thought, but as always she was both right and wrong, which was what made her so maddening.

'Of course I'll come,' he said to Laura. 'I'll be glad to. It'll bring the old life on board back to me as well, though I may be a little slow on the key at first. My life in any case gets pretty dull at times.' Except when malevolent sunspots suck away the vital parts of a message. 'Though I do have to go to London from time to time. Or on a boat trip.'

'It obviously would be whenever is convenient for you.'

She was as pleased as a schoolgirl. Charming. Amazing how soon you could make those happy whom you had just met – or who you hardly knew. 'Give me your telephone number, if you like. I'll call you when I can, to see if it's a good time.'

'It will be, I'm sure. Blast, I don't have a pen.'

They stood apart, to let someone go inside. 'Here's one. I have to be off soon, though. I have a business appointment in half an hour. But I'll be sure to call.' He most certainly would, though it wasn't easy to say when. 'I'll be very interested to meet your husband.'

SIX

Howard had many acquaintances on shortwave, except that while he knew them they didn't know him. They could have suspected him but probably didn't. They were recognisable by the text, and by the idiosyncrasies of the sending. He felt the spring in the wrist or the ache at their elbow. Those with speed and rhythm were artists at the game, whereas he spotted some by the slow and awkward delivery, though they weren't necessarily inexperienced, merely taken over by a spirit of syncopation out of boredom, or they were drawing attention to themselves by showing off, and maliciously wanting to drive people halfway potty who had to take down their message. Operators by trade were often naive regarding the big world beyond, and neither knew nor cared what effect they had on others, all of which helped Howard in his recognition.

Sometimes they sounded as if touching two pieces of electrified wire together, a feat he remembered seeing in a film as a youth, when a train going into the far West was wrecked in an Indian ambush. The telegraph operator, who happened to be on board as a passenger, climbed up a pole by the line, cut a wire, and by touching the two pieces together to make morse, sent a message to get help from the US Cavalry. Howard couldn't recall whether the man had been struck by an arrow at the end of his effort, and fallen from a great height, or whether he had survived for a hero's welcome.

He knew the various radio operators also by the tone of their equipment, whether it came from the steely precision of the Royal Navy's sublime telegraphists, or the bird-like slowness of machine morse giving airfield weather conditions from the RAF. He could tell Soviet operators on ships and at shore stations bouncing telegrams to each other by the ball-bearing quality of the transmitters and the record speed at which they were sent, too fast to write but not to read, though he suspected the messages were tape recorded on reception and slowed down at leisure for transcription. He knew the various nationalities from the language used, able to read (but not understand) Greek, Turkish, Romanian and German, though French was easy enough.

Fingers on the key called for a flexible wrist. The amount of energy pulsing from the elbow varied as much as a snowflake or thumb print. Energy was fed from the heart and backbone, an engine sending power to the hand, so that he could tell when a man (or, who knows, a woman?) was tired, or irascible, or lackadaisical, or slapdash, or indeed calm, competent, conscientious, and incapable of exhaustion. Maybe the latter played tennis, or went swimming, or sawed an uncountable number of logs to keep his fire going. The difference was minimal but always detectable. If a man was tired he might be unhappy, or at the end of his stint. If someone was easy and competent they had no worries, or they had just come on watch and weren't yet jaded. Some operators had a natural sense of rhythm, and rattled on like talented pianists, while others, a minority, laboured in such a way as made them tiring to listen to, and he couldn't imagine why they had taken up such a job, though it was certainly better than working on a motorway or building site. The behaviour of the fist was mysterious, but with earphones clamped Howard became a remote and all-knowing god, skilled in interpretation but, like a true god, unable to help anyone avoid their fate, even supposing he would want to.

He knew from experience that the most difficult place from which to send morse was an aeroplane. Though seated at a comfortable-enough desk, albeit most of the time cramped, your fist was at the mercy of vibration and turbulence, not to mention the vagaries of height and aerial. He had heard Chinese operators flying between Peking and Urumchi sending hourly position reports, a fluke of reception because after a few weeks the signals faded. The Russians also had radio men on board civil and military aircraft. He understood them because they used – as did the Chinese – the same international Q signals which he had used in the Air Force, detailing times of arrival and departure, height, speed and geographical locality.

The station most persistently monitored was that of the direction-finding system near Moscow, which he first came across during a morning's idle trawl. The operator in a plane would tap out a request for latitude and longitude, and the man in Moscow would ask him to press his morse key for ten or so seconds of continuous squeak. This the man in the aircraft willingly did, and a minute or so later, Vanya (as Howard called him) on earth near Moscow, had worked his technological magic and the position was sent.

After recording each message Howard fixed a metaphorical pin on a map of the Soviet Union displayed in his mind. In the beginning he'd had to ask Laura for help in placing such coordinates, until he became familiar enough with the geographical graticule to do without her. The operator who communicated the result of his bearings did not have the lightning dexterity of his marine counterpart, and an aircraft would often have trouble making contact. The fist of Vanya on the ground was sometimes erratic, while his correspondent in the plane was occasionally affected by turbulence.

Such interceptions allowed Howard to play a game called 'Spot the Bomber', and if Laura came in to say lunch was ready he would laugh: 'Shan't be a moment. I have a bomber on the line.' She read him an item about Soviet planes trying to manipulate the weather over the Arctic Ocean, and he heard some from that region asking for their position. Others were so far north they must have been on 'Bear Patrol', and he'd even heard the hesitant squeak of planes on the Vladivostok run.

The Moscow operator suffered from ennui, because in eight hours of keeping watch not more than a dozen planes would ask for their position, and each transmission did not last for more than a few minutes. Howard assumed that Vanya closed his eyes now and again, for a plane would sometimes call and get no reply. On the other hand either the plane didn't hear the land station, or the land station didn't hear the aeroplane, which could happen if the latter's equipment was a few kilocycles off frequency. Cannier airborne operators would try to catch Vanya out by sending a single letter V, but he would invariably shoot back rapidly with: 'Who's calling me?' and contact would be made, with no evidence of sloth at all.

He pictured Vanya, at his direction-finder's Consol, as a man with

54

cropped fair hair and, of course, blue eyes. He was underpaid, and became more and more bored as the hours went by and the airwaves stayed empty. What kind of person was he? When a contact was made he displayed a very individual style, would start by sending with painful slowness and then, suddenly, maybe to fox or catch out the other operator, whom he considered to be an interloper till proved a friend because he had need of his services, speed along like a virtuoso, overall erratic but good even when bad, unwilling to be constrained by the age old parameters of Samuel B. Morse. Perhaps he even wished at times that the genius inventor of the telegraphic code had stuck to his painting and had not come up out of nowhere with his disciplined style of communication.

Laura had taken a biography of the great man out of the library, and read a chapter a night to Howard till the book was finished – the only entertainment she had known which had kept him away from his 'precious wireless'. 'More about Samuel,' he would say after supper, knowing she smiled on reaching for the book.

Samuel B. Morse had been the white hope of American classical painting, and earned a fair living covering enormous canvases with the dignified faces of the worthy.

Returning from a tour of Europe on the steamship *Sully* in 1832, Morse conceived the idea of an electric telegraph, and a couple of years later he had devised a working model which sent letters from one side of the room to the other. As a concept it seemed to others a step into the white and empty spaces of the unknown, the blank future that their imaginations could not envisage, and certainly not colonise with science. But Morse had a practical mind and overcame the setbacks. 'If we knew the how and why of such a brain even the secrets of the universe might one day be revealed,' Howard thought, after the author of the book had said: 'His inventive brain, nurtured by painting, putting what the eye can see onto canvas, helped if not actually propelled him to make the leap, art being ever the precursor of invention.'

From that point the narrative became thrilling, and Laura was some-times persuaded to go on reading till nearly midnight, taking him through the inventor's struggle to have his idea accepted by the US Congress, though it didn't happen till 1843, by which time he had constructed the famous code 'which will forever bear his name.' Howard lived, as the code was put together, in the light of inspiration, Samuel no doubt making a chart so that he could alter and modify, until the perfect arrangements of dots and dashes for each letter and number was fixed for all time.

The triumph of the first transmission on a line between Washington and Baltimore, a mere thirty nautical miles, called forth the immortal phrase from the Bible, which Morse chose to send: 'WHAT GOD HATH WROUGHT,' because he modestly believed, like all artists, that neither praise nor responsibility could be accepted whatever was achieved in his name.

Howard used the phrase from then on as an exercise when his key was plugged into the oscillator, a way of flexing his fingers and warming his spirit, on no better concept than Morse's chosen words.

The vision of Morse was of the earth being circled and criss-crossed by lines of more-or-less instant communication, and this eventually came about when cables were laid under the sea. A more complete girdling of the world – which Morse imagined but did not live to see – occurred when the equally great Marconi invented a method of signalling without wires. The ability to send news and save life at sea was achieved.

After Vanya had tapped out the plane's position, thanks to Morse and Marconi (in some sort of homage, though he didn't know it) boredom once more threw its woolly blanket over him. When no requests came for his assistance the sky must have been clear across the vastness of the Soviet Empire, all navigators knowing where they were by looking out of the window, only asking the radio officer to use the facility as a final resort, when cloud went from nought to forty thousand feet over Siberia and the Northern Ocean.

Most of the time Vanya sat with earphones around his neck instead of clamped where they should be, and brooded at not having any money in his pocket. He didn't give a damn anymore, tilting his chair so far back and knowing that the legs would eventually break, but telling himself there were plenty more where that came from, and if not, so what? He looked boggle-eyed at the morse key and receiver needle, and hoped for another call on his expertise to stop him going berserk and breaking up the table as well.

Listening to the uninhabited wavelength was, for Vanya, like being blindfolded in a room with no roof. A hissing phase of atmospherics scribbled across the sky, and then for no reason – Howard tried guessing at the import of what came next – a rising crescendo of noise filling the earphones like being inside the thrust of a passing comet, gathering power until tipping into *diminuendo*, when its disintegrating tail vanished into the firmament, beyond all range, as if God had been about to say something but had changed His mind. He was coated with the irradiating and gaseous pitchblende of despair, when a quick whistle passed like a bird, mocking him in his blindness.

Behind the static, what seemed like a ghost plane would start sending morse, indecipherable, too distant perhaps, tinkling to someone on the far side of Moscow. He listened for a while, till he doubted anyone was there at all. Some wizardry of atmospherics was deceiving him, as a mirage would trick the eyes of one in the desert who could see. He thought, when the signals again floated towards him, that because he couldn't read the message it must be one of the most important ever sent. Meant for him alone, it was unreachable, he had missed it, had not been sufficiently alert, or he had been maliciously deceived.

Vanya, leaning forward and putting his cigarette in the ash tray made by himself from an old tin lid, tapped the key, as if he had got the pip, you might say, sent a dot, one squeak into the aether which flitted over half the world, a single pulse liberated, picked up by Howard with a smile, the letter E, for Easy when he'd been flying, but now E for Echo in the modern phonetic alphabet.

Then Vanya went back to musing on the charms of his girlfriend (we'll call her Galya, Howard decided) or he resumed reading his magazine until, fifteen minutes later, he tapped the key three times, three dots in a row, and artfully spaced, rhythmically plinked without reason but as if to show he was still alive, was impatient in fact, and craved to be communicated with.

His idea of heaven would be to have a dozen aircraft calling at the same time for their position, the wavelength sounding as crowded as if a big buck rat had gnawed a way into the parrot house at the zoo, but the most Vanya ever got was when one plane came on a few minutes after the other, and then he had to pay for the luxury by waiting more than an hour for the next client.

Goaded into action by an unquiet spirit he sent random dots, yet diffidently now because Big Brother (Radio) might be listening for such infringements. You couldn't be shot for it any more, but might be posted to one of those remote mosquito-infested places in the Tundra which, from ten thousand metres above, he was occasionally called to give a pinpoint. Best not to take chances, however, by letting yourself go completely but, oh! if he could, what a tale Howard might hear! Such pips and squeaks were not necessarily proof that Vanya was an alert listener, though Howard assumed he was, but it seemed obvious that because the dots were so brief, albeit chirpy, he could be a very smart sender whenever called on to communicate.

Such operators were easily bored, and jittery when alone for too long. Having the spark gaps of the morse key only a foot or two from ever itching fingers, the temptation to give a tap now and again is more than flesh and blood can tolerate. Howard recalled flying over Germany as a long period of monotony, because radio silence had to be kept in case some German listener picked up the signal and beamed guns or fighters onto you. He had yearned to give a tap or two, even to call up a nonexistent station and send a fictitious message, but aircraft keys had a wider gap in case the bouncing should close the contacts and cause a ripple, and to tap the key meant a positive press, thereby discouraging the impulse.

Laura had read that every telegraphist in the Japanese fleet, on its approach to Pearl Harbor, was wisely ordered to put a slip of paper between the contacts in case an operator accidentally touched the key and revealed the presence of their ships before the surprise attack.

Vanya had received no such order because Russia wasn't at war. Maybe he knew an operator in one of the planes, a woman perhaps, because the pattern of his dots, three in a row, like the tiniest of sparks, were as quick as if coming from a half-burnt log which had rolled off the fire. It was merely Vanya's form of identification, to let her know he was on watch and thinking about her. Perhaps he would come out one day and make his statement of intent, go mad, in other words. No chance of that, so Howard had to do what he could by thinking for him, building a 3-D identikit picture, which could only stay in his world because no reciprocal chit-chat was either permitted or possible.

Every wireless operator lived in Ionosphere Gardens, and Vanya was no exception. Maybe he didn't have an airborne sweetheart, but he sure had one, if not several, in the place where he was born. He goes there every month or so. At the bus station, having not quite shaken the radio dust off his feet, he drums morse with his fingertips on the window pane, scorched with impatience. If he's lucky he can stay a few days in the village, where he earns extra roubles repairing the peasants' broken radios, being a dab hand at finding valves and even transistors from street markets in town. With Marconi fingers he is seen as a young man made good, and everyone loves him. The aerial blues don't get at him in the countryside, a magic bucolic heaven compared to the grim buildings near Moscow surrounded by aerials.

When the bus lands him back there and he sits down, and tunes in, atmospherics make sounds as if someone is sobbing far away, the breaking of a heart in deepest misery. You need earphones to hear the fully nuanced music of the spheres, so he puts them firmly on, even living out a pestilential itch in his groin to keep them there in case he should miss something. No distraction of family, neighbours, traffic or sweethearts until Grushenka, the station slavey in headscarf and baggy clothes, brings him, halfway through his stint, a slice of black bread and a glass of lemon tea. Whenever she does he manages somehow to touch her bottom, and she slaps his hand before going huffily out – though Howard couldn't spill this part of his fantasy to Laura, because even the blind must have their secrets.

It took Vanya some time to get sense out of a plane with a faulty transmitter, a dull and rusty note, albeit sharp enough for him, fitful mews morsing from the outer world. He pinned it down like a butterfly in the specimen box and, still on a lover's wavelength, sent a position report to set it free.

Laura tapped the shoulder of someone on a comparable wavelength, so he stood for a hug-and-kiss, glad to be released from his peculiar bondage.

'You were a long way out,' she said.

'Too far, maybe. I've got you to thank for bringing me back. I often wonder where I'd end up if you didn't.' He would sit without food or sleep for days until he died, except that he would have to come away from wherever he was to go out to the toilet, she reminded him, as he followed her into the kitchen for tea.

'I had a puncture coming back from Bracebridge, and a very pleasant man changed the wheel for me.'

Even when she only went to the bottom of the hill he would hear about all that was seen and heard, every incident no matter how minor or irrelevant, she decided, to keep his mind alive with things other than radio listening. Sometimes by a slight downward movement of his lips, he showed impatience at such trivialities, maybe thinking she ought to invent a few occurrences to make her revelations more interesting. But that kind of talent would be too close to lying, and common sense hadn't equipped her for it.

The lid made a satisfying clunk onto the big teapot, then the sound of the cake tin being opened. 'He was a gentleman, then, to help you.'

'He was. It was a muddy lay-by. I'd never have got the wheel off. When he'd done he asked me to have a drink in The Foxglove, though I suspect he only wanted to wash his hands. He was about forty' – she made a picture for Howard to see, of more details than she remembered. 'We chatted over the drinks – I had an orange juice – and do you know, he told me he'd been a radio officer in the Merchant Navy. When I mentioned your hobby he said he'd like to meet you one day. I didn't know what to say, but couldn't really rebuff him. He'd been so kind.'

Howard, on his second cup of tea, decided that listening was thirsty work. 'You should have said yes. Anyone who is good to you is my friend for life.'

'Oh, I didn't put him off. Couldn't really. He said you and he belonged to a fraternity. I liked that. We exchanged telephone numbers. I suppose he could have some fascinating things to say.'

He assembled crumbs from around his plate. 'What's his line of work now?'

'He didn't say exactly. We weren't in the pub for long. But I gathered it was something to do with boats.'

'Would be, I suppose. Did he tell you when he'd call?'

'He didn't promise. Seemed uncertain, because of his work. But I think he was quite keen on it, because he said he would as soon as he could.'

He had wondered why she was so long away, often did, though in this case the adventure was worth it if he could one day gab with an ex-Merchant Navy key-basher. He often had the dread that Laura would go out and never come back. Just like that. She would be spirited away forever. Hard to know why he should think so, though if you'd had one disaster another was always possible. Maybe that was it, no other reason at all. To make it unthinkable he told her about his fear, and they laughed at such an impossibility, an evening taken up with speculation as to what he would do if left alone in the house with no money. The fantasy enthralled them through twilight and into supper. He was inventive, as if he had heard the solution suggested by a message on the radio.

'If I was alone, and had to get by, you know what I'd do?'

'Can't imagine,' she said.

'Nor me. But it's just come to me. I'd take my morse key and oscillator, and a groundsheet, which I'd sit on outside the big supermarket. I would have a notice on a bit of cardboard beside me, having got Arthur the postman to write it, saying: "GOOD LUCK AND LONG LIFE TO YOU ALL." I'd sit there, and send it in morse at maximum volume over and over again, my cap in front for passers by to drop money into. It'd be such an original way of begging that I'd be bound to make several pounds a day for my food, especially if I went into the supermarket at closing time to scoop up stuff that had passed its sell-by date.'

'A brilliant idea,' she laughed. 'You wouldn't be a beggar, though, you'd be a busker, an entertainer. Perhaps you'd be spotted, and you'd make a tape, and get into the top ten. You'd be interviewed on the radio. You might even go on television.'

'Well, you never know, do you? Maybe I should do it anyway. It wouldn't be a boring life, because I'd hear some very interesting remarks from people as I sat on the pavement. Children with pretty young mums would be the best givers. They'd be spellbound at the music from my morse machine, and have to be dragged away screaming because they wanted one to play with as well. Maybe an ex-service wireless op would be so intrigued he'd drop me a quid, and even stop for a chat. What a life it would be, as long as the police didn't move me on.'

'You could go somewhere else,' Laura said, 'couldn't you? Outside the church, or the library. I'd certainly put something in your cap. In fact I might be so amazed by your act that I'd fall in love with you and carry you off.'

'And we'd soon be back where we started,' he said, 'which is no bad place to be.'

'I do hope that chap calls,' she said.

A careless and wayward signal came like a fly into his web – VIP from *Lux Australis*. He asked Laura to look the call sign up in his manual. Sensitive fingers were for splitting kilocycle hairs so as to get aircraft captains giving their position crossing the North Atlantic, a constant coming and going.

The cannon shell that had swept through the Lancaster over Essen smashed the radio and blinded him. The smell of metal and burning wires in a cold darkness threw him to the deck, on hands and knees looking for his eyes, for a place to see and cool the heat of his flesh, to find a window to the outside and discover what happened. He wanted to know where he was, even to leap from the plane and find out on whatever part of the earth.

Under his radio desk, locked in a box which Laura might know about but had never asked him to open, were his training manuals and discharge papers, the last resort to riffle through, as he used to, though no longer necessary. They lay there, best left alone in the hope of being forgotten. A life of action was no longer open to him, had been over from the age of twenty, but you didn't complain. It wasn't done. Life in an aeroplane had been all he wanted, made for no other, and when it was taken away he no longer felt any connection with his past or himself. For a while he was drowning in black space, happy that no one could realise his pain. He seemed normal, but the clock had stopped, pendulum and mainspring gone. Like others no doubt, he smiled when tea was brought, or his bed was made, or the MO asked how he felt.

'Fine, Sir. Never felt better.'

'Good chap.'

It was the only answer. Wanting to die was lack of moral fibre, and when he thought of Laura he craved even more to float into extinction and never come back. Yet when she came, and he heard the gentle plain words she had to say, he decided to live. Her tone suggested that a similar disaster had happened to her, and there could be no greater sympathy than that. He couldn't but want to live with a young woman who had such miraculous powers of empathy that she would match herself so equally with him.

Even so, the mind was too often in turmoil, though no matter, as long as he kept it to himself. The *Flying Dutchman* was ever at the helm. What would he have done and been if he had led an ordinary life? The question hadn't popped up of late, meaning that his existence had become normal. One less architect or clerk in the world made no difference. He could have been anything, but now he was everything because he was himself again, had been for a long time. Put your hat on in the House of the Lord, and say how do you do to the German Numbers Woman.

Perhaps it was her day's break, but trawling the higher reaches of the shortwave spectrum, he put his fingers to the typewriter and recorded that: 'The Indian Government has produced a macabre plan to clean up the polluted Ganges where hundreds of corpses are brought each day and floated down the river on makeshift funeral pyres. Now three thousand soft shelled turtles are to be introduced into the waters around the Holy City of Varanasi (which he assumed was Benares) where they still feed off the corpses.'

Such a gem made his day, better than taking down screeds of gobbledegook which blighted dreams and damaged otherwise untroubled sleep. The scriptures of the aether shape the heart. He tapped that too onto his typewriter, as if it had come through in morse, though what government would send that out? – signing off with: 'What God hath wrought.'

SEVEN

Richard focussed his Barr and Stroud 8 x 30 binoculars on the block-like radio and television detector van parked in the lay-by at the end of the lane: two straight aerials to one side, and a Bellini-tosi system above the driver's cabin. Windows blacked out, the only identification mark, apart from licence plates which he could not see, was a POLICE sign on the side.

He looked down on a grey stone wall, covered with ivy and overgrown grass. The wooden lattice fence at the end of the kitchen garden had gone mildewed. It was a bloody disgrace, the whole plot surfaced with a thin layer of dead leaves, and a few upright stalks of etiolated currant bushes. Green-trunked trees beyond were tangled with last autumn's twigs, and made a silhouette between him and the neighbouring hill. Ken was supposed to keep the place tidy, but was only interested in growing vegetables they didn't need but he did.

If they were searching for a transmitter they wouldn't find one, but he switched off the communications receiver in case a microphone was beamed at the open window. He passed the time sending a few paragraphs from *The Times* on his morse key, after disconnecting the oscillator, just the rhythmical clicks to keep him occupied while wondering what the hell the car was doing there. After five minutes his wrist ached, and he was making mistakes. It wasn't easy, without half an hour's daily practice.

He supposed the van was parked so that the crew inside could rest from their work of looking for clandestine television sets. They were no doubt eating sandwiches, and drinking coffee out of flasks. On the other hand maybe they were investigating him. Perhaps his more-than-ordinary aerials had attracted their attention, or some local snooper had reported hearing suspicious noises. Well, it was a free country, and you could tune in to what you liked in the privacy of your home. As long as you didn't write what you heard or show it to anybody else. Some hopes of that. Anything sent in plain language was fair game as far as he was concerned. Reception would be just as good if he dismantled the main aerial and threw a piece of inconspicuous wire out of the window.

They drove away ten minutes later, so he returned to his work on the highly forbidden frequencies, reflecting that they had nothing on him. He was always careful to renew the television licence.

He opened a manual from the United States which gave the police and security frequencies, and checked them one by one on the radio. They were silent for a while, or mere oddments on short wave bounding up to the heaviside layer and coming down and leaping up again, invisibly around the world and diminishing in potency to vanishing point. Then one of the Interpol frequencies became active, allowing him to pull in a choice item of a ship that had departed from a port in Turkey. The message queried its load of phosphates, and gave the boat's appearance: 'Structure just aft of midships, twin funnels aft of bridge, hull dark blue with bright green bulwarks, fore and aft funnels dark grey with black top. Keep a sharp look out. Thought to have destination Trieste.'

To prove he was earning his keep he took the weather for that part of the Mediterranean: 'Aegean and south of Crete sectors, northwesterly wind, Force 5, increasing. Scattered showers, moderate visibility, slight sea, outlook changeable,' and so on for another half sheet. If the ship was known about, its progress could be realistically monitored. Should any message be due from its master he would keep watch on the maritime channel. Maybe the ship had nothing to do with them at all, but every scrap of information had to be passed on in case it was useful. He phoned the signals through, then posted them for confirmation in the box at the end of the lane.

Back in his room he thought it hard to know how long his spying could go on. Sooner or later an astute organisation like Interpol would wonder if their plain-language signals were being intercepted. Didn't they know someone was always listening, and that hand-sent morse wasn't secure? Seemed not. Maybe they were being cunning, running fictional texts so as to fox people like him, plotting to lure the mob into a trap. What a web of deceit he would have spun in their place, the best and neatest spider in the business, purely on the offchance, so subtle, so complicated, so certain to get the drug smugglers to a pre-arranged spot where launches and armed helicopters would be lurking on red alert – with an alacrity that chilled his spine.

Circumstances and accident had put him on the opposite side, because his intelligence reports were better paid, not to mention the boat trips. Working for law abiders would have been more permanent, possibly more absorbing, not to mention – he laughed out loud – there being a pension at the end. Well, they could stuff their perks and pensions. All he knew was that drug running would go on forever, and the money was better for whoever got involved.

The trouble was that sooner or later Interpol would modernise its communications, though he would try to keep up with them. They would go radio teletype, or send a message in a single burst which couldn't be deciphered, but he would be ready for them because the clever and enterprising Japanese already had decoders on the market, and one was on its way from a shop in the north of England. He would only be defeated if they came up with a cipher he could not break, one-day message pads impossible to disentangle. It would be little enough trouble for them, and he was expecting it at any time. Five-letter groups would rip across the screen of his decoder, money spent for nothing, bugger-all left but to confess to his contacts in London that their spy branch would be closing down, at least on the telegraphy spectrum.

For a month or so he might pass on messages out of his imagination, based on the knowledge he'd so far acquired. He would tell them about phantom boats heading for secret coves, and ghostly small aeroplanes alighting on disused airfields, or the arrival of teams from Colombia about to flood the airports of western Europe with false-bottomed suitcases stuffed with the latest paradise powders.

The chaos would set them to hunt him down and kill him, unless he never went to sleep and sat at the window with his two-two rifle beamed in the lane. *Boys' Own* stuff. He would explore the aether for other stations. There was always something to pick up, with scanners coming on the market.

Trouble was you couldn't tune in to every frequency at once, though maybe the blind man who had been doing it for far longer had stumbled on a few items Richard didn't know about, wavelengths or stations providing priceless gen he couldn't have found by himself. Blind Howard might be someone who, in his innocence, would boastfully babble on about what he had alighted onto like a cloth-footed fly in his darkness. Any signals fed to the boss would keep the pay-cheques coming, so it might be the best idea he'd had for a long time.

Amanda came in with cups of tea.

'This is my lucky day.'

'You can say that again, though I don't know why you sit all the hours God sends at that bloody silly radio.'

'I'm hoping to find out how long I've got to live.'

'Tell me if you do. I'll want to know.' She laughed, and sat in the large padded armchair, balancing her cup. His table was laden with books full of figures and letters she didn't understand, notepads, and three (three!) radio sets. He had placed the table in front of the window so that he could look out while listening. The floor was covered with a tough grey cord, though the strands were shining through under his table at the wear from his nervous feet. The windowless wall was taken up by a chart of the radio facilities of the British Isles, a map of northwest Europe, and a chart of the Mediterranean. He liked playing captain on the bridge, between his yachting trips. 'I expect you're going to live forever, anyway, so why bother to find out?'

He faced her, hoping not to miss anything good on the waveband while talking. 'Is that what you want?'

'I love you, don't I?'

'Do you?'

'I must, if I say so.'

'I love you, too.'

'There's nothing like hearing good news.'

She often threw at him that he never talked, so he disproved her now by dredging up the incident while driving back from Bracebridge. 'I saw this woman in a lay-by. Her car had a flat tyre, so I pulled in and changed it for her.'

'Your good deed of the year. Was she pretty?'

'I suppose she had been in her time. She was still good looking, but a bit over forty.'

'A really good deed, then. I'll bet you didn't know she was that old before you pulled in.'

'No, but I was glad I helped her. We went to The Foxglove afterwards for a drink. It turned out that she was married, to a man who's been blind since the war. He got shot up in a bomber. Sounds a lonely old cove, but the coincidence is that he's also an ex-wireless operator, and spends all his time listening to morse. She begged me to call on them when I could, and talk to him. I'd cheer him up, no end, she said.'

'Another good deed?'

'I might do it.'

'Why not? Before your next trip, I suppose.'

'I don't have one lined up at the moment.'

'As long as you let me know when you have.' She stood, kissed him on the lips, as if in thank you for the story. 'I must be off now. I'm going to call on Doris in Angleton.'

'Have a nice time.'

'I'll try.'

In such a good phase she was bound to.

'Love you,' she called.

What they got up to he couldn't imagine. Probably went to a pub and had a jolly time. His mood for eavesdropping had misted away. The front door banged. Her car bumped over the ruts on the lane. He liked being alone, not listening to the radio. Strange, though, that all his best transcripts came when Amanda was in the house. Maybe she provided the electricity that gave persistence and brought luck. When she was out he was dilatory, got up too often and looked mindlessly at the charts, or switched on the wireless for music, and wondered why the hell he was where he was and doing what he did. Much better to be crewing one of the mob's small boats, in at the sharp end with all the risks of getting caught, the beer cans going overboard like confetti for a fish's wedding, and banter to keep you amused on changing watch.

If anyone asked where he came from he always answered 'Shithouse-on-the-Ouse.' You don't have that sort of accent, they might reply, and he would tell them that's because I was brought up properly, meaning mind your own business, which they usually did. Where Shithouse-on-the-Ouse was he had no idea, but it must have been a seaport somewhere because the old man had been a pastry cook on a liner, and they were always on the trek from one place to another.

His father had seen no greater success in life than for Richard to become an officer in the Merchant Service, but Richard could only get as close to that heavy level by going back to college and training to be a radio operator, with which the old man had to be satisfied, and more or less was, since it gave him officer status on board. Poor old sod thinks I'm still connected with it, and would walk off the end of Southport pier if he knew what I was up to.

His first job was on a trawler, but he had to give a hand with the catch now and again, and didn't like the smell. Then he worked on a series of superannuated tramp steamers that took him around the world, each billet varying from poor to awful, nothing to do but call it experience. As second radio officer on tankers he enjoyed dodging pirates in the Far East. He carried a service revolver, but they were ordered to offer no resistance and just hand over cash, cigarettes and whisky to any cutthroats who got on the ship. He would often lie in wait, a one-man ambush, and regretted that no Lascar mob had ever thought to climb on board in the night, so that he could shoot them down.

He went from ship to ship, but didn't get far enough, or quick enough, up the so-called ladder of success. For him there seemed to be no such thing. Maybe there was some defect in his character that others saw but he did not. He wasn't unhappy. He could wait. Life up and down the Gulf Stream on his last ship was cushy enough, until one evening in Maracaibo, after they had loaded, someone approached him behind a shed on the quayside and offered five thousand pounds if he would take a bundle to an address in England. He hadn't imagined it to contain soap, and that was a fact, but so much money never came amiss, and he got the packet through without being stopped, the first indication in his life that, while not cut out for honesty, he must have an honest face. He liked the bright light in his head, and the rhythmical buzzing that marked time with his legs as he went through the customs, an experience more intense than any to be got from a taste of whatever the parcel in his kit contained.

Honesty and naivety went together, he had to suppose, because when asked to do the same again he turned the proposal down. The young thug in dark glasses made it plain that if he didn't take another consignment they would shop him for the first transgression. Richard let the man know he had only refused because he needed a hefty upping in the pay. The man swayed off to use the telephone, which brought a higher up from across the street. To them Richard played a normal hand, merely business sense, showing they dealt with someone hardening to the realities of the trade. Because he seemed no fool they paid half as much again. After the third trip he said let's be cunning. Nobody's luck lasts. Let's find other ways, other routes. From then on he was in too far to either get out or want to.

He never knew whether being frightened came first or feeling guilty at taking drugs into the country. Success made the query irrelevant. Kids had no self control, or they wanted to see how close they could get to auto-destruct, or they needed to get drunk quicker and travel further out than was possible on half pints of bitter; or they had to blast a way with the dynamite of coke, crack, hash or acid to a part of themselves they wouldn't understand or very much like when they got there – a method towards self knowledge which, once tried, or even more than twice tried, would stop them ever getting there by normal means such as jogging or swimming forty lengths in the swimming pool, or holding their breath for five minutes. Maybe they ought not to splash out their giros, dole, wages, pocket money, or fat salary from the bank, or corrupt handouts gained by public office, on something so disagreeably lethal. It was a free country, however, so forgive them, Lord, they know only too well what they do.

But there was no excuse for what he did, nevertheless, plenty of articles in the papers to put him right, should he need it, with such money rolling in. No use telling them anymore that he wanted out. He didn't. If it wasn't him it would be someone else, never a shortage to volunteer as a pack mule from the poppy fields. He was up to his neck in it, thousands every trip being good enough reason to carry on.

For the captain to call him to his cabin had been an out-of-the-ordinary command. He stood up from his table, all six feet four of him, as if he might come forward for the pleasure of throwing him

70

overboard. 'I want you off, as soon as your contract's up, which it will be when we get to Southampton in two days.' The matter was so important he even paused halfway through filling his pipe. 'You can go to hell in your own way.'

Richard never knew how he had found out. A response wasn't called for. The captain was a bastard, straight as they came. No beard or moustache for him, all clean shaven, and no damned nonsense either. One of those menacing peepholes glared as if finding him no better than a dung beetle that had crawled up a hawser to spatter his immaculate ship, too low to shop, though he might have given him to the hangman if he'd had sufficient proof, and if that was the regulation punishment for the crime.

'You heard me. Out of my sight!' in a tone suggesting he would bark at someone afterwards to mop the floor where his shoes had been placed – and who could fault him? Such a man wouldn't act without a picture of Richard taking the parcel from his contact. He'd been shopped all right, maybe a couple of times, which finally set the captain onto him. 'Clear out.'

A hard spark in the old man's eye indicated relish for the play whilever he stood there. Better a yes sir, not even that, only an about turn and head on fire with chagrin at his stupidity at having been caught, wondering how many seamen and officers the captain had thrown off ships during his lifetime.

That was it. No more Merchant Service for him. The more occupations you had, the longer life seemed. There was a lot to learn, so he went into the game full time, and nobody had made the connection with him yet. Few got caught out of many who did it, and he soon gave good if not plenty of unique service, especially with his intercepted wireless material. The only way to get caught – apart from redhanded, which would put him down for twenty years if the consignment was a big one – was if whoever moved the pieces wanted to get rid of him, and put a few words in the right direction. But he would never be such a one, having built up his own intelligence file, and should they ever pull that kind of stunt he'd tear such a large part of the fabric down that the sound of ripping would be in their ears forevermore. He wasn't the naive tourist recruited in Bangkok or Turkey. If and when he got out of the trade it would be under his own terms, and in safety, the only assurance on his side that he would keep his lips tight forever.

Called to the flat on Harley Street, where the crew assembled before a trip, Richard caught a glance of deference from Mr Waistcoat, looking like a prosperous surgeon who had made pots of money pulling the tonsils out of rich Arabs. Richard called him Mr Waistcoat because he wore such a garment of the fanciest design. Richard would like to ask where he got them, except he wouldn't be seen dead wearing one. In any case, it was best to act as if you knew your place, which at crisis time would be a more rarified locality than such a ponce could ever know about.

Waistcoat sat on the mock-Jacobean Harrods sofa and, by continuing to manicure his nails and not inviting Richard to sit down, showed his origins as rather different to those which would have led him to becoming an eminent Harley Street surgeon. Neither did the timbre of his voice suggest as much, and Richard wondered how many years in jail had been necessary to make the transformation. He was no longer a person who would feel at ease weaving through the crowds on Oxford Street, but the sort to grow pettish if a Rolls wasn't waiting to ferry him from place to place. He was one of those who looked as if he didn't need to shave yet shaved twice a day. As for his age he could be anything between forty and fifty, forty because he had spent twenty years inside, and fifty because he had struck it rich too young, with the canny ruthlessness never to get caught. He put his well-cared-for hands in the pockets of his open navy-blue smoking jacket so that you couldn't see how short his nails or how burnt his fingers were.

Either way, he could be tricky and dangerous to argue with, though Richard, strengthened by years in the navy, when he hadn't given a toss for anyone since he felt indispensable and therefore untouchable, and because his work at the wireless gave him a certain mystery (and due also to the natural power of his self-esteem) felt no need to argue. He stood, waited, and listened out of habit as much as desire, an attitude in no way allowing Waistcoat to think that not being asked to sit down meant anything to him at all.

Even so, he wasn't surprised, or didn't show it, when a chair was pointed out to him. 'Take a pew.'

He didn't care to sit when Waistcoat stayed on his feet. 'I'd rather stand. Naval habit.'

'I like that.' Waistcoat leaned against the mantel shelf. 'I like it.'

He would have to like silence as well, till he explained what he wanted. The other man, whom Richard hadn't so far met, sat four square on an upholstered chair, by a mahogany corner cupboard whose shelves were laden with old pewter mugs and plates. Across the room was an oak chest, and an oak cupboard above containing the same sort of pewter but behind glass. Against another wall was a dwarf chest of drawers with an oval mirror on its top, the whole place like an antiques clearing house, confirming his assumption that Waistcoat had done a course or two in collectables while banged up. He felt an impulse, couldn't think why, to come in one day with a sledge hammer and take such relics to task, half of which were no doubt fakes, the only way to get confirmation as to what sort of person Waistcoat was.

A foolish fantasy, of course. Times were good, and the future impossible to imagine, so you hoped it would go on being good, which gave no alternative except to live in the present, and since that was the only way he had ever been able to live, it posed no great difficulty.

'It's a short boat ride he's got in store for us this time,' the other man said, 'but it ain't through the tunnel of love.' Richard thought if that was the case he should size the man up, who introduced himself as Jack Cannister: long greasy hair tied back in a tail, a dark three-day growth, and a ring in his left ear – steel rather than gold. He was in his late thirties, and Richard wondered where he had been dredged up from, though he had worked with worse on the boat jobs so far done. The fairly lavish payment was for sailing with such people, as much as for the quantity of stuff he helped to deliver – whatever Waistcoat might think.

'It'll be a little boat,' Waistcoat said.

Cannister gave a slit-mouthed laugh. 'Saving on petrol, are we?'

'Shut up, prick!' Waistcoat snapped. 'It's a big job for us. Simple, though, if you listen to me.' He opened the chest of drawers, and took out a chart of the Eastern Channel, spread it on a rosewood folding table in the middle of the room. 'Your skipper will be waiting in Rye. And he won't be bringing back baccy for the parson nor brandy for the squire. The goodies are scattered a bit more among the population these days, if they go thieving and mugging to pay for it.'

Richard waited for him to say that England this day expected every man to do his duty, but maybe he was saving it for another time. He walked to Victoria, liking the exercise, a hundred and twenty paces to the minute. Good to rattle the limbs and test the breath, knowing he could coax some of it back on the train going home.

The mission would be an easy one, Waistcoat had said, a piece of piss, though it didn't do to think so till it was over. Three men on a thirty-two-foot boat sailed out of Rye Harbour, set for a weekend of pleasure in Boulogne, where they would pick up a consignment and come back as if on the last leg home. When the motor got them clear of the canalised river Cannister hoisted the sail, and the skipper, whose name was Scuddilaw, gave a course. The sea, fair to calm, made progress pleasant if not easy. Richard felt sufficient apprehension to know they would bring the job off, though the others, half tanked up even when coming on board, fetched a crate of lager and sent empty tins flying over the stern.

Visibility was soon a bit off centre, when they needed to cross two lanes of Channel shipping, but Richard found the beacons on the radio, separated Boulogne from the rest, and called a course to set them straight. Scuddilaw scoffed at his fancy position system from the Consol beacon in Norway, and said he didn't need it. He could get there blindfold. 'And as for beacons, you can stuff 'em. Just keep your eyes skinned for the light. My glasses aren't as good as they used to be.'

Cannister altered course towards the wake of a tanker without being told. The weather worsened, the boat chopping up and down, but at the entrance to Boulogne harbour, nearly four hours from Rye, Richard felt obliged to do things by the book and put on the courtesy act, which meant getting on deck to haul up the French tricolour on the starboard halyard. He thought the Jolly Roger would suit them better, but the rain was horizontal, and the rope tangled, became stuck halfway, so he brought it down again and went through a clumsy unthreading with wet hands. Scud called that he should wipe his arse on it, but he reduced time into slow motion and threw back the hood of his anorak so that he could at least see, till rope and flag slid up the mast without hindrance.

They found a berth in the yacht harbour and tied up. Cannister went loping into town for a few flagons of red wine, to drink while in port, as well as get fags and booze for their duty-free, while Richard and Scud sorted out the galley to produce a fry-up and brew tea. The French harbourman called to collect their dues. 'We'll have to stay up all night,' Scud said when he'd gone. 'They could bring the stuff any time, and we have to be on hand to stow it safe.'

Richard took the weather forecast in morse from Portishead, the paper on his knee, legs twisted at the chart table so that the others could get up and down. They didn't like his news, that by tomorrow the wind would blow up to five or six, maybe on to gale. 'Whatever it is, we've got to clear out.'

While steering outward bound across the harbour Scud was suddenly aware that an Enterprise cross-Channel ferry was coming straight at them – and not too far off, at that. Richard, cursing the French flag down, heard Cannister shout through the squall: 'Wipe the wet off yer glasses, Skip. We've got a visitor at the door.'

The huge white building, all lit up and merry, came head on for the crunch, and Richard thought, well if this is how it's got to end, so be it. The life jacket might just keep him afloat, but at least he could swim. People fishing at the end of the pier looked on, as well they might, laughing at such stupidity, or misfortune.

How they missed it he would never know – God protect me from such shipmates – but Scuddilaw jeered as the escarpment went by, comic-book passengers with big eyes and red hands looking at them through the murk – and as welcome a slice of luck as Richard had so far known.

Bracing themselves for the wash, the boat went up and down like a piece of balsa, though it was nothing to when open sea struck them beyond the harbour walls, a prelude to the leg back, which was the worst small-boat journey he'd ever put up with, eight hours of corkscrewing through high waves, when the next was always hungry enough to tip them over and under.

After four hours edging way from the French coast Scuddilaw set the engine going while Richard pulled down the jib and put two reefs in the main sail, but left it up to steady the yacht under power. They stayed by the wheel, leaving chaos below deck to look after itself: better to be in the open than go down and sick your guts up, which didn't stop Cannister spewing before they were halfway across. Richard, who boasted guts of concrete, said it must have been the meal they had in town – when Scuddilaw went to the rail as well.

Under the lee of Dungeness the sea was quieter, all of them happy to reach the welcoming arms of the river mouth that had been in sight for over an hour. The tide took them neatly between the red on port and green on starboard, and suddenly into calm water. 'We won't stop for the customs,' Scud said. 'We'll do a Lord Nelson, and go straight on into town. Let the bastards come for us.'

The neat concrete walls to either side, holding the mounds of shingle and sand beyond, channelled them reassuringly back into nanny England, though adrenalin beat through Richard at the thought of what they carried. Even before reaching the berth a man from the customs post followed them along the straight road on his low-powered motorbike.

Tying up was quick and efficient, slotting in without trouble. 'Here he comes,' Scud said. 'Let me talk.'

'Didn't you see my signal? You should have stopped at the harbour,' were his first tetchy words.

'Come aboard. To tell you the truth, we didn't. We've had one hell of a bloody crossing. I think none of us had eyes except for the berth. We're just about done for. It took eight hours from Boulogne. Some pleasure trip that was. I thought it was going to be the last.'

He looked down into the saloon, and Richard could have laughed: a mass of dirty bedding, food, pots and pans, radio, charts and logbooks, all Swiss-rolled into a disgusting mess. 'What do you have on board?'

'Our duty-free's somewhere down there,' Scud told him.

'I'll get it.' Cannister jumped up. 'If you like. It's in them plastic bags.'

The customs man was halfway down. Let him cut into it if he was in the mind to. He'd need a sharp knife. Going the rest of the way, he opened a cupboard or two, and came back up. He might have been suspicious, but couldn't take the boat to pieces on his own. 'Next time, stop at my signal.'

When the noise of his half-stroke put-put bike diminished along the road they brought out the bundles. Rain came warm and wetter than wet from seawards, but they had something to sing about as they took them under their coats to Cannister's Land-Rover so that he could set off for London.

'He'd never have found it, anyway,' Scud said when he and Richard sat down to a meal in the galley after a quick tidying. 'I've never known such weather for this time of year.'

'Maybe that's what saved us.' The thought of surviving another such trip put him in a low mood, yet they were all the same, and none exactly alike. As the spaghetti and rich meat sauce went down, helped by two bottles of wine, he could only look forward to collecting his pay. Hard to know how Waistcoat had been so sure they would accomplish what he'd sent them to do in such foul weather.

'Bad trip, I hear?' Waistcoat said the next afternoon.

'It was all right.'

'Smoke, if you want to.' He offered a cigar. 'I'm glad you were with them. You might not think you're essential, but you are. You keep them in order, just by being there.'

So that was it. Thank you very much, fuckface. Without him they might run off with the stuff.

'Or do something silly,' Waistcoat said. 'You never know.' He flashed the gold lighter under Richard's cigar. 'But a chap like you, well, they feel safe. Anyway, it's good to have a radio officer on board.' He took an envelope from the pocket of his smoking jacket – plum coloured this time. 'I hope this keeps you happy.'

Best to be a man of few words. Make him think he's got a bargain. 'Thanks.'

'The next trip will be in a bigger league altogether. Much larger boat. All engine power. We'll fly to Malaga, and bring it back from Gib.'

'I'd like a date.'

'Don't know myself yet.'

'As soon as you can, let me have it, then.'

Meeting over. The next stage was to face Amanda's righteous anger for not having told her where he was going and how long he would be away. He brought that one off as well, in spite of them screaming at each other that there was nothing else to do but end the marriage.

'Next time,' he said, a shake in his hands as he fitted the corkscrew into a bottle of wine from Boulogne, 'and for me anyway it'll be hemlock before wedlock.' Which made her laugh, the crisis over, leaving him to wonder how many more times he would get away with it.

He sat again at the radio and checked all frequencies. Nothing was coming through that could be used. At half-past six everyone had signed off, so he picked up the phone and dialled Laura's number from his address book. She had a young woman's voice, and seemed more than happy when he said his name. 'If it's all right with you I'll knock on your door tomorrow evening, sometime after supper.'

'About eight o'clock? You'll be able to have coffee. Howard will be thrilled when I tell him.'

EIGHT

Sunspots had given so much trouble that Howard hadn't heard Moscow for a week, no sound of Vanya on his usual *qui vive*. A wobbly-wobbly note, like the noise of a bathtub eternally filling, might turn into his reappearance, but the sound died, though he listened assiduously and long for anything intelligible. Ionised gases and the sun's ultraviolet rays in the upper atmosphere, bending the radio beams back to earth, were troublesome at dawn and dusk, and solar flares played havoc for days.

The magician's cabin was full of complications, a test bed of patience needed even from the most devoted. He became angry when things weren't perfect, always hoping for something, maybe a signal from God's miracle department saying that the application in triplicate to get his sight back had been approved. Neither the in-tray nor the out-tray held any such plan. The condition had been so long with him that he was beyond that kind of hope, more an animal longing he ought not to need anymore, but necessary for him to go on living.

You could always hope, because sunspots altered by the hour. A special radio station devoted to news of them morsed out periodical bulletins from a place called Boulder:

'FORECAST SUN ACT LOW TO MODERATE. MAG FIELD ACTIVE TO WEAK STORM. HF CONDITIONS NORMAL TO MODERATE,' followed by a long dash from the beacon.

Atmospheric conditions varied with the equinox, yet he doubted this was the reason for Moscow's demise, because certain random whistles and occasional taps at the key were beginning to come back, or the tuning-up of transmitters (that fizzled to nothing) or muffled voices too far out to identify.

Either there was no work for Vanya, or no planes were flying because of bad weather, or everyone was on holiday, or the system had been discontinued for lack of use, or the frequency had been changed for security reasons, or the transmitter had broken down and Vanya had gone back to his village till a telegram arrived by landline saying the equipment had been mended.

Whatever the reason, Moscow came back, and Vanya was his unmistakable, competent, idiosyncratic self. Howard's typed log soon filled with latitudes and longitudes, and the serial numbers of Russian aircraft grew into a column on his typewriter. He recalled kids on street corners before the war writing on penny jotters the number of each car that passed, a futile pastime he'd laughed at, but which he now seemed to be following with his collection of Russian plane numbers.

Last year at the end of the tourist season Laura had taken him to Paris, and he resisted the temptation at both airports of asking her to note the numbers of any Aeroflot planes she might see on the tarmac. At London Heathrow, going through the security screen, the man took the morse key and oscillator from Howard's bag and asked what it was for.

'Looks like one of them little tap-tap things,' the girl assistant said.

Howard explained that indeed it was, and gave a demonstration to prove it was no part of a secret terrorist weapon.

'I've always admired blokes who can use one of them,' the man said. 'It must be wonderful to send messages like that.'

Howard was gratified at being wished a good journey.

'He's blind, as well,' he heard the girl say. 'Did you notice?' as Laura led him away for coffee.

At evening in the hotel he took out his key to send an item or two to himself. Rich days of different air and unusual food, and going around galleries with a hired commentary plugged into his ear – perfect for a blind man – demanded some therapy before going to bed, a few paragraphs of impressions:

'Light comes out of darkness as I see the paintings, according to colours conjured up by myself. The shapes, too, face and bodies, seascapes, buildings and sunsets and harvest fields. I smelled petrol but we leaned over the bridge and caught an odour of water. I touched the stones of Notre Dame, their surface like the sides of a well-used matchbox. Inside, the world of peace expanded in all directions.'

Sitting in a tearoom on the rue de Rivoli, after a couple of exhausting hours in the Jeu de Paume, he heard the German Numbers Woman counting in her precise and authoritarian voice. He flushed red and felt a thudding beat of the heart. How could she be in Paris? Her employers were so happy with her year-in and year-out duty at the microphone that she had been awarded a special excursion to France. They even paid a woman to look after the children while she was away.

Laura was frightened when he half stood for no reason, clattering his cup, a spoon falling. 'Oh, it's her!' he cried, then sat, because the recitation of numbers had stopped, the bell of the till rang her off. 'Does she have children?'

She couldn't think what he meant. 'Who?'

'The woman going out.'

'She's only a German tourist.'

'What was she like? Tell me.'

'There was a man with her. They were deciding what tip to leave. I hardly saw her. Tall and blonde, I think.'

His hands shook. Something had upset him, the heart pounding through his shirt. Her happiness was in knowing he couldn't see her tears, surreptitiously dabbed with the napkin. 'What was she wearing?'

'I'm not sure. I only saw her in the mirror. A red see-through mac.'

'Did she have a hat on?'

Such holidays were difficult, but she wouldn't give them up. 'I don't think so.'

'Weren't you sure?' He turned his head in the direction of the door, hard to stop himself blundering out to follow her. Perhaps she was in Paris with the American boyfriend he had given her, and someone in her small German town was taking care of the children as a favour, without payment. From then on he imagined her a few paces behind, or one room in front of them in a museum. Where had she gone? Useless and hopeless. He would never catch her in the crowds. The darkness grew more sombre than it had for weeks.

Laura noted that for the rest of the holiday he was edgy, moody, and apologetic about his behaviour, which upset her even more. Back home he couldn't find the German Numbers Woman on the airwaves for a week, proof if he needed any that she was still in Paris.

Hearing Vanya again was like resuming touch with an old friend. Maybe he hadn't been off the air at all, simply that his services were so infrequently needed that Howard hadn't tuned in at the right time. As simple as that. He often lost patience while waiting for transmissions, moving from atmospheric emptiness to a search for equally interesting items, of which there were still many. But here was Vanya, bouncing out his wares with the usual alacrity.

Astute due to his aircrew training, Howard made guesses as to where planes were going to and coming from. If a plane received two positions within a certain time he could, with Laura's help (though he called for it as little as possible) calculate the airspeed and work out the plane's direction, and speculate on what was being carried if it was not travelling on a usual airline route. One vector suggested a flight to Tripoli in Libya, taking God knew what, then Vienna, to bring back vintage bottles of the Blue Danube maybe, another to China for chopsticks and tinned dog, one over the Himalayas to India for tea, and one to a place in Afghanistan, no doubt a bit of private enterprise for drugs.

He plotted one to Archangel, and one to Spitzbergen, while still another was on its way to Yakutsk for a cargo of smoked reindeer meat. The speed of one plane was calculated as so fast, at 1175 miles per hour, that it must have been the Konkordski, going from Rostov to Samarkand. Another plane trundled along so slowly it could only be piston engined – or the wind was so strong it almost stood still. Or was it going in circles? Or it had landed somewhere and taken off again between the two calls. Or Vanya's mechanism had got the second position wrong, which sometimes happened.

He went into the wireless room instead of waiting for Laura to read him the newspaper he had just brought back, and picked up stations so far west they were still belting out good mornings. With others it was good afternoon, so by knowing the time zone of their messages he could guess the longitude. The radio officer of a ship coming up Channel fixed his oscillators to tinkle out the first bars of 'My Darling Clementine', a ruse to wake the coast stations. Another ship's operator was sending 'Three Blind Mice' to get himself into a social mood. Howard decided to concentrate on the eight-megacycle band. Let the spectrum live for me. I don't care when I die. Short wave will go on pulsating after I'm dead, and even then my soul will find a home between the earth and the heaviside layer.

At tea Laura told him that the man who had changed her wheel in the rain had phoned to say he would call after supper tomorrow night. 'I'm glad he kept his promise, aren't you?'

In one way yes, in another no. 'Of course. There's a lot to thank you for.'

A stranger in the house on such a pretext would highlight his disability, bring it to mind in relation to the non blind outside his wireless room. 'It'll be nice to have a chat.' Laura helped him to be king of himself, but he was a Lord of the Universe when concealed within his earphones. He felt no excitement at meeting someone with the same radio aptitudes as himself but who had his sight as well. 'It's marvellous you've fixed it up.'

He listened until ten o'clock to chatter among the stream of cargo planes coming over the Atlantic, then turned the wheel slowly through the static till alighting on a recognisable voice. Lighting a cigarette to take his ease, he heard a woman calling someone who couldn't hear her. She was on a boat by the name of *Daedalus*, and her friend was on the *Pontifex*. Hearing both, he willed them to come together. Loud and clear, they called through space. The woman with the gruff voice and heavy foreign accent suggested they change to another channel, but as the English and younger woman, who sounded as if she came from somewhere north of London, couldn't hear there was no complying, but she persisted in calling: '*Pontifex, Pontifex*, can you hear me? Over.'

Their powerful transmitters, especially the Englishwoman's, brought them together. 'Where have you been, Carla? What were you doing with your radio? I could hear you all the time.'

He didn't get the answer, because Carla was talking on one frequency and the Englishwoman on another – working duplex it was called. When they occasionally changed to get better reception Howard decided to stay with the Englishwoman. 'I miss you a lot. The others on board joke about when I was with you. I'm happy when I'm with you. When I got back on board everybody said how happy I was, but I was ready to cry when I said goodbye to you. They were watching me saying goodbye so I said goodbye quickly because I didn't want them to see me cry.'

He wouldn't make a typescript in case of missing something, and cursed the static that threatened to diminish her voice.

'Carla, I want to stay with you forever. I want to do everything with you. Whenever I go on shore alone I imagine you're with me.'

'I love you too, Judy,' Carla said, now using the same channel, 'but I must go on the bridge.'

'I could talk to you forever. I'd love to be able to talk your language. We've known each other for over a year and haven't been together more than one month. I can't tell you over the radio how much I want you.'

Howard couldn't wheel off it, though knew he should. Eavesdropping on a private conversation was different to recording impersonal morse. It wasn't a ship-to-shore telephone line either, only a boat-to-boat chat, which didn't diminish the sensation of excitement and theft. Maybe Judy did most of the talking because it saved her friend the effort of trying to be fluent in a foreign language. 'I phoned you at home, but your husband answered.'

'He not my husband. Boyfriend.'

Judy laughed. 'Don't you know?'

'I no tell.'

Dynamite if whoever it was had a communications receiver and knew how to tune in. The airwaves were public property, after all. Maybe he knew already, or at least suspected. Could even be he didn't mind, different if it was another man.

'I'm hungry,' Judy said, 'so I'll take some bread to my cabin, with sausage and an orange. I can't talk tomorrow evening because we don't sail till one o'clock. We'll talk on Wednesday, though, the day after tomorrow. Don't forget. I know it's difficult, but we'll try at eleven, though wait till twelve because other crew sometimes come in the cabin where the radio is and I don't want to talk with anyone listening.'

'What about skipper?'

'Oh, he's in bed, and the others have gone to a disco. They heard me last night and said why do you want to talk to a Spanish woman? She doesn't understand you. And I said: "She's a very nice person." But they only laughed. They tease me, but I don't care. I love you very much. My hand is painful when I have to press the button to you. When I have a chance I'll bring my camera to the radio corner and take a picture so you'll know where I am. The men on board say: "Why have you got a woman lover?" And I say: "Haven't you heard how nice Spanish women are? She's fantastic. I see her every two months, and I'm more happy than if I see an English person every day." I tell them you're married, and we're just friends. Oh, my finger's gone to sleep. Can you hear me now? Say again? It was good to see you in Valencia. I was happy.'

'We meet again soon, then?'

'It's very difficult, and a long way to come. Maybe we'll meet next in Barcelona.'

'I don't know.'

'Why not? When you're with your boyfriend you forget me, I know. I'm going to my cabin now to eat French honey. Then I'll have a drink, and one cigarette. I'll be on my own. When it's dark the reception's better on the radio, isn't it? The frequency's clear.'

'I want to go to sleep.'

'Typical! I could talk all night, even though I have to get their breakfasts at six in the morning. I don't like to get out of bed either. After lunch I have to be on again at four.'

'Must go now,' Carla said. Howard thought she sounded weary.

'OK, speak to you on Wednesday. Love you, Carla. Goodnight.'

He heard the sound of kisses.

The voice of Judy enchanted, went deeply in, he couldn't say why. The tone spoke to him, more he hoped than to her lover. Though they had signed off he waited for more, a forlorn hope that she would come back. Laura came in to tell him it was time for his drinks before going to bed, so he plugged in the tape recorder in case there was more talk on the wavelength, not wanting to miss a word of their conversation.

NINE

Richard downhilled into town towards the sea, the morse key squeaking intermittently in its box. Contacts were too close, no hidden message made out of such electrical dribble. He smiled that if it went on much longer he would feed its canary spirit to the cat, or cut down the ration of birdseed for breakfast. He had practised using it during the afternoon, testing for digital dexterity and the flexibility of his wrist. It was a little ex-post office model, all shining precision of brass-made parts except for the Bakelite thumb and finger hold.

Lights spread along the front and, parking by the church, he unscrewed the key to stop the contacts mewing, unwilling for the battery to waste. Stars pushed from ragged cloud, and he knew he needed a drink when half a dozen lucky youths rocketed from a pub and went singing towards the amusement arcades. He climbed steps between the houses, undrawn curtains showing dolly-mixture coloured screens ogled by those who had nothing better to do.

Drizzle blew from behind, kept at bay by his trench coat and cap. No bell, but a solid knocker on the door of a Queen Anne house, no more than a glorified cottage, windows curtained though blades of light whitened the edges.

The television went off, an outside bulb glowed on him, and Laura opened the door. Her tenseness made him wonder why he was here. Perhaps the most important actions are done for no apparent reason, in spite of or even unknown to yourself, whether for ill or good. He recalled Amanda's laugh at his intention to do a charitable deed, her remarks seeming irrelevant, even spiteful.

Laura's poise and superb figure told him that if she had been twenty years younger he would have regarded her as the love of his life, and even now he felt regret at seeing what he had lost. Maybe I'm here to find out, which says something about me, though I should be too old to wonder.

She took his coat and cap, surprised at how vacant he had looked for a moment. He handed over the plastic bag with his morse key, and took the bunch of Dutch roses from its swathe of white paper. 'Some flowers for you.' He enjoyed her blushing amazement. 'I couldn't come empty handed. It was kind of you to invite me. Not much, but they're all I could find. I hope they keep for a while.' He supposed he had little chance of staying favourably in her mind after the flowers had wilted.

'You shouldn't,' she said, though liked him thinking he was under an obligation. In the living room there was an air of long-lived domestic comfort. A black cat sleeping its length on top of the still-warm television didn't stir as he came in, though the man got up from his armchair by the fireplace and strode so quickly that he was ready to step aside in case they collided.

Howard stopped a couple of paces off, and put out a hand. 'I'm pleased you could make it. I'm Howard. Laura's told you about me, I expect.' The horizontal voice makes him about my height, not a bit puffed after climbing the hill, so he's in fair condition, though he smokes, and obviously likes his tipple. He sensed the uneasiness at being in a strange house, and though not able to see, and never would, fixed a face to match words and gestures. Fair, neat hair, alert features enhanced by a small clipped moustache maybe. A curious and enquiring face, intelligent and perhaps devious, a bit like the bomb aimer in the kite that was crippled. Beyond that he couldn't go. Have to check with Laura.

Richard felt an intruder into their long-fixed relationship, but since he was there he'd have to relax and be at his best. At least he could stare at Howard for more than long enough to take him in, though not too intently with Laura looking on. 'I'm sure you want coffee,' she said.

He did. Howard sat down, pointing to a chair as if the plan of everything was firm in his mind. 'It's a lousy night. Did you come far?'

Pots rattled in the kitchen. 'Only from near Bracebridge.'

'It was good of you to help Laura with the car.'

'If you don't mind me saying so, I'd do the same for any woman. For a man as well if he was having difficulty.'

Howard thought about this, then went on: 'Is your house up, or down?'

'I'm on a fair hill.' He'd imagined Howard to be tallish, but he wasn't much above medium height. The solid arched forehead looked as if much was packed behind, but whether profitable grey matter or as a result of suffering it was hard to tell. With glazed eyes and seemingly dead much expression was gone, but he felt a central all-seeing eye somewhere. The chin jutting beneath full curving lips suggested a temper well controlled. He wore a polo-neck fisherman's blue jersey, corduroy trousers, and carpet slippers.

'Good for the antennae,' he smiled. 'Do you get much time to listen?'

'I do a bit most days,' Richard said.

Howard passed his silver cigarette case. He'd filled it himself. 'You can't keep away from the wireless gear, eh?' Going to the table in the middle of the room, he put an ash tray on the arm of Richard's chair. 'I know I can't. There are so many interesting things. You'd think the whole system was designed for a chap like me. It makes a pattern in my universe.'

Richard wanted to encourage him. 'And mine, you might say.'

'I suppose you believe in Fate, then? Predestination, and all that.'

Richard examined the large coloured print of a Lancaster framed on the wall. 'I don't know.'

'Looking at the old bomber, are you?' Howard said. 'I got my come-uppance in one of those. Over Essen. Twelfth of March, in 'forty-five. Beware the Ides of March! I should have known I'd get the chop, especially with the number 12.3.45. Easy enough to remember.'

'Nice plane,' Richard said.

'Roomy,' Howard laughed. 'For bombs.' He visualised the plane as if with the power of both eyes, even more clearly, the twin tail and sturdy Rolls Royce motors, long camouflaged body and angled wings (dihedral they called it), gun turrets and greenhouse cockpit, a strong craft to look at, but he remembered it feeling as flimsy as paper among the flak. He saw it right enough. The last home before the dark. Nothing more vivid. He also took in the photograph of Laura in its silver frame close by, every feature responsive to the fingers he now and again ran over them. He would pick it up, saying to himself, or aloud if she wasn't close: 'What a lovely young woman you are,' then wonder in what way age had altered her, which he could confirm as he touched her actual face.

'Fate, you said?' Richard turned. 'Predestination? If I think about it I suppose I do. You have to in a way, don't you?'

'Life's treated you all right?'

The abrupt change of topic showed he had to be alert in dealing with him. He hadn't expected to talk on such matters, and the older man seemed to be guiding him, as if he thought being blind gave him the right. 'Yes, certainly.'

'Not that you'd complain, eh?' Howard laughed. 'You're not the type. Nor am I. I'm a lucky man in many ways, having something to cope with which shapes my life. No arguing there. The eternal test of ingenuity keeps me alert.'

And young, as if both man and wife had stopped dead in their tracks. Richard took in the portrait of Laura, a palimpsest of youth. You could see from where her present beauty came. 'I hope listening to the wireless does that in any case,' he said, wanting to escape the topic.

'That's a bonus for me.' Howard opened the door for Laura to come in with the tray, and Richard marvelled at his sharp hearing.

The cat slid from the telly to lap up a saucer of milk. 'I hope I'm not butting in on your conversation.'

Richard took his cup. 'We're only on generalities. No shop yet.' Behind the Lear-like aspect of the blind telegraphist was a lot waiting to be said, and Richard wondered how much he would be able to salvage from his long-stored accretion of radio clutter to meet it.

Laura enjoyed the accomplishment of having brought them together, already as familiar to each other as acquaintances who had met after some years. Their uncommon hobby had cemented two people who on the street would have seemed utterly different – and passed each other without thought. Yet a whispered word of mutual interest, and they would stop and talk. 'What generalities, though?'

Richard laughed. 'Oh, Howard happened to mention predestination, though I'm not too sure what it means.'

'I always thought it had something to do with God knowing every step of your fate,' Howard said. 'It's written out even before you're born. And whatever you think might happen, or would like to happen, when you're young, there's nothing you can do about what will happen. You just do your best, enjoy life if possible, and get on with it.'

'He sounds a rather indomitable old God.' She came around with the milk, not altogether liking the subject, Richard thought, who didn't know it took her back to the hospital where Howard lay wounded and blinded after the raid, when he had said much the same thing. They hadn't talked about it since, so his ideas had altered little in all those years, though why had such talk come up at this moment?

'No one can kick against Fate, in any case.' Richard drank his coffee, hot as it was, even if only to have something to do in putting the cup down. Faced with a man who had been more in its grip than most he didn't feel predestination to be the right subject so early on. Or maybe it was best to get it out of the way.

'True,' Howard said dryly. 'Funnily enough, though, I dwell on it every day. Not for long, but I do. A survival exercise you might call it. Still, it's strange the subject came up.'

'Maybe it's the common denominator of those who have a life long attachment to wireless,' Richard suggested. 'You can't help but feel everything is foreordained, every dot and dash sparking the details of somebody's fate into your ear.' He turned to Laura. 'Now we are talking shop. Didn't take long, did it?'

She liked his levity of tone, as well as skill and diplomacy in keeping the chat going. 'I'll leave you both to it. I must put those lovely flowers in water, and tidy up the kitchen after supper.'

Richard tapped the rim of the cup with his spoon, as if she had taken their talk with her. Howard looked, if he could be said to, at the door through which she had gone, then lowered an arm to stroke the cat which, though silent, he knew to be there.

Richard saw him as being all the time alone in a place Laura could never reach. When they weren't together Howard was somewhere on his own, unreachable and curled into himself. It was the only way he

90

could get by, but even if he had never been afflicted he might still have been an unreachable loner. You couldn't tell, though he imagined Laura got into his spirit and lodged there for her solace as well as his.

'You sound as if you're trying to send me a message.'

He lay his spoon in the saucer. 'Same old restless fingers.'

'Like all of us. The French call wireless operators "*pianistes*", so I hear, because they play at the key and make a peculiar rhythmical noise. I suppose it does sound weird to other people, but to us it's like listening to plain language.'

Richard thought it charitable to let someone do the talking who lived a virtual hermit much of his life. Which is good as far as I'm concerned because he'll have little to judge me by, though it could be I'll learn more from him than he will from me.

'You might call us the high priests of morse. Funny how I sometimes feel one myself,' Howard said. 'We're members of a secret society because we have access to spheres which let us clip into their traffic – unknown to those who are communicating. I often envy the way they go on so blithely, not suspecting a thing.'

He spoke slowly, yet a subtle urgency lay behind his words, sometimes as if he would stumble over the next, though he never did, choosing each phrase as if rehearsed beforehand in the darkness of his mind. Perhaps Howard thought he was speaking to someone who lacked one of the many senses developed through being blind, or who was without at least one extra sense which a man with sight couldn't have. At the same time he seemed unaffected by Richard being a stranger, unselfconscious to an extent that he was on his own, or talking to a mirror in which he couldn't see himself. Though finding it a peculiar experience Richard was neither offended nor embarrassed, simply standing to one side while Howard did the talking. He assumed he would get used to it, if he came to see him again, and for Laura's sake, after another glance at the photograph of her as a young woman, he very well might.

'For instance,' Howard went on, 'there was a time when I heard Chinese operators on the Peking to Turkestan run. Very peculiar morse they sent. Most had no idea of the rhythm, and it was hard at times to make sense of. Then Laura read me from the newspaper that when a

Chinese airliner was hijacked the wireless operator killed the terrorist with an axe!'

Richard laughed with him, saw the smile lift his cheeks, an extension of the lips, the sound unnerving, like a hand scraping on cardboard. 'Served the bugger right. Hijackers will become the unacknowledged legislators of the world if we're not careful.'

'It's wonderful that the sparks did it,' Howard said. 'It must have made his day, after being bored so long at his key. I wish I'd been tuned in at the same time, when he sent his SOS. I'm always on the line for learning something new about the human soul. A peculiar wish, you might say, because I don't suppose I'll ever be able to, at least until I've learned all there is to know about my own – assuming that's possible, which of course I have to doubt. I'm not even sure I would want to know myself completely, though the wish is always there.'

Richard sat again, resisted taking up the spoon in case he tapped out something incriminating. 'I don't imagine it would do much good to either of us.'

'It might make me a different person, and that couldn't be bad, under the circumstances. The thing is, that all the time I listen at the wireless I feel myself changing, but so subtly I don't really notice at the time. That's what keeps me going. Though it can be disturbing it's also like a balm, twenty years measurable only in micro units. I tune in on the wavelengths we used in the Air Force, hoping to hear something vital, but there's nothing there anymore, just silence, or atmospheric mush.' He was quiet for a moment, and for Richard to fill it would seem too brusque an interruption. Then he decided: 'Let's have a whisky. We can take our glasses to the wireless room.'

The cat followed them. Howard switched on to the French merchant marine station, a call sign endlessly repeating. 'Such a noise would send most people mad, if they were forced to listen.'

'Me as well,' Richard said. 'Maybe they used that sort of thing in Northern Ireland, to get people to talk. A chap went mad from hearing it when I was at radio college. It can be a good weapon. For instance I was in a hotel room once, and a party was going on next door. It was after midnight, and I couldn't get to sleep. Luckily I had a portable shortwave radio I was taking with me to join a yacht, so I plugged it in and held the speaker against the wall. It only needed two minutes, with the loudest possible morse belting away. Cut their jollity dead. Didn't hear a murmur after that, though I did get a few funny looks at breakfast.'

The room was neat, custom built for the purpose, a narrow table from wall to wall, and a small window for taking the aerial outside. The wall was covered by a coloured Mercator map of the world, and a plotting chart of Western Europe similar to his own. Maybe Howard liked to feel the paper.

He was put in the spare chair while Howard fiddled with the controls of an old RAF Marconi, to the left of his typewriter and the modern equipment. A morse key was screwed into the table and wired to an oscillator. Richard imagined him being helped into his flying jacket, hitching on a parachute, and sitting hunched at his wireless as in the old days, re-living the trip of his final devastation over Germany. He might also wear a suit and beret, and play a resistant *pianiste* in occupied France, keeping a loaded and cocked revolver by his sending hand should the Germans break in, aiming to kill them but reserving the final bullet for himself. Such people were taken alive if possible, tortured to make them spill codes and contacts before being killed. 'Been hearing anything interesting?'

The magic eye of his twenty-quid junk-shop radio was a button of green flame created out of electrons and neutrons, which produced a small circle of living light held to a constant glow, not an identity button for the blackout but one for the overcoat of a wandering wizard – fixed into the left side of the wireless. If the magic eye dimmed out the circuit would go dead, the world stop, all movable animal and geological life be sucked into space. Every morning Howard put his finger close to make sure it was at his bidding, and thanked the Deity – whoever or whatever that might be – for keeping him healthy and well provided for, except that he couldn't see the green glow in the same way as everyone else, didn't need to, because there was a greener eye inside him, an eye that could penetrate everything, which he now turned on Richard.

'A fair amount. It's hard not to, if you're persistent. I'm at it all my spare time.' The first rule in the procedure book at radio school was: 'Intelligent cooperation between operators,' but to share what he heard would be like leaving a hole in his body never to be closed. All he heard was his alone. To betray Judy and her friend, or the German Numbers Woman, or Vanya in Moscow, or the *Flying Dutchman*, or any other character culled from the network and allowed to grow and become real in his mind, wasn't part of his wish. At the moment they were beholden to him for their secret existence. On the other hand, perhaps Richard already had them in his books, and to mention them would make no difference either to their fate or his. But he was taking no chances.

Richard sensed his reluctance. You only got what you gave, nothing more and nothing less. 'I still have the speed to take everything, even the Italian news at twenty eight words a minute. It's amazing how it stays with you. The Italian weather comes in pretty fast as well. It's good practice, and keeps the brain sharp. That's the reason I do it.' He wondered at the red pins scattered across the Russia of *Mercator's World*, deciding Laura must have put them in, places Howard had heard calling on the radio perhaps, though none were on known towns. A pile of sheets were stacked behind the typewriter, and he tried to see what was on them. 'Is that how you keep your log?'

'I do.' Howard shuffled them, put them aside. 'Though there's no method in it, unless I get my sight back and one day want to remind myself how things were. A tape recorder's better, which I use for voice mainly.' He turned the needle from where it might alight on Judy calling her lover.

Richard, leaning against the chest of drawers, noted a plastic globe of the world, surface slightly raised for coastlines and mountains, which made it easier for Howard to read. 'I like to hear ship-to-shore telephone conversations, though they're mostly Russian or Italian. Trawler skippers come up as well. Can't say I record much of that, or type it up.'

'I'd like to be able to.' Howard lit his pipe, more apposite for the wireless room, blowing smoke upwards, head tilted as if to look at its changing shape. 'That's one thing I miss – seeing my handwriting. I could read a lot more from how that changes than from what it's actually recording. Did you bring your key?'

Richard reached for his plastic bag. 'And the oscillator. I'll send something if you like.'

'It'll be music to my ears.'

One at each end of the table, but as if separated by five hundred miles, Howard locked the fingers of one hand into the other, cracking his knuckles into a state of flexibility. Very professional, Richard smiled.

'You go first,' Howard said.

'What shall I be? Ship, plane or land station?'

'Try land station, and I'll be a plane, unless I change into something different halfway through.' His laugh was like that of an infant embarking on mischief. 'This will give meaning to life, but it'll be interesting to hear morse from a person I know. You can use the call sign RIC and I'll be HOWAR. How's that?'

Start with something short, Richard decided, smoothing thumb and forefinger together, surfaces as if dried with chalk dust. 'Where are you?' he tapped.

The signals came back with exquisite tone and well practised rhythm. 'Over the Ural mountains,' Howard played, 'heading west. You'll hear me louder soon. And where might you be?'

Howard must fiddle with the key at a set time every day to send so perfectly, a man of habit and timetable. 'On a Greek island, listening out for the sinners of the world. What are you doing?'

'I'm the radio officer on the *Flying Dutchman* of Eternal Airlines, going round and round the turbulent earth. It's dark up here, all the time. Sometimes the ailerons or an elevator get struck by lightning, and we spiral down, livid with fear, but before we hit the deck God makes everything right and pulls us back to thirty thousand feet. He needs us alive, though I often wonder why. I'd like us to find a neat runway and come into a perfect landing along the flarepath, but God won't let us.'

The gaps between the contacts of Richard's key were wide enough for the clicks to be heard, as well as the oscillations, and his sending at the moment was less perfect than Howard's. He tightened the screw to avoid occasional repetitions. 'Yes, God is a hard man. Do you want me to have a word with him?'

'Wouldn't do any good. His wirelesses are turned off for people like us.' He gave the wireless operator's laugh. 'The Lord ain't got no radio gen. But tell me about yourself. Keep me busy.'

Richard took a piece of paper from his pocket. 'Irrelevant and inconsequential chat between operators is expressly forbidden but, frankly, I don't give a toss. Of course, somebody's always listening, though only you and me, in this case. So let's carry on. You have my permission, if I have yours.'

'Granted. Trouble is, there's always a third person taking everything in,' Howard responded, 'and we know who that is, don't we?'

'That old grandad God. Let him listen. We can't say anything that would surprise Him.'

'Maybe not.' Howard laughed at the cat going out because it could take no more. 'He's a lot older than we are.'

'I know, but it's saying it that's the point, and you can bet everything's written in the Good Lord's logbook, to be held against us whenever He thinks fit.'

Richard paused, at Howard's intention to give away no secrets – which is why I am here. Hand over the key, he had to break out of such crap talk. 'There's not much to say about myself.' This was untrue, but the speedy response startled him:

'We don't listen to morse on the wireless for hour after hour for pleasure. There must be more to it than that.'

Richard's hand trembled, missing a beat and needing to repeat a word. His wrist ached, and he wanted to pack it in, but they had just started. It might be impossible for anything but honesty, not the sort of situation he liked. He looked at the other side of the paper. 'I'll send you the latest weather from my Greek island.'

'If you like,' Howard rapped, face towards him.

'Here goes, then. Rain later Karpathio east south-east. Five. Moderate. Rain later east Karpathio east to south-east. Five. Moderate. Rain later. South-west Aegean north north-east, six. Moderate. Rain south-east Aegean Ikario north to north-east. Six. Moderate. Rain later. Saronikos north-east. Five in the south.'

Howard scratched his nose, and sped back with: 'Too much rain. Rough sea, as well. You must be cut off. What do you think about when alone in your little concrete blockhouse?'

More a demand than a request, so Richard could only send a list Howard would believe in. 'My wife, my work, my past, and my future.'

'Anything else?'

I should be questioning him, but he's blind so there's little to ask. It's all up to me, and he knows it. 'What I'm going to have for supper when I get home. Whether I've got enough cigarettes to last to the morning.'

Howard pondered the list. 'What you do to earn a living would be more interesting to hear about.'

Rain splattered the aerial window, a draught from the gap cooling Richard's cheek. It bloody well wouldn't, though it was difficult to think between messages tapped out in morse. The immediate response was all you could handle. You had to be quick and seemingly instinctive, so it was apt to come from a deeper place than intended. With so little time to decide you sent whatever sprang into your mind. Trying to formulate a considered statement would not only delay too long – with the risk of not being believed – but the mechanical expertise needed to work the key went awry and could betray you in any case. This sudden realisation hardly gave him time to wonder, let alone regret, how he had got into the situation. He felt as if in a confessional or on a psychiatrist's couch, giving in to relaxation and a false sense of trust, induced to speak whatever came. He must be careful. 'It's quite simple. I hire myself out as a crew member on yachts, which have to be taken from A to B, by a rich owner who can't be bothered to do it himself.'

Because of Richard's hesitant rhythms at the key Howard knew that something was being held back, perhaps nothing important, yet maybe a text which Richard would feel better having brought into the open, and Howard knew that his duty was to give him the peace of mind all men should have. On the other hand he saw little use badgering him into revealing his trouble, if trouble there was, because that would only confuse or harden him. Kinder to come out with something personal of your own by way of encouragement:

'I sometimes dream I can't open my eyes, that I've lost or broken my glasses – which I never wore, however – that my lids have congealed together, but I know I'm in a dream and that everything will be all right when I wake up. But when I do it isn't, which is the closest I get to nightmare. Luckily the dream has come only a few times in my life. I remember it blighting me as a child of eight or so, which may have been a sign as to what would happen later. What puzzles me is why I still have the dream as an adult, because what can it indicate for the future?'

Sending was more relaxed when a visible person was receiving your messages, but after his long paragraph Howard's fingers began to falter. Richard assumed it was the content which disturbed, and doubted he could respond at the same intimate level, didn't want to at all, though felt himself tangled in a net he couldn't fight free of:

'I received a distress call today concerning a yacht that was sinking. I tried to contact it but failed. Think it was sunk deliberately. Sea was calm at the time. Men were arrested on the beach.'

He was surprised at the speed with which Howard demanded: 'Was there a woman on board?'

'Not specifically mentioned.'

'Are you sure?'

Not having received such a signal made it easy to calm him: 'I'm certain they were all men.'

A tremble in Howard's hand, and a minor error in sending, suggested to Richard that he had caught him on a disturbing point and, more important, that Howard had heard something on the radio he didn't want to share.

Indulging in such secret yet musical talk, Howard felt more sure of himself. He was captivated by being in control of a rare experience. Darkness fell away in the light of enthusiasm. Thoughts were exchanged with Richard in spite of himself, which was how it should be, for it was futile to be afraid of revealing what gems of intelligence he had picked up. Something may well have happened to Judy's yacht to shatter his inner confidence and peace. Perhaps her boat was employed in projects which were against the law. The rest of the crew knew it but she did not, though if they were caught there was a risk of her getting ten years in jail as well.

His mood changed by the moment, and in spite of a touch of exhaustion he sent to Richard: 'As the *Flying Dutchman* goes around in circles without hope, I hear Russian transport planes crossing and recrossing Europe and Asia. Some appear to be going to Kazakhstan, Turkmenistan, Uzbekistan, Tajikstan, and maybe even Kyrgyzstan . . .'

Richard broke in excitedly: 'All the Stanleys, in fact. And what do you suppose they were carrying?'

'It could be anybody's guess, but I get their positions, routes, speeds, and heights from a direction finding station and a command traffic network. Sometimes a plane goes to India, or Nepal, or even beyond.'

Now he was talking, so we'll give him a bit of encouragement: 'To Poppyland, do you suppose?'

'Drugs, you mean? Why not? I sometimes think so.' But let's get off that subject, though not too obviously. 'I also play "Spot the Bomber" now and again.' He couldn't help himself: 'Even they may be on the drugs run. It's every man for himself over there.'

Which explained the rash of pins on his map. He's got more up his sleeve than he's letting on, so it's time to give a little encouragement. 'Myself, I keep watch for smugglers of cocaine coming from Colombia to Europe. In my time I've learned they bring matter concealed in false bottomed suitcases. In fact a party of six is expected soon. Information from the informer is unidentified, though I assume Intercop will be waiting, unless the intrepid six are warned beforehand.'

Howard laughed at the way things were going. If he and Richard put their materials together they would have an even more exciting game than Monopoly or Cluedo. Richard wanted him to think so. Imagination was a wonderful thing, could be put to many uses. 'The time is right for searching the aether assiduously for arcane morsels of morse,' he went on, 'and we can post the transcripts to each other, or collect them as and when we meet. Life is too short not to need the benefits of collaboration in our rare pastime. It would double the results of our efforts, a two-man GCHQ no less.'

'We'd have been great assets to that establishment,' Howard beat out. 'I'd have been happy working there.'

'Me too,' Richard flashed. 'One of us would have been in charge by now. But to stay on the subject of our future correspondence. We can even suggest to each other the frequencies that ought to be watched.

These might include voice transmissions as well as telegraphy. We might listen in to trawlers, for instance. You never know what you might get from them. I see you've got VHF. You could pick up cross-Channel small boat traffic, or even the coastguards and their choppers.'

'No problem,' Howard said. 'I can get VHF. I'll give it a go. We'll have fat files on all the villains of the universe, or know things about people whether they do anything against the law or not.'

He was too far ahead, so Richard pushed his advantage in another direction. 'What I suggest is that when I write to you I don't do it on paper, for obvious reasons. I'll tap it onto a tape so that you can listen to it with no difficulty.' In that way Laura wouldn't know what was being communicated. 'And you can tape record a morse letter to me whenever you come across something interesting. The post should get it to me overnight.'

'I like that idea.' Howard drew him more surely into the alliance. 'We'll have a perfect interception system.'

'For economy's sake,' Richard tapped on, 'we can use the same tape over and over again' – rubbing out each text as soon as it's read, which is good for security.

Howard decided on a little mischief. 'I might want to file your letters, I would if they were written. I'd keep them in a shoebox like an old lady,' he laughed. 'I don't see why I should destroy them, because they'd be in the sort of sound bytes I like. In any case I might want to refer to them later on.'

'Just as you wish.' You can't win 'em all. 'I only thought it would save the expense of buying new tapes.' Shouldn't have said that, because he and Laura obviously lived on more than whatever pittance he got for a pension.

'I'm not short of a bob or two,' Howard told him.

'What about space for storage?'

'I can always put them in the loft.'

Something else he thought of: 'If you get a report that's really interesting and amusing, and you want to share it with me, you can always get me on the phone.'

'What if we're listened to?'

Not yet they wouldn't be. 'Hardly likely.'

'You've done me quite a favour tonight. I can't remember enjoying myself so much.'

He was getting tired. Keep it short. 'Nor me.'

'We'll close the wavelength down, if you like.'

'Agreed.'

'Funny how pastimes wear you out as much as real work,' Howard commiserated.

They exchanged the appropriate signals, switched off, disconnected, and pushed their chairs back. The atmosphere of the room died on them, colder in the silence. Surprising how working the fingers heated the body, with the effort of using your arm and the whole right side. Throat and mouth speech seemed strange after such intensity with ears and fingers, more shallow, less significant, more formal even.

Laura was in the living room, a book on the table by her hand. Richard felt relieved at coming back into the real world. She stood up. 'You look as if you've had a hard time at the tappers. I could hear it vaguely rattling away. I'll make another pot of coffee before you go.'

There was a too-saintly aspect about her face, and the blue peculiarly bruised eyes that went with it. Something had happened in her life that had harmed her crucially, and Howard didn't know because he couldn't see it, never had and never would. He had seen a similar look of blight in Amanda's features on saying the unforgivable during a quarrel, but after making up it wasn't there any more.

'It's a blustery night,' she said, 'so you must have a hot drink.'

He saw no make-up in the bathroom when he went there, just utilitarian Kleenex, an electric shaver for Howard, and a razor. Amanda's tubes and bottles spilled over the whole place, but he liked that untidy part of her. No proper shower here, but a rubber pipe attached by two leads to the taps.

Laura met him by the kitchen door. 'You must come again. I know he enjoyed it.'

He followed her in. 'I will.'

'He's a busy man,' Howard called.

101

'Not all the time,' Richard said. 'I'll send you a tape. It'll be good practice for me to fill one. Then I can look forward to yours.'

Laura thought Howard would go to bed after Richard had gone, but he went straight back to the radio, thinking he might hear Judy talking to her lover.

TEN

When Richard finished listening he screwed up the papers written on and burned them in the stove. This time he hadn't, in too much of a hurry to get into town and spend a couple of hours with that blind telegraphist. She wondered what they could possibly find to talk about for so long.

He had left after supper and wouldn't return till near twelve, a perfect alibi for seeing a girlfriend – if he needed an alibi. She had one as well, come to that, though there was no call at the moment, which made existence rather a bore – him being away so often.

He was the love of her life, but it was no use telling him, could only let him know in her ecstasy while making love, when he assumed the words didn't mean much, said the same back, as if he hadn't thought of them till she put the notion into his mind by crying out. At such times the truth didn't come into it. For him that was what you said while making love, and because she had done so already he had to make some response. A man must do what a woman had to tell him, but it was better than him not doing anything at all.

She knew him to be one of those men who loved women, and knowing that women found it easy to love him back, made him a difficult man to deal with. The more women love men like that the more such men loved women, and if you were married to one you never knew where he might be when he said he was visiting so-and-so for the evening. Luckily she wasn't jealous, only suspicious, knowing his secrets weren't necessarily to do with other women – at least as far as she knew.

She smoothed the papers over and over to get them flat. No love letters anywhere, not yet anyway, but what was on them must be important because he had taken care to make sure nobody got a look in. Much of it seemed gibberish, or in code, letters and figures in tidy groups, an orderliness not altogether characteristic, so confused and uncertain was he much of the time about his life, rarely knowing what to do with himself between mysterious jobs with boats he was called on to man.

His handwriting for taking morse was more legible than on the occasional postcards he sent her, as if he was an altered person at the radio. She supposed handwriting varied according to what you did with it, and knew he could be quite a different man to the one she knew in their normal life.

She was amused therefore to think that in his secret activity he wasn't the person she knew him to be, that what he did was so confidential he must become someone else to do it. Unless that person was the greater part of him and all these years she had been knowing only an offshoot of his true personality. Such might be the case with some women's husbands, and with many husbands' women as well. Who knew anything about another until words or actions provided the evidence or proved them wrong?

Her back ached, so she sat at his table. Some of his writing was in French, a simple officialese to do with weather, and no trouble to make out. Another sheet had a more puzzling content:

'*L'homme n'a que la mot "dieu" pour essayer de voir clair en ces vestiges, pour avoir la force d'aller au plus simple et au plus juste, mais il y a autre chose. Et c'est précisement l'homme qui sait à tout moment comment on s'inquiet et à quoi on aboutit. C'est précisement la lucidité . . .*'

And so on. Where did he get such stuff? It must have come over the radio because he couldn't write French so exactly, unless he got it from a book, though none such were hanging around that she could see. She puzzled over the sheet, and could just about make sense of it, after her O Level in the language. Was it a code, containing hidden instructions for a *coup d'état* in some Third World country? It was hardly fair of him not to have written down where it came from.

The paper underneath, in Italian, looked like press material, nothing strange about that, each paragraph headed Rome or Paris or Berlin. She picked Mrs Thatcher's name out of the item from London, thinking what a strange world he must live in when not in her presence, though it wasn't one she envied him for, floating around from one boat to another when he wasn't sitting at his silly radios or looking speechless out of the window at the horse in the field, or at a tractor going up the lane, or spying on the neighbour's house at the junction where the farmer's wife made jam.

She couldn't expect him to think about her at such times, but if he did he would surely say something about his work, hobby, interests, ambitions, the world situation, but above all his love and concern for her. It would be nice to assume he knew more about her than she could imagine, even more perhaps than she knew about herself, but if he wasn't capable of talking on this level then he was fundamentally less than she wanted him to be. At the end of everything what did it matter? Mutual love was rarely based on knowledge but on deeper factors which neither were capable of putting into words.

Perhaps it was better they couldn't, or wouldn't, or didn't, because then the spell would be broken, the mystery demystified, the relationship empty and over and out – which she didn't want. They weren't incompatible because nothing was revealed which if it were could only throw them apart. It was the unknown, the unspoken that kept you together; better they knew just sufficient about each other to stay enthralled.

She couldn't get rid of this eternal need to know, however, a perpetual knot of frustration inside her that, when it became intolerable, produced a sexual excitement only spun back to point zero after they had quarrelled and made love. Otherwise it was the desert in between.

An intense erotic feeling came into her now, but she resisted it on picking up another clutch of papers, one of which gave the weather forecast in the Black Sea and the Sea of Marmara: 'A northeasterly wind, and visibility moderate in the latter, while in the former there would be poor visibility locally in the morning with a three to four wind. No significant change expected.' How peculiar to be interested in such rubbish.

A stair creaked, a foot on a broken nut shell, maybe a floorboard, which often made a noise in the house, even though Rentokil had done its stuff and they had a certificate to prove it. Such old houses had to be alive, but the place was empty except for her, at the moment, and she hadn't heard his car coming down the lane, didn't expect him anyway till much later.

Maybe she would surprise him and have a meal cooked and laid out: lamb chops from the fridge, a couple of scrubbed new potatoes, a packet of broccoli, fruit yoghourt and sliced banana for dessert. Might be quite an adventure, to play nice little wifey. But he would be so late that maybe an omelette would be enough. She didn't believe any meal ought to take more than half an hour to get onto the table. All in all it was best not to bother, because when she had last done so they'd ended up having a fight, her fault mainly, for she hadn't considered his appreciation of her effort to be genuine, or calmly and sincerely enough expressed, when it certainly had been, coming from him.

So and so was to be arrested on arrival at Amsterdam airport. Here was something more interesting. A woman would be with him, both carrying Samsonite suitcases with false bottoms. Cocaine was suspected. Then followed their dates and places of birth, as well as times, and details as to when they had previously broken the law. The man sounded very interesting: he'd been caught for pickpocketing, embezzlement, highway robbery, manslaughter and, of course, smuggling. At the bottom of the sheet came a series of numbers and letters, followed by a note in Richard's hand saying: 'Send through.'

She supposed he had to pick up such items now and again, he spent so much time at it. Now she knew why he was so interested and amused. A message on the following sheet told of a yacht coming out of Salonika and heading for Izmir in Turkey. Among the crew was a woman called Judy, though the cargo was unspecified and merely to be watched.

Page after page showed what clever Richard had his ears latched onto, so much turmoil for his own amusement. Now she knew why he was intent on listening, and could see it must be fascinating for a sailor to know so exactly what was going on in the criminal world. Another sheet listed the directors of The Puritan drug company, and gave the name of a boat which, luckily, wasn't one she had heard that Richard had ever been on, though she couldn't recall him mentioning any names.

If he had known people high up in government she might have thought him a spy. He would have made a good one, though he had nothing, as far as she could tell, on which he could send morse out. On the other hand he could be getting instructions, at the risk of fourteen years if he was caught, unless he had been to Cambridge and knew the Queen, like that man Blunt, or unless he took a plane somewhere and never came back. Hard to imagine him betraying his country, though a man capable of cheating on his wife might not think twice – well, three times, say – before doing so.

In the kitchen she stood a cup of coffee in the microwave, took it out at the ping, and sat on the stool to sip. What was he really up to? She also wondered about his puzzling phone calls, frequent enough to ask. 'Put them down to business,' he said. 'I have to make a lot, fifty or so for every job I get.' She had never seen him as a sailor yet could picture him in his jaunty and nautical mode, for he was always happy and loving before setting off for some seaport or other.

'Want to come with me?' he chaffed between kisses.

She didn't. 'There are two places I wouldn't be seen dead. One is in a tent, and the other is on a boat.' She liked her comfort, as much as could be got from this draughty old place.

Uneasiness told her that an obvious connection had to be made between what he took from the radio and his expectations. The coffee was scalding but her body was cold. He said he had saved a lot in the Merchant Navy, and was still living off it, plus what he had got in cash from the owners of the yachts, who paid well for his skill. 'All on the black economy, you understand?' he told her. But she must have been blind to think so much could be earned or saved. The way they lived, in spite of what she earned at Doris's, needed far more than that.

The temperature of embarrassment was never so high as when you had been deceived, except when you deceived yourself, when it hit the roof. He was so obviously up to his neck in the smuggling trade. To think so explained more than she was comfortable in believing, but having fixed on the fact – she spoke it out loud – so much of his behaviour fell into place: his unwillingness to let her know where he was going, and what exactly he had done when he got back. The few bits he let drop had obviously been lies, for her own good, he might have said.

She would rather have found out that he was having an affair, a storm they had weathered before, on her part as well as his, because this threatened to end the only world that mattered. She had been brought up to assume, and experience hadn't told her otherwise, that all criminals were caught sooner or later. A mistake would be made, luck would run out, and whoever was involved would be rounded up and sent down for twenty years. So far she had only anguished about an accident at sea, till his reassurances, and the number of times he had gone, dulled her worries. On that score she had to regard him as indestructible, if she wasn't to practice walking along the ceiling to while away the time during the long absences.

She wanted the plain evidence to mean something else, yet only by asking could her mind be settled – which she didn't need at all, since the truth was already known. When the worst situations in life had to be lived with, those which were tolerable you hardly knew about. He didn't trust her because he was afraid of her, not for her. If he brought her out of the dark she would make a fuss, which would not only shake his resolution but might erode his run of luck. He must suppose that Fate would take a turn against him if too many people knew what he was doing, or that he knew that the person closest to him disapproved. She couldn't imagine him giving up his work (if that's what he called it) so there would be little point in letting him know what she'd found.

The discovery made her an accomplice, or accessory after the fact (as it was quaintly put, though it made the blood run cold) and from now on she would be equally responsible for his nefarious activities. There was also the morality factor of bringing drugs into the country for the ruination of poor fools who craved them, which was horrible and inexcusable. The thought of living off such gains made her angry and ashamed. She wondered what he felt about it, if anything, though she supposed he'd long since reconciled himself with his conscience – if ever he'd had one. To tell him what she had found out, and what she surmised, would certainly test his ingenuity in evading the truth.

Part Two

Spinning the Web

ELEVEN

Madagascar came in loud and clear, but that wasn't what he wanted to hear. Laura had put herself to bed, the cat comfortably installed at her feet, until he joined her and it had to go. Meanwhile he picked up a rogue station on a wavelength where it had no right to be, an Albanian emitter with a kolkhoz bully boasting of the overfulfilment of the pigshit quota for the current five year plan.

Sometimes he would alight on the pirate station of Chang the Hatchet Man, a warlord loose around the headwaters of the Yangtze River, shouting exhortations of liberation, his followers no doubt shouldering the latest heat-seeking missiles behind crags overlooking the gorge, waiting for a steamboat of tourists to feel its slow way along . . .

He wanted to hear Judy and her Spanish friend, would wait as long as necessary, and in the meantime contemplate sending on his key the Old Testament scriptures, a task which, at twenty words a minute and for an hour at a stretch, would occupy about four hundred days, a heavenly task indeed if he saw it as a suitable penance for eavesdropping, perfect for a recently installed mediaeval monk wearing rough garb and sitting in his cell expiating previous misdemeanours – except he couldn't believe in such a process, would only send the Bible as a gift to God but not for balancing the books of his ups and downs. Nor would he bother to tap out the New Testament, for to credit that a man could be a God seemed the worst insult to God – who in any case Howard wasn't altogether sure he believed in, though he had called his name a few times during trips over Germany.

But to hear Judy and her friend he wouldn't have to wait so long. The weather forecast from Voronezh taxed his wits, likewise that from the North Atlantic. Search and rescue messages told which if any sailors

111

were in peril on the sea though not, dear God, that one of them was Judy. A voice in the night, calling her Spanish lover, sweetly through growling static, was as yet unheard. Their recently discovered method of communication galled her when she called to no avail, the aether making difficulties which might in the end do little for their relationship. The maleficent sunspots played bedlam with communication, much, he supposed, to Mercury's disapproval.

The cold coffee, sickening but drunk nonetheless, was Laura's last gesture before giving him up to the airwaves, knowing it was more kindly than scorning his mundane searches, convinced she would never lose him no matter how many light years he travelled.

Aware of the wavelength on which to find Judy, he even so skated across other stations so as not to come under the influence too soon. But he heard her, anyway, couldn't resist, as if he had crept helplessly into a listening position close by.

'Miss you a lot' – clear words came out of mush that sounded like fat bubbling hectically in a frying pan. 'I've just been on shore for a glass of vermouth. Can you still hear me, Carla? Maybe you have a problem with your transmitter.'

Carla: 'No, it's all right.'

Judy: 'I want to see you. Anywhere will do. Can I see you in Izmir?'

Carla: 'Not possible.'

Judy: 'Typical! Where are you tonight?'

Carla: 'Ajaccio. Where you?'

Judy: 'Naxos, hundreds of miles away.'

Carla: 'Bloody 'ell!'

Judy: 'It's nice to hear your voice. I really miss you. I want to be with you. I want to stay with you always.'

Carla: 'Me too. I hear you very well tonight, as if you close. I want to kiss you.'

Judy: 'It's terrible that we can't. I was lying on deck today in the sun, thinking about us in Corinth, when you first kissed me. It's too long ago.'

Carla: 'Like yesterday for me.'

Judy: 'I want to find some way of seeing you. There must be some way. The thing is, we might come your way in two weeks. They don't often tell me where we're going next, but I sometimes overhear them, or I can work it out.'

Carla: 'You busy now?'

Judy: 'Yeah. We have six people on board at the moment, which means a lot of work for me. I have to do everything for them, but it's my job anyway. Will you stay long with your boat?'

Carla: 'I suppose.'

Judy: 'Maybe we'll run away together. Or perhaps I'll come and try to get a job on your boat. I have a long list of things I want to do with you. I miss you so much. I want a nice dance with you.'

Carla: 'I too. But this is our life. I can't see you in Izmir. Or Naxos. Not my fault.'

Judy: 'I know, but I love you, you sexy thing. Love you, love you. Can you hear me better now?'

Carla: 'There's much electric.'

Judy: 'That's atmospherics. There's been a lot of shooting stars here, all evening. Beautiful. I wish we could see them together.'

Carla: 'Every guest on board here asleep. We have accountant who wears waistcoat always, even when hot. He's got a lovely blonde with him.'

Judy: 'I suppose you can't keep your eyes off her. How many more women are there?'

Carla: 'Only two. The men are ugly. Tomorrow we go ashore. We go every day nearly, to buy food, and catch other things.'

Judy: 'I don't want to know. Same with us. And I have to look after everybody. I eat so much I'm putting on weight.'

Carla: 'You can be more for me.'

Judy: 'I don't want to. I need more exercise.'

Carla: (laughing) 'I give you plenty when we meet.'

Judy: 'We can do it in the day as well. I can't say all I want to over the radio, but I love you so much.'

Carla: 'Don't say anything. I know what you think. Just remember what I say. You tell me when we meet. Lights are on all over the harbour. A plane is going in to land. Wish you were on it. Another one leaving. Wish I was on that. But I'm happy to talk to you. I

dream about you every night, unless very tired. I can talk all night if
you want.'

Judy: 'No problem for me, though we're very busy these days, going
from one island to another, picking things up, seeing things.
A lot of telephone calls. No problems, though. I don't know
what the skipper's up to. I don't want to know. I just do my
job looking after them.'

Carla: 'I like when you tell me things.'

Judy: 'Love you, stewardess. You're my sailor.'

Carla: 'Love you, too. Wish you were here. Tell me in a letter how
you feel. I like your letters.'

Judy: 'I'll send you another. Do you want me to buy you anything
in Izmir?'

Carla: 'Maybe you buy nice underwear.'

Judy: 'The black? I don't know about Turkey, but I'll try. It's so nice
speaking to you. You know what I want to do now? I'm shaking.
I have to smoke a cigarette.'

Carla: 'Me too. You sleep now?'

Judy: 'I don't want to, but I think I have to.'

Carla: 'Me too.'

Judy: 'Alone?'

Carla: 'No, with girl.'

Judy: 'I'll kill you.'

Carla: 'I love *you*, OK?'

Judy: 'Thanks a lot. Get your boss to buy a helicopter, then we can
meet anytime.'

Carla: 'Maybe we meet in Izmir. I know good restaurant there. I want
you in my arms.'

Judy: 'Don't torment me. We'll be zig-zagging around here for another
two weeks. Talk to the man with the waistcoat and maybe he'll
suggest it. Got to go now.'

Carla: 'Me too. I don't want to. I love you too much.'

Judy: 'Not enough. Love you too, Carla. We'll talk the day after
tomorrow. Make sure you're there.'

Carla: 'I listen. Love you.'

Static, atmospherics, mush, the heavenly code for silence. He was in a different country after they had signed off, on his own, in a stranger's skin, an altered person, bereft of more than sight, sat without knowing how long, hands by the morse key as if to tap out a message and get Judy and her lover back on the air or, better by far, to talk to Judy alone, though she wouldn't understand the medium. The call had been taped and he could play it back when he liked, though felt no wish to at the moment, it would make him feel more isolated, more desolate. Despair enriched a darkness he would not be without, painful though it was. But he reached for the key, and tapped away his misery at not being close.

'Dear Judy, I know more about you than you can know about me, though if you were able to hear what I've just listened to you would undoubtedly know more about me than I am allowed to know about you, or about myself. Or would you? Forgive the maunderings of a blind man. You are the chosen heroine of my night hours, and I am your unacknowledged swain of a listener, who knows more about you than you can know about me because I can hear you while you can't hear me, though we're on the same level in that neither of us can see each other. You don't even know when I listen to your voice electrically pulsing through the air. I know you have a lover, but I am infatuated by you so intensely that I might call it love as well, besotted hopelessly by your voice and personality coming into focus before my empty eyes. There's no one I can tell it to, which makes the pain worse, yet for that reason richer and easier to be endured. To confess it to Laura would put her into despair, or she would have me sent quickstep into a lunatic asylum, and who would blame her? To admit it to myself makes me laugh with a cynicism I haven't known before. There's a helpless yearning inside me which is new, as if I'm just born, ready to go into the world, a new man filled with hope and inspiration, willing to set out on any journey, however long and difficult, to find you, and see what you look like, though I can't, so maybe you would fall in love with me, so that I could touch you, know your shape, feel your kisses . . .'

A traffic list from a China coast station couldn't divert him from the amalgamation of misery and illumination. Nor would the German Numbers Woman have consoled him had it not been her night off.

Nothing was able to disperse the miasma of light beyond his barrier of darkness. Some Japanese ships on call completed his dislocation. He was an island of flotsam in the mist, the coastline indistinct as on a part of the ocean not yet properly explored, or seen even by the *Flying Dutchman*'s ever-searching telescopes, that ragged weevil-rotted and eternally turning craft, privileged or bedevilled in having some of the latest technology to keep it going.

He twirled the knob, searching for the night frequency of the Moscow HF-DF station. For months he had been hoping to find it, done all kinds of mental calculations to bracket the exact band of the spectrum, but with no success. There obviously was one, because planes in darkness over the vastness of Russia would need even more to know where they were, flying as blind as he was for the most part, and dependent on electrical assistance, just as he was, sitting at the radio trying to track them down. Nor could it be that planes weren't up at night, no more than he didn't listen at night. His eternal searching had put him onto Judy, but he still wanted to hear the Russian night planes asking Vanya where they were.

When the lamp was on he sat in the light though couldn't see it, reaching for the switch to press it off and cut away even from his little world within the house, stronger around him than if he had been in the deepest prison, and as alien a piece of territory as the fact of his blindness because it prevented him from travelling to Naxos and Izmir.

His blindness was a cloth pinning him to the ground and stopping all movement, mental or otherwise. With normal sight he could have found her, maybe even spoken the time of the day while passing between the tables of a café on the quayside, close enough to reinforce his imagination and call it sight, yet giving no hint of his love. He would know more what she looked like, or at least decide which of the many pictures that had passed through his mind's cyclopean eye was closest, an accomplishment sufficient to send him home, having foolishly wasted time, money and effort.

He was embarrassed, almost ashamed at the juvenile intensity of love that forced him to sit in the darkest dark unable to think of anyone but Judy, not even to move a finger, a still figure that had no will to get out of her thrall and go to bed.

If I had not been blind, he wondered, would I have left home, work and wife, and set out on a fortnight's jaunt to look for someone whose voice I'd only heard on shortwave, a voice belonging to a woman who already had a girlfriend but whom I had, like a schoolboy, fallen in love with? Why not? How can you be in love, and prove that you are, if you aren't prepared to ruin yourself by advancing matters further? Especially if it was the first time you had fallen in love which, coming at any age, was bound to strike you like a thunderbolt into paralysis. Nothing could be done, and it was yours to endure till the overwhelming wave diminished in power and broke itself – if you didn't break first, succumb to despair at the powerlessness of your life.

He did not know what got him on the move, but he was halfway to the kitchen before smiling at the fact. The kettle was filled for breakfast so he had only to throw the switch to get water for tea. Cups also were set out, as would be marmalade, cornflakes, plates and cutlery, orange juice glasses. Laura liked as little as possible to do in her somnambulist state before a drink and something to eat in the morning.

He thought of himself as a man with two lives. One was rooted here, with Laura, while the other was enclosed within a mind which was his alone, the whole reason for his existence, making his blood run faster than it had since the night over Germany had put the full stop on him. If he hadn't been blinded, and was still the same person, he would have abandoned everything and gone on his mad escapade, a thought which bridged the gap between then and now.

But when you cannot see, when most of what occurs cannot be seen, you can't affect the course of action. Neither on the other hand could you see the leaping cycles of the aether, the megahertz and geigerhertz containing speech and pictures, messages and weather maps and morse, the calling of and replying to aeroplanes, police, firemen, ambulances, ships and people, life within that immense span of the planet going on since the genius of Watt, Volta, Ampère, Hertz, Morse and Marconi had set it going. You couldn't see it, but it was there.

Laura's arrangements for breakfast were signs that one day would follow another exactly – items that hadn't been touched by him before because he had never needed to make tea at such a time. Any change of routine disturbed her, though she always denied that it did. She would wonder what had been in his mind for him to make tea on his own in the middle of the night. Let her wonder. He sat until he was too tired to move, and then moved.

TWELVE

'You never take me anywhere,' Amanda said. 'I like to go out now and again.'

'You go out all the time.'

'With you, I mean.'

He wanted to belt her one, because her accusation was only too true, but you didn't do that kind of thing, though he was ashamed to admit that the impulse came often enough. Luckily they were outside, which made the charge easier to take.

He knew every weed and corner of the garden, but was no gardener, except that he had tied a sickly tree to a pole to stop the wind pushing it down. It didn't seem to thrive, had no will to grow or even live while fastened up for six months. Ken had advised him to do it, but in spite of such countryman know-how his sensibilities were too elementary to realise that what a tree needed was tender loving care. Noticing the tree from his window one day he went out with his Leatherman knife and cut the cords so that, in the next months, it thrived, easily able to withstand the winds. 'Let's go somewhere today, then. We'll find a nice pub, and have lunch.'

Surprising how few words made her happy. They only ever went to bed after she had passed her bleak mood onto him, though he knew that to suggest they go there wouldn't work at all. He could wait, not denying that her own terms usually made the experience a notch or two higher than memorable.

'That'd be lovely,' she said. 'I like to see the sea now and again.'

'So do I,' he smiled, 'from land,' making himself happy too. He stood in the frame of the back door, looking across the lawn and hearing the languid hot day whistle of the birds from the belt of trees surrounding

119

the house except where the lane led up to the road. The trees there never had any difficulty, plenty of mutual support, lived and died among each other. But a tree on its own needed special treatment.

She had always thought the car a good place to ask her questions, so when into the clear of the main road said: 'There's something I've been meaning to ask you, Richard.'

No problem in taking Sunday off, because messages didn't come through on that day, proof that government agencies liked their leisure hours. Nevertheless he had flicked on the radio, idly between getting out of bed and shaving, to hear that the French cops were ready for Pentecostal traffic being dense towards EuroDisney. Whenever she used his first name he knew something was on its way that he wasn't going to like. 'What about?'

'Well, you might say I've been snooping.'

He overtook a Mini on a bend, just made it. Mustn't do that again. Don't let her think she's got you concerned about whatever the asking's going to be. He pushed in the cigarette lighter. 'How, snooping?'

'I was in your room a few days ago, to see if it wanted cleaning. You'd gone off to do your good deed for the blind man. Your wastepaper basket was full. You always empty it to save me the trouble, I know, but I couldn't help noticing what was written on the sheets.'

A queue of traffic stalled them on the way to Rye. 'Oh, it was just rubbish for putting in the stove.'

'Why burn it, though? They collect waste paper in the village. Every bit counts.'

'Only newspapers. Anyway. I like to burn it, because strictly speaking it's against the law to write such stuff, even though I only do it out of curiosity. I've a passion for poking my nose into other people's business. The world's full of shortwave listeners doing the same. It passes the dead hours when I don't know what to do with myself, between getting work on the boats.'

She saw little point continuing because, after all that, it was his problem, or business. Even so, he had stopped talking, and somebody had to break the silence now that the air inside the car thickened, and not only from cigarette smoke. She could tell he was worried because, going towards Folkestone, he drove as carefully as if the car had L plates.

'These transcripts, I found them absolutely fascinating. I'd never known they were like that.'

'Like what?'

He sounded irritated, or nervous. He was both, but she went on: 'All to do with smuggling, from various government stations it looked like, and the police in France, as well as diplomatic traffic. Priceless. But dynamite as well, I should think, wouldn't you?'

'What else do you expect me to take? Weather forecasts get boring after a while.'

'But couldn't all that information be useful to somebody?'

'It could, I suppose.' The Merc in front seemed to be slowing, so he flashed and shot out. As he drew level the Merc, with four youths inside, increased speed, and both went nearly a ton along the flat before Richard got in because another car was heading towards them. Then he noticed the Merc behind trying the same trick on somebody else. No use slowing down, and starting a fight with four of them.

'I'm hoping to get out of this car alive,' she said. 'I don't fancy life as a basket case.'

'You can't blame me for that.' He picked up the new mobile phone and punched in 999. 'Police? There's a Mercedes' – he gave the number – 'with four lads inside on the A259 east from Rye, playing murder games when people try to overtake.' He put it down. 'You saw what they did.'

He didn't like people on the road who broke the law, she knew. 'But those papers, don't you pass some of the information to other people?'

Changing his mind about stopping on the coast, he turned onto a winding lane towards higher ground in the distance, as if starting a circle to get back home. 'I hate that road on Sunday.'

'I see what you mean.'

'No, I don't pass it on.'

'Is that the truth?'

The truth was what he told her whether it was true or not. A woman who didn't believe your lies when you said they were the truth ought to be sent packing because there was no greater injustice. The relationship was intolerable from that point on. He might not believe certain things that she told him but he could never let her suspect it. He pressed the tab to let fresh air into the car. 'Why should I lie?'

She only knew that he was lying. 'I wouldn't know.'

'Have I ever lied to you?'

'Only by not telling me things.'

'There was never any point in telling you what you didn't need to know.'

'There is that, I suppose.'

He laughed inside, which gave his face a grimmer expression. 'There certainly is.'

'On the other hand,' she said, 'we *are* married, which means we're fairly close, shall I say. Everything that happens to me, I tell you.'

'That's not the same.'

'I like to think it is.'

So would he, but wasn't able to. Silence was the best policy, though once something had a grip on her mind there was little hope.

'For example,' she said, 'when I read such things from those papers I wondered about the smuggling part, and wondered whether you have anything to do with it.'

'You would, wouldn't you? That's normal. But the answer is still no.' He hoped that would satisfy her, but it didn't. It never had. He took a sharp corner in the lane and bumped a verge below the hedge, which was just as well because a car coming overfast barely missed him, a mere tick on the wing mirror. The answer had to be no, and no again, till the end of time.

'I can't believe it.'

She was doing well as an interrogator, so would he have to stop the car and tip her out, as the only way of bringing it to an end? 'Why not?'

'It's a feeling.'

'Oh, well, is that so? We all have them.'

'Based on evidence. I've got to believe what's before my eyes. You don't sit at that radio day in and day out for fun. I can't believe it. I don't think I ever did. The stuff you take is lethal. You sell it to whoever it's useful to. They must pay you a pretty high price. I would, if I was in their game.'

'You have a good imagination.'

122

'I don't need much of one to think that.'

'I'm sure I would.'

'You're not me.'

'No, I'm not.' If they fell to bickering maybe the argument would go away. He joined a B road heading towards a village, the church tower visible. 'We'll find a pub there. I could do with a drink.'

So could she. To question him further would be futile, and demeaning since he would admit nothing. In any case she knew the truth, and would have to be satisfied with that, and with him knowing she knew. Like so much else in their life it would remain unspoken, just another sore festering in the relationship, but one so charged with danger and ruination that destruction seemed the only prospect. She couldn't live in peace with it, which he didn't know, or didn't want to know, or was incapable of knowing. Or he just didn't care, or couldn't afford to care.

When they first got together and she had taken him to meet her father he had said, as soon as Richard went down the road for some cigarettes: 'What do you want to marry somebody like that for? I wouldn't trust him an inch. He's as sly as they come. I can see it in his eyes. I'll be worrying every minute you're with him' – or words to that effect. Well, he didn't worry for long, because a heart attack took him off three months later. But it was galling that he'd been right. 'I'm hungry as well.'

They gave their orders for the meal, and stood at the bar, Amanda with a pale sherry, and he a vodka with a cube of ice. 'You know I love you, don't you?' he said.

'Yes, but I wish you trusted me as well. Or doesn't your sort of love include trust?' She'd intended not harping on it anymore, but was upset, fighting back tears, so it just came out. 'I always thought it did, or at least I hoped, but I know different now.'

'Oh, don't say that.' He felt like throwing the vodka into her face. Nothing less would stop her, so he had to stand there and take it till she packed it in. The pub was full of the green wellie brigade, as he had known it would be from the phalanx of Volvos and Land-Rovers outside. Braying voices made it hard to hear, their faces too close. 'I trust you as much as I would trust anybody.'

'Oh, thank you very much,' she scorned.

He turned, to look across the dining section. 'They're taking long enough with our bloody meal. I suppose they want us to order more drinks. They never miss a trick in these places.'

'I think I'm going to need another, in any case.'

'I can't, though, because I'm driving.' A number was called. 'That's ours.'

She was no longer hungry, but split the fillets of fresh mackerel in two, and ate a piece with some bread. Lack of honesty had given him an appetite, not surprising. He was empty but for the telling of lies, and it seemed as if his body was also empty, the way he was eating. In his certainty he had all the answers, and therefore more inner peace than she could ever have with him. The distance was increasing between them, which touched her with despair, and made her wonder whether she shouldn't walk out now, just go, leave him to it. Surely one of the green wellie brigade would give her a lift back to town. The older she got the more she needed to be close to him, but as time went on such a necessity had less importance on his part. He didn't want it, and maybe never had, though there had been some promise in the early years.

'You're being unreasonable, in quizzing me.' His first course finished, he was disturbed at her not eating. 'I thought we were coming out to have a pleasant meal.' He refilled her glass with white wine. 'But something has got into you.'

'It's nothing.'

'Oh yes, it is.'

Now *he* would put on a show of understanding her. Either that or he would be angry. He was so simple it was impossible not to know him, and they had been through the same pattern many times. After needing to be close she no longer wanted his sympathy, or whatever it was. She only wanted to finish the meal, clear out, and go home. 'Let's not talk about it.'

'A minute ago you wanted to.'

'Now I don't.' He looked miserable. No doubt he felt it. She hoped so, but that too was a show. 'There's no point talking if you can't tell the truth.'

Their plates were taken away. 'I wish to God I worked in a bank, or some sort of nice nine-to-five office. You'd like that, I'm sure. Then I could amuse you with all the scandal and tittle-tattle I'd heard during the day.'

She laughed at the idea, not wanting to, but it tripped out. 'I just expect you to be what you are.'

'That's exactly what I am. But you don't like it.'

'No, but I like you.' All said and done. 'And I love you, that's what I know.' She asked herself if it were really true, whether she was telling the truth only to emphasise his lies, but if she wasn't, which seemed more and more likely, let him be deceived for a change. She would say anything at the moment to ensnare him and get a straight answer. After she had read those sheets of incriminating paper she had screwed each one up and thrown it back into the basket so that he wouldn't know they had been disturbed. He must have burned them the following day, all but the most blatant drug-related transcript, which she kept hidden, without knowing why. Anyone she showed it to would realise straight away what it was. She imagined the police going crazy at the sight of it, and sending a dozen squad cars to get him. But oh damn, they could take her away as well, on the assumption that even if she wasn't as deep in it as he was she might well have something to tell them.

'I just ask you to trust me,' he was saying, 'because if you can't, there's not much point in staying together.'

It was as if she had caught him having an affair. Once she had, and he insistently denied it, his last ditch ploy for defence was that he would pack his bags and go if she didn't believe him. Such ultimatums were childish and base. Those without trust and honesty were never able to grow up, be mature, responsible, and truly loving. 'I don't trust you,' she said, by now enjoying the rack of lamb. 'How can I? If you tell me I'm wrong, in the face of such black and white evidence, what can I think?' He really wasn't worthy of straight talking, didn't deserve it, was best left alone.

He wondered if others in the same game had this kind of trouble with wives or girlfriends. They probably told them all about it, boasted even, but threatened to disembowel them if they breathed a word. Either that, or they kept their mouths firmly shut. It was a career exclusively for button lips, as Waistcoat had said. They told their women to mind their own business, and they did because they didn't want to lose such an easy going life. He couldn't trust Amanda because she was a different type of woman. Reaching across, he laid a hand on her wrist. 'Look, since you know about it, why keep on asking me if it's true?'

She smiled. 'All of it, though?'

'Up to my neck.'

There, it was done, said. She would never breathe a word, of course. Maybe someone else would have taken his messages and plastered them all over the district as handbills, but not her. They went on eating. 'You're a difficult bastard.'

He seemed about to laugh. 'Am I?'

She had always known it, but hadn't thought to tell him. What greater proof of love can there be than that your partner gives you something to churn up your liver about? 'You certainly are.'

'I try not to be. I just don't want you worrying.'

'Oh thank you very much again.'

Neither of them could do anything about that. If his boat went down she didn't want to go with it. Love was love, but self sacrifice was unhealthy. 'I feel much better now it's in the open.'

'So do I,' he admitted, unable to know whether he did or not, but there was no doubt he felt better at having made her happy, marvelling at how easy it had been, though far from assuming he had been right to capitulate, wondering if she realised what she had got herself into. At least he'd make sure to burn everything in the basket from now on. Lifting his glass, he looked into those palest of blue-grey eyes which he had found so sexy in the beginning and still did: 'Here's to us, darling.'

She clinked his glass. 'Who else? We have to stick together' – though I hope not till the edge of doom, at least not if I know it. Her hard won victory brought a steely attitude into her thinking not known before. He still didn't trust her, and never would, even though it might be to his advantage to do so. He was just hell bent on destroying himself.

THIRTEEN

After dark, when nothing more of significance could be expected to come through, Richard thought of sending a morse letter to Howard, but he hadn't reckoned on the difficulty of filling a half hour tape, or deciding what sort of items to mention. Nothing in common between them beyond the hobby of shortwave eavesdropping, he had no notion where to start. In any case he had never written a letter of more than a few lines in his life, and to concoct one at eighteen or twenty words per minute by morse code would have to cover at least two pages of transcript. He needed to think of something that even Howard hadn't heard on the radio. Ordinary chatter of everyday life would be too much like cheating. The main thing was to begin.

Following the address and the date he sent: 'Dear Howard' – and stopped. His morse was crisp and clear. The beginning always did sound musical, fresh on the ears, notes evenly spaced, rhythmical, in the best professional style – a concert fist, as they used to say – but to send morse for half an hour without cease and not to make an error would be something of a feat, though he could stop the tape recorder whenever he did so or his hand grew tired.

Even so, thumping out banal generalities by such a method hardly fitted the effort that went into it, or the uniqueness of the means used. He wound the tape back, reached for a pencil so as to write the letter first and send it from sight as a long message. That way he would be less likely to make mistakes, or give out anything he regretted.

Yet that also was cheating, and he couldn't get further again than 'Dear Howard,' wondering why he had suggested such a revealing and difficult means of communication.

He threw the paper away, set the recorder going, and reached for the key. 'Dear Howard, for the last week or so I've intended calling on you again, but I've been much of the time in the sort of mood that wouldn't even let me leave the house.'

Not a good start, but it would have to pass. 'Not knowing what to do with myself I spent several hours a day at the radio, and usually got something interesting to ease the mind. To sum up, there was diplomatic screed on the eighteen-megacycle band, as well as government stuff knocking around on various other wavelengths. I have to be careful of course to shred the stuff afterwards, having no further use for it. I don't suppose you'd care to see it, either, if I sent it to you, which I won't unless specifically requested. This obsessive attachment to radio stops me going bonkers.

'You do it for different reasons, I know, but it stops me thinking of things which aren't pleasant to dwell on. What are they? Well, how I got to the stage of life I'm at now. After I'd had enough of the Merchant Navy there were lots of shore-related jobs I could have taken. I might even have gone on a course and become a teacher in a comprehensive school for the rest of my life, but that seemed too much like a living death, and in any case what would a character like me have to teach? I'm an all or nothing sort who, when I end up with nothing, as I sometimes have, diverts into something easy to do, and has such rewards on the payment side that at least I can have a good life, and enjoy myself while it lasts.

'And there's the rub, you might say. Nothing good goes on forever, only the ordinary, the humdrum does that, and who wants that kind of existence? Your life isn't anything on those terms, with your unique disadvantage. But my life floats along between one high moment and another, each moment (which might last a fortnight) packed with sufficient excitement to keep the adrenalin short-circuiting very well between times.

'The boat trips are what I'm talking about. In the last two years I've been to the Med a couple of times, across to Holland more than once, also to the Canaries and down to Madeira, to pinpoint a few. I mix with people I wouldn't be seen dead with on shore, but it's the sort of trade in which one can't choose one's companions, and since I'm paid well I can hardly complain.

'In spite of the ideal life I'm telling you about, I can't but think there's a better and more fulfilling one waiting for me somewhere. Why I'm going on about it I don't know, but at least it's in morse and is filling the tape, exclamation mark! though I realise it may be of no interest to you at all. Doing such top secret work as I do, which I can't even talk about to my wife, makes what you might call a lonely man out of me, but I like that, because it matches perfectly with my temperament, whatever of course that is.

'Having made your acquaintance improves my situation, because at least there's someone I can talk to without inhibition or limit. Maybe we are equally cut off from the world in our different ways, when we're not at the radio and in touch with more than anybody can realise.

'It's a different world, and that's the attraction. I often wonder when the point came in my life that made me what I am today. The more I dwell on it, the less I can decide what it was. This suggests to me, perhaps as an easy way out, that such a decision must have taken place before I was born.

'In other words, it's in the genes. We're born more than made is what I mean, and what I've thought for as long as I've been capable of thinking – or asking questions – which may not go that far back. In one respect you are lucky because you can say exactly where and when that special something happened which made you what you are today.

'Forgive such rambling. The tape runneth over. I'm not stuck to the radio every hour God sends. Another exclamation mark! I walk over the hills, and through the woods when the paths aren't knee-high in mud. Sometimes I drive in the Bracebridge direction and call at the pub where I took Laura for a drink – to whom best wishes, by the way. Occasionally I take Amanda to London, where she does a bit of shopping, and we enjoy a night out.

'But it's time to stop. Wrist's aching like the devil, as you must twig from the number of erasures. Let's meet. Call you soon. Best regards. End of tape, which alas can't be endless, Richard.'

Sweat plastered his hair, from the effort of prolonged sending. He'd pumped more than expected, or that he had intended, felt uneasy at having let the words sparkle out and not thought once of censorship, and hoped he hadn't revealed too much of himself. Spinning the tape back he played it through to hear what had been said. Amanda knew all of it and more already, but it would be interesting to know what Howard guessed on listening in.

The replay, all the same, seemed to concern someone quite different, not another person exactly, but a sidestepped version of himself who both puzzled and fascinated. A fool in the grip of cosmic forces couldn't avoid being who he didn't want to be.

He smiled however at the similarities which couldn't be disowned. Tapping out more such missives would illuminate himself to himself, both versions eventually turning into one person so that he would finally know. He might even find a clue as to what he wanted to do in life, and then do it.

Howard, a man made wise by his inability to know what went on in the physical world, would be his correspondent. Whatever comments came in return should be interesting, if you thought about it, because a person was just as blind when it came to dealing with the world as was a man who had lost his sight, though the man without normal vision would have known it all along, and had no illusions about the benefits of seeing. Therefore he developed alternatives of which a man with eyes could not conceive.

A man who had eyes to see blundered around without thought, without vision, imagining he saw everything, whereas in many cases he was more blind than the blind man. The man who was blind, due to impacted sorrow over the years at not being able to see everyday details of the world – either to love, hate or wonder at – had cultivated, in order to stay sane, a deeper connection with the human heart because he moved around in subterranean emotional strata with more surety of perception. Even though he might not be able to put the experience gained into words, he developed an instinct which allowed him to endure in equilibrium – something all of us wanted to do – and bring important matters to the surface now and again when it was important, to himself and even others, to do so.

Richard conjectured as to whether such thoughts came because a change was taking place. They seemed benign and helpful, whatever was happening, bringing calm to his recently disordered condition. If a blind man could get on so well in the world, without being a burden to it, and be even less a burden to himself, how was it that he (though the state was not apparent to Amanda or others) could be harrowed at times with confusion and anxiety?

On the other hand that's not me at all. I'm making it up. It's a game. If I didn't take life as a game I couldn't exist another minute. I'm playing with a phase of mind that has no connection to me, which comes easy because whoever I'm with I have to pretend to be somebody I'm not; neither with those on the jobs I go to, nor with Amanda, nor with Howard and Laura. If a third personality shoulders its way in to claim me I ought not to be surprised. Two, three, or even a dozen could make no difference when I've never been the sort of solid man with an innocuous career, a character of substance and probity, honest in every fibre, plain to myself and to everyone with whom I come in contact.

That's the sort of person his father had wanted him to be, but then he would, wouldn't he? The old man has never been happier than when a 'person of substance' just one notch of the ladder above, complimented him on his work or merely gave him the time of day. You could expect the sons of people like that to be anything but certain of their place in life, lone wolves and wanderers all, spoiled and disloyal, beholden to no one yet itching to make money and get rich, camouflaged jackals moving around the periphery of the jungle and ready to pounce on anything easy, having long since learned to avoid the traps which society sets in the form of law and order. Partially blind Richard may be, but his eyes had served him well enough up to now.

Since there had to be a reason for everything, such thoughts might come as a warning. He would take more care, check and recheck (and check again) the details of every seagoing operation, make the most of the time allowed instead of slinging back drinks beforehand as a form of celebration for the success of what they hadn't yet pulled off. They relied on him to be painstaking, and he would be, for their sake but most of all for his own.

Shadows dimmed the room, and when it was dark he cut himself off even more from the world by drawing the curtains. Lighting a cigarette, he sat at ease in the armchair. A morning phone call had told him to be in Glasgow by tomorrow evening. Something 'big' was on, maybe a delivery from one of the East European fishing ships beyond some

131

remote point of the Hebrides. Or they would beat their way out at night on a high powered yacht to meet one even as far off as St Kilda. To intercept spot-on they would have to navigate by homing in on the ship's transmitter, a radio beacon to be used only sparingly, and by changing wavelength every ten minutes, so that no suspicious interception could pin them down.

All his expertise in radio would be called on to get them to the exact meeting point, and his mood in the days beforehand swung between anxiety and excitement. He wanted to be off, and joining the fray, to be on deck at night in uncertain weather (it was invariably bloody awful) earphones clamped and senses well tuned as he gave directions to the man at the wheel.

Such primitive excitement was hard to come by. A head on meeting with a distant ship showing the faintest of lights, their smaller boat beating a way through wild and inhospitable seas, was always an achievement. It was a medium in which the half dozen crew knew how to survive, having been in the game so long that if they couldn't do it neither could anyone else.

While anti-drug agencies joined efforts against those smugglers from South America and the Middle East, the door was open – and had been for years – from Russia and Eastern Europe. The main transit routes flowed from the central Asian republics and converged on Moscow, then spread by barge down the Don and Dnieper rivers to the ports of Rostov and Odessa. Or stuff went north along the Dvina to Archangel, then by Onega and across the Kola peninsula to Murmansk. Nobody had known about that arm of the business, or they hadn't been able to do much to stop it.

In the trade it was known as the Snowflake Route, and boats setting off from such places unloaded their cargo by devious and indirect means throughout Western Europe. What began as a trade had turned into an industry, and too many were making a living for it to be dented, even if the odd person was caught or the occasional boat stopped.

Morality, he reflected, knows no bounds. Nor, to be realistic, does necessity, because if it wasn't drugs it would have to be another commodity, and if there was no something else: 'I would have no way of earning a living. Evil is in the eye of the beholder, and though I am not a beholder anymore, but the activist, I can still take the place of one and see myself for what I am, or for what others think I am, and laugh.'

He only ever felt guilt when he went north to see his father, and played at being the son of a disappointed man. Last time he had taken a Leatherman tool knife, and half a pound of duty-free Gold Block tobacco. In spite of himself old Len had been unable to resist being pleased as he took the knife from its small leather case and opened the various implements, from the main blade to metric screwdriver. 'I can throw my tool set away now.'

'You can, Dad.'

'And you've brought me a good smoke as well. I can let myself go for a month. The old puff-stuff keeps me happy. A bit too expensive for me to smoke all I'd like.' He lived in a bachelor ground-floor flat in Southport, and Richard had called because he could hardly avoid it, down from Glasgow on his way to London.

'Still messing about in boats, are you?'

'I make a living.' He had already told him that the radio officer job had gone bang. As you can see from what I've given you, you stupid old bastard.

The presents in his hands, Len stood as if he might throw them into the fire. 'Big ships are better. You were doing well as radio officer.' He put the things down. 'I'll make you some tea, anyway.'

Instead of following his tall well-built figure into the kitchen Richard looked around the room, at the pathetic artifacts on shelves and dressers, and photographed groups of becapped putty-faced pipe-smoking men on decks or quaysides. The photograph of his mother, who had died of cancer when he was sixteen, had been set in the grandest frame, the enlargement of one taken on Formby beach when she had, apparently, been happy. Not much use looking at her, since she had been so long gone.

By the settee was a pile of library books: A.J. Cronin, P.G. Wodehouse, J.B. Priestley, and accounts of sailors' travels, and Richard wondered with a smile why the old man's favourite writers always had to have two initials.

'I don't suppose I need to say that you've always been a great disappointment to me.' He came in with the tray, tea things immaculately laid out, cream biscuits on a plate with a doily underneath, two paper napkins and, when Richard tasted it, the very best tea.

He banged the point home on every visit, and Richard couldn't think why he had bothered to call, unless it was that he needed to hear it for the good of his soul. Or was it necessary to strengthen him into going on more trips to do with his nefarious work? The old bugger said it either because he was senile and had forgotten about the previous time; or he knew very well what he was saying, and wanted to show that he hated his son's guts.

'I'm sorry about that, but I have my own life to live.' He always made the same response, so that his father could come back with the rejoinder:

'It's wrong to live for yourself. Every man's duty on this earth is to live for others. Those who live for themselves end up living for nobody. They die bitter and disappointed, and alone.'

Like you, he thought. 'I'm a long way from that yet.'

'You won't say so when you're there, in thirty years' time. Today will seem like yesterday.'

Time to get out of his presence, steam down the road in a happier state. All the same, the old man fascinated him, and he couldn't deny there was a profound connection between them, nor feel altogether unhappy about it. He hated to admit that he loved the grumbling old bastard. 'What would you like me to be doing?'

Len smiled as he put down his large cup. 'I don't know much about anything anymore. You've always been your own man. I give you that. But I've always felt you were perfect on a ship. You'd have had a good position by now, on a cruise liner even. Or you'd have had a good job on shore, with Marconi's maybe. It's never too late to change, and get back on course.'

'I'll have to think about it.' Humour the old dog. 'But how are you, these days? You look well. In fact I don't think I've ever seen you better.'

He winked, a heavy lid covering his blue eyes. 'I feel good, I'll say that much.' He flexed the muscles under the sleeve of his shirt, and pressed to show how hard the flesh was. 'Not bad for seventy-five, eh?'

'I'm glad to see it.'

134

'I walk five miles a day, all along the sea front and back.'

He must be healthier than I am. 'You'll see me out.'

'No, please God, I don't want to do that. That would never do. I couldn't imagine a world without you.'

'Nor me you,' he forced himself to say. Not to have spoken would have been vicious, what Amanda called lying by omission.

'I don't enquire too closely into what you do on your small boat journeys, but I hope it's all four square and above board.' He put a whole biscuit into his mouth. 'That's all I say.'

'It is,' Richard told him. 'You can rely on that.'

'I'm glad to hear it.'

Lies were useful in stopping people assuming what you didn't want to hear, though they only deceived good and simple people like his father – except that it didn't seem to stop him worrying, or continuing to get at him. 'You seem to be leading a fine old life. Just look at that car outside.'

'I'll take you for a spin if you like.'

'It's all right. I've got my old banger, though I don't use it much, except for shopping once a week, or if I want a trip in the country. Sometimes I call on an old shipmate in Bootle. He's bedridden now, so he's always glad to see me. Silly bugger's younger than me,' he smiled with obvious pride.

Richard usually departed thinking he would write as many letters as were needed to get a regular shore job, but by the time he was coasting around Birmingham he knew that his destiny was fixed, his life set, his feet locked onto the course until disaster struck or he had so much money put away that even excitement wouldn't tempt him on another trip.

Amanda's car came down the lane, back from her work at Doris's hairdressing shop in Angleton, so he went down to put the kettle on and make her some tea. She would feel welcome, and like that. He couldn't wait to set off in the morning.

FOURTEEN

A sound, as if produced by the idle trawling of fingernails along a corrugated tin fence, came into his earphones. Was outer space trying to get in touch? If so was he the last person they (whoever they were) should want to reach. Yet maybe only a blind man could make sense out of the chaos they would need to know about.

What produced such a noise? Aerials and the superheterodyne stage plus the magnetism of power pulled it in. Molecules were so small that not even he, using the best of his mind's eye, as well as infallible equipment (and what could be a more acute combination?) was able to see them. Yet we can, Howard thought, contemplate the universe in which they function, imagine the most elegant of their trajectories breaking off and free-going beyond all vision, while nevertheless imprisoned within our horizons.

Tracking the molecules by their patterns was a form of prayer to the Great Creator, trying in his blindness to understand the unleashed energy of the universe, the dust in motion whose scattered structures were called atoms. Electricity sent protons and neutrons on a journey to the infinite, never to disappear. Science might not solve the final mystery. Only the heart can explore beyond the range of mechanical contrivances.

Besides the electric heater, he wore a white wool sweater (knitted by Laura), a padded parka (blue with a white band at the back), a woollen rainbow hat, and fishermen's socks tucked into long johns, as well as boots. The Persian Gulf was warmer, morse hammering through in plain language, but he looked forward to Christmas, the New Year and Easter, when the mariners of the world would have loving and friendly greetings sent to wives and relations, telegrams of goodwill and hope for the future, in all languages but especially Russian and those of Eastern Europe.

He would mull on this in his next morse letter to Richard, for want of anything else to say, because Richard's shallow communications in the code did not help to suggest an easygoing, though interesting, response. To begin with, Richard's character was difficult to get into and sort out. He was no ordinary man – though who was? – or maybe he was ordinary enough yet lived so unconventional a life that Howard wished he was an ordinary man. Hard to tell, for he could hear his voice, and had a strong sense of him when he was present. Maybe his occasional boat journeys were no harmless excursions, and perhaps he was in some sort of trouble, for he had caught the change in his voice, almost a catch, when he related his experiences. He wasn't telling the truth, and that was a fact.

On the other hand his morse letters were slightly different, because he made an effort to be as straightforward as possible, by which Howard concluded that he wasn't normally truthful. His 'fist', his style, his sending of the symbols was suspect, if only because he tried to make it as machine-like as possible, impermeable, hiding any trait or peculiarity of character that less precise sending might reveal. Clear and easy to read, his sending was too perfect.

One way to break down the palisade surrounding such perfection was to send a letter with a mass of false information about what he, Howard, was receiving on the wireless. To make the text plausible he would build up a special letter piece by piece, mix in a true item now and again, and hope such a ruse wouldn't be too subtle to bring the required response.

There was certainly no shortage of time on his part, though he wondered how much there would be for Richard, who was out in the world and trying to make a way for himself. Nor did Howard altogether like constructing such a web around a so-called friend, but excitement in the kingdom of the blind was hard to come by, so the project seemed valid.

He would claim that the falsehoods came to him in agitated morse and through the most difficult curtain of atmospherics: 'Let me introduce myself. No, perhaps I'd better not. You might not want to know me if I did, and I'm not the sort of personality to waste time and energy, since everyone comes to me in the end, or I go to them, it makes no difference. No, I'm not a miller, a monarch, or a millionaire. And no, "no" is not my favourite word.'

'Can't make anything of it,' he would say to Richard. 'So you tell me. He faded at that point, went right off the air. I tried to follow him, searched all over the spectrum, but he'd packed up and gone. Where to? Who can say? Your guess is as good as mine. At first I thought he was the chap from the *Flying Dutchman*, then I didn't think so because he didn't seem at the point of death. People in the worst situations go optimistic when they think it will save their lives. It sometimes does, I expect.'

For what came next he would say: 'The last six months I've listened mostly on one frequency out of the whole radio range. Don't stop reading this *morscreed*. Everything will be explained. This is a sort of confession, to tell you I've fallen in love. I'm not used to disembowelling myself, but telling you has got to be done, because who else is a blind man to confide in but his best friend? I'm a perfectly happy person, but have strange dreams which lead me over oceans I alone know how to find. All I will say is that it's a very special wavelength I've lit on, and hope I'm the only one who has. Her boat, called the *Daedalus*, does erratics in the Dodecanese, trundles around the coast of Turkey, slides in and out of rock bound gulfs of Greece. I'm on their track all right! This woman talks to someone every night in the *Pontifex*, and wouldn't it be a strange coincidence if you had been on one or both of these yachts?'

He would send it when the time had come for the net to be cast out and drawn in. Such work would be too much of a self indulgence on this cold night, and in any case it was almost the hour for Judy to come on schedule. Morse news in Italian could go by the board, likewise the RAF weather, and material from the Gulf, as well as navigation warnings from the Caribbean, and five figure groups from Haifa. Time for Judy to be calling her lover, and nothing else mattered.

He took the bottle of whisky from the sideboard, where it stood between Gin and Sherry, and poured a small glass, the liquid so warm it came out like nectar. What he wouldn't have given for such a tot in the Lancaster, flying at eighteen thousand feet over Germany on that last winter of the war! He filled the glass, a finger at the rim to feel its progress, so full to the top he saw the liquid as convex in shape, his hand so steady that nothing spilled as he lifted it to his lips. Another one warmed his insides as he made ready to search for the star-crossed lovers.

Everything was unclear at first, mush swamping the earphones. He thought he heard her voice but couldn't be sure, an oscillation halfway between morse and speech, increasing to Donald Duck chatter as he turned the wheel at such slow speed the gradations would hardly be measured. Russian talk was mixed into their interchange, and by the time he found them they must have been on the air for some time.

Judy: (haughtily, about the Russian speaker, as if Carla could) 'Tell him to go away.'

Carla: 'He not hear me. He go soon. Your transmitter too weak.'

Judy: 'Flippin' hell, it's on full. Do you hear me properly now?'

Carla: 'I hear you.'

Judy: 'Last night we went ashore, and had a meal of couscous.'

Carla: 'Don't you eat that *fackin'* thing.'

Judy: 'That's not nice language. You shouldn't swear.'

Carla: 'You swear, some time.'

Judy: 'I know. But I try not to. The couscous was delicious. Then we had sherbet ices.'

Carla: 'In my flat, when my boyfriend not there, you make me fish cakes, remember?'

Judy: 'Oh yes, I remember.'

Carla: 'They good.'

Judy: 'Wish you were with me now. I have lots of ideas.'

Carla: 'Flippin' 'ell! I want to sleep with you all night.'

Judy: 'I want minimum one week, OK? I'll hijack the yacht and come and see you – all on my own. I don't think I could manage it, though. I'd probably end up on the rocks somewhere. You'd have to come and rescue me.'

Carla: 'I come and meet you.'

Judy: (laughing) 'If I took the boat they'd kill me. It's full of valuable stuff. Know what I mean?'

139

Carla: 'Judy, I worry about you. What if you get in a lot of trouble?'

Judy: 'No trouble. Just come and get me.'

Carla: 'Turkish prison no good.'

Judy: 'Don't talk about such things. People on pleasure cruises don't get into trouble.'

Carla: 'It makes me glad to hear it.'

Judy: 'Just give up everything and come to me. Leave your man.'

Carla: 'I can't.'

Judy: 'If you loved me you would.'

Carla: 'I do love you, more than anybody.'

Judy: 'So you say. You're all I have.'

Carla: 'Judy, I love you. You got to believe me.'

Judy: 'I do. But I feel like crying. We've had such a busy day here, I can't tell you. I can only talk to you like this because the others have gone ashore. I expect they'll be back soon, probably drunk.'

Carla: (sounding worried, almost angry) 'And what happen to you?'

Judy: 'Nothing.'

Carla: 'I think of you all the time.'

Judy: 'I want you, as well. Why can't we be together always instead of just a couple of days every few months? I sometimes think I want to die.'

Carla: 'Me too. I love you. Don't like to think of you on that boat, only one woman.'

Judy: (laughs) 'You needn't worry. I don't fancy any of them. Anyway, what about you and your crew?'

Carla: 'Nobody want me. I'm forty, but you young.'

Judy: 'Don't *worry*. They're all too busy here. Anyway, they go after the local variety, or look for tourists. They know I've got you, so they leave me alone.'

Carla: 'I kill them.'

Judy: (another laugh) 'I like it when you're jealous.'

Carla: 'No good. Love not jealous. It's just I worry about you.'

An excitable Russian, as if he was in difficulty trying to steer a container ship through the Corinth Canal, drowned Carla's voice for a few moments.

Judy: 'There's that man again. I can't hear you.'

140

Carla: 'Me change channel?'
Judy: 'I always hate doing it in case we don't make contact again. Up
  to the next OK?'

Howard trailed after them, step by step until he overshot or passed,
nothing to fix on because they had as yet made no contact. He saw
them both, on the bridge of their yachts, or maybe down in a cabin, in
the dim light anyway, hearing nothing but lost in the thrall of calling,
drowned by annihilating atmospherics, and the ever expanding crush
of iron filings, an aural snowstorm from earth into space. Morse got
through, but voices had a hard time of it, till he heard Judy clearly
enough: '*Pontifex, Pontifex*, this is *Daedalus*, can you hear me, over?'

Again and again, voice close to frantic, often with a note of pleading,
as if the Almighty might hear and, out of sentimental feeling, turn
down the static: '*Pontifex, Pontifex*, where are you? Carla, can you
hear me?'

Howard picked up both when they were deaf to each other, a
common failure between two people trying to make contact. Their
transmitters were no doubt accurate in definition, pre-set and spot on
for the required number and decimal point of kilocycles, but the voices
working through them failed to meet. Vanya didn't always hear aircraft
wanting to know where they were, and ships working on different
wavelengths failed to get in touch. In spite of technical perfection and
acute professional ears contact was often difficult, Howard amused and
gratified with evidence that scientific man was not always master in his
own house, and that a greater Power could foil what was supposed to
be certain – no bad thing for the sobering of whoever assumed they
had chained the forces of nature.

But now he felt woeful that Judy couldn't hear Carla nor Carla Judy,
call as they might. Judy's tone was fretful, though her voice was loud:
'*Pontifex*, this is *Daedalus*, can you hear me?'

Carla was exasperated: '*Daedalus*, no can hear you. Where are you?
Can you hear me?'

They regretted not having struggled along on the previous wavelength, in spite of shrill interference from the Russian captain, who
persisted in manoeuvring his vast ship through the Corinth Canal for

a bet. They had searched for improvement, if not perfection, as if the power of such love would bring them physically together – and who could blame them? He wanted to hear Judy as if she were in the same room, and with whatever senses he could muster try to imagine what she looked like. Knowing such a meeting to be impossible – at which he might be able to ask her, or get someone else to describe her – he felt a pain at the heart, an ache which could only be alleviated by another tot of life giving whisky. He would crawl to bed if he had to, meanwhile resuming his brush-like sweeping of the aether, and wondering whether he would give an account of his tribulations in the next morse letter to Richard. Then they were reunited.

Carla: 'Now I hear you. Top strength. Wonderful.'

Judy: 'I hear you too. Where have you flippin' been?'

Carla: 'Nowhere, here.'

Judy: 'I've been on this frequency all the time. You must have been somewhere.'

Carla: (sound of annoyance) 'I can't tell. Where have you been?'

Judy: 'I'm not telling you. It was very nice. But I needed a shower afterwards.'

Carla: 'I kill you.'

Judy: 'I was with my lover, Carla, the best woman on earth.'

Carla: 'What we do?'

Judy: 'I'll tell you when I see you.'

Carla: 'You drive me mad. I love you today.'

Judy: 'Love you, too. Tomorrow we'll be going to Salonika. Can you come?'

Carla: 'No, we go to Sicily. Trapani. Much work.'

Judy: 'I'll call you at midnight.'

Carla: 'Don't know if possible. Not if captain on bridge. We try, though. Also lots of people on board. We take horse to Naples.'

Judy: 'Horse! What do you do with a flippin' horse?'

Carla: 'Boss likes.'

Judy: 'Funny boss. Do you know Salonika?'

Carla: 'Empty place. But we did much work.'

Judy: 'Don't tell me. Just say you love me.'

Carla: 'I love you. I remember when in bed.'

Judy: 'Do you want me to come now? No, I'll meet you on the quay in the morning. In Italy. Italy! We'll find a café and eat breakfast in the sun.'

Carla: ''Olding 'ands!'

Judy: 'How can we eat when we're holding hands? We'll just look at each other, and smile. And when we're finished we'll go upstairs, and stay in bed all day. It'll be a café with rooms.'

Carla: 'At night we eat again, and have bottle of wine.'

Judy: 'We're tormenting ourselves.'

Carla: 'I can't hear you.'

Nor could Howard. She had faded, overwhelmed by atmospherics and interference. They called each other in the wilderness but heard nothing. Using their lovers' intuition they would both, without telling the other to do so, change to the next wavelength down, which Howard had already reached and knew to be clear. If he were Carla he would know what to do, but neither were wireless operators, and nor were they blind. Then he heard Judy, who came in as loud as if she had made a thousand-mile leap closer to Howard: 'Hello, *Pontifex*, can you hear me? This is *Daedalus* calling *Pontifex*.'

Her lover was lost, or still at the previous place, and Howard was happy to know that though he couldn't talk, he now had Judy to himself. He felt the pain of her forlorn pleas for her lover, anguish lodging in him for her. She went back to the old frequency and began calling there, telling Carla to change to lower down, as if trying to lead her by hand into clearer skies and greener fields. Howard heard Judy on one and then the other, sensing tears behind an ever despairing voice. When she was calling on one frequency Carla was calling on the other, and each would think to change at the same moment, Howard turning the wheel and hearing their voices going futilely into space. They no longer used the names of their boats, Carla calling for Judy and Judy for Carla: 'Can you hear me? Carla, where are you? This is *Daedalus* calling *Pontifex*.' Howard poured another whisky to celebrate.

*   *   *

Judy: 'Hello, I can hear you. It's so hard keeping in touch, and now it's nearly one o'clock. I have to get some sleep. I dream about you, but I would dream more if I could stay in bed in the morning. I love the woman I can't have, that's all I know.'

The separation had worn away her normal ebullience. Carla spoke into the silence.

Carla: 'OK. We are in love, but what can I do? I think it all my fault.'

Judy: 'I don't know. What do I have to do? You don't want me enough.'

She was crying, tears to rend Howard's heart, so what could it be doing to her lover's? Perhaps not half as much.

Judy: 'What do you want me to say?'

Carla: 'You don't want to talk anymore? I hear this noise. I don't want you to be unhappy. It's not my fault. What I have to do now? Nothing. Don't be upset, is all I say.'

Judy: 'What do you want *me* to do? Go out with somebody else? I can't. There isn't anybody else. You have the power, telling me to do this, do that. What's it all for? We've got to do something.'

Carla: 'You know my situation.'

Judy: 'I know. You can't do anything. You never can.'

Carla: 'All right, don't wait for me anymore. Find somebody else.'

Judy: 'You don't understand me. I don't want somebody else.'

Carla: 'Judy, how we get in this quarrel?'

Judy: 'I don't know. But what can we do?'

Carla: 'Now *I* don't know. When you finish on the yacht we find a job together.'

Judy: 'I don't know what I want. Oh, there's that voice interfering again. Let's change up, but don't get lost this time.'

They found each other immediately, and went straight on.

Carla: 'I'd like to do something for you.'

Judy: 'I know what that is. But you're not the only one who's upset. I'm more upset than you are. You can only say go and find someone else.'

Carla: 'No, I understand now that you love me.'

Judy: 'It upsets me when you think I'm not serious. I love you, and

144

try to make you feel better. Sometimes I go out with the crew, and we go to a café. Maybe I have a dance with a man, but it doesn't mean anything.'

Carla: 'I come to your boat. Maybe they give me a job.'

Judy: 'No, I want you to come to England. I'll show you around Lincolnshire. Lots of nice places, Stamford, Boston. We can go to Cambridge and Ely. I'll take you around, my old woman! I'd love that.'

Carla: (shouting) 'Flippin' 'ell, I'm only forty.'

Judy: 'Well, I'm twenty-eight, so you're a lot older, but don't worry, I'll keep you young, though I know I don't need to. You're all right. I only see you two or three times a year, but I get so that I can't wait anymore. I want to dance with you, even though you tread on my feet. I want to go to a restaurant with you. I want to walk along a beach. All those normal things. In England we'll find a cottage by the sea for a month. I want to bring you your breakfast in bed.'

Carla: 'Me too. I want all those things. I love you deeply.'

Judy: (laughs) 'Your voice has gone very gruff, so I believe you. It makes my spine tingle. Must go soon, though. I'll try to call you tomorrow night.'

Carla: 'Love you, darling.'

Judy: 'I love you a lot. This minute, and all the minutes after. All today and all next week and next month, all this year and all the next year. To love you anymore than that would destroy myself. I only want to hold you, Carla.'

Carla: 'I love you, Judy.'

Judy: 'Love you truly. Not hearing you too well. There's a horrible noise coming on. It's that Russian again. Let's change.'

    They switched, but only to say goodnight.

Carla: 'Time to sleep. Boss coming on bridge.'

Judy: 'Good night, Carla.' (sound of kisses) '*Buenos noches*!'

Carla: 'I light last cigarette. Love you, darling.'

Howard couldn't move, unable to say for certain where he was. In spite of the whisky his feet were sleeping, as if his body was solidifying and would be launched like a stone out of the world's orbit. He tuned in to the call sign from China (XSG) and let the rhythm go through his mind, as if the repetition would bring his senses back.

If he didn't make a move he would fall asleep and be found in the morning, a piece of old rock. The cat would jump on the frozen lump and run howling to Laura. He exercised his faculties on picturing Judy: fairly tall for a woman, maybe five feet six or seven, a good full figure, grey eyes and rich brown hair of medium length. She wore slacks and a white shirt, the two top buttons undone, sat on the deck of the *Daedalus* in the sunlight smoking a cigarette, engrossed by a Turkish fort on the hill behind the small harbour town, thinking not so much about her lover as of life in general, and what would happen in the future.

He sighed, though she was worth more than that, would hear her if they met, a warm accent with a level of north country still discernible, suggesting Derbyshire, remembered from a fortnight in Matlock ten years ago. Perhaps she had been born there, and her family had moved to Lincolnshire when she was a child. Everything was possible, and whatever you imagined could be true.

The door opened, and he knew the main light went on. She would be wearing her heavy dressing gown, and furry carpet slippers. 'Howard, come to bed.'

'You'll have to sleep with an iceberg. I forgot about the time.'

'I'll warm you up. What have you been listening to all these hours?'

'One thing and another. I think I'm going to hear a message that will change my life, but I never do. Nor ever shall.' He hadn't lied before, surprised at how easy, no guilt to ruffle him. 'It's just one of those mad dreams.'

She trembled with anguish at the idea that he would want to alter his settled existence. 'Why should you want to?'

He caught the tremor in her question, as she had known he must. 'I don't.' A few words heedlessly brought out. 'There's no better life than this. But you're right. I'd better switch off.' Once he was in bed, thoughts of Judy would bring back warmth. 'It's just that I get carried away with some of the irrelevant things I hear, and can't leave off.' Judy would be sleeping, wrapped in her pyjamas, or maybe even naked, enclosed in a narrow bunk and dreaming of the unworthy Carla.

146

They walked through the hall. 'I worry about you,' she said. 'You might catch cold.'

'I had a few drams of whisky.'

'I know. I can smell it.'

He laughed as they climbed up the stairs. Nothing could destroy his awakening spirit. 'It's not often I have more than one or two.'

'Yes, it was good of Richard to bring it. I'll help you to get undressed.'

'No, you go and warm the bed. I must call at the bathroom first. Shan't be long.'

FIFTEEN

He filtered right from a line of traffic, in front of a man and his girl-friend entering left from the opposite road. The vile morning of frost and mist called for navigational lights, and though as yet on the outskirts of Glasgow, he was in a hurry to get south in the hope of more human weather. The breakfast of scrambled eggs, kippers and two large washbowls of coffee would take him beyond Leeds and well down the M1 without stopping.

But the man he had placed himself in front of, driving a low grey TR7, presumably disliked Richard's alacrity and, when the traffic thinned further along the road, shot by on a straight bit, and drove in front of him at thirty miles per hour. Funny devil, Richard thought, being forced to overtake before getting on his way. The TR7 came scream-ing by again, to resume his previous crawl in front, even slower this time.

The swine's trying to teach me a lesson, where none is neither welcome or warranted. Hasn't had his morning crap yet. With a sigh, Richard passed him again, and speeded up a little so as to get out of his way, but the man, either a fool or a fanatic, managed the same manoeuvre. Richard caught a millisecond's glimpse, no more, but he had the picture clear: a man in his thirties with short ginger hair, pencil moustache of the same colour, and a reddish well-fed face. He wearily got by him once more, and went somewhat faster to avoid his dangerous game.

He came on, roaring by. He went so fast that, able to place himself in front of Richard only by a too-abrupt reduction in speed, and a too-sudden swing to the left, he lost equilibrium, wobbled, struck the embankment and went halfway up it, then overturned twice on the way down before settling, minus a few bits and pieces, on the hard shoulder.

Richard considered stopping, in case the man and his girlfriend (or perhaps she was his wife) were injured, but because no part of their cars had touched, meaning he couldn't be held responsible for what had happened, he drove on and left them to it, convinced that a fool must pay for his folly.

The contest, if such it had been, had unnerved him. For a start the man, no doubt even now too stupid to realise that everything was his fault (if he wasn't too dazed to think of anything at all) should have had more sense than to tangle with a BMW. He probably thought himself king of that stretch of the road because he drove along it every day, and had the right to try killing whoever he felt was getting in his way. Perhaps I was a bit precipitate at the traffic lights, Richard thought, but certainly not more so than most motorists at such a junction.

A further notion was that maybe the man had known him, that the awkwardness had been no accident, that someone was aware of what he carried in the boot. He hadn't noticed another car close enough behind to be in cooperation, so as an attempted hijack the tricksy business would have turned out very clumsy. No, it was a common near-accident of the road, and he had been lucky to get off – as it were – scot free.

The road was good through the Lowland area of dismal hills, not too much traffic, visibility a kilometre and therefore reasonable for speed, though he kept close to seventy in case a cop car was planted in dead ground, always law abiding at the wheel because it would be ridiculous to get pulled in, even supposing the boot was empty, which it surely was not. He could either regard the stupid man's accident as a bad omen for his day, or think of good times coming because the bad thing had already happened. Superstition was a weakness, but he looked forward to the luxury of getting to Carlisle and into England.

To pass the miles he mulled on his recent stint on the water, something of a killpig, as Scuddilaw had accurately termed it, a trip out and in whose incidents made his duel at the traffic lights seem like the pleasant arsing about with an old friend. He had arrived at the hotel in Glasgow in time for breakfast, as a sailor home from the sea after having been, it seemed, almost to Iceland and back. 'The Cod War's got nothing on this,' Scud said, another swig at the whisky when they were halfway there, though no one yet knew exactly where there was.

'Rockall, it's supposed to be.'

'Fuck all, not Rockall. Here we go again.'

And a thousand times they went – but who was counting? – up the hills and down into valleys of malevolent water. And who had the heart to calculate after the first, in any case? Cannister looked knife-blades at Richard who had taken down the weather forecast. 'This is yer force-fucking-two, is it?'

'Well, we're on our way,' the skipper said, 'and we don't come back without the cargo. It's the Barbadoes for me next week. Sweat blood now, and get a touch of the sun later. If we aren't beaten, we've won.'

Richard, to himself, agreed. It was a mood to his liking, but every trip seemed to hinge on an all or nothing gamble, the ever expanding peril of a forlorn hope, and he more than once saw the next white topped emerald wave as his last, except you thought of nothing beyond staying alive.

The Polish skipper wouldn't risk his rusty old ship too near the Hebrides, or the eyes of the customs men, but Richard's radio navigation got them to the rendezvous, when the real trouble began. Had they come all this way for nothing? They weren't fighting for their lives now. Money was involved, millions, and though only a comparative pittance went into their pockets there was a fortune to be counted out for the gaffers.

The ship's flank was a rusting cliff, they were one moment bottomed out, in danger of being keel hauled and then, whoops, you bastards, they were staring boggle-eyed right into the buttons of a sailor's coat on the bridge, who was looking back at them no doubt wondering what creatures had come out of the deep. After the captain had grabbed his single tea chest of payment (and not before) the stuff came up and over, and they didn't lose a bundle.

Set for home, no one dared to think so. The risk of being caught was subsumed by the danger of being drowned, but Richard could only see such a picture by looking on it from safety, like now, steaming effortlessly down the dual carriageway. Wet, hungry, and cramped at the bowels, the power of concentration had threatened to evaporate any second but was kept in check, only he and the skipper at times holding the boat on course. Could Waistcoat and the big men in London know what the crews went through?

He took them back part way on the Omni Range beacon at Tiree, but kept well clear when in the pull of the islands. No one had seen them go, and no one would spot them sliding in. So they hoped, and so it turned out. The night was long and, despite the sea, the powerful boat landed them far enough into the cove to start the welcome work of humping bundles up the track and into the cars behind the ruined bothy, so that the material could go by various cars to London.

Mulling too long on the hard night, he bumped the centre studs for a second or two, which told him he was getting tired. Ought to stop soon and stow my head for twenty minutes. But the exhaustion, if that's what it was, put him into the Republic of Euphoria, only welcoming after all had gone well, setting him up for another hundred miles.

Beyond Carlisle he overtook a steady Eddie Stobart on its way south, glided by the usual Wallace Arnold and Shearing coaches, Dodd's pantechnicons, and various self-hire vans. The odd car coming the other way had lights aglow as if playing Volvos. Then he was overtaken on the outer lane by a vehicle of the Freebooter Transport Company doing well over eighty.

He pushed in the lighter and felt for a cigarette, a simple-minded gloat that if all the cars overtaken in his life had been given to him he would be rich indeed. To while away the miles he pushed in Howard's morse tape which had arrived before leaving home, slotted it into the cassette deck. He'd carried it in the pocket of his duffel coat out and back, and wondered at Howard's amazement if he knew the nature of the trip.

'Dear Richard, these are cold days, and it gets cold at the heart sometimes, though Laura and I are weathering it – you might say. The wireless has me in its grip as much as ever. Usually it cools any sparks of passion a blind man might have, but these days it has a nasty way of stoking them up instead. It's always hard to get through the winter, and seems like a victory when I do. Long nights mean too many long journeys. I'm working on a certain voice frequency, but can't tell you much as yet, not being sure exactly what I've got onto. It may be of interest to you, perhaps not. A woman is talking to her lover, another woman, a few hundred miles from the yacht she works on. Their business might be something to do with smuggling – immigrants or drugs, who can tell which? Probably neither, just my imagination running away with itself. It occasionally does, the one luxury I'm allowed.'

A sliver of burnt out tyre lay across the motorway. He stopped the tape to get by various weaving wagons, a lorry churning smoke like a haystack about to flare up. A bus overtook him on the inner lane at ninety. Accident black spots move around and settle themselves temporarily in certain places for no apparent reason.

A few more miles, and he felt safer. Someone always gets killed on the last day of the war, or the final lap home. In a car one loses the feeling of being at the whim of the elements, of crossing a rainswept field with little between you and dull cloud on a winter's afternoon. He supposed there were people who never knew such a sensation – lucky or not he wouldn't say.

He set the tape spinning, to find out whether Howard would be more explicit about the smuggling, but the silly blind devil waffled on about something else until: 'I walked down the hill to get a sniff at the sea, just before midday, well wrapped up because a fair wind was on, mostly from the old south-west, telling myself I wouldn't like to be at sea in such a blow. My cap went flying once, but some kind soul brought it back. The only fit haven was a pub, and a pint was soon set before me. A large coal fire burned, a few of the regulars sitting around. I was familiar with their voices, and heard them chin-wagging about a local character called Charlie (no surname mentioned) who had been arrested by the revenue men (that was the term they used: would you believe it?) coming back from Cherbourg in a fast launch with half a dozen other chaps a few nights ago.

'Rumour had it that they had stuff stowed on board worth millions. They'd always wondered where Charlie got his money, because he never seemed to do much, and always had plenty. Now we know, they said. You can imagine how I enjoyed such talk, saying to myself here is a bit of tittle-tattle to tell Richard in my next communication. I usually have precious little to say in such an ordered life. I'd give my right arm to go on such a trip as you now and again take yourself.'

Richard switched off the morse a few moments to wonder if Howard had made any connection between the two but, though with some unease, decided it wasn't possible.

The rhythm soothed him so he let the tape play on. 'Not being able to see anything wouldn't rob me of the pleasure, you can bet. But of course, it's out of the question, and I can only work on the imagination till it seems like reality, as if I've actually done the thing. Then it calms me, and I'm happy enough to get back to the radio, which does its job by living for me.'

Break time. The clock goes slowly not the miles, and landscape stays more or less the same, so there are times you do A to B and have no memory of the scenery at all. Your mind has submerged itself, yet your reactions work if they have to. He thought he was getting a cold, feeling a notch below perfect, which could be dangerous if he didn't lock his perceptions onto taking care, so he signalled to reach the inner lane, and slowed along the one-two-three white marks for the service station, lorries already cutting along to his right.

The parking space was fairly full but he found a slot not too far from the cafeteria entrance. The wind freshened his cheeks, and he put on his mackintosh because the sky was low and grey. Preferring to eat little and often, rather than scoff a debilitating sleep-inducing meal, he sat in the smoking section with his cheese roll and pot of tea. Two women across the way were talking about how to make life happier for someone who had recently tried to kill herself. They sounded like social workers but he couldn't be sure. The pill victim could have been a sister or cousin – a world away from his own life. He was glad of the empty table, for in his line of business it paid to be alone if you wanted to stay in the game.

A man further along was so untidily bearded it was hard to tell his age. The hair was mostly ginger, with frontier wisps of grey. Exhausted and filthy, wearing a blue jersey, checked jacket, and jeans, he looked like someone who could sleep with his eyes open, and certainly didn't have a car in the parking lot. Down one side of his face, only partly covered with hair, was a scar still streaked with congealed blood. 'Going far, are you?'

Richard knew who was meant.

The man stared at an empty cup and crumb-strewn plate, a small ruck-sack beside him with a woolly hat on top. 'I said are you going far?'

'Far enough.'

'I've been here four fuckin' hours, and nobody'll gi' me a lift. Yer know what kind of life that is?'

He didn't, wasn't interested in finding out, finished his food and swigged off his tea. The country was full of such people, on the road for London, where they could beg and sleep rough.

'It's nay life for a man who only wants to work. Up every fuckin' mornin', and I walk the arse off me feet looking for it.'

Richard buttoned his mackintosh: 'I'm turning off at the next junction,' but set two pound coins on the man's table, in case he was genuine, then walked to the exit without hearing a thank-you. Only now, as the achievement of the sea trip swept over him, did he realise his life was one long bottle of champagne. He started the car, and drove to the pumps to fill the tank, check oil, water and tyre pressures, then go inside to pay, have a piss, and buy a newspaper.

The same trampish man stood by the lane when he slowed down on turning from the pumps. Richard stopped, leaned back to open the rear door. Served him right for handing out the two quid. 'Come in, then.'

'Ah, ye're a gentleman.'

Like hell I am. He shot off to get in front of a juggernaut and into the middle lane, already regretting his action, in that good deeds never came cheap, or did much for you. He had put him in the back because on giving someone a lift a few years ago the man had managed to purloin some earrings from the glove box which he was taking to Amanda.

'Where the fuck are we?'

'Cheshire.'

'Where the fuck's that?'

No point telling him, in case it strained his vocabulary, but he passed over a cigarette, which the man lit with a brass Zippo. The face was scarred, pockmarked, veined, ruined by want and self-indulgence, a face whose movable features, even if they had been washed and cared for, would not have made him pretty. An ugly bastard, and no mistake.

After a few more miles he threw the cigarette out of the window, then seemed to doze. Richard liked it that way. He pushed the button to hear more of Howard's morse.

'You see, there is something to write about after all. That little bit of gossip in the pub made my day, but I don't really find life's real until I'm tuned into the two lovers on their yachts, one among the Isles of Greece, and the other somewhere between Corsica and Sicily. I'm particularly attracted to one of the women, but then, I would be, wouldn't I? It's the sheer mystery of her that appeals to me, and what also whiles away the time is the fantasy I spin, of one day going in search of her, to try and find out what she looks like.'

'What the fuck's that noise?'

He switched off.

'Sounds like fuckin' morse code or somethin'. Drive yer fuckin' mad.'

Richard slid along the wall of a bus doing seventy, and in the mirror saw his passenger rolling up his left sleeve. He took a primed needle from the side pocket of his pack, and jabbed it among the knotted veins. Services, seven miles, Richard noticed, as the man snorted, head back, struck Richard's spine with his knees and laughed: 'Yippee! London, here I come!'

Not in my car. Against expectations, the miles went quickly, and he jinked beyond a sports car and a builder's van, onto the inner lane by two lorries, and shot up the slipway onto the car park. He didn't bother to look for a space, but stopped at the steps leading to the entrance. 'This is as far as you go.'

The man, head back and looking with rolling eyes towards the sun roof, as if to coax it open so as to see heaven more clearly, heard nothing. Hazard lights on, Richard got out, pulled the door wide open, and took the man's arm in a twist too powerful for him to resist. He pulled him onto the tarmac. 'You don't shoot drugs in my car.'

'What the fuckin' hell's going on?'

A happy family group – mother, father and two children – coming from the cafeteria with chip butties instead of hands, looked on as if a piece of street theatre was being provided especially for them. The man's rucksack hit him in the stomach, Richard now knowing why he'd had to wait four hours for a lift. The scumbag even tried to get back in. 'It's London I want, not fuckin' Cheshire.'

Richard evaded the heavy punch, and gave one back which, with the power of an angry sea built in, sent him scuffing across the steps. Very Merchant Service, as the captain once said when he'd laid out a man who had gone berserk on the bridge.

You goddamned fool, he told himself on driving away, how can you be so brain dead as to pick up a hitchhiker, and a hop head as well? He fumed for the next fifty miles, until he knew himself lucky compared to Howard and his sky-empty life, which reminded him to bring the morse rattling back:

'There is a demon in me trying to break out, to let fly, to fragment my existence in return for I don't know what. This is the first time I've expressed myself openly as an adult, believe it or not, since the full stop put on me in March 1945. Whether the demon, or the impulse, is evil or not I wouldn't like to say, but certainly it could be destructive, though not while the thought is unable to change into action. In that sense I'm safe and can talk to you, or tap rather, freely.

'Perhaps my ideas as to what I mean, and what might be possible, will have clarified by the next letter, though the agitation does diminish somewhat while I try to describe my feelings to you. At the most, or worst, I envy the fate of old Charlie, who was nabbed for smuggling. To sum up, I sometimes think we have to look on life as tragic because otherwise it would be too dull to be acceptable. By way of banalities, Laura and I are well, and hope that you are, too. Until next time. Signing off. Howard.'

Fringing the dereliction of the Black Country (though there were signs of resuscitation) he thought it not a long letter, though there was quite enough in it to make him sweat. Spaghetti Junction posed no fears, after the ins and outs of such a missive which, far from the old boy going off his chump, showed he was on to something bigger than he realised by having picked up Judy babbling away. Howard couldn't know what kind of tramcar he was jumping onto, in passing over such red hot gen, because if that big silly lesbian wasn't stopped she would have the Mediterranean end of the game wrapped up by Interpol. She wasn't cracked enough to blow the gaff on anything knowingly, but any slight clue could get the dogs of the law on the lot of them. Since Howard was picking them up loud and clear there was a chance others were as well. Waistcoat had always had too much affection for tenuous social connections, more than was good for him or them, having fitted her as a general slavey into the outfit to prevent her doing worse mischief to herself than she had already.

Couldn't think why, but he changed his mind about the M1, rolled around the Birmingham conurbation to the M40 turn-off, and headed southeast for London. He pressed the window button, to get rid of the beer and druggie stench of the hitchhiker, glad of the cold air to keep him awake. By-passing London, he would drop his load as arranged at Tonbridge, and keep on for the coast.

Howard couldn't know that, on the other hand, he was worth his weight in gold for his latest intelligence, that he was now part of the decision as to what should be done with it. Or when. He would ask Howard to type up a log of what exactly he had heard, or maybe only a résumé, giving black-and-white page proof, so that nothing more incriminating would be spoken by Judy or her girlfriend after it was handed in.

Stopping at the next call box to inform Waistcoat would be seen as another startling exhibition of his power, for them to marvel at. On the other hand to wait a little longer might mean getting more information which he could use in some way for himself alone. To hang on for a typed log would make the matter easier to credit, while to delay telling what he knew would give more time for Howard to play his sentimental game. You could only handle Howard with the velvet touch, because he was the sort of person who had a mind that talked to him all the time, and so had to be treated with respect.

No need to spoil Howard's life unnecessarily, though at the same time he didn't want him to spend all his listening hours on this one matter. He needed him back on day work, where he might for example find something more useful about the Afghan and central-Asian traffic. In that case it would be better to stop Judy's mouth sooner rather than later. Yet Howard seemed so besotted that if she went off the air his despondency could put him out of action for a while.

He had to be handled carefully. Being blind, he was a man of feeling, and it was strange that he had become his only friend after Amanda, a person he could talk to more or less freely – which he couldn't always even with her. It had come about because of his attraction to Laura, though how far she looked on him as friendly – apart from merely charitable – was hard to say. She was even more of an enigma than Howard, as if she knew that to become open might let slip a deadly secret gnawing inside her. If such was the case, only some kind of psychic dynamite, of the kind well packed in the back of his car, would solve her problem.

In spite of their long married life he thought Howard wasn't as aware of her secret self as he imagined. Every woman had a secret self, and that was a fact. If you thought about it few people did or could get close because if they did there would be nothing to hold them together. Such a truth struck him as bleak, but obvious. With Amanda, their most violent quarrels occurred when the final barrier before mutual revelation was about to give, but they always kept it in place, by embarking on a wonderful bout of bedroom love. Perhaps they knew each other better than they thought, an observation which was not so bleak. He enjoyed long distance driving because the monotony allowed him to think, but he only wanted to deliver the packages and get home as soon as possible, so that he could rattle off a tape letter to Howard. He didn't yet know the text but was confident that one would come as soon as he sat down at the key.

SIXTEEN

White gulls mocked him with their freedom, squealing in the unlimited blue. They concentrated on the area as if waiting for a house to break free, head for the open sea like a ship, and begin discarding choice leftovers for them to eat.

He took off his cap to feel the wind. Instead of wondering what he would do if Laura went shopping and didn't return, he thought: what if I didn't go back from my morning walk? What if I was hit by a car, was incinerated by lightning, or strolled off the breakwater and drowned? Better still, what if I took a train to London, got to the airport, and boarded a jet for Brazil? Secret preparations would be necessary so, like a prisoner of war, I would work at my escape for weeks.

On the other hand, how far can a blind man get on his travels? Hard to disguise myself as someone with sight, and clever is that man who can act blind without detection. The alarms would go off as if I really had escaped, and I would be brought home like a mental case, shackled to a triumphant social worker, a number painted on the back my jacket in case I made a run for it again. Even the gulls would become part of the search, circling the copse in which I had crawled to hide or die.

He sat on a low wall halfway down the winding steps, relishing the touch of spring breeze. A man was digging in his garden, and Howard knew that the soil was rich and black from the easy sound of the spade going in. The leaf mould of last year and the emerging leaves of this had a cool vegetable smell, reminding him of his infants' school when the teacher managed them across the road and into the hedged field for a lesson on how to recognise flowers and trees.

Before leaving he had taken a signal from his wireless telling of nine stowaways who had been arrested some miles inland. The captain of the ship they had come on, now at sea again, was disputing the fact that his company should pay for their repatriation. The local police had checked the ship before leaving Casablanca, and found no stowaways, so how could it be his responsibility?

Everyone in the world was on the move legally or without formality, and it was easy for those who had the will to get up and go. Even if the stowaways were sent back, their journeying would fill part of their lives, and the memory stay to be talked about. No doubt they would set off again, an enterprise to envy.

He walked on when the man rested from his rhythmical digging, and the sea breeze took over from the smell of earthy life on rounding the bend, counting the taps with his stick so as to know when he was about to reach level ground.

The igniting signal had lit a way through a lifetime of regrets. He would rather not have heard it, except that he could pass the message to Richard in his next morse letter. There was little to tell. Even the story about old Charlie coming back from Cherbourg with his launch full of drugs, heard supposedly in the pub, had been invented. A man must say something amusing when writing to a friend, and such items as smugglers getting caught appeared often enough in the newspapers. Still, it wasn't good to spin a lie, and he wished he hadn't done so, regarding the unease as an indication that he would not do so again.

Instead of continuing to the beach at the bottom of the hill he turned and climbed slowly back, impatiently counting the steps so as to know when he reached the house. He imagined Laura's lift of the eyelids as he opened the door. 'What have you forgotten?'

'I had my walk.' He put his stick in the rack and took off his cap. 'I got to the bottom, but suddenly felt it was futile to go any further.'

'I'll make your coffee, then.' To think of her concern as worry would be extreme, yet his breaking of habit was always done for a reason. For weeks, instead of shutting down his wireless at eleven, he had stayed as if mesmerised till well past midnight. He no longer told her stories about what he intercepted. Was what he picked up responsible for his reticence, and if not then what could be? Nothing ever received had been of the sort to chill her, or surprise her, or alarm her, but it wouldn't do to question him about a world they had agreed should be his own. A blind man needed more inviolable territory than anyone else, but what afflicted him must have something to do with what was part of him and not of her.

A few days ago she'd heard the hum and click of morse as she stood in the kitchen. He must have been sending for at least half an hour, and on asking him why, he responded in a tone of not liking to be asked, which she hadn't heard before. Then he admitted it was a tape letter to Richard, who sometimes wrote to him in that same way. They exchanged information about what each had heard on the radio and, if there happened to be nothing of interest, just what came into their heads.

She didn't therefore see how that could be the reason for his morose state, since they had been communicating for months. Nor did she think that if she knew morse she would gain any enlightenment by listening to Richard's tapes. Another reason for his moods could be that the year-in and year-out sameness of existence preyed on his spirit.

She laid the coffee before him. 'Perhaps it's time we had another holiday.'

'I'm happy enough here.'

'I sometimes think you might not be.'

He put sugar into his coffee, the first time in years. 'I'm as happy as you are, my love,' touching her wrist and joining thumb and finger around as if to gauge the span, one of his oldest caresses.

Today the gesture annoyed her, though again it was too strong a word, merely that together with his new remoteness he was shackling her into a situation he wouldn't explain. 'I know, but I worry. Stupid, probably.'

'I'm well, except that a shadow goes over me now and again. But it'll pass. It always has.' He wanted to get back to the radio, a drug impossible to do without, by day now as well as night. Judy might come on at any time.

'Maybe we should go for you to have a check-up.'

The cat brushed his ankles, and he pushed it forcefully away. 'That won't be necessary.'

He was putting on weight, but eating gave pleasure. No harm in

161

that. He had so few, apart from her. Going on a diet would seem too regimented to put up with.

'I don't want you to worry about me.' He laughed, his old self. 'That would really make me ail. I'll go for a long walk after lunch, and it would be a pleasure if you'd join me.'

He stroked the cat, and its rattling harmonised with her agreement. 'I'd love to. We can go to the Pot and Kettle on the front, and have tea.'

'We will,' he stood. 'In the meantime me and Ebony will listen to a few funny squeaks coming out of the wireless. Won't we, pussy cat?'

'We'll get a novel on tape from the library later, to take your mind off things.' She watched him go, no diverting him from whatever it was, and feeling still more desolate, though she couldn't think why. There was no reason, except there must be. As he had often said, there was a reason for everything.

A shake of the hand as he readied himself for the search. She hardly ever came on during the day, being busy in the galley serving three-course meals for a boisterous and hungry crew. The waving bush of atmospherics on her frequency sounded like the wash of water around the boat as it plied tricky channels of the Dodecanese. He consoled himself with the weather forecast: 'A moist and unstable air circulation is still affecting the eastern Mediterranean. Patchy cloud and moderate visibility. Outlook similar.' And so, he thought, is my future, though similar to what?

The ten-o'clock transmission from France was useful for honing his brain. Even when I'm close to dying, or halfway to being ga-ga, I'll still be able to take morse and work a typewriter. If my brain loses its sharpness for that it'll prove I'm going into a darkness greater than the one I'm in now, and I'll enter it quietly because there'll be no option.

The French station emitted a few score groups of letters, cunningly throwing in a figure now and again to fox whoever was taking it. Then came ten minutes of prose, which Howard got the gist of because he had taken the language for Higher School Certificate. Every little endeavour or event before the age of twenty had been drawn on to reinforce his life-long effort of survival.

Laura once remarked as a compliment that only the simplest people could live their lives to the full, but he had never known till now how right her observation was, recalling it because today's French transmission ended with: '. . . *l'homme le plus simple du monde, ce n'est pas assez dire, il est avec les autres comme il est dans l'obscurité silencieuse de sa demeure*,' which he rendered as: 'The simplest man, needless to say, remains, when among others, in the silence and obscurity of his own soul.'

He moulded the daily aphorisms to the demands of his own mind, messages from God manipulated to distil the basic beliefs of his life, an innocent conceit, but supportive all the same. Some he recorded on tape for listening to whenever he needed to speculate on who he was, and ponder the reason for being on earth. They were more relevant than if coming through in English, for his imperfect French could suggest meanings that may not have been intended, or weren't there in the first place. They tested his wits, prompted him to formulate questions and search for answers, unable to deny that any disturbance elevated his often deadened mind into a higher state than boredom or the mere transcribing of morse.

He sometimes forgot the station for weeks until, one morning, without knowing that he needed to, he would give up his walk, and tune into the half-hour transmission, the hundred or so code groups inducing a mindlessness which prepared him for the gnomic utterance of the prose.

The older he got, merely inhabiting himself wasn't enough to satisfy his existence. The blister of discontent, there since birth, plagued him more because he was blind, an anguish of uselessness sometimes close to madness, as if he were an animal in the zoo and he the only member of the public looking on.

An undignified picture but maybe it would guide him towards making a better situation for himself. If he could take morse, he was still sane, which was good. If he told Laura of his lack of moral fibre she would say he was restless, needed to see a doctor, or could do with a holiday, so he wouldn't hint that anything was wrong because nothing was. Rather, in some ways, it was more right than since taking off for that last bombing raid over Germany. The flimsy covering of renewal was lifting with an effect as painful as when plaster was taken from a healing wound. He could only endure, knowing that uncertainty and discontent could be tolerated as long as you gave no sign to anyone else.

He pressed the radio button, and put on earphones. A crushing phase of interference, like a load of gravel sliding from the uptilted back of a lorry when a new road is being laid out, obliterated a few words of the weather forecast from the Gulf of Mexico. What electrical machine caused the disturbance was impossible to know, the noise not lasting long enough to give clues. He heard the voice of Judy, the tone as if she was in danger, though most likely from exasperation.

Judy: 'Still don't hear you very well. I woke up at four this morning. I had a bad dream.'

Carla: 'What it say?'

Judy: 'Horrible. That's all I remember. Then I thought about you, and went back to sleep. It was bliss.'

Carla: 'What do you do?'

Judy: 'Don't be rude. It's you I want, not me. It's driving me crazy. Maybe it would be good if we didn't talk like this nearly every day. I'd feel more settled perhaps. I hate the radio sometimes.'

Carla: 'If you want.'

Judy: 'I don't want. It's you I want, but I can't have you. I want to be near you again. In two weeks I fly to England, and stay a fortnight at my aunt's place in Boston.'

Carla: 'Boston in America?'

Judy: 'No, silly.' (laughs) 'Boston in Lincolnshire. That's where the people came from who went to America. So they called their town Boston. Don't you know about the Pilgrim Fathers?'

Carla: 'Don't like fathers.'

Judy: 'Nor me. Somebody will take my place here on the boat, then I can leave. Maybe you can come with me.'

Carla: 'I can't. I work here.'

Judy: 'Ask your boss for leave.'

Carla: 'Maybe not possible.'

Judy: 'I'll see you in Madrid then, on my way up.'

164

Carla: 'Yes, I think. Two nights, I can. You meet old boyfriend in England?'

Judy: 'Don't worry. I've only seen him once since I met you. He took me out to dinner but I told him he was wasting his time. It's no good, I said to him. Forget me. I only love you, Carla.'

Carla: 'I'm jealous.'

Judy: 'You needn't be. We should live together.'

Carla: 'We can't. You don't understand.'

Judy: 'I do. I know we can't live together. Anyway, I like this job, but only for a few weeks at a time. But why can't we live together, I should like to know.'

Carla: 'We damn lovers. In autumn yacht go in dock. I have more time. Maybe we see more each other.'

Judy: 'Yes, that'll be good. In September we're going to do things in the Azores. I can't say more.'

Carla: 'Tell when we meet. If long way away, in Atlantic, no radio talk, too far, maybe.'

Judy: 'We'll have to write letters.'

Carla: 'Difficult for me. Telephone could be. We find way.'

Judy: 'You'll have to come to England.'

Carla: 'No good for me.'

Judy: 'I know. You'll be with your man. You never talk about him.'

Carla: 'What the use? You know about him from start. No secrets.'

Judy: 'I know. I love you. I don't want to upset you. Lots of mosquitoes in this place. I swat them. I see all the rooms we've been in, I go through the list of places we've been together in, every night I do it, over and over again, so that I can get to sleep. It always works.'

Carla: 'I think of you. Much pain, though. I think of restaurants we eat in. But time to go to sleep. Siesta time for me.'

Judy: (laughs) 'You don't love me anymore.'

Carla: 'I do. I prove it when we meet, OK? What about your crew, what they do?'

Judy: 'Oh, don't worry. The captain's forty-eight years old, and he's got a girlfriend called Brenda. She goes back tomorrow. I can't hear you very well. Maybe I'll let you go. Let's talk at the same time tomorrow.'

Carla: 'All right. I'm sleepy now. I call you.'
Judy: 'We call each other. Love you, Carla.'
Carla: 'Kiss, kiss, Judy.'

A Niagara of atmospherics scraped his eardrums to an itch. Able to hear both voices on the air, which neither of them could, he caught a tone in Carla's that Judy missed, and something in Judy's that Carla wouldn't notice. Judy was infatuated (you might say almost in love) to the point of destruction. Carla no doubt liked her, flattered to have her on the line, and proud to have such a compliant English girlfriend, though they met so rarely – and she may not be the only one. She's a sailor, after all. He speculated as to how long the affair would go on, and hoped not for much longer. They were near the end, but who would break first? He noted impatience in Carla's tone at Judy's importunities, which she couldn't control, or didn't care to. From his God-like position he felt the threads weakening, yet hoped they wouldn't break because he wanted to continue listening, keep them under control. On the other hand he would like them to separate so that he could have Judy to himself, at least in memory.

At lunch he said to Laura: 'When I was young my parents used to take me to the Lincolnshire coast for holidays. Well, they did once or twice. A time or two we went to Llandudno, but mostly to Skegness. I had a vision of Lincolnshire just now while I was sitting at the radio, a place called Boston. I don't know why it came to me, but I'd like to have a sniff at the old place.'

'Funny you should think of your boyhood.'

'Isn't it? Maybe I'm getting old.'

'We both are, if you think about it.' He had turned her down point blank at the mention of a holiday that morning, and now he was back on the subject, though in as courteous a fashion as he could manage. She would like to know what lay behind his change of mind, if anything did. Things often flashed into his consciousness, and into hers as well. Hardly a day went by without a glancing return of her horrible powerlessness under the sweating rage of the man she had trusted, who had 'interfered' with her, and done what she still could not put the right word to. She used to think that every miscreant was somehow redeemable, but the older she got, and the more her torment grew rather than lessened, the more she believed that some people were damned even beyond the grave.

'We could go there, perhaps in three weeks' time,' he said. 'And stay a few days. Won't cost much, if we do it by car, and take a midweek bargain break.'

She wondered why now, and why the excitement in his voice. It wasn't something he had picked up on the radio, or heard on the street, since he hadn't even gone into town from the bottom of the steps, yet the insistence was too strong to have shot out of the past as he claimed. Nor was he merely agreeing to her suggestion that they take a holiday, and leaving her to say where they should go. In any case there was nothing wrong with the idea, they had the time, and could afford it. Paris was the last place, and Malvern before that, but now he stipulated Lincolnshire, and she was always glad to go along with him, to improve the life of darkness and boredom he fought so well. 'Yes, I think I'd like that. It'll be a pleasant break.'

He touched her hand. 'Everything good in my life depends on you.' But would it be so wonderful? The obstacles to getting close to Judy were like sheets of black cloth. They would surround him, zone on zone spreading out and impossible to break through, yet there was no problem in motoring to Boston, lodging there, and walking around, and even if he didn't find her he would be happy at being within a mile of her whereabouts.

'I'll look Boston up on the map,' she said. 'I expect it'll take most of the day. I've never been that way, so I shall enjoy it.'

'We'll go through Cambridge and King's Lynn. Should take about five hours, unless we stop off in Cambridge for tea.'

She marvelled at how thoroughly he had absorbed the geography of the country before his injury. He was never so happy as when they were planning a trip, though there was something unusual about this one. Adding the word fateful as well, she told herself not to be silly.

Excited at the prospect of an adventure, he tapped out his letter to Richard: 'All I want, all I can have, is to hear her voice unframed by a monsoon of atmospherics. I may not be able to talk to her, but it might enhance the platonic acquaintance if I get in any way close. And perhaps I'll end up with some idea as to what she looks like.'

167

He ran the tape back and started again, trusting no one to guess what he was planning, even regretted mentioning Judy and her lover in a previous letter, surprised again by his competent recourse to subterfuge. In a normal unblind life this is what I would have been like, he told himself. Near-fatal wounds distort the character, delay development, keep one in a still pool of inertia and quietude so as to give the strength to live from day to day. Such is my way of justifying the instinct of self preservation, rather than admitting to a lack of moral force in my character. An obsession forges its own rules, or acknowledges none. A man with nothing but his private world to keep him going needn't share thoughts with anyone else.

The downward slide was sudden and complete and, far from damaging his morale with vain regrets, he was buoyed at being able to act even in this small way. Though realising what he was doing, his state seemed preferable to how he had felt a year ago.

Something had to be sent. A rule of civilised life was that you always responded to a letter.

'Dear Richard, I hope your trip went well. Nothing worth reporting has happened to me. It was quite otherwise, though, on the radio. I intercepted a telegram from a ship's engineer in mid-Atlantic to his wife saying he would be coming ashore at Southampton in four days' time, and that she was to meet him at a certain hotel. Armed with her name and address I went to the library and had someone get her number for me from the local directory. Not knowing what to do with it, I nevertheless wondered how such information would allow a blind man to play God. On the way home I sat on low wall by a telephone box. All kinds of wicked plans went through my mind. I could call the police, like an anonymous informer, and say that the man was a smuggler of heroin who should be intercepted. I could contact the wife and, posing as an old friend, tell her about her husband's infidelities. Or I could phone the man after he had got home and pretend to be the wife's lover. Knowledge would become power, yet if it didn't improve my position in life it would stay as malice.

'I had no wish to do any of these things. It would be the height of evil to do so, which just isn't me, though I suppose you could say that even thinking in such a way shows evil enough. In any case it is only the evidence of an exploding mind, a minor temporary eruption that subsides and, I hope, leaves no trace.'

He was telling a story, having received no such signal, not recently, and similar ones that had come his way in the past had vanished into the mulch of so many others. He wanted to fill the tape, put marrow into the bone of his letter, out of polite reciprocation that mutual confidence called for. It was more a missive to himself, as they all had been, which made them instructive by putting his mind into a state of fermentation. It only mattered that you knew what you did, and squashed the temptations arising out of what you thought. Truth lit a way through the labyrinth, kept you close to yourself, and stopped you doing harm to others, but the light was yours alone, whatever its fuel, illumination known only to the Almighty who, he hoped, would forgive a darkening soul suddenly finding it necessary to use whatever light came close.

'All in all, things are good with me. I still listen to the German Numbers Woman, and hear the Moscow latitude and longitude merchant trading position reports with aircraft toing and froing with cargoes of poppy dust between Europe and Central Asia. Some planes have four slow engines, while others do six hundred miles an hour on three or four jets. The traffic goes on, and I suppose the world goes down, and we can only make sure good people such as us don't go with it. From what I hear on the news, and from what Laura reads to me out of the newspapers, the prospects for the world are dire, but we have to stay part of that rock of ages which holds the swamp back, hoping there are enough of us on earth to do the job.

'An item on the news said a blind man was knocked down and robbed by some lads. Such mindlessness is appalling, and my response would be, if they were caught, utterly Biblical. Maybe they were drugged up, as many are these days, but that shouldn't alter the quality of retribution. I do not say: "Forgive them, Lord, they know not what they do," because everybody knows very well what they do. I become less of a Christian as life goes on; if ever I was one, that is.

'I'm rambling, but what's the point of a letter to a friend if you don't say what's on your mind? The troubled spirit needs the solace of communication, as I've always known, and it's better to be in touch rather than talk all the time to yourself, as I suppose most people have to do, blind or not. I shall be away for a week as from the thirteenth. Laura and I want to have a break, and explore the Wolds (or is it the wilds?) of Lincolnshire. Which is all I have to say for now.'

SEVENTEEN

'Any flowers by the roadside?'

'Only dandelions, as far as I can see, otherwise fields, green of course, but a sheen of orange from that few seconds of sun. Pleasant, though. Rich agricultural land, by the look of it.'

'Petrol fumes must put the prettier flowers off,' he said. 'They run for the woods.'

'There aren't any,' she said. 'It's better in spring, though, on the lanes.'

'Dandelions are tough. Yellow and gritty. They thrive anywhere.' He turned his head left and right, as if seeing their dull mustard faces, not knowing they were too far off. Such gestures used to bring tears to her eyes. 'You are a lovely soft-hearted thing,' he would say, 'and I adore you for it, but don't weep for me, dearest. I'm as hard as nails.'

'I'm sure you are not,' she said, and he loved her even more for disbelieving him.

'Another roundabout, a straight road now. Still flat, of course. Enormous bales of straw piled on a lorry turning right. Electrical pylons we've just gone under. A cabbage field to the right.'

'Are we going very fast?'

'Only fifty. I'm way behind that lorry in front. Another roundabout.'

'We'll call it Roundabout Land,' he smiled.

'Six miles to go,' she said.

'It feels smooth.'

'A line of houses, but we aren't there yet.'

'I like flowers in the spring,' he said. 'Also to smell them in cottage gardens.'

171

After a silence she announced: 'Boston, three miles. And yet another roundabout coming up. I can see the church.'

Howard breathed, and she felt his excitement at picturing it more clearly from her description than if he hadn't last seen it as a child.

'I'm slowing down.' Tarmac was slippery after the rain so she trailed behind a lorry, clearing the windscreen continually against an oily backwash. Impossible to know why – since it seemed to have meant so much – he had waited all these years to come back. Maybe he had met a girl before getting to know her, a storybook experience of unrequited juvenile passion. Since mentioning the trip there had been an atmosphere about him, and between them, that had never been there before. She wished her intuition wasn't so finely tuned as to feel it, but having been married so long such nuances were hard to avoid. Life with him called for the sort of unremitting care and vigilance which demanded that she live within his skin, as much as he sometimes seemed to be in hers. She had never been discontented, having had the prescence of mind in marrying him to expect the kind of existence about which she would never be able to have any regrets or make complaint. Was there a firmer prison than that?

'Can you still see it?'

'There's the lorry in front,' she said. 'A line of lorries, in fact.'

'I thought there was, from the noise.'

'We're almost there. We've just passed the Boston Coat of Arms by the roadside.'

'I can't wait.' He was revealing too much. 'I mean, it'll be good to get out of the car and stretch the legs a bit.' Both arms would be so far apart, as if trying to get them around the earth and pull it sufficiently open to let daylight pour from the middle – a common dream, or nightmare.

'Same here.' The subterfuge was plain, but what if I'm wrong, she thought, and things are as he says, and I'm tormenting myself into a kind of madness? 'It was a good idea, to come up here. We certainly needed a break.'

'I'm glad you think so. I can feel houses.'

'A sign for the town centre. Over the river now.'

'Muddy?'

'Not sure. I think it was.'

'It always was.'

So he had been there before. The tide was out, water retreated from steep banks. 'We're turning towards a bridge.'

'It smells the same. Mud, tobacco, beer, smoke. Cleaner, I suppose. It takes me back more than I can say. I first came in from the west side. My father had an Austin, and I was in the back. Ten I'd be. It was a real job winding the window down. No electrics then. But I managed it. My father had a leather map case, a special uniform set of England and Wales. I remember the smell of its leather. You opened the case with a little key, and whenever my mother told him she thought we were lost my father would stop the car by the roadside – you could in those days – and get out and say: "All right, lost are we? Unlock the maps! We'll soon find where we are!" My mother went into stitches at him sounding so pompous, but he had said it like that on purpose, so that we could laugh together. We had wonderful times in Lincolnshire. At home, she would stick out her bosom and say: "I haven't the foggiest notion where we are. Don't you think you'd better unlock the maps, dear?"'

More reason to believe him. He sounded like the boy he remembered being.

They went around the town and came into it as if entering by the back door. 'Looks a very old fashioned place,' she said. 'Handsome buildings. Most beautiful town I've seen for a long time.' In the early days she used to wonder how far she ought to go in praising memorable scenes, because she didn't want to make him too depressed at being unable to see, but quite soon she recovered from such a nicety, and described everything so that he could see almost as well as she.

She turned a corner, and there they were. 'Well, I shan't have to unlock the maps, because this is where we are going to stay. It looks a very pleasant place. I'll go in and register, then come out with someone to help with the luggage.'

'And I'll wait here, just to smell the place.' He felt people going by, found the edge of the pavement but decided not to wander, strained all the power of his ears to hear a voice that would be Judy's, or even Carla's. Far too early for it to happen, but even the harshest exchanges registered like the best of music.

'What we'll do,' she said, when they were in the room, 'is rest an hour before dinner. We usually do.'

He stood by the window. 'I feel rather restless. I'd like to amble around the town while it's still light.'

The veins on his lids were dark, as if he was under some sort of stress. But then, he always was. 'I don't think that would be a good idea. You look so tired.'

'I'm not at all. It'll be pleasant to exercise the limbs. I know the name of the hotel, so I can ask if I lose my bearings. You know my navigation is good, though.'

Not always, in a strange town. It was all according to his mood. Malvern had been easy, either up or down, but even there he'd needed a few outings on her arm. 'I'd better come with you.'

He couldn't say no. Could, but it wouldn't do. Besides, he could walk more quickly with her, cover a bigger area, hear more voices, sense more. Luckily the rain had stopped, and people were out in the main street. 'The air's clean. I'll sleep tonight.'

'Would you like to see St Botolph's? It's famous.'

The more places the better, but he wouldn't know if Judy was in the church, unless she walked with a companion and he heard her talking. Maybe her voice would sound different to when on the radio from two thousand miles away. It was so with Laura who once phoned the house to say she would be home late. He'd noticed a higher tone, not apparent when close. When he'd first heard his voice on a tape recorder he couldn't believe it was his.

He took in the local accent on hearing two men talking outside a pub. The hotel manager had come from somewhere else, and his staff were foreigners. 'You'll have to explain it to me.' Graveyard mould was rank to the nostrils. 'I must have gone into it in the old days, because my father insisted we call at all the churches. He ticked them off from a guidebook. Whenever he stopped the car my mother liked to annoy him by saying: "Make sure you get the right one!" But I don't recall going in here, though if you describe it the memory might come back. I don't think anything can be forgotten.'

He could tell no one was inside, so didn't care to waste time, but couldn't say so because she was already reading aloud about the wood carvings, going on to explain the tombs and a chapel as they walked its light and spacious interior, with its lofty arches, which he felt went up forever into a sky she couldn't see, towards a God he had no feeling for. Bored and impatient, he stayed close, chilled at every step. Judy would never be seen in such a place, not even to get married, which he supposed she never would.

He wasn't interested, and she was glad when he said: 'We can go, if you like.'

'I think so.'

'Churches are much the same.' They walked back towards the High Street. 'I can't say I've ever had much time for them,' which was perhaps churlish, because Laura went to church occasionally. The frying of fish and chips brought a shock at the notion that Judy might be in the queue. 'I salivate so much at the smell I feel like getting a bundle and eating them on the street.'

'We'll be having dinner in the hotel,' she said.

'I know. But I used to do that as a youth. We'd go into a pub for half a pint, then go out to eat fish and chips. Very daring, because we weren't eighteen. Young people don't bother about that these days.'

'Yes,' she said, 'there is more freedom about. Maybe we'll have some for lunch tomorrow. I've nothing against it. We can even sit down. I saw tables inside.'

'Were there many people?'

'About half full.'

'We'll certainly sit, then. The purpose of being here isn't for me to re-live my childhood and youth. I'm not that old.' He was chagrined they couldn't go in now, but consoled himself by hoping that Judy might come to the hotel for dinner, though she wouldn't be staying there. Carla would have flown up from Corsica, and they would put up at her aunt's house. Unable to tolerate the cooking, and not being welcome to, they would go out for something to eat, and because Carla was a stranger to England Judy would want her to sample the local fare. Or the food of a typical provincial hotel. There wouldn't be much on the menu to pick from, though neither would worry about that. Even so, he would rather encounter her voice when she was on her own, though that was impossible unless she talked to herself.

175

Not being at home put him into a tense state. He spilled his soup more than usual. 'I'm getting shaky in my old age,' he smiled.

A Nottingham couple at the next table was giving the waiter more trouble than Howard thought necessary over selecting the wine. When the bottle came his wife said it was like vinegar, so the man ordered champagne for her and drank the wine himself. Both turned quieter in the process, which enabled Howard to tune in to what others were saying, though with everyone talking at the same time it was hard to separate words which, like broken strings of beads, clattered around the room and were difficult to pin down. Catching at the tail of one, the words of someone else butted in.

He thought a woman said: 'I don't believe you, Carla,' anything further crushed by a woman's laugh at the joke of a man who thought being amusing was the best way to win her love. The clash of plates put his senses aslant a promising conversation. No good. 'Any young people here? Or are they all like us?'

She was looking. 'A woman in her thirties is eating in the corner on her own, that's all.'

'Does she look a bit nautical?'

'She's doing *The Times* crossword, it seems. But why do you ask?'

'Boston's a seaport, isn't it?'

His soup slopped again, the hazard of such an affliction, though a man with less control might have spilt more than his soup: 'Can't think what's wrong with me this evening.'

The next course came, and she cut up his steak, which for some reason annoyed him. 'I like this place,' she said, eating her own.

'Me too.'

He was set apart, unusually so, had been even before they left home. He'd been determined about booking a room on the front instead of at the back which they normally liked because of the quiet. On her asking why, he merely said it would be a change. He could pick up voices from the street instead of listening to the sound of plumbing and the shouts of people who worked at the hotel. 'We must come here again.'

'Any time,' he said.

'Did you put up in Boston in the old days?'

Couldn't remember. He thought not. 'Just a jumble of rooms. We stayed a few days at a boarding house in Skegness, which my father didn't like. Said the place was too common. So we motored around. Went to Louth (which mother called *Loath*) and Horncastle.'

'Would you like to see those places?'

'If we have time. But I'd like to concentrate on Boston. A lot comes back to me here. Atmosphere, if you see what I mean. Can't quite put it into words.'

'You're not doing too badly. I'm getting to know more about your childhood, and that's nice' – glad he was managing his main course better. He came out so naturally with his reminiscences, having nothing to hide. Nor had she, if caring to go so far back, but blocking her from such days of innocence was an obstacle to all speech and reason, a permanent and constant bewareness, and she thought what sort of woman would I have been if that ghastly event hadn't happened? Perhaps I wouldn't have married Howard – the first time such a dambusting idea had occurred to her, shocking, but brought out by the puzzling disturbance in him. She wouldn't have worn herself into this mood of stern quietude but for that. There could have been gaiety and laxity instead of a spirit tamped by secretions of bitter ash and fear, keeping her under the lock and key of endurance.

'I love you when you smile,' he said.

'Did I?'

'Right out of the blue. I saw it in my mind's eye, you might say. As if you were looking at a Charlie Chaplin film, and waiting to laugh when he really got going.'

It wasn't a smile, rather a tilt of pain at the lips, and even that she had instinctively covered. He hadn't seen it, but he would have guessed. She sometimes thought he had one-second flashes of actual vision, too quick either to notice or for him to think it meant his sight was coming back, which was not thought joyous, though it should have been. 'I always smile when I'm happy,' she said. 'It's quite involuntary. Don't think too much of this trifle in a glass, do you?'

'Bit too sweet.'

'We'll sit in the lounge afterwards so that you can smoke your smoke.'

'It wasn't a bad drop of Bordeaux. A smoke tastes good after the wine.'

'I feel quite tipsy,' she laughed.

'It could be you're tired. You've driven a long way. Why don't you go to the room and rest? I'll just pop outside the front door for a breath of air. I'll get back all right.'

Uncanny if he knew the lie of the land already. She would have to believe him, but was more than uneasy at the notion of letting him go. 'I don't like to think of you wandering around.'

There was something determined in his laugh. 'Like a lost soul?'

'Well, not quite like that.'

'You can't lose me, never fear. Nor can I lose myself. Wouldn't want to, in any case.'

He didn't seem altogether convinced, but to respond in the same mood would only increase her anxiety when he came back with an untruth. He had decided, so she would give in, though not before a last try. 'Wouldn't you rather spend half an hour at your portable wireless? You might get something different, being in another part of the country.'

He had been looking forward to that, a length of aerial wire slung out of the window to bring in the east coast stations on medium wave, not always easy down south. 'I'll give it a try tomorrow night.'

No stopping him. 'I'll sit in the lounge,' she said, 'and look at the paper. It'll be easier for you to find than the room upstairs.'

'I'll beam in on it all right. Don't you worry about me.'

She would, though. A blind man had been knocked down and robbed, she had heard on the wireless. They were an easy target for thugs. 'Oh, I shan't.'

'Just ten minutes or so.'

He must have been measuring the distance and direction between table and door throughout the meal, remembered it exactly when coming in. On her way to the lounge she saw him, still standing by the door, uncertain which way to go.

He felt her presence, and turned to the left, went slowly along the

High Street. Navigation must be precise, and for every turn-off he transferred a coin from the left to the right pocket. There wouldn't be many. A gang of youths jeered but made way.

'Somebody's nicked his dog.'

'He's off on the razz!'

'I bet he can see as well as I can.'

'That ain't much, yer cunt.'

Laugh with them, though with impeccable sight he would never have done so. 'Are you lost, duck?' a voice called when he hesitated about turning back to the hotel.

'Judy?' he cried.

'I'm not Judy,' she said. 'I'm Tracey.'

Judy wouldn't have called anyone *duck* for a start. 'It's all right, Tracey. Thank you, but I know where I am. It's just that I once knew a girl here called Judy.'

'I expect there's lots of 'em,' she said. 'Are you sure you'll be OK?'

He turned left into a narrower street, hearing the odd tangle of sounds from a pub, under the window a good place to stand, being out of breath from hurrying more than usual. Or from excitement, though traversing an ocean of blackness was no way to find anyone. If he was a sailor adrift in an open boat during a moonless blackout he would be as keen sighted as the next man, except he was in the middle of a lit up town where everyone could see. Would shouting her name loud enough make her hear?

He pushed the door, and a couple of taps with the stick opened a way to the bar. Beer following wine wouldn't do, but had to when he was asked. 'Half a pint – best bitter, I suppose.' He could stay half an hour over that.

'Yes, sir.' Light pushed against his senses, though the noise made it hard to tell who was by his side. 'It's a nice night after the rain,' he said, to find out.

'I like a frost, myself,' the man put in. 'You can't beat it in winter. Healthy, as well. Wind straight from Siberia. Puts your back straight it does, but rain gives a man the ague. A good sharp frost sets him on his own two feet.'

'If he don't slip on his arse. But you're right, Lionel,' another man chimed in. 'If yer can tek this climate yer can tek any.'

'Mother's milk to me,' Lionel said. 'As long as you're brought up on it.'

'Are you visitin', then?'

'Yes,' Howard told him. 'For a couple of days. Motoring round the country. With my wife, that is.'

'A nice county, as well,' Lionel said, 'even in the hilly parts. I see you're blind, though. Or can you see a bit?'

'Not a thing. My wife tells me all she's seeing, and I get a good idea from that. I got her to stop in Boston because I'm trying to locate a woman called Judy, friend of the family.'

'Lives in Boston?' the other man asked.

'So I heard, when we last met.' His hand shook as he put the empty glass down, gone quicker than he'd thought. 'She works on boats, small yachts that take people around.'

They didn't know, couldn't say, the landlord adding that he would know, if anybody did, but he couldn't say, either. The question went around the room, till a woman said she used to know her but hadn't seen her for over a year.

'Do you remember her address, where she lived?'

'Can't say I do.'

'Could it be down Skirbeck way?' Lionel said.

'Shouldn't think so. Might have been. Could be anywhere,' the woman said. 'You never know, do you? She went away. That's all *I* know.'

They were talking about her, so she was real, not just a voice. He was suspended in hope, yet cursed the darkness. Turning to go, as if to get outside would give more light, he said: 'Thank you for your help.'

'Shall you be all right getting back?'

'Yes, thanks, it's just around the corner and up the street a bit.'

'Bloody funny bloke,' a man said while he was still at the door.

'You'd be bloody funny if you was blind. He must have second sight, going about like that. I'd have led him back to his hotel, only I didn't want to push myself. He might be a bit touchy. They are sometimes, if they're blind.'

Howard didn't know whether he'd heard or imagined it, and he let the door go and paced back to the wider street, didn't much care, because though he hadn't found anything firm about Judy, there had still been the achievement of sauntering into a pub and talking with people who seemed to have known her.

Laura threw the paper down. 'I was worried.'

He was tired of being worried about. He could live in the dark without any help. Being worried about all his life had stopped him learning to live properly on his own two feet. Being blind, and worried about as well, doubled the pain of being alive. And now that he had put it into words it would get worse because he didn't know whether the real him was the loving and long-suffering husband of this wonderful woman who looked after him, or the petulant self-engrossed burden that these new revelations and his search for Judy would make for them both.

'You needn't have been.' He sat by her. 'It's the sort of adventure I have to indulge in now and again.'

Shouldn't have said I was worried. Must control myself. She had noted before how the difficulties were at least doubled while travelling, a strain on them both. 'Was it good?'

He laughed. 'I went in a pub, and had half a pint. Chatted with the locals. I felt very sociable.'

'What about?'

'The weather. What else? One of them offered to lead me back, but I said I could manage, which I did, as you see. They were nice people. I'll have something to tap out when I send my next morse message to Richard. Where did *you* go for your holidays when you were little?'

'Oh, to Cornwall mostly.'

'We'll go there next.'

Her uncle had stayed at the same hotel. 'Cornwall's a better Riviera than the French one.' He held out both hands. 'Time for a walk along the cliffs,' glittery blue-grey eyes fixed on her, a beam of love and a command making for nothing but obedience, the relinquishing of her will that stunned her like a rabbit before a reptile. But she ran to take his hand, all innocent and loving in white socks, buttoned shoes and blue frock. And now in Boston – though why here? – she wanted to scream, but locked it in, thanking God Howard couldn't see her twisted features.

'What's wrong?'

'Nothing.'

'Funny, I felt it.'

A denial might warp his intuition, do him no good. His peace of mind depended on knowing when he was and wasn't right. He looked as if he had eyes to see, and the longer the pause the more he would know his guess to be accurate. Then she could say less guiltily what was not the truth at all. 'I didn't like Cornwall, so won't want to go there again.'

'Fair enough, my love.' There was something she couldn't talk about, but he was neither concerned nor curious, since he was unwilling to say what was in his own mind.

'There are so many places to see,' she said, 'especially abroad.'

'Like Turkey,' he said, not sure he wasn't in a dream. 'Or Greece.'

Anywhere, except Cornwall. Or here, though she did not entirely dislike the place, which wasn't after all to blame. The first few days on their trips were always difficult. They needed time to adjust after the too-settled life at home. 'Yes, maybe we should go abroad again.'

'All the same, I'm enjoying this more than I can tell you, especially that visit to the pub on my own. I love you to be with me, you know that, but it's such a treat for me when I go somewhere alone. I know you don't mind. Probably gives you a rest, too. It satisfies a deep instinct in me to wander, to get out on my own two feet. In normal life we'd have gone on exploring holidays, to Africa or the Himalayas, but since that's not feasible the closest I can get to it is to be on my own now and again.'

'That's all right. You know I understand.'

'And I understand you, sweetheart.'

'We have a bond between us.'

'So I'll want to go out on my own tomorrow.'

'Oh.'

'A stroll, no more. I get an authentic feeling for the place when I'm alone. It brings things back.'

She stood up. 'I have a headache. I must go to bed.'

'It's probably from driving.' Some of the exquisite pain of searching for Judy had passed onto her, yet he felt remorse at not keeping the evidence of his obsession more to himself. 'Yes, that must be it.'

He was like a man who had met another woman and made up his mind to run away. Or he was in the coils of wondering whether to do so, as my uncle had pleaded with me after he had raped me. 'Come with me to the ends of the earth,' he said. 'I'm game. I'll cut myself off from everything. We'll go away together. We'll even be happy. It's our destiny.'

What harsh, stupid, unruly words they sounded. She had wanted to say: 'Yes, take me then. I'm yours till either or both of us dies. We must be made for each other after this. I'll stay with you till I've poisoned you, or driven you mad, which I'll have the strength to do in the years to come.'

He didn't mean it, wasn't serious, was testing her, taunting her, tricking her into silence, and into going on with him so that he could do with her what he still craved to do. He played with her out of weakness, and the injustice cut her off from the world so that she wailed half mad in her dark corner, hearing her never ending rhythmical cries that she didn't know were hers till the flesh plank of his hand struck her to make her quiet in case the neighbours heard. Her screams frightened her back to sanity and remorse, and from that time her true mind had hardly spoken. Nun-like, she had taken on the healing burden of guarding Howard for life.

They had booked a room with single beds, but got a double, and between the sheets held each other as if some cosmic force might try to wrench them apart. When she took off her night dress he turned to face her. 'What colour?'

'White,' she said, though it was blue.

'Thought so,' her tears an unmistakable signal that she wanted him in the old and most effective way. 'If only you could see.' Cruel to say, but he would imagine even better what was there, and feel her soon enough.

'Love you,' he murmured. 'Love you.'

'Love you, too.' Her anguish dissolved. 'It's the only thing.'

He lit a cigarette, put on his cap, and set off to find the public library. Laura had read a street plan to him in the lounge, and indicated which way to turn from the door to reach the middle of town. 'Ask,' she said, 'if you lose track.'

'I'll show you,' a woman said when he did. 'It's not far. I go past it to get home. Take my arm, if you like.' She was young, no doubt personable, her accent like Judy's. But she wasn't Judy, nothing so miraculous. 'I was in Turkey last year for my holidays,' he said. 'Have you ever been?'

'No, but I went to Majorca once.'

'I met a woman from Boston called Judy.'

'Lucky devil! Here we are. Mind the steps. I'll get you to the door.'

A youngish woman inside helped all she could, but Judy came nowhere on the electoral rolls. Another girl said she knew her, but she wasn't in town at the moment. A pressure at the heart caused him to sit down. 'She's supposed to be.'

'Well, I haven't seen her lately.'

'What does she look like?'

'Tall, and well built. Blonde hair coming halfway down her back in a ponytail. She always wears trousers, and a blouse. Sometimes a sweater folded around her neck, if it's going to be chilly. She wears small gold earrings, and walks quickly.'

'It sounds like you know her well.'

'She's a bit too stuck-up for that, but I always see her walking by the house, when she's around. You couldn't mistake her.'

'She was nice enough when I met her in Turkey,' he said.

'I suppose she would be, out there.'

'What sort of work does she do?'

'I couldn't say exactly. She goes away for a few months, then comes back for a week or two. Something to do with boats, I think. She's always got nice clothes. Must cost more than she could afford if she worked here at the library. Last time I saw her she was walking along the street eating an ice-cream. I must get back to my work now.'

He stood. 'Can you tell me how to get to the street?'

She explained, but he caught the tone of disbelief that he would find it, or get much satisfaction if he did.

Success discouraged him, had taken the heart out of his search while making his slow way along. He was afraid. He didn't want to find the place. He felt embarrassed, almost ashamed at being so close in his tracking, wouldn't know what to say, felt an impulse to turn back, to leave the issue unresolved, in the air, so as to have something to regret for the rest of his life. If he met her he would have to confess to his clandestine listening, reveal himself as a snooper, a stalker, a dirty old flasher, a sneaking eavesdropper. He would invent a story. 'You met me and my wife at a café in Antalya and told us to look you up.'

'Did I?'

'Yes. We'd had a few drinks.'

'I don't remember. I meet so many people.'

'Oh, well, sorry to have bothered you. Maybe I've made a mistake.'

'No, it's all right. It could have been me. Come in for a moment. Now I think about it I do remember meeting someone like you.'

'I wondered if you might.'

He smelled the mud of the river. A man took him to the gate saying: 'That should be the house.' Disembodied voices sometimes brought tears. Or they hardened the steel in him. The range could be unimaginable.

He walked along a path between dead flowers, till his hand found the knocker. Anyone passing would think him a burglar, or a beggar – a bit of both. He let the knocker drop three times, holding onto the lintel to stay upright. A dog barked from the next house. He looked up, as if to see something, as if to sample the comfort of rain, his throat as if a cloud of wool surrounded his neck. Houses and traffic melted away, and he was alone in the middle of a plain, no human life for miles, only the ever renewing howl of the dog. Doing something alone made him feel more isolated, floating and unattached, his own island.

Another hammering echoed through the house. Inside were chairs she had sat on, a bed she had slept in, a mirror she had seen her unsettled melancholy face in. Nobody in. She had gone shopping. She had gone to meet Carla. She had gone for a walk to the sea. She wasn't there, and never would be. He knocked, called her name, couldn't believe she wasn't there. She was telling her aunt or whoever not to open the door, though why should anybody want to do that? Why should she be afraid of a knock at the door? She had turned the curtain aside and saw who it was. A man with a white stick and obviously blind couldn't be dangerous, unless she thought he wasn't blind at all, afraid it was the police come to talk about smuggling.

He walked slowly away – inanity to persist. Having tracked her to her den was more success than he had hoped for.

Waiting for their cod and chips, pot of tea and bread and butter, Laura said: 'Howard, I want you to tell me what's going on.'

'I don't understand you.'

'It hurts me to put it like that, but you're up to something. I've never been so mystified in all my life. It's making me miserable.'

Understanding her plight – only too well – raised the level of his irritation, but he was adept at keeping it down. 'I'm sorry you're not enjoying the holiday as much as I am.'

'Well, so am I. Which is why you must explain what's going on. I feel I'm being driven mad since we came here. We only arrived yesterday, but it seems like years. I can't take feeling that something's wrong and not knowing what it is.'

'Ah, here's our meal. I'm as hungry as if I hadn't eaten for days.' He separated fish from bone, making a mess of it, batter spilling from the plate. 'I suppose you'll think it silly, if I tell you.'

'Not as long as it makes sense. It won't be silly to put me at my ease.'

'It's all to do with radio.'

She sniffed. 'I guessed as much. What else?'

'For the last few weeks I've been listening to a couple of boats in the Mediterranean talking to each other – by voice, not morse – and I'm sure they're up to their necks in smuggling. A woman talks to another woman, and one of them comes from this town. The other's Spanish, and I'm not sure what place she's from. Anyway, I thought I'd play detective, and look the Boston woman up. The last thing I heard she was supposed to be here on a fortnight's leave. I wanted to hear her voice, confirm that she existed, listen to what other people might say about her, see if I could dig up any clues, get another angle on the puzzle as to what she's up to.'

He used his hands more while talking, but as if to calm his excitement.

'Why didn't you tell me this before?' she said. 'We could have been in it together. I would have helped.'

'I wanted to concentrate my own mind on it, accomplish something by myself.'

She thought there had been too much of that lately. 'And did you?'

'I found out where she stays, but when I went to the house, no one was in.'

Hilarious and pathetic. He was biting on the sky of nowhere. The right words wouldn't come, but she let what cared to, which could be the right ones after all, though none she would reveal. There was a vein of slyness in him, worst of all, but was she being repaid for that quality in herself? 'That's quite a feat, to do so much. I wondered why you wanted to go to the library. Where do you intend to go from here?'

'I don't know. Seems there's nowhere else. I might have to leave it, listen to the radio when I get back and see if any further light comes from that. It's my only hope. The whole thing may be a fantasy, about the smuggling especially, though I don't think so.'

She should have been glad of his independence, and in a way was, but secrets from each other had never been expected in their life together. The singularity of his quest led her to wonder whether he was telling the truth, that it wasn't a smokescreen hiding something else, but common sense told her that though he might be sly he was in no way subtle. The two never quite went together. In any case it was so bizarre a notion, to imagine he could ever catch anyone smuggling, though if it made him feel part of the world then she must admit and appreciate the good it might do. On the other hand he seemed a little too far in the land of obsession, which was most unhealthy, to do all he'd done unbeknown to her, unless she was going too far in the same direction by thinking so. 'You must keep me up to date on your investigations.'

'I'll have to now, won't I? I don't suppose I'll really learn anything up here. Enjoying your meal? I know I am.'

She poured tea for them both. 'It's a pleasant change.'

'It's just that my mind is rather taken up by trying to track her down.'

'So it seems.'

187

'Whether I like it or not is beside the point.' He enjoyed talking to someone else about Judy, though without giving anything vital away. 'I'm just going where my inclination leads me.'

'Do you have any feeling that you should resist it?'

'Since there's no possible harm,' he said, 'I don't. It's like a game, and I'm enjoying it.'

'Well, of course, it's all right listening to the wireless out of interest, as a hobby, and even making up stories from what you hear, but trying to fit something into a reality you can only imagine strikes me as a little unhealthy.'

'You can hardly say I make a habit of that kind of thing.'

She was going too far. 'I didn't mean to imply you did.'

'Wouldn't your curiosity have been aroused?'

'It might have been. I can't be sure. I would have waited for more information before coming up here.'

He spooned hot apple tart and custard. 'We needed a holiday, as you said, so I suggested we come.' Their talk was embarrassing now that she had decided his venture was weird and futile, not fit for her approval, but he saw no way to convince her, especially since the quest was peculiar even to him. He controlled an unfamiliar annoyance, though spoke as openly as possible. 'I didn't tell you why I thought we needed a holiday because I assumed you would see the reason as a bit daft, and I'd get discouraged.'

A response would lead into the unusual territory of a quarrel. He had wanted to do without her, even to deceive her. If she hadn't asked he would have told her nothing. He was suggesting it had been a mistake to ask, and perhaps he was right. Rules in such a marriage had to be made up as you went along. Because every day was the same there was always the danger that one day would be different. 'What shall we do this afternoon?' she said, after the silence.

'I'd like to walk the town a bit more.'

She folded her paper napkin, and reached for the bill. Only one thing was on his mind, which it seemed nothing could move. 'It'll be tiring, you know, and boring for me.'

'I'd be happy to go alone.'

More than happy, no doubt. 'What I mean is that it will be boring for me without you.' The girl took the twenty-note. 'I have some ideas about our holiday as well, and I'll tell you what we're going to do. We'll go to a place called Somersby. I read in the guidebook that Tennyson was born there. I'm sure you'll enjoy it. I know I will. We can both walk around the town some more tomorrow.'

Such negotiations over disputed territory brought them closer, gave something to talk about at least, laced with the unfamiliar frisson of infighting. He would relent, allow chance to operate in the hope of it bringing unforeseen results. 'Fair enough. We'll do it your way.'

She gave him his stick. 'Not my way entirely. If you aren't going to like it, we won't go.'

'Oh,' he smiled, 'I'll enjoy it.' Judy must know about Tennyson, and it was more than possible she would want to show Carla his birthplace.

'And tonight,' she said, 'you can try to get the east coast stations on your radio.'

Between tea and dinner he lay down to sleep. So did Laura, on the other side of the bed. Somersby, embosomed (a word she used) in early greenery had exhausted them. 'All those Tennysons,' she recalled, 'half mad, and doped on laudanum!'

'I want to hear his poems again,' he said. '"Tiresias" is the one I like, but it would be, wouldn't it? How did it go?'

'Like this, I think.' Years ago she had thought it apposite to learn:

'I wish I were as in the years of old,
While yet the blessed daylight made itself
Ruddy thro' both the roofs of sight, and woke
These days, now dull, but then so keen to seek
The meanings ambushed under all they saw,
The flight of birds, the flame of sacrifice
What omens may foreshadow fate to man
And woman, and the secrets of the Gods.'

'I forget the rest, though it is rather long. What a pity I didn't bring the book. I could have read all of it.'

'I can't wait,' he said. 'Maybe we'll leave the day after tomorrow.'

189

If he couldn't find Judy by then he would conclude she'd gone elsewhere, maybe taken Carla to Scarborough, or Blackpool, or to the Derbyshire hills.

After dinner Laura stayed in the lounge with a couple telling her about their holiday in Israel. Upstairs Howard put his radio on a chest of drawers under the window, threw out a length of wire, and plugged in, using earphones so as not to disturb anyone next door, leaving him alone with the ionosphere hissing and crackling, talking and morsing as the needle swivelled through scores of stations.

A hotel bedroom was more clandestine than his own mock radio shack, and the last two days of speculation were erased by the streaming of bird sounds into the brain, a relaxing therapy never known to fail.

The east coast transmitters, loud, brash, and a delight to listen to, nevertheless gave out little of interest. Messages from tankers requested pilots to guide them to their berths, sounding so close he had to decrease the volume. He soothed himself for half an hour with North Atlantic and Gulf of Mexico weather, such clear and easy to read rhythms transferred to his hand held tape recorder in case anything was worth putting onto the typewriter at home.

Switching to short wave, he trawled the usual frequencies and fancied, with a shock that went through his whole body, as if he had touched a naked cable, that he heard Carla calling her girlfriend. He twitched the needle, to go back slowly over an arc of almost silence. The aether played party tricks to bemuse and deceive. There were footpaths, bridleways and lanes through the static, no terrors or lack of navigational know-how for a blind man. Distant laughter on the half wane mocked him to return and look for it, but he was adept at playing ring around the moon, went up wave and down wave, waited on the edge, smoothed in and came out again, sneaked as slowly over the frequency as if a voice he wanted to hear, and which knew he wanted to hear it, could feel him changing kilocycles, each one passing like the clanging of a door.

Carla must know something I don't know, or she's calling another boat and another woman. Maybe a man, because you couldn't always tell with such people. A Slavic voice poached on the wave but didn't stay, and Carla's urgent requests fell into the silence, then came clear enough from the whirlpool: ''Ello, *Daedalus, Daedalus*, this is *Pontifex*. You hear me now, over.'

Judy couldn't, or wouldn't, or she wasn't anywhere but in Boston, which Carla seemed not to know. Again and again she called, as if convinced Judy was somewhere waiting – pleading for her to answer. He felt angry at such importunity, at such clamouring for Judy when she knew she couldn't possibly be there.

But she was. '*Pontifex, Pontifex*, this is *Daedalus*, this is *Daedalus*. Now I hear you. My receiver wasn't tuned in properly, but I found the trouble.'

Her voice was nowhere as loud or clear as on the larger receiver two hundred miles further south, but he heard enough, wanted to bang his head against the wall because they had conspired to deceive him as to where in the universe they would be.

Carla: 'I thought you in England.'

Judy: 'I should have been, but they stopped me. I couldn't go. The other woman didn't come out to replace me, and they had to do a job which was urgent. I lost my airline ticket, but it means nothing to them. They'll pay. I cried when they told me. It's getting too much. I sometimes want to die.'

Carla: 'You no die.'

Judy: 'I know. But I feel like it. I wanted us to go to Boston. I wanted you in bed with me.'

Carla: 'Me, as well. What we do?'

Judy: 'Don't ask me.'

Carla: 'I do. Who else ask?'

Judy: 'I know, but not yet, please.'

Howard felt their pain overwhelming whatever had been in him, and could hardly bear to listen. Their plan had misfired, been smashed. What was fate playing at?

Judy: 'I can't wait for the Azores, though. Big thing.'

Carla: 'You no say about that.'

Judy: 'Yes, I know, but I only say it might because I want you to come as well.'

Carla: 'I don't think it possible.'

Judy: 'Love you, Carla, but I can't help this situation. It's killing me.'

Carla: 'No kill. We meet soon.'

Judy: (as if she will weep) 'But when?'

Carla: 'Soon. In London maybe we meet.'

Judy: 'I long for it. But I have to go now. The skipper's found out about me using the radio, and he'll be back soon. He doesn't like it. I'm for the big chop if he catches me. I'll call you tomorrow, but only for a minute. Nobody will notice that.'

Carla: 'I listen, then. Call you anyway.'

Judy: 'And I'll pick up your wonderful voice, even if I can't answer. Love you a lot, Carla.'

Carla: 'Love you, Judy.'

At least he knew what she looked like, had enough details to sketch out a vivid comic-book picture. Tall and well built, with fine features, shiny blonde hair ponytailing down her back, a loving woman who liked a good time with her girlfriend. She wore pale grey trousers and a white blouse with a colourful silk scarf casually knotted, leather sandals on elegant feet, a gold buckle the colour of her earrings. After signing off with Carla she would smoke a thin black Turkish cigarette, and pensively wonder what direction her life could take now that their plan to meet had gone for a burton. Perhaps the cigarette made the roof of her mouth hot, and called for an ice-cream – another human touch to her appearance.

He couldn't deny how slipshod she was to think nobody could overhear her conversation. She used the radio like a telephone, with no notion of its vulnerability. Most people were similar in their faith, if they weren't wireless operators, and knew nothing about radio, looking on the phenomenon as a kind of magic, and as if their words went securely from one ear to the other. No wonder the skipper had told her not to do it, though such carelessness with regard to radio could only make her more interesting.

192

'We're wasting our time in Boston,' he said. 'I heard her on the radio. She's still out there. Something went wrong with the crewing arrangements, and she couldn't make it.'

He was infatuated with her, though she supposed detectives often were with their prey. Stalkers would be certainly. 'Shall we stay on, then?'

'I don't see any point.'

'Let's have another night,' she said, 'and then we'll go back. We can drive to the Wash tomorrow, and hear the birds. We brought the binoculars and the book so I'll tell you what they are. I've also been looking at the map. There are some curious names for sandbanks – whole families of them.'

'Like what?'

She spread the map on the bed. 'Oh, there's Bulldog Sand, and Pandora Sand.'

'I expect they're married. A right couple they must be.'

'Perhaps brother and sister. Then there's Roger Sand, and Old South, not to mention Westmark Knock. You couldn't find better names on your radio. There's Peter Black, and Thief Sand, and Gat, and Trap, and Hook, as well as Stubborn Sand, and Macaroni Channel.'

He laughed. 'You're right. What I wouldn't give to hear names like that,' wondering if somewhere among them he would find a clue to Judy's antecedents, though it could be she wasn't born of the area, only connected to it by some branch of the family. Not here now, maybe in two weeks she would be, walking the streets, haughty and set apart among the stay-at-homes yet glad to be in a place known since infancy. He would be on the south coast, the radio blank because she and her girlfriend were in Boston. He ached for a sight of her, but fate was as blind as he was. To beat the painful tension he must assume they would never meet, though in his imagination he would keep her a prisoner behind a jumble of kilocycles, locked in an electric cell, pristine and never aging, a picture for himself alone, no one able to release her from his radio hideaway.

But if ever he did get close, and he had to foresee the possibility so as to live in hope, he would touch her face in recognition, establish a memory in case he should meet her a second or third time, would guide a hand from nose to lips, over the contours of the chin and around to that tactile place at the back of the neck. Then she would be his.

'We should go to bed,' Laura said from her seat at the dressing table. 'I'll help you get your things off.'

The promise of her body between the sheets had never failed to displace even the room he was in, but now, shamming enthusiasm when her fingers began their work, the word 'Azores' lit his mind like the flash of a beacon, repeating itself across the shining water.

He saw himself performing self-destructive actions of which he would normally never approve, tried to ignore the word 'Azores', pull away from its dangers, and get back to being the person he had always supposed himself to be, but he was no longer in control and, happy enough in such a state, was helplessly pulled along.

EIGHTEEN

'I don't want to do anymore of this,' he would say to Waistcoat, who was sure to come back with: 'I'm afraid you have to, yellow belly. Nobody retires from this game till I press the buzzer. If they do it before then they are likely to find themselves up the creek without even a teaspoon. In Essex most likely, face down in the ooze. Or you'll be a waiter for the rest of your life at the Scarface Hotel – as I myself might if I wanted out.'

He knew it, so would keep the cosy chat to himself for some time yet. In any case there still wasn't enough in his Malta account to provide a comfortable beachcombing life till he popped his clogs, and he hadn't the right to go poor due to moral scruples, whether or not he assumed that Amanda would stay with him if he did.

All the same a few more trips and he would be justified in hinting that the job was too hard, and it was time a younger man took his place. He was too loyal, he would say, to allow his body to let them down in a crisis. And his present loyalty could be proved by blowing the gaff on that big gorgeous Judy yapping to her Spanish girlfriend. Love isn't only blind, it's dangerous, and she ought to be put down.

He stood by the gate at the end of the garden, a heavy two-two air rifle sighted across the meadow, ready for the next plump rabbit to come sniffing out of the hedge oh so full of the joys of life. Amanda had gone to put in some time at the hairdressers, and he would surprise her with a stew for supper. The only time he liked to cook was after skinning, disembowelling and cutting up what he had killed himself. Howard's morse letter had arrived with the morning post, showing on second reading that the old telegraphist was going even more off his trolley, in spite of his precisely rhythmical sending. The clicks of

195

the key were audible behind contacts which were slightly more apart than usual.

Not one, but two rabbits. Let them play. Plenty more where they came from. There were ten born every minute, and he could take one whenever he liked. If they were lovers – and what two rabbits weren't? – he saw no reason for them not to enjoy life a little longer. They chomped the grass, came together and nuzzled prettily. A shame, really, but where was the morality when you wanted something to eat? Their flesh was even fresher than at the butcher's, and probably cleaner.

Talking about drugs the other day, Waistcoat said that bringing them in was part of the excitement, a perk of the trade. 'Look at it this way,' he smarmed, 'if it's not us channelling 'em onto the streets to keep the dregs under control, the government would have to provide something else.'

'It's good to know we're doing a public service.' Richard smiled.

Waistcoat puffed on his long thin cigar. 'And you're well paid for it. Don't forget there's something big coming up in the Azores this autumn. A lot of cash and carry, a spin-off from the eastern trade. The Russians are getting greedier. Too many on the take. It's getting easier, though, in some ways too easy.'

He was right. They were living close to the clouds, business for everyone, so that at times you would think everyone was in on it. The organisation was getting ragged at the edges, because here was Howard, as unknowing as that prime rabbit gambolling in the sunlight as if its life was going to last forever, obsessed with the notion of tracking down a voice on the radio. If in his madness he made contact God knows what might pass between them.

The weighty two-two lead slug sent the rabbit spinning, kicking in the air till Richard locked its back feet, held it level, and sent the blade of his hand on a blow to the neck. Amanda hated to see him kill them, was even more sickened during the preparations for the pot, but she was always happy with the meal that followed.

After a long day in London he came home to see her packing two suitcases on the bed. 'What's all this about?'

'I can't take it any longer.' She sat on a stool, her face ugly with despair. 'I didn't marry a commuter, nor a dope smuggler, either.'

'Bit sudden, isn't it?'

Her laugh was pure vinegar. It wasn't, but no use telling him. 'Not for me.'

The Azores operation would be the most profitable ever. For all concerned, Waistcoat added. The length of time planning it told Richard as much. He went to London every day with energy enough, but the work of going over and over the minutiae of organisation wore him out. After every recent trip, when he'd thought to pack the trade in, he recalled the frequent saying of his father: 'Can you tell me one thing that thought ever did?' All the same, after the Azores trip he would.

The arrangements still had plenty of holes left to plug. Everything depended on planning and security, and though he had never known a lack of either, watertight was no way to describe the care they were taking. Yet what boat had ever been watertight, and what plan either? The crew was made up of freebooters to a man, in rough weather or smooth, brothers in arms no less, all of them tight lipped for fear the tighter rope they walked on would snap. You either ended in jail, or cursing the sky at fifty when an ulcer burst. Richard wanted neither option, though none of the others, as far as he knew, were glued into his kind of wedded domestic relationship. And now he wasn't to have it for more than a few minutes longer.

He lit a cigarette, watched her opening drawers to decide what was worth taking. Whenever a wife or girlfriend left the reason was never the one they threw at you, but he was too tired to figure it out. It was light and tranquilly green across the garden, the birds still musical, which would have been soothing if she had been glad to see him. He couldn't understand why she had chosen this particular hour to leave, instead of during the day when he was absent. A note on the kitchen table would have served, unless she was making the gesture now because she hoped he would argue and plead, though she ought to know that wasn't his way.

'I'm absolutely unable to put up with the so-called work you do. It's not work at all. It's horrible.'

'There's nothing I can do about it. Not yet, anyway.'

'I know there isn't.'

'The next trip will be my last. I promise.'

'You always say that.'

'I mean it.'

'It's too late already.' She put layers of clean and newly folded knickers over her dresses in the second case. 'Anyway, it always was.'

'Then why did you wait?' He had never known she had such quantities of underwear, and wondered who it was for. The sight made him want her in bed. 'Is there somebody else?'

'You know why I'm going.' He would ask that, wouldn't he? Walking cocks can't imagine you don't want to be bothered with a man anymore, not for the moment anyway, and never again with one like him. 'I'm off to Doris's. She'll put me up, till I decide what to do.'

So that was it. You couldn't win 'em all, though it would be gallant to ask her not to go, even if only for the sake of her self esteem. As if she needed it. And how egotistical could he get? They used to joke that when they were rich they would each have their own house built, a grandiose back-to-back, one for him and one for her, each residence with its separate door. The only communication between the two would be via a false bookcase, as in the old movies, to be used by prior telephone agreement when they wanted a romantic meeting. The rest of the time they wouldn't be so intolerably close.

He smiled at the memory of better days. Let her go. Best not to argue. Even so: 'Why don't you stay? I love you, you know that.'

'It makes no difference anymore.' She remembered how, not long after their first meeting, he did funny things with a razor blade while sitting at the kitchen table. Looking closer, she saw he was dividing each match into four, hadn't seen him so diverted before or since, and wondered where he had learned the skill, not to say the technique. It wasn't long before he told her, and now she thought: 'Once a jailbird, always a jailbird. I'm getting out while the going's good.' She closed the case. 'I don't want to stay with you. I can't take it anymore.' She began to cry, which he didn't know whether to take as a good or bad sign. 'I've had more than enough.'

He went to comfort her, knowing she would say, as always when he did: 'Keep away from me.'

They had given each other so much during the best times that at parting they owed each other nothing – a perfect separation. He was going to tell her, but didn't because it wouldn't stop her going. Living in Dropshort Lodge was over. He offered to carry her cases to the car, and when she agreed he knew it was final. She had been on the verge of leaving him from the very first day, so he had grown to assume it would never happen. Now it had. Her car bumped gently over the ruts to the road, then accelerated ferociously to the left.

He pulled the plug out of a bottle of wine from the fridge. Nothing like a glass or two to settle the gut. The ring on a tin of sardines snapped off, so he opened it with the ordinary tool and jagged his finger. He sucked the globe of blood, and popped a slice of bread in the toaster, then settled to his first course. Leftover rabbit stew did for the second, with fruit and cheese to follow. Luckily she'd always believed in having plenty of food in the house. Because he was hungry even iron rations tasted good, but in what commodity would he find the poison? Into what dish had she poured a distillation of her dislike? Coffee, a glass of Cointreau and a cigar erased the devastation, yet kept him in a mood to think about what had happened.

Luckily he was too engrossed in providing for himself to suffer annihilation at her scarpering. Time enough when he got back from the Azores, though it might seem old news by then. He switched the telly on, then off. Cointreau as always blended ambrosially with the cigar. A tape from Howard had laid on the table since the day before yesterday. The silly bugger took the game seriously, kept pumping them out, though Richard knew it was a plaything for them both.

Howard had the perfect life. Being totally dependent on Laura was a small price to pay for his blindness, even much to be envied, though envy wasn't – Richard considered – one of his especial sins. But to have a wife of Laura's calibre must be a wonderful comfort. He carried his glass upstairs and plugged the tape in, stretched himself in the armchair to listen.

'Dear Richard, my life has been full of incident lately, full of thought as well, though where to start and tell you about it is the difficulty. You'll remember I was listening to those Mediterranean yachts. The woman called Judy was due to go to Lincolnshire on leave, and I got Laura to drive me to Boston so that I could make contact. The plot thickens, you might say, and though I didn't actually get to her it was a worthwhile trip, because I found out quite a lot. You might wonder why I wanted to talk to her at all, and the reason is that, apart from other things, I had to put her wise about the Azores, the big event (if you know what I mean) coming off soon, which she and maybe even her girlfriend Carla will become mixed up in. It's not so much the text of her messages I'm going by as the tone of her voice. She's certainly not ignorant of what's afoot, and what it could all mean, but I suspect she'll go into it nevertheless. There's a fecklessness about her that's almost enviable to someone like me. All the same, I wouldn't really want her to get into such a venture up to, or even deeper, than her neck.

'Who she is I don't know, but I'm in thrall to her. It began out of curiosity, but now it's gone close to infatuation, so much so that yesterday I went into a travel agent's and asked about prices and services to the Azores, thinking it might be possible for me to head her off, meet her there, and get her away from whatever danger she could be in. Of course, it's out of the question because Laura would never let me go on my own, so I'm left with one possibility, which I really don't want to pursue. Or I can't make up my mind whether to or not because I could never be sure of the outcome. I want to get her out of the fire, not land her in a pit of dung.

'Being blind I love a plot, but I seem to have landed in one that's hard to get out of. You're the sort of person I can confide in, being a fellow wireless operator (a member of the fraternity, as Laura told me you said) because who else could understand the extent to which one can become involved in some chance interception? The decision I'm talking about is whether or not to drop a suggestion somewhere – Interpol, maybe? – as to what's going to happen in the Azores. Whether or not it would do Judy any good is another matter, which makes me hesitate, and hence my feeling that the best thing would be to fly out to the Azores and see what I can do. That she's in danger I can't doubt, because smuggling is a wicked and perilous occupation, from all points of view. I just feel I ought to try and do something.

'I apologise for worrying you with my problems, but at least I have something to communicate instead of just talking about the weather in the Gulf of Mexico. I could ramble on, but won't because I'm sure you have your own problems. Everyone does, and that's for sure. I can't see the point of tapping the key simply to fill up the tape. So – signing off. Yours Ever. Howard.'

Richard reached into the cupboard for his special bottle of Jack Daniel's, and poured a good glass, thinking-cap stuff, considering the state he was in after hearing Howard's letter. He sweated and shivered, and swore. Anxiety was too mild a word. The lid was falling shut on him and all of them. Howard couldn't know what problems he was making for himself.

He laughed, but wasn't amused, sorry not to be dreaming. The reasoning of the letter was full of holes, yet the whole fitted together, deliberately plotted by the cunning devil who had nothing better to do and all the time to do it in. He sounded as if he knew even more than he let on, but whether he had guessed, or had pulled in piquant extras from the radio with more shit-hot skill and instinct than Richard could ever muster, was hard to say.

He certainly wasn't giving his sources or methods away, just letting drop by worrying drop fall into his letter and cause maximum anxiety. Perhaps he was part of a subtle law-enforcing plot to put the kibosh on the biggest drug transaction of the century (as Waistcoat liked to brag) and had been in it from the beginning. Laura had played the decoy by putting a knitting needle in her tyre at the lay-by, knowing he would be passing on his way home from the pub. A policeman in a bush across the road would have been there to witness that all went well. Either it made sense, or a fit of paranoia was coming on – or both. Such a trap was easy to imagine, and tempting to dismiss, but it would be unwise to do either.

He was sweating again. Someone had fed Howard just that little bit of information to make his letter convincing, or at least disturbing. What a fuck-up he was in. Everyone. Or they might be. Whatever way you looked at it something needed to be done, or discovered, or confirmed – and quickly.

Another wouldn't help, but when he poured and swigged off half, it did. He knew what to do, would call Howard in the morning and say he'd take him for a pub lunch – if he was free. Talk to him, it was the only way, though Howard obviously knew so much that no amount of gabble would set anybody's mind at rest. At least Richard might get some idea of the situation before confronting Waistcoat and the men in London and telling, rocking back and forth as the shit hit the fan, that their security had been cracked.

No aches, no pains, but Howard felt weak and weary. Being blind made you quickly tired. He smiled, nevertheless. Listening to startling and fascinating words from the radio was no longer the cure, unless to hear the divine voice of Judy. His magneto didn't provide enough energy to work his fingers at the typewriter.

And yet, out of the house, only a cap between his head and the sky, he was sufficiently clear-brained and wide awake not to care about whatever had reduced him to impotence at the radio. On such walks he was more at peace than when in the house with Laura. No reflection on her, but the lid was off, was how he put it. He sometimes wondered if she wasn't yet born, had stopped living or being herself from the moment they were married. She had either been fixed for all time by his so-called helplessness, or there had been an event about which she had never told him. There sometimes seemed as big a blind spot in her as in him, though the notion was hardly credible, such a thought leading him to doubt any wisdom he might have. He shook his head, and a passing man must have said to himself: 'Oh no! not another bloke off his chump due to the stress of modern life!'

Even so, he was learning to see more and more with his own unseeing eyes, and went as fast as was safe back to the radio for fear of missing Judy. Some singing's going on that I can't hear; I only know it's singing but the meaning won't come clear. He sang to himself. A flick of the wheel, and it stopped on gobbledegook. Radio roulette was a favourite game. A fervent whistling bled away, a tormented soul free-falling into the inferno. He could imagine himself a turtle that the Indian government had let loose into the Ganges to clean up corpses from the ghats of Benares. Wasn't he a turtle who did that voraciously to whatever was heard on the radio? His spirit ate all the material with such greed that he consumed himself as well, never knowing when to stop.

His position in life was cocked up by three bearings closing on nothingness. The captain of the spaceship told them calmly they were lost. You could only find out where you were by going in a straight line. Avoid circles or any deviation, no matter what. But there were no straight lines, and even less in space. If you didn't want to lose yourself you must never let the ever-diminishing circles pull you into a maelstrom. Doubting that either earth or space existed, he wondered how he had got where he was. Nothing could be worse than being drawn into a fatal whirlpool without a bottle to put your last message in. Whatever happened, or wouldn't, he must get away, make distance, find a new space for himself and his body to inhabit.

An unknown station on the upper reaches of eight megacycles sent only numbers, perhaps the morse equivalent of the German Numbers Woman. Her employers had sent her on a course to learn the trade of dots and dashes, and she was happier now that she had a lover, and more money to spend on her children. He was chasing phantoms, as if he might be blessed with ordinary sight should he meet one of them. Being on the *Flying Dutchman* might bring him close to what he was looking for, whatever that was, but the vessel never landed to let him climb aboard.

How can what you think have any effect unless you act? He wanted to go on a boat, a small boat, smell the raw sea, hear the hull bump against wave after wave, feel water splashing his face, be terrified at the awesomeness of the ocean, be the first blind man ever to solo around the world. Such an adventure would quell his inner turbulence. He yearned to head for a point of no return, and come back as someone he would recognise as more of himself than before he set off. It had happened in the Lancaster bomber, and he hadn't returned as the person who had gone, had come back no longer young, because whoever lost the use of his eyes was suddenly turned into an old man, or quickly grew into one so as to go on living.

You couldn't break out of yourself, become someone you were not. Fantasies were all the better for staying in the mind. A blind man couldn't hoist sails, or shoot the midday sun with a sextant, or plot the position on a chart. Even with eyes you had to learn, and yet – the yearning was unremitting. He wouldn't be useless, would hear beacons on the radio, steer by them, guide and navigate. In the midnight of the ocean all men were equal. He imagined countless feats to be performed, his imagination playing with possibilities till the Black Dog leapt disappointed from his back – though leaving the marks of its claws.

And then he heard, the voice more remote, less confident: 'Hello, *Pontifex*, can you hear me? Carla, are you there?'

Carla: 'Yes, no problem. Don't use names anymore.'

Judy: 'I know. Can't talk long, in any case. I'll be in big trouble if I do. Did you have a good day?'

Carla: 'Boring. On small island. Seven on board. I try to get new job, big yacht in Malaga.'

Judy: 'Better not leave me.'

Carla: 'You crazy? In September. He need Spanish crew.'

Judy: 'I'll come with you.'

Carla: 'Maybe. Give me a kiss. Dream me this night.'

Judy: 'Love you too. Had a dream about you and me in Boston.'

Carla: (laughing) 'What I do?'

Judy: 'Everything.'

Carla: 'You dream again, then.'

Judy: 'I will. I want more than dreams. But I must go now. Somebody's coming. Maybe we got shopped. In fact I'm sure we did. The skipper was livid. I denied it black and blue but he only half believed me. So I can't talk anymore today. Same time tomorrow, though. Just a one-minute burst, all right?'

Carla: 'I understand. *Adios, carina.*'

He saw them going to work about their boats, Carla the competent deckhand and stewardess, and Judy the cook, provider of food and comfort. Someone who had been listening, apart from himself, had betrayed them. Yet it was hard to believe in unsolicited malice, for betrayal always had its reasons. If the usual shortwave enthusiast heard the lovers how would he be able to inform the skipper of Judy's yacht? He wouldn't. Such eavesdroppers, as he well knew, culled secrets only out of a dispassionate sense of curiosity and perhaps power, but wouldn't do anything for fear of revealing their illicit pastime. Satisfaction, as they sat in the entrancing half dark of a desk lamp, came from knowing they could while being aware that they wouldn't. The ordinary shortwave scourer, with its effective decoding equipment – the sort that Howard could neither use nor afford – locked onto newsagency, embassy or weather and shipping traffic, and would pass the gabble of telephony voices with contempt.

Anyone who found such unregulated traffic morally distasteful could inform the Post Office Telephony Authority, and get the lovers stopped, but Howard thought it unlikely that such trouble would be taken. In any case what listener would have the know-how to guess the real importance of Judy and Carla's talk, as he had done? If someone *had* given their game away they should be dropped out of a plane minus a parachute, except that such a fate would be too good for them.

Judy would converse for a precious minute with her lover tomorrow, against all common sense, and Howard was only sorry that longer chats were no longer possible. Caution had come too late. The two boats were heading for the Pillars of Hercules bumping through a grumbling sea (according to the latest forecast) from one landfall to another, across to Sicily, by the rugged coasts of Algeria and Morocco, and along to Spain. They might pass within fifty miles of each other yet not be able to meet or even talk.

He could easily believe he had been the only one to hear them, so who could the informer be? The droning of the German Numbers Woman led him to wonder whether Laura had done it out of pique. She hadn't liked his infatuation – and who could blame her? – therefore you could say she had a motive. On the other hand you could say she was aware that the women were too involved with each other for her to feel jealousy, so would hardly think it worthwhile to betray them.

An account of his interceptions had almost filled a morse letter to Richard, who was the only person able to stop their shortwave trysts. By sending extended telegrams on tape, the medium of morse had put an ebullience into Howard's revelations, which excluded all caution. Richard must have known this would be the case, and like a fool he had fallen into his trap.

He recalled solving his first simple jigsaw as a child: thick wood, bright colours, not too many pieces, and all too obvious joinings, an easy and satisfying picture to put together, of the Big Bad Wolf chasing three little piggies from their burning straw-roofed house. He felt angry at not having thought of the explanation before. The time scheme fitted. Two women chatting, and giving hints of their future shifts, could be threatening to someone, possibly fatal, and Richard wanted them stopped because such talk pointed to criminal activity he also was involved in, or people he knew were involved in, matters to do with small boats going around Greece and the Middle East which, as Howard already knew, signified smuggling.

The forlorn inexorable tone of the German Numbers Woman mocked his obtuseness, but she had put the edge back into his thinking, and was no longer needed. He wanted to hear Vanya's erratic and slapdash morse on the Moscow frequency, an operator who would find Howard's mistake easy to say never mind about, but who was doubtless in some downtown bistro knocking back the vodka with his radio cronies. All Howard heard were hideous crackles of static, no help to a mind in turmoil.

When evil creeps up on you, ignorance of its power is no excuse. Stupidity is alarming, unknowingness worse. The damage had been done, but the lesson could be learned, provided it wasn't too late and no one paid for your lapse.

All the same it remained to be seen whether or not he had made a mistake. Perhaps the subconscious which had led him to act foolishly would yet take care of him, since he had fitted together the puzzle connecting Judy and Carla to the skippers of their yachts, and now with Richard, who also went on small boat trips for a living.

The fatal tape letter had revealed most of what he had assumed or concocted, and if Richard read it carefully – he certainly would – Howard expected him to telephone and say that they had to meet. When they did Howard would appear certain about his solution of the puzzle, but play the amateur who did not know the importance of what had come into his ken. The theme to choose was that which would not put Judy into more peril than she was in already. Other than that the conversation would have to follow its own rules.

He had sent the tapes, and awaited the response. Perhaps it was no more than his unworldliness and isolation that had led him to fabricate such an outlandish plot, but if that was so, he reasoned, it was because a blind man must try in every way to enrich and extend his life.

NINETEEN

A call came during breakfast, the old post-office bird chirping MMM between cornflakes and the cooked part. 'Thought you might like to come for a drink,' Richard said. 'About lunchtime. We can have a bite in Rye or some place. That is, if Laura can spare you an hour or two.'

'Sounds good.' The thongs of the web were firm, its spider working sufficiently to draw Richard in. 'I don't have anything on.'

'Pick you up at twelve-hundred hours?'

'I'll be waiting.'

'Who was that, dear?'

He sat at the table, cut into his food. 'Richard's coming to take me out to lunch. Says he knows a nice place, though I think he mainly wants to talk.'

'About that woman you heard on the wireless?'

Judy must be on her mind all the time. 'Possibly.'

'He knows about it, then?'

'I mentioned her in a letter some time ago, but I can't see how it can be of any interest to him.'

He was still on the woman's track, unwilling or unable to leave his plaything alone, but Laura was consoled by knowing that his pursuit couldn't go on forever, though it was hard to know why she hoped for the demise of something which kept him so enthralled. It was touching, when he had little else. 'That's as maybe,' was all she could say.

'She's hardly on the wavelength anymore,' he went on. 'Only for a minute or so, and not always every day.'

'I expect you'll be sorry when it's finished.'

'There's always something else. Anyway,' he sensed her disapproving

207

mood as she stood to collect the dishes, 'it's only a pastime. You're my rock and my staff. Nobody else but you, my love.'

She kissed him on the back of the neck, which he liked, looked at him enjoying his sausage, egg and tomato. 'Well,' she said, 'we have a pact, and it's a wonderful one as far as I'm concerned.'

'When we went over Germany in the war we got a fried egg for our breakfast afterwards. That's why they always taste so good to me. Every time I have one, even now, it's as if I'm eating the one I didn't get when I came back wounded. Even better, because you know exactly how I like them cooked.'

He ate well, always enjoying his food, and ever hungry for meals, as if wanting to show that while such an appetite prevailed there could be nothing wrong or devious about him. Even so, the unease that had lately come between them proved that something unusual was happening, and to separate the warp from the weft and make sense of it was impossible for her.

Richard was on time, to the minute. He half apologised for the inconvenience of being punctual: 'Naval habit, I suppose.'

'A good one,' she said, stepping aside. 'Howard's in the bathroom. He won't be long.'

He felt the same shock at being half in love with a robust haughtiness he would relish breaking down. Her staunch beauty, concealing a passion she seemed afraid of, turned more ordinary at her smile of welcome. 'It's terrifically good of you to take him out. He has so few opportunities.'

He laughed. 'I'll bring him back in one piece, never fear. I'll be driving, so shan't drink much. Never do, in any case.'

'Oh, I know you'll take care of him.'

'Why don't you come as well? You're certainly welcome to.'

The offer was tempting. 'I have things to do.' The response was a little too sharp, so she added: 'Reading, mostly. I like to keep up.'

Show an interest. 'Oh, on what?'

'It's a funny Kingsley Amis novel. I'll read it to Howard when I've done. He'll like that. I read him books from time to time because he prefers my voice to an actor on tape. I suppose I've become quite good at it.'

He had no doubt that she could act tragedy to good effect, wanted her to go on talking, would rather listen to her than hear what Howard had to say. But here he was, a kiss for Laura, and they were on their way down the hill.

Driving towards the coast, Richard was too preoccupied to describe the scenery, as he had heard was Laura's custom, while Howard was happy to interpret winds and smells drifting through the open window, enjoying the rush of air as the road turned inland. Richard seemed anxious in his silence, in a hurry either to eat or talk.

The unseeing figure beside Richard seemed more like an exhibit meant for an art museum than a person of flesh and blood. At the most he might be a wise Buddha too all-knowing to speak. The phenomenon made him feel more alone in the car than if he'd been on his own, and he said when approaching Rye: 'Be there in a few minutes.'

'Going northeast, I think.' He moved from arms folded to hands on knees. 'It's a long time since I was in Rye. Another of the Cinque Ports. Crossing the Rother, are we?'

'That's right. We'll soon be at the trough.'

'Makes me hungry, this sea air.'

Small talk was necessary to start with, though there was no saying how small it could ever be with Howard.

'Up the cobbles, and onto the High Street,' he said.

'You know it, then?'

'Laura's brought me here a time or two, though not lately. The place pullulates on market day, and in the summer holidays.'

'Here we are.' A few steps to the door, and Richard cleared a path to the bar, feeling strange being a blind man's minder. 'A pint first, and then to eat. Will that suit you?'

Howard gave a little laugh, almost feminine. 'More than all right. You get thirsty, living in the dark.'

They sat by the window, light gleaming in. 'I must say, you're a skilful listener at that wireless of yours, the wonderful things you pull in.'

Howard drank, wiped his mouth, an unnecessary motion but it kept his tone neutral, surprised the subject had come up so soon. 'I'm glad you think so.'

'I do. It's been a real treat, getting your morse letters. I always look forward to 'em.' It was like talking to someone dumb as well as blind. Must be living with him that makes Laura so noble and enigmatic, though a woman of few words would seem that way.

Howard said something at last. 'I think you know Rye much better than I do.' The voice was unfamiliar, almost caressive, as if not certain of being heard, putting the onus on whoever he was talking to. 'I expect you've made a few trips, in and out.'

'One or two.'

Silence again, until sitting at the table over their pâté and toast, when Howard said: 'I don't know what I've done to be taken out and treated so handsomely. I'm certainly enjoying it.'

'No special reason. But I did think it was about time we talked at our leisure, without the inevitable morse code between us.'

A touch of mischief wouldn't come amiss. 'You mean with no one else to listen?'

He seemed uneasy. 'Maybe.'

'I'm not very good at conversation,' Howard put in. 'I sometimes wonder whether it's because I'm a wireless operator, or because I'm blind. It could be both. A wireless operator listens all the time, so doesn't have time to talk, or feel the inclination to. A blind man can't see, and so has less to talk about what he's heard, which often isn't much, and he's not supposed to reveal most of it, in any case. A blind man has only what's inside himself to draw on, and he sometimes finds great difficulty in doing so because it's too complicated to disentangle.' He pushed his plate aside with a laugh. 'You seem to have got me talking, and maybe that's what a friend's most valuable for.'

You're not saying much, all the same, Richard said to himself.

A little more than you, so far. Howard went on: 'I could ask you, of course, what it is you want me to talk about.'

'Anything that comes to mind. What else?'

Richard was a man who always lit a cigarette between courses. Or was it only now, with Howard, who wasn't surprised that so much was on his mind. 'And if nothing does?'

'I know, it takes two to talk. The only thing that's happened to me recently is that my wife's left me.'

'Oh, I'm sorry.'

Or was he? There was a slight envy in his tone, at the ups and downs of other men, of men who could see and had to take all that was thrown at them. 'Don't be. She'd been meaning to do it from the first moment she saw me and, since I'd been waiting for it, it came as no surprise. Life's calmer, which is no bad thing.'

'Is that the truth?' Howard said. 'Has she really gone?'

'Ah, here's our steak and chips.' He pressed out his cigarette. 'She certainly has. Nothing like it for clearing the decks. I'd been dreading it every minute for years, but now it's happened I feel light-headed with freedom. The only thing is, if I get too happy I might not do my work so well. I could get careless.'

'I shouldn't think there's any chance of that with you,' Howard said. 'Happiness takes more care of a man than misery.'

'Ah! You think so? In my trade it's better to have neither one thing nor the other. Nothing to think about except your work.'

'Do you have much these days? Will you pass me the salt? If I search for it myself I might knock it for six.'

'A certain amount. Time goes by when there's nothing, and suddenly the big trip is on. Shall I put the salt on for you?'

'I can do it. You'll be going far?'

'Maybe. It's a millionaire's yacht, a hundred-and-fifty footer, with good engines, and I'll be part of the crew.'

He was a quick eater, Howard surmised. 'It sounds a good life, but I suppose dangerous at times.'

'I'm used to it. But you're right, though I wouldn't want to do anything else. Nothing else I'm fitted for.'

'That's a blessed state. At least you're fixed in your purpose, and know where you stand.'

Howard felt him smile. 'You could say that. I'm handy of course with the radio on such trips, and you can understand how they appreciate it.'

'You mean using beacons for navigation?'

'Oh, all sorts of things. I listen out for the good and the bad, you might say.'

'If I'd had my sight I might well have gravitated to the same sort of work. I'd certainly give at least one of my arms to do what you do.'

Richard felt pity for him, though only for a moment. 'Are you sure about that?'

'As much as I can be sure of anything.'

'You'd have been good at it, no doubt about it, with all those juicy items you pick up.'

Time again for a little silence, Howard decided, even if only to eat. He turned his head as if to look around the room, then concentrated on getting food from plate to mouth. The room seemed full, which explained Richard's low tone while talking. He wanted no one to over-hear. Well, neither did Howard, who felt comfortable in the controlling role of the conspirator.

'For instance,' Richard said at last, 'these women you were hear-ing.'

'Judy?'

'You seem to base a hell of a lot on that contact.'

'Well, I got in on the picture, didn't I? But you had my report, and know as much as I do.'

Richard seemed to think about it. 'Perhaps. But it was like a story you made up.'

Howard laughed. 'Exactly. That's what I told myself, and yet it all dropped into place. I imagine you would have come up with the same story, based on the evidence I got. Your intuition would have led you onto the same track.'

'Maybe. But how right would I have been?' He tapped his glass. 'Another drink? I'm having one.'

You're going to need it more than me. 'Half a pint, then.'

He went to the bar and, while waiting, Howard surmised he was being looked at, so went on eating as if knowing he wasn't.

'But how much of a story do you think it was?' Richard put the tankard into his hand.

Howard set it down, quite capable of picking it up himself. 'Don't think I told you one half.'

Richard's pint clicked against his plate. 'You mean you could make up an even more fantastic tale?'

'Certainly. One which might get a good deal closer to the truth than fantasy. The more my mind worked on it, that is.'

'I wish I'd waited till your next letter then. It would have made another of my days.'

'I dare say it would. It might have made several.'

'Well, tell it to me, if it won't wait.'

'Oh, it will wait right enough. Me having so little meat to put in my letters, I prefer to spin them out. That was certainly a nicely cooked steak. And the chips were just how I like them. You picked a good place.'

'I sometimes come here with the crew, when we're back from a trip.'

So he'd been more than a few times to Rye, and bringing in what? 'You can read me the dessert menu, if you would.'

He seemed glad of a hiatus in their indeterminate chatter. 'I can recommend the hot apple pie and mince tart, with cream.'

'I'm ready when you are.' Howard was also calm, and happy to wait for confirmation of his ideas about the future. He tasted his beer while Richard gave the order. Soon enough there would be time to tell Richard what he knew, or thought he knew, which was the same, or it would be in the end. Loud talk came from the door, and a clash of cutlery from the bar.

'I need another drink,' Richard said. 'But that will be my last. How about you?'

'I could run to the same again.' Maybe he couldn't, but he lived on two levels as far as drink went, alcohol kept in one compartment and clear faculties in another. Unless he had too much, which he never would. To be abstemious about his drink might bring suspicion, or distrust. All the same, much of him regarded Richard as a friend, a fellow sparks, a comrade in arms who'd had the generosity to invite him out, and who in the last months had made his life more interesting, probably more so than since he had been blasted into sightlessness. He liked him as much as you could like someone you would never fully know, and probably never be able to trust. A certain density of friendship had settled around them, in a situation so fraught with unknowingness that it could only strengthen the connection.

213

He put the glass into Howard's hand. 'Here's to your health.'

'And yours.'

They forked at their dessert. 'I have a liking for sweet things,' Howard said. 'And this is delicious.' Certainly more palatable than Laura's often too health-conscious food. 'It must have been good, coming here when you had landed, after all that salt water.'

Richard laughed. 'Yes, we had plenty of that, smack in our faces at times. But about this woman talking to her girlfriend?'

'There's no more to tell than I've let on already. She was on a boat called the *Daedalus*. You know who Daedalus was, in the old Greek mythology?'

'I've forgotten.' He hadn't. 'A blacksmith?'

'Something like that. Artificer. He had a son called Icarus, and he made them both a pair of wings to fly to Italy. The father told the son not to go too close to the sun in case the wax melted. Of course, the bloody silly youth did, and he falls into the drink. Father flies on. I love those old legends.'

'So her boat was called *Daedalus*?'

'That's right.'

'You're sure of that?'

'Still is. I must have heard her say it fifty times. And the other woman was – is – the *Pontifex*. Which means pope or priest. But what's in a name? Judy and Carla had a natter every night, until recently. They were sweet on each other, you might say. But from the few hints I got they were involved in some very funny business, going from one place to another.'

'What business, do you think?' He had finished his dessert, and lit a cigarette. 'Did you get any idea?'

'You seem to like the story. It's got you hooked.'

'I'm just interested.'

'So was I. Who wouldn't be? You can see how it would grab me, can't you?'

'Here, have one of mine.' He passed a cigarette, and held the match. 'The whole thing sounds fascinating, just the sort of storybook thing to talk about over lunch. And you said you weren't very good at conversation!'

214

'The thought of boring people horrifies me.'

'You'd never do that. But what business did you decide they were in?'

'It isn't what I decided. It's what I gathered.'

'But not definite?'

'Oh, definite enough for me. They go smuggling, from one place to another. Unloading stuff from Turkey and the islands. The cargo comes from Russia and places in central Asia. Or maybe from the Far East. The Golden Triangle, isn't it called?'

The silence was heavy, didn't last, though long enough for Howard to know that he had scored: a bull's-eye, with buckshot.

'That's a lot to assume, all the same.'

'You wouldn't have thought so if you'd heard what I heard.'

'But what, exactly?'

He shifted in his seat, as if to get closer. 'Unfortunately, I didn't have my tape recorder on, otherwise I would play it so that you could hear why I knew they were working the rough powder trade. Opium maybe, mostly.'

'Opium? Did they say that?' Anything more specific, and Howard would be lying.

'As far as I heard.' Keep it indefinite. 'Tons of it. More than you could get from all the Flanders poppies put together, it seemed.' The fact that Richard kept him on this topic, as he had known he would, told Howard more than he had been certain of before the meeting. 'I suppose if I was a right thinking law abiding citizen I might put a word in somebody's ear about it.'

'And why didn't you? Don't you, I should say?' It's because he's still not sure, or he's lying. He's in the airy realms of yarn telling. But if he isn't, and his intention is hinted to Waistcoat, there'll be a contract killing on his head before he can find the Belisha beacons to cross the road.

Howard felt hot ash on his wrist, a bit of cigarette paper attached, but let it burn out – Richard noticed – without flinching. 'It's because that isn't all. I could be waiting for something more to develop.'

'Like what?'

'Like what? Something so big it gives me palpitations.' He regretted more than at any other time that he couldn't see Richard's face on coming out with: 'The Azores.'

'I'd better get the bill.' Richard knew that if he couldn't stand the heat he had better get out of the kitchen. The blind man was playing cup and ball, and scoring every time, the only good being that he didn't see the jolt of his hand when he said *Azores* – though he recovered sufficiently to say: 'We were made to recite a poem at school about the Azores. Didn't it go something like: "At Flores in the Azores Sir Richard Grenville lay" – I forget the rest. I hated it.'

'Tennyson,' Howard said.

'Yeh, the old bastard. But what about the Azores?' he went on, calmly now.

'Oh, yes, well, there's going to be the biggest pick-up of the lot from there. Isn't that enough?' He stopped, feeling a fly on his hand and waiting to swat it. It flew away, as if disturbed by the tension in his veins. 'Very big, all lined up.'

'You heard that?'

'In no uncertain terms.'

No more fucking about, he decided. 'When?'

'In September, late, towards the end. But even they don't know the exact date. Not yet. I'll find out. I'm glued to the radio every night.'

'They're still talking?'

'Why shouldn't they be?'

'I don't know.'

'They're in love, you see. Indiscreet, perhaps, but not too much so. It's just that someone like me can put the bits and pieces together, and come up with the right answer.'

Richard had to play the only card possible, though with little hope of winning. He lit another cigarette, in spite of a sore spot in his chest, sent the smoke drifting over Howard's empty plate. 'Supposing I were a detective putting all the pieces together. I have to assume so, to be part of the game.'

'It's certainly absorbing us,' Howard grinned.

'Well, it's such a good story. The end of it all for me would be that, finally, I wouldn't believe there was any reality to it. Absolute garbage. I'd like it for the story – who wouldn't? – but not for the truth.'

'Why is that?'

'I wouldn't believe two people chatting on the radio would be so careless, and give away a scheme that might put them and a few others away for twenty years.'

Howard moved spoon and fork around on his plate. 'You could be right.'

'I'm sure I am – would be, I mean.'

But why so sure, on any terms? Truth was often, as he had heard, stranger than fiction, and instinct a sure guide to sort out both, the final lock on what was what. He was tiring of the cat-and-mouse zig-zags, 'And yet.'

'Yet what?'

'My deductions are spot on. A few holes left, but not many. When they're filled in I shall know what to do.'

All was lost for a moment, with knobs on, forcing Richard to say: 'Will you promise you won't do anything until you've talked it over with me?'

It was hard at times when you were blind not to think that others couldn't see either, so Howard's smile was more than ruthlessly put down, Richard only catching a figment of pain on his lips. He knew now all he needed to know. 'If you'd like me to, out of friendship, yes. I'll keep it to myself.'

A laugh was necessary, to cover the fact that he felt a mere child. 'Not that. Why should it be? I only ask because maybe the final story will be more finished if we put both our heads together. It's such a good one. I like talking about it, that's all.'

'All right. I'll keep to that,' regarding Richard's request as an attempt to save face.

Which promise was the best Richard knew he would get out of such a subtle antagonist, at least until he had spoken to the others. 'Before going back, let's drive down to Dungeness.'

'I'd like that.' He knocked a chair over while standing up, which Richard righted in an instant. 'We can watch the fish swimming in the warm water from the power station. Laura told me about them when we were there before.'

TWENTY

On the way to town Richard thought he would listen, for entertainment, to the latest morse letter from Howard. Each note's absolute regularity could almost have been made on a machine, but after the initial greetings, and enquiries after health, he realised that the forthcoming text would be special and create no laughter. There was something eerie about the self-assured patter of his sending.

He spun the tape back several times to check that he had heard correctly. Can I credit it? he asked himself, and a solid no was the response. The aura of a bad dream was hardly calculated to calm his mind. Certainly a fantasy on Howard's part, though he couldn't deny that it was one which cemented their relationship even further.

He had been thinking, Howard said – he certainly had – but what he proposed, what he in fact demanded in a way not much short of blackmail, must have been in his mind far earlier than the time of their lunch together. That Howard had a unique mind compared to his own he had never doubted, though whether it was because of his affliction – so called: he was beginning to wonder – or because he would have been that way as a perfectly sighted man, he didn't know. All he was sure of was that the association might land Howard in such a quantity of drek that it would bury him even above his unseeing head.

As far as Howard went, and Howard was more than acute enough to know it, he had nothing to lose or, being as blind as a bat, assumed he hadn't, but Richard, as far as he himself was concerned, had everything to lose, which could also be said for the rest of the crew. Howard must obviously realise as much, but didn't bring the factor into his calculations. Had he been normal, and sent a handwritten letter, there would have been something to hang him by,

218

but the clear and imperious morse, which only the two of them in the local circle could read, enclosed them in secrecy and implicated Richard also, which Howard well knew, in his peculiar and illuminated ruthlessness.

Richard didn't know what to do, yet there was only one thing he could do. The sentences came clear and pat, no more dissimulation or hiding what Howard wanted. And what he did want was preposterous. It was unbelievable. 'I seem to have the whole key to your expedition in my hands, even down to the details.' He was lying, but that wasn't significant anymore, though a blind man lying could be alarming enough to set the klaxon shrieking.

Howard would know that Richard would know that he was lying, which was all part of the net he was casting. 'It is up to me whether or not to blow the gaff on you and the rest. I could do it at any hour I chose, whether you go on the trip or not. Nothing would be easier. As you know, however, telling what I know to the police would put me on the wrong side of the law for listening, an anomalous position with regard to my conscience, but I expect they would forgive me for that.'

What a mealy-mouthed old bastard! though Richard admired his subtlety and dexterity, especially when he went on: 'Informing a third party would in any case allow me to get used to being against the law, so having contemplated such a course I can feel no qualms by going even further, even the whole hog, you might say. In my life a little chaos, and even danger (though I don't anticipate that) can do no harm. Rather, it has an attraction which I find hard to steer away from.

'What I propose then, want, demand if you like, is that you somehow or other take me with you to the Azores, on any pretext – I don't care which you have to choose – but get me on that boat. If you want absolute secrecy from me as to why you are going then I can guarantee it hand on heart. After all, what can a blind man be witness to? That I go with you is the only condition for my silence, and from then on I will take my secret to the grave, as melodramatic as that may sound. I'm all set for it, nothing will stop me, and you have no other way out except to make sure I go with you.'

Oh, yes there was a way out, but it was one which Howard's imagination seemed not to have thought of, unless he just wasn't saying.

He lacked one of his five senses already, but could be deprived of the others, could lose even the use of his legs, or his hands or, worst of all, his ears, which could cut him off from life and mischief altogether. Maybe he knew this, well aware of the odds but, as before, thought he had nothing to lose, and because of one paltry affliction was prepared to gamble his empty life away.

In the tape he went on to indicate – and Richard even in his mind saw the rather large but delicate fingers manipulating the key with a certainty that he would get what he wanted – that since he poured all his thoughts on the matter into such a message his obsession would have to be satisfied. He ended by saying that on the kind of trip he envisaged – a little sugar on the pill – he could act as second radio man and tune into any station whose information might be vital for making the trip safer for all on board. He thought of everything, this final snippet at least giving Richard a line to suggest if Waistcoat's reaction turned out to be rougher than he hoped.

Richard regretted getting to know him, yet if he hadn't he would not have won his confidence, and found out what he listened to. Also, it would be a godsend for the others to be aware of a break in their security. A man with the use of his eyes may have thought little of the chatter going on between two women, but the one in a million chance of a blind man hearing it had let him put clues together and figure the whole thing out. Richard had been on hand to know, luckily, but he hardly saw himself being thanked for the priceless information that had been hammered into his brainbox.

Going into the flat on Harley Street, he couldn't imagine the redecorations had been done specially for the penultimate countdown briefings, though Waistcoat may have had such an object in mind, since he would be coming on the boat with them. He never thought he had much aesthetic taste (having left it to Amanda, who had) but puke yellow in the recesses, offal white for the ceiling, and snot green for the rest, obviously seemed more than all right to Waistcoat, who stood by the mantelpiece beneath the fake 'Last Supper' with a finger in each lower pocket. Such bizarre choices didn't much matter to Richard, whose stance was bolstered by a little private knowledge about the forthcoming expedition, something they would learn soon enough.

Waistcoat was as close to an affable mood as he could get, as he poured white wine, even though he thought it much too good for them, since they wouldn't know mouthwash from the best Bordeaux, or a vintage from recently established vineyards in the north of England.

Richard glanced around the room as if seeing everyone for the first time, a villainous lot of proficient seamen whose faces he hoped belied their true character. On the other hand it was often difficult to decide whether the face showed its true self, or whether the true self was hidden by the face. All he knew was that the right behaviour was guaranteed in a crisis. He had sailed with them before, had no qualms, and supposed it was likewise, their glances so quick as he came in that no optical instrument could measure them.

Killisick's large head and small body made him look frail, but Richard knew him as a strong little man, in that he had once slung a vat of boiling stew over someone who, he found out, had taken his false teeth – resting in a mug on the bread bin – and wouldn't say where they were hidden. Bald and fair skinned, always with a smile while working at his stove, he was known as so ingenious a cook that if need be he could produce a cordon bleu blow-out in a force nine gale from a couple of seagulls and a bucket of kelp.

Richard was so engrossed in weighing up his shipmates' qualities that for some moments he wasn't aware of Waistcoat talking, though didn't suppose he had missed anything important.

'It's a long time since we had such a big job on, and I've called the six of you together just to make sure you know it, and how vital it's going to be. We're taking a big boat, which signifies you'll be in the lap of luxury. But I'll need all the hands I can get, so I'll be on board from start to finish. You'll have to watch yourselves, that's all I can say. We don't want any fuck-ups this time.'

Waistcoat's choice of language made it easy to know what ran through his mind – a cross as he was between a panther and a south London slum kid. A certain tension among the members of such an organisation – if you could call it that – was healthy enough, and Richard had no difficulty plugging into it, knowing that in any emergency they would fuse into an acceptable unity rather than the other way round – except that introducing the matter of Howard's demands right now might have a spectacular effect, Waistcoat's temper always fragile when any grains of sand fell into the meticulousness of his Swiss watch arrangements.

'There've never been any fuck-ups,' Scuddilaw said. 'That's not what we're here for. Never have been.' Richard had seen him do the most backbreaking work for longer than anyone else, without complaining. He had a squat compact body, thick ginger hair low on his brow, and grey glinting eyes that gave nothing away. All they knew about him was that he exercised several hours a day to make himself look more and more as if he had nothing inside but concrete. 'We all know well enough what to do once we're at sea.'

'I know,' Waistcoat said, 'but we're motoring a long way this time, and I'm not telling you where it'll be yet, because of security.'

A belligerent murmur came from George Cleaver. Over six feet tall, wary and erect, in his conventional three-piece suit, with a gold watch chain leading into a waistcoat pocket, he always stood by the door of whatever room he was in, as if ready to jump clear at a sudden inrush of police. He spoke little, but when he did those nearby listened, especially at sea when they wanted to know where they were, because he was known as the best Atlantic navigator in the trade. 'We aren't a bunch of school kids.'

'Nor old women, either,' Scuddilaw said. 'We don't just want to know where we're going the day we get on board.'

Cannister, an ex-trawlerman who, Richard smiled, seemed to have polished his earring, and shampooed his ponytailed hair to come to the meeting, backed him up.

'All right, then,' Waistcoat said. 'I know I can rely on you lot as far as security is concerned. But I'm only not telling you yet in case there's a change of plan. I don't expect there will be, but you never know. All I do know, though, is that none of you will be disappointed. When this trip's behind you, you'll all be plenty satisfied.'

Since Richard had been told a fortnight ago he wasn't much concerned whether the others knew or not where they were going, but he didn't want to openly announce that security had already been cracked by a blind man at his wireless. He must wait for an opportunity, meanwhile hearing Waistcoat say they would be crewing for him on a pleasure cruise, but that the boat on the return trip would be packed with four hundred kilos of cocaine in watertight kitbags which, Richard reckoned, would be worth something like forty million on the UK market. If they were caught with such an amount they would never walk on daisies again, but if they brought it off the pay could only be called retirement money – though it was hard to imagine any of them getting out of the game. They would go on for more, and more, and still more, not solely out of greed, but because buccaneering was in their blood.

'It may be,' Waistcoat was saying, 'that we'll be shorthanded on such a big boat, so I might ask Oswald Beck if he can spare a couple of weeks from his posh pub, see if he can't tear himself away from them ivory-handled beer pumps, and his barmaid with the big tits.'

Hard not to laugh, or be seen not to. 'He won't come,' Cannister said. 'I called there for a pint last week. The bastard made me pay for it.'

'He's gone soft,' Paul Cinnakle said. He paused in filing his nails, a man whose clothes almost matched Waistcoat's expensive style. Richard had heard him scornful of those who in their gear could mix freely and unnoticed among people on the street – at least they could these days, with so many weirdoes about. Maybe for such an attitude Waistcoat sometimes seemed suspicious of Cinnakle, though he had no reason not to trust such a proficient engine man, unless he regarded him as being after his job, or at least that he would like to give it a try, though Richard knew there wasn't a hope of him coming to within a sniffing distance of a skipper's aftershave.

'That's for me to decide,' Waistcoat responded, his look as if to say: 'And don't you forget it. In any case, it's no business of yours, fuck-face.' He came over to Richard, who held out his glass for a refill. 'You look like you've got something on your plate.'

The others were talking among themselves, as if no longer interested in the trip. 'No, I'm all right.'

'Any comments on the arrangements?'

'They seem fine to me. We've been through them often enough.' He drank, more to be sociable than for the quality: Waistcoat's posh wine merchant had filled the bottles with acidy plonk, and stuck fancy labels on them. 'I'd prefer a word with you afterwards, Chief, if that's in order.'

'With you it always is. Anything serious?'

'Could be important, though I expect it'll be all right.' Might as well let him have an indication, though the momentary shade on Waistcoat's face showed that he suspected something disagreeable. A man who had pulled himself out of the mire to become more than a millionaire was alive to every nuance. The only thing in his life was a controlled drive for the visible yet unattainable object, not seen by anyone else but to their cost if they knowingly – or unknowingly for that matter – stood in his way. So he kept ahead of others with an energy common in those who had dragged themselves from the lowest of the low, the sort who thrived on the versatility of his malice (which was as close to evil, in Waistcoat's case, as a person of limited intellectual ability could get) and also luck, as well as a certain off-hand skill when dealing with someone more powerful in the game.

'I'm dying to hear about it, so I'll get rid of this lot,' which he soon did, for there was no one who wasn't glad to go. 'All right, the show's over – but finish your wine first, if you like.'

Richard's problem was how to begin.

'Sit down,' Waistcoat said. 'The hoi-polloi's gone to the steak house, so tell me what's on your mind.'

He pulled his chair close. 'You know I've been sending in wireless signals over the years, from various places?'

'You've been well paid, haven't you?'

'It's not that.'

'What the fuck is it, then?'

'I struck up an acquaintance a few months ago with another chap, who does the same thing as me. He just listens, but does nothing with what he gets. Out of interest, you might say. It was a chance meeting, and just as well it took place. I kept tabs on him, got to know everything he pulled off the air.'

224

'Yeh, well, so what?'

'He didn't only get Interpol and such things. He heard small boats, yacht traffic, people chatting to one another. He also got Russian planes on the eastern runs, and much else. In short, he's cracked our whole operation. He knows we're going to the Azores, and has a good idea of the date. He also knows why we're going. He's more than clever at putting two and two together. I'm sure nobody else could have done it. But he's priceless, and we've got to take him into account.'

Waistcoat's complexion was far from rubicund at the best of times, but this revelation downed it a notch or two towards the wedding-cake colours of his interior decoration. He unpeeled a cigar, twitched flame out of his lighter. 'Does he know your line of work?'

He'd been expecting the question, though not so early on. 'No chance. He hasn't a clue. I know more than anybody how to hide such things.'

'I'm sure you do.'

Richard would take no side from him, chief or not. 'Yes, you can bank on that.'

'Well, who is he?'

'An ex-RAF chap. He lives on the south coast. He's the best wireless operator I've ever come across.'

'Apart from yourself.'

'You could say that.'

'Even better, by the sound of it. But what are we going to do with him?'

'There's no chance of him giving us away.'

'You mean he wants paying off?'

'We could kill him,' Richard said quietly.

'You keep your suggestions to yourself.'

It was a reasonable one, but good to dispose of before the notion came to Waistcoat. 'I may be able to come up with something helpful.' Calmness was the only way to keep Waistcoat from your or anybody else's throat.

'That'll be the day.' He snapped the cigar in two and prepared to light another. 'The whole fucking trip jeopardised. It's all set up, and there's no way out. I can't credit it. You're the bringer of bad news.'

225

Richard lit a cigarette, glad to note that his fingers were steady. 'He'd be a first rate hand on the boat.'

'What are you trying to tell me?'

'I'm not suggesting anything, but there's going to be a lot for me to do at the wireless, and standing watches as well. Precautions are going to be necessary, and I'll have more than a job on. I can't attend to everything.'

'Does he have a sheet?'

'Clean as laundered snow.'

'Would he be willing?'

'He put it to me himself, but I had to turn him down.'

'Stupid bastard. Always keep people on the hook.'

'How was I to know? I couldn't give him any sort of go-ahead, not without talking to you first. But he'd be willing, I know. I could soon win him back, talk him round. Wouldn't cost you, either. So much a day maybe, and a bit of bonus when we got back.'

Waistcoat appeared to think, unusual when with someone else, afraid the workings of his face would show too much. He looked beyond Richard, into the wall, as if seeing to the horizon beyond; much as he must have done to while away the days in his prisons of the past, hoping his endless animal stare would burn through concrete. There was no disturbing him. Leave him alone, let time and the information take its toll. Don't offer a way out but rather allow his brain to grow its own ideas, the more the better, and whatever he comes up with, imagine the choice is his – if you're happy for your judgment to be based on his apparent cunning.

If Richard's mind could be compared to the circuit diagram of a radio set (as unfortunately so could Howard's, which had started all the trouble) you could base Waistcoat's on the cruder mechanism of a one-armed bandit. A radio set, though more complex, could throw you half across the room with shock if you made a mistake while powering it to the mains. A one-armed bandit might fall and crush your foot after a too-enthusiastic pull at the handle, but at least there might be a river of money in its wake. As a piece of engineering it was far simpler, and more old fashioned, less useful from a worldly view than a high-powered multiband radio.

'I'll have to leave it to you,' was all Waistcoat could say. 'But you say he's all right?'

It was the moment to faint, or run screaming from what looked like becoming the ruination of his life, but an inborne sense of destiny, which he in no way liked, forced him to say: 'I've never known a man more like one of us who isn't in it already.'

'That's all right, then.' Waistcoat seemed almost happy, as Richard had to be, but he added: 'It's your skin as well as mine. If I didn't know you were one-hundred-per-cent reliable I'd see him myself beforehand, but we're too close to the day, and I've still got a lot to do.'

The glint in his eyes never died. Even when he slept their piercing tipped beadiness was live under the lizard lids, burning into his dreams, the eyes of a killer, and whoever they were turned on in anger knew the threat they posed, and felt lucky to walk out of the door unharmed. Richard wondered whether he had been born with such malevolent eyes or they had developed out of a lifetime of circumstance. One thing he knew: Waistcoat had a villainous soul, and Richard wondered about the state of his own in that he recognised it so clearly.

Driving through the rush hour of south east London, in fits and starts from one set of traffic lights to another, and jammed in a queue to get through New Cross, he surmised from what he knew that Waistcoat had been a south London youth, brought up in the sharp brutality of its ways. He had been through the hardest time any kid could, was maybe one of seven or eight, with the old man on and off in prison, at which times his mother would go on the game to make ends meet, and savage treatment she got for it when the man came out.

He pictured Waistcoat bright and innocent in appearance, but eternally on the lookout for anything of use or value, holding back from outright muggery through fear of retribution at the copshop if caught. Even so, he was kicked around by his parents when they were together, so knew what violence was all about, until he learned to avoid such trouble. At the age of eleven or twelve, when his father stood up to boot him, he took out a flick-knife lifted that afternoon from a stall in Bermondsey – and was never threatened again. Whatever tolerant softness had been in his eyes – and it could only have been enough to cajole, wheedle or deceive – faded on knowing he had to be in charge of himself before he could control others.

Thus Borstal was a better school, where he absorbed the rules quicker than any of his intake. To know something was better than not to know, or to pretend not to know, and promised an easier time than if you were ignorant or resentful. To be more aware than others was an advantage. The more you knew the better. Those who ran the place had power, and if you didn't try to break yourself against it they made life easier for you because then they didn't have to work so hard, and a better time was had by all.

In any case, in the phrase of the time, he had never had it so good. Such assurance of food on the dot, clothes and a roof made it a doddle to tolerate a place where he could look after himself with no trouble. Not that he liked the screws or the governor. He didn't have to. He wanted to get out as soon as they would let him go, and meanwhile learned new ways of thieving, though not so useful because how come those who gloated over them had got caught? They were only useful in pointing the way to tricks that would be more successful.

In prison – where Richard had met such characters during his fortunately brief incarceration – Waistcoat would have learned many things that were more profitable. He made connections, got into the real world and found advancement on going free but, even then, had to come back a few times before falling in to the drugs trade. In twenty years he had become rich, changed his name, appearance and accent (as far as he could) and certainly his style of living, which had helped him not to get caught so often.

Traffic smoothed its way more freely beyond Sidcup, but he held back from driving too fast. Keep your distance, sideways as well as to the front and back. A scarlet biscuit tin on the starboard bow overtook, came on as if pulling a wall of rain with it. The wipers conducting like a metronome, he lit a cigarette. Shit's creek without a paddle would be paradise compared to the Howard connection. Hard to know how serious the old bat was about getting on board, though he seemed determined enough. He hoped so, because if he backed out the best to be expected would be driving an ice-cream van for the rest of his active life with half his fingers missing.

Then again, if he did manage to inveigle Howard onto the boat his time might be up when Waistcoat realised he was blind. Richard had no enemy as far as he knew (except Amanda, and she had flitted) and decided that if he must have one it might as well be Waistcoat, who wouldn't be difficult to deal with because he regarded everyone as his enemy, and of no particular importance unless that person had something specific against him.

Howard had to come on the trip because he knew too much, but if Waistcoat found out he was blind he would be done away with before he could get on board. Or he would find a grave in the water soon afterwards. Orders had ever been orders, but he didn't want to see Howard damaged, a man who represented everything that was the opposite of himself, a probity so thick you could scoop it up with a spoon and sell it in jars. He didn't envy Howard, or think he could ever have fitted into his sort of character, knowing from early on that such a moral life was not for him. Howard had moral quality, he decided, and could never be anyone other than who he was.

And yet there was enough of Howard in him for him to know that he could never be Howard, and what there might have been of Howard in him at the beginning had been overridden by an impatience forever nagging at his vitals, till it had landed him in a fix so tight he wished he had got out of the drugs game years ago.

Approaching the end of the Maidstone bypass, the notion came to him of saving himself even now, of turning the car round at the island and making his way northwest to call on his father. He would stay and look after him, a safe place to hide in any case, and let the Azores trip go to disaster, or success if they were lucky, which they probably would be without him or Howard on board.

He wasn't the sort to run away like a frightened rabbit, knew himself to be the keep on keeping on type, having at least that much of Howard in him which said that a contract was a contract and must be kept, even with the worst of people and for the worst of reasons. You didn't desert when things got difficult, and nor would he expect Howard to let him down. If either made a run for it Waistcoat and the others would pursue them into everlasting hell.

Such a gridlock could not be broken. He was so much part of one that there was no decision to make, nothing but to go on; unless to tell Howard, who had probity and fine sense, that he had been playing with a dream, and should be satisfied to keep it at that. Men of probity were made for dreams, such visitations sustaining them on their straight path. Howard would call to say he couldn't come on the boat, it would be impossible to cope, he would be a hindrance, and so would like to keep the idea as a dream. Out of friendship, his lips would stay clamped. He would give nothing away.

Richard laughed on rounding the island, to drive across the Weald at dusk. Such an outcome could be little more than a dream he himself was having, as if trying to snatch one from Howard. The dream was going to happen, and he was giving in to it, a thought which did not help, since he realised, turning on his headlights – and in their beams saying goodbye to bellies of cloud overhead – that he did not know anything about Howard who was as complete a blank as if he – Richard – was the blind man. Howard was a code he hadn't so far cracked.

TWENTY-ONE

Gulls, aeroplaning above the chimney pots, were calling that he must talk to Laura about his plans. He needed no telling, for once in tune to their outlandish cries. Judy had sent her final message, as the yachts closed on their routes. The boat would stop at Gibraltar for water and provisions, before leaving for you-know-where. She would go by hire car to Malaga for a day to keep a well-planned tryst with Carla.

The frantic, one minute burst ended by her saying there would be no radio contact for an unspecified time afterwards. Howard taped their talk to use as encouragement for making his way onto Richard's yacht. His spirit floated in suspense, but with the confidence of a compass needle always sure where north and therefore every other direction was to be found.

The tension in him resembled the adolescent state of mind before he had gone blind. More than halfway in thrall to that previous existence, he felt the unacknowledged emotions of a young man, forever impatient to get from one minute to the next no matter what would occur. Life had been normal then, exciting but tolerable, above all easy going, the play of uncertainties utterly different to the present routine which he would learn to live without, by letting the past come back and help him to face the changes that came.

He leaned on the gate, pausing in his 'constitutional' – Laura's word, which he disliked, knowing she would see nothing tired in him when he explained where he was going. Walking made up the mind with a firmness that would not be undone however she objected. The exercise stilled his secret fears, after years of not needing to make up his mind about anything. Though there had been no final yes from Richard, an illusion of increased visibility in his dome of darkness convinced him

231

there would be. For the barely imaginable to become reality meant climbing out of the pit he had inhabited for so long, like a mole in its comfortable burrow, and going into the second great trip of his life.

The gulls told him he was on his own. One squeal a yes and the one that followed a no. Either way, he lived in an indifferent universe, and smiled at the notion that the universe itself might mirror the complexity of a single human being – if there was anything to it at all – and by giving himself up to it he became the controller of the earth and every star and planet, if only for a second in astronomical reckoning. The gulls would be fixed in the swoop and circle of their intimidating cries till the end of time, and because Fate cared nothing for either him or them he enjoyed their eternal disputations.

A steady downpour of warm rain came from the direction they would chop towards when the boat motored into Atlantic spaces. The homely smell of the house would be hard to leave, yet less so because of it, a break to be welcomed whatever his adventure led to.

After checking that the table was laid in the dining room he followed the smell of cooking into the kitchen. Laura noted the increased confidence of his approach. He stood by her side:

'We'll have smoked mackerel and toast,' she said, 'to start with. Then new potatoes, with cauliflower and a thick lamb chop. I've put a bottle of wine in the fridge, which we can share. I'll serve the first course now, while the rest finishes on a low light.'

He had noted her concern, how she provided an extra newspaper for reading aloud in the evening, set out nicer treats for his meals, gave unsolicited embraces and kisses. What else could she do? There was nothing worse than not knowing.

He heard the apron coming off, for a more formal meal than usual, as if knowing he had something to tell her, though how could she? She held out the chair, but he pulled it under himself. Over the years they had developed an idiom of signs, graded by the subtlety of pressures from one to ten, you might say, shades of the heart's wish easy to express, yesses and nos without the help of words. An unacknowledged lexicon of smell and touch had built between them, by now of a certain bulk. Misinterpretation was a call for laughter, though not this time. His brooding staled his appetite, but she gave him the sound of cutting into her fish and toast, and was not pleased by him pouring wine which came exactly to the brim. He held the glass towards her: 'Let's drink to having lived so long together.'

She fought the tears, as if he might see them. Making no sound would deceive him, but the touch of their glasses covered the catch in her voice. 'Yes, I like that.'

'You see,' he said, 'I've decided to go on a trip. Richard has asked me to go with him to the Azores. I might be away for some time.' He sighed, not for himself, but for the thing completed. The darkness seemed to have opened, a faint glow shimmering where his sight once was, so that he had less feeling of being blind.

Half his wine went in one swallow. 'Richard wants me to help with the radio.' He ate so easily, as if he told her such preposterous news every day. 'It's a big boat, a motor yacht, a hundred and fifty feet long. There'll be a crew of seven or eight, so I'll be well looked after.'

The fork fell against her plate. 'How long have you known about this?' She needed no special faculties to realise that his behaviour had changed since their outing to Boston. He tied himself less to the wireless, had become impatient with all activity, sat at his dials for no more than half an hour of an evening, not always that long. A change of habit when she didn't have one of hers to vary was disturbing. He sat for hours as if half asleep, but she picked up the intensity of his thoughts, knowing he would never tell her what they were. Now he had. She was frightened that such snapping of routine meant the end of their life together, but to question him would solve nothing. She must let him talk further, as he certainly must, though the suspense put a stitch in her side.

He filled another glass, spilled some this time. 'Oh, I've told you as soon as I could.'

No post had come today, no phone calls either, so he had known for a while. Or was it another fantasy, like the pipe dream that had led them on a wild goose chase to Boston? Richard couldn't be such a fool as to take a blind man to sea.

'I know what you're thinking,' he said.

'Do you? Can you?'

'Well, what's strange about my plan to have a little outing? It'll take two or three weeks, that's all. I've always wanted to see the Azores.' He heard her go into the kitchen, to stop the chops scorching, no other response possible, though he couldn't think why, since he only wanted to go on a sea trip with a friend instead of with her.

Topside, they were a little overdone, but their celebratory meal had gone into the wilderness. Draining the cauliflower steamed the glasses as she tipped it into a colander. If the trip had been with anybody but Richard the scheme might have sounded feasible. 'What sort of people will be going on the boat? And what is the real reason for the voyage?' she asked, back at the table.

Howard poured another drink, as if it would be better for her to comment that he was becoming an alcoholic. 'It's a rich man's yacht, and he's cruising for pleasure, to the Azores.'

She put her unfinished mackerel aside for the cat. 'What's his name?'

'Does it matter?'

'Of course it does.'

'I'm not sure at the moment, but I'll tell you as soon as I find out. It's all open handed and above board, so I wish you'd stop worrying.'

'Worrying?' she said, with an anger he'd never heard before. 'Don't you know I worry about you every second of the day and night, especially when you go down the hill alone each morning on your walk? Don't you know it's been the same since the day we were married? Always hoping you'll be all right, that you'll come back safe. Maybe it was unnecessary – it obviously was – but it's been a lifetime of anxiety nevertheless. And here you are, suddenly announcing that you want to go away for weeks on a small boat into the Atlantic, with people I know nothing about. And you don't seem to know anything about them, either.'

'I wish you would eat your food before it gets cold. All this is rather unnecessary. It's even irrelevant.' She would have made the same fuss if he had been going on a bus trip to Brighton, because by having gone everywhere with her he had dug his own grave into absolute dependence. In spite of her disapproval he found the silence benign, though not unaware of his callousness.

'Has this got anything to do with this woman you were hoping to meet in Boston?'

His tone was flat. 'No.'

It was a lie, at least a half-truth. She knew it had started then, and that this voyage was another stage in looking for her, and said so.

Easy to slump back into ease and go on with no event to mark the time between now and death. Is that all life would be? Those glorious moments of feeling the laden bomber lift sluggishly under him from the runway as a youth couldn't be all there was to it. He had paid for them over and over by vegetating ever since, and now he must get into the world again. He didn't need anyone to tell him whether he was doing right or wrong: not even the German Numbers Woman, or Vanya, and not Judy either. He was alone with his own voice saying that not to go would pitch him into a living death till the end of his time, unless he weakened and soon enough died by cancer or a blow at the heart for his pusillanimity.

'All I can do is repeat myself. Richard has worked hard to get me this place, and it's an opportunity that won't come again.'

She laughed with such bitterness that he wondered what part of her it had come from, where it had been hiding all these years, and why. He saw no reason for bitterness. Parts of her she hadn't shown before, having no reason to, though there must be more to it than that. He also had zones never revealed, but that he found encouraging.

'I thought you'd be happy to let me go, and do everything possible to help me on my way.'

'Why,' she said mockingly, 'do you intend to make a career of it? Surely not!'

'Would to God I could. But no, I don't.' He laughed at such an idea. 'I'm not going off into the blue forever. There'll be radio facilities on board for me to call you every day or two.' He wasn't sure this would be the case, didn't much care, though hoped it was possible so that the separation wouldn't hurt her for too long. On the other hand the disturbance of calling would break into his sensation of being free.

She wanted to lie down, from weakness, out of shock, in total surprise at his ruthlessness, at his denial of everything they had lived by, marking the end of their world, a confession as if he had announced he was going to live with another woman, nothing less than a stark betrayal of trust, destroyed by one plain announcement. 'Do you think it will make me happy, knowing that every minute might be your last? I don't suppose there can be any worse position for someone like you being on a small boat in a rough sea.'

If it meant getting killed, what better way to die, though it was only her unreasonable fear that suggested such might happen, while his premonition of danger was due only to a childish dread at being apart.

'You're denying me a holiday,' he said. 'It's as simple as that. I'll go away for a few weeks, and then come back. We'll have something to talk about for a change.' It was impossible to do anything without being cruel. He was seared, but unrepentant and more determined. If Richard called to say it was no go, this anguish would be for nothing. Yet nothing was for nothing. Everything that happened was good in a life where nothing happened, and no more so than to a blind man. She disliked him, therefore he was noticed, more real to her, a more separate person than he'd ever been. He said as much, assumed he was becoming like the man he would have been if he had come back from the air raid with no injury. She was the only obstacle to this progress, but the power of his infatuation with Judy wouldn't let her stop him going to sea. Judy was the glow drawing him on, and no amount of resistance could deflect him from the beam.

'It's not so much that I mind you leaving me, though I do, wouldn't be human if I didn't, but it's what might happen. You surely see that.'

He touched her hand, but she drew it petulantly away. 'Nothing bad will happen. I'll have a wonderful time. I can't tell you how much it means to me, how much I'm looking forward to it. You'll have to trust me.'

'It's not that.' There was steel in her tone. 'I just can't let you go. Won't. You can't go. It's not a matter of you leaving me on my own. Anywhere else. But not to sea. I couldn't bear it. I won't let you go.'

'Well, I shall.'

'I'll talk to Richard. He'll understand.'

'It was his idea.' Lies had become easy because the limits to his freedom had fallen down. 'He wants me on the boat. He thought I needed to get away for a while.'

'I don't believe it.' Richard was man enough of the world. He would never make such an outlandish offer, but if it were true she had only herself to blame for having introduced them. And if Howard was lying, which he probably was, how could she hold it against him when she had married him to escape the pain of what she could never mention, thus lying to him by omission? It was as if he guessed, or definitely knew, and felt free to crush her with this kind of revenge. The possibility of him having found out gave her more strength. 'You can't go, though. I'm quite determined. You're not fit for such an adventure. There are ways of stopping you. I'll discuss it with a social worker, to see what we can do.'

'The cat's going to eat well today, if you don't finish your meat. He's putting on too much weight as it is. Everything balances out. How can you think anything will happen to me, or that I won't come back? I don't see it.'

Her instinct was as good as his. The journey might be easy to set out on but hard to get back from, or perhaps the obstacles to going were so difficult that the return couldn't enter the mind. Departures for her were fraught with terrors and desolation, while with him they stimulated and filled with joy. Her despair was understandable, always worse for the person left behind.

If he fell in love with a woman on the street, say, and she showed a sudden (though unaccountable) passion for him, both knowing it was forever and that a break must be made with their present lives, say, for instance, that he met Judy and they went away together: Laura would feel the same when he told her he had found someone else. She would have preferred that, as being more understandable according to her views, while he felt the same whatever it was, a liberation from which no one could deter him.

'I understand how you feel, my love.'

'You don't. You can't possibly.' She clattered the chair back and saw herself whitefaced from surprise and chagrin, from a powerlessness which must be caused by more than his announcement. She should smile, indeed she should, and kiss him, arms around his neck: 'Yes, do go. It's an opportunity not to be missed. It'll be so wonderful for you. It'll do you good to get away from the house and dull old me for a while. I know Richard will take care of you.'

237

'I do understand,' he said, 'but I still can't think of a valid reason not to go.'

She couldn't respond. Wouldn't anyway. There was every reason for him not to go. He was in the coils of some madness. God knows, she felt close to it herself, but with his obsession pulling her more deeply, words could do nothing, though there was little else to use. No doubt she ought to talk calmly, like a doctor perhaps, or the kind of guru people went to when they were in spiritual trouble. A guru would only confirm him in his determination, tell him to live it through, such people so unscrupulous. 'I don't understand.' She sat down to face him, hands and legs trembling.

'There's nothing to understand. It's all very plain and straight-forward.'

'No, it's not,' she said sharply, 'and you know it.' She couldn't get the right tone into her voice, the effort almost strangling her. The windows shivered in their sockets from the gale, rain smearing the panes. 'How would you survive, in weather like this?'

No problem. A lightness of spirit made him a different person, reconnected to his youth, as if that youth had led a conventional life all these years. He wasn't certain what had done it, only that some kind of magic must have fused him and that other person together, finally mysterious, as if the seed had been there all along and waiting only for certain factors to enrich the soil from which the unity could flower. He felt irresponsible, accountable only to himself. What you can't see you feel, and when you feel you act, and when you act you see more than if you had stayed still.

'We have a radio to warn us,' he told her. 'You go around the worst of the weather. And there's always a harbour to run for. I'll get the atlas out soon, and show you where the Azores are.'

'I don't want to see. It's the end of the world for me. You'll never get there. I feel it. Or if you do you won't get back.'

'I'm sorry to have to tell you, but you're talking nonsense.' He sometimes felt he would never see the place, either, but supposed you always did think that before you left for somewhere, confident he would feel differently after the first day at sea.

'I only wish I was. I'm in a bad dream.'

'And I'm in a good one, and wish you could share it.'

'I want to wake up from mine.' Hard to believe she wasn't going to. 'But let's not talk about it anymore. Not for a while. I can't think properly while we're talking.' She was hungry but unable to eat, famished but didn't know for what, in an altered mental state to an hour ago, isolated, floating in uncertainty and misery, everything that was comforting and familiar blown away. She began to cry.

We've woken up, he thought, into the real world, and it took so little, an announcement that I intend setting out on a trip without her. Her crying was muted, made dreadful by her fight to control it. 'Please, my love, it's no big thing. I'll be gone and back before you know it.'

Not one word of concession, of giving in on a single point. 'I can't take any more. I can't listen to you.'

'Yes, I see that.'

It must be a practical joke, a test of loyalty and love. Perhaps he had found a way of getting into the locked drawer of her armoire and read the diary account of the times with her uncle, and all the details of the abortion – but how could he, without eyes to see? She had kept a diary as a solace to her distress, written through tears. At the worst of times she recalled the scratching of her pen, the speedy turning of pages, words scribbled so fast that some lines were a jumble impossible to make out whenever she was forced to look at it again, trying to still her mind. She ought to have known that nothing in the past could be buried.

She had always assumed the book to be safe, because even if she forgot to lock the drawer, and Howard looked inside, the words were braille only to her, though maybe he had secretly taken the diary to Richard, who had read everything to him in his measured uncaring voice. Or Richard, with new-found malevolence, which she supposed every man to have, had tapped out the choicest excerpts in morse and posted the tape back for Howard to run and re-run.

He was bringing up this detestable stunt of a boat trip by way of revenge for her lifetime's silence, not knowing that in doing so he was parting them forever. And yet revenge wasn't part of him – no matter by how much he seemed to have altered – because even if he knew he would understand and forgive. There would be nothing else for him to do.

Such a fantasy showed how low one could fall in the face of the unexpected. Her mind raced cruelly, not letting her alone. It wouldn't from now on, a horrifying thought. Even if he suddenly laughed that his plan had been a joke, and he wasn't going on any such trip, the damage could never be made good. Out of the blue, just like that, he had blasted their lives. 'I don't think you'll ever be able to understand,' she said.

Nor would she. He felt young enough to no longer know himself, laughed at his severed connection from whoever he had been a few months ago. The mechanism of how it had come about was clearly part of him. He had been two people most of his life, even before the disaster of going blind, and the dormant person had emerged at last from Sleepy Hollow, the two fusing into himself, not knowing how or why it had taken so long, a transformation impossible to explain.

'I think I do,' he said. 'I understand very well. But I would rather go with your blessing than without it.'

'I know.' She noticed a blackhead on the left side of his forehead, couldn't think where he had got it in the clean sea air, but decided not to tell him. 'And you never will.'

'I'm sad about that.'

'Give me time,' was all she could say. 'I'd like to lie down' – being as sleepy as if she had taken a drug.

'We could have some coffee.'

'That won't do it.' He had been well looked after for so long that the reason for her being upset was beyond his power to comprehend. How long would they have stayed together if he hadn't been blind, and if this was what he was really like – making up his mind on such an important issue without any discussion? Not very long. The storm had slackened, birds whistling in the bushes, glad of better weather. 'I'm your wife,' she said. 'I have rights in these matters.'

If the modern trend of women's liberation hadn't passed her by they might not have argued like this, and he would have been on his way with her approval. But any article on women's lib in the papers, or something mentioned on the radio, had always brought scornful remarks – he would never understand why, though now he did. It was loggerheads, and no mistake, neither of them with any more to say, until:

240

'I'm going upstairs to sleep, though don't suppose I shall.'

But she did, fell off immediately, every corpuscle so weary she didn't even dream.

Planes weren't calling for Vanya's electronic pinpoints, so no hope of playing 'Spot the Bomber'. The German Numbers Woman was having her day off, and Portishead told of front after front coming in from the grey Atlantic. On Judy's wavelength the crackling mush was interrupted by a Russian operator sending widdershins in morse.

He hoped for better weather when the boat set out, wondering how he would take to the turbulent water, since he had never been on a small boat. At moments he had wanted to tell Laura he wouldn't go, to forget it, he was sorry, I love you, and everything's all right, so forgive me if I've tormented you, and let's carry on as before.

No one could say that he would still be going. Things went wrong in any enterprise. He could tell Richard that such a jaunt was out of the question if it meant the end of his marriage. And Richard, knowing he must come on the trip because of all he knew, would make whatever obstacles disappear. Some ingenuity in persuasion could do no harm, even if not really necessary. To cause Richard worry was an exercise in power, and he felt no shame in stating it. Let him also believe nothing was certain. He couldn't think of anything to prevent him going, but if some factor did arise, there was a pressure moving him forward that couldn't be resisted.

When Massachusetts tinkled in he found the sounds banal, couldn't sit still, paced up and down the familiar room, picked up books and earphones and various pieces of equipment, wanted to go this minute, saying no goodbyes, oblivious to objections or tears, get his stick and walk down the hill with a song on his lips, relishing a madness that was more to him than life itself.

On Judy's frequency again he found, as expected, nothing. Emptiness. She was with Carla in Malaga, and he could only hope they were happy. He missed the throaty richness of her voice with an intensity that almost made him faint.

TWENTY-TWO

'Richard?'

'That's me.'

'Howard here.'

'I was going to get in touch.'

'Beat you to it. I'm in a phone box on the front. I got a woman to punch in the numbers for me. Could have done it myself, I suppose, but I didn't want to take any chances, or delay matters.'

Bloody fool, to let a passer-by have my unlisted number. She might have been following for just such a clue. 'Why all the urgency?'

'I have to talk to you.'

'Don't say a word about you know what. Somebody may be listening in. You never can tell.'

He managed a laugh, to reassure. 'Who would know better than me?'

'That's right.' Who indeed? 'Me as well, you might say.'

'We're two of a feather.'

'As long as you like to think so.' Let him talk, even though time was crucial. He had to be pulled on board, with no argument, otherwise the trip might be called off. It would be like walking into prison if they left him behind. 'Are you ready for the big sea trip?'

'Well, you see . . .'

'All I see,' he monitored the pause with his watch, 'is that I'll pick you up at thirteen-hundred hours on Monday the fifteenth, and take you to the boat.'

'I was going to tell you. I can't go. It's off.'

Richard had always known how to be the king of silence. The mouth moved so that only you could see it. The voice box boomed but only you could hear. He looked around the room, naming every gewgaw and object of furniture. When that inventory was finished he glanced at the window, and lit another cigarette at a distance from the telephone to keep the line quiet. He would stand all day if necessary, waiting for Howard to say something further, would drag the bastard out by the short and curlies if it had to be that way.

Waistcoat had told him to get the potential danger on board or he, as well as his old and upstanding father, would be scuffed off the surface of the world without ever knowing they'd been on it. Waistcoat had a way with words, but one day they would choke him. In the meantime he had to wait for Howard to say something, and though Howard was just as capable of waiting in silence till the end of time he didn't think more than a decent interval was necessary for what he had to say.

'The reason is, that Laura objects to it.'

'Is that all?'

'Well, it's something.'

'Amanda used to get like that, all bossy and tearful. I understand how you feel. But she lit off, and a good thing I think now. Women shouldn't be allowed to interfere without reason with what men want to do.'

'Agreed. All the same, they need to be considered.'

'But not obeyed. I have to tell you I haven't much time.'

'Neither have I. I'm putting another fifty pee in.'

'Do you want me to hang up, and then I can call you?'

He saw through that one. 'I've plenty of change. The main question is whether or not you still need me on the boat.'

'You said you wanted to come, didn't you? Almost insisted on it. So I made arrangements. They're expecting you. I'd look a right charlie if you didn't turn up. The idea is that you help out with the radio. I sang your praises so much they're counting on it.'

Another pause. 'All right, I'll be there. I just wanted final confirmation.'

Show a little more anger. 'How much final confirmation do you want, for God's sake?'

'No more, but Laura's still got to be dealt with.'

'I have to leave that to you.'

'My problem, is it?'

'Well, it's not mine.'

All Howard wanted to know was whether they were definitely going, without him or not. 'The trip's on, then, and nothing will stop me.'

Richard tried a bit of Air-Force slang. 'Good show. Zero hour's not far off. You'll have an interesting time, believe you me.'

'I know I shall. She may contact you, though, come to see you.'

'I don't mind.' He'd expected it, hoped for it, knew she'd be on her own. 'As long as you're ready on the day.'

'You can depend on it.'

'Bring what you think you'll need. A kitbag and a hold-all. There'll be plenty to eat and drink on board.'

'I can't wait.'

'You won't have to. I'll pick you up, and all your worries will be over.'

'I owe you more than I can say. It's as if I suddenly had a brother. Sounds crazy, but it's true.'

More crazy than you think, though Richard shied at a fitting response, felt none of the right emotion. At the same time wondered what sense or truth there was in it. 'It's a favour I knew you wanted. Wasn't easy, but we were friends.'

Howard had said no more than he felt. He was going on a drug smuggler's jaunt, inviolable because blind, and assumed he could depend on Richard to get him on board, from which moment he would be at the mercy of so many unknown factors that it didn't bear thinking about – an adventure not to be refused. 'I'll be waiting.'

'And I'll be there to pick you up.'

The sign-offs were simultaneous.

Richard wondered what he had done, but knew he could have done nothing else. He had taken responsibility for another human being so completely that part of himself had been cut away, and he didn't like it. Nor would Howard, no doubt poking his way back up the hill for another bout with Laura. Not hard to know who would win, though that part of the scheme was no fight of his. He had drawn Howard into his web, and Howard had lured him into an equally tangled snare.

It was unusual for Richard to be discouraged by success, because he suspected – being no fool – that anything as easy as getting Howard to come with them couldn't fall out well. Such self-indulgent worry was more intense than the trip deserved, and who had entrapped who, and how it began, was no use going into, must be accepted and forgotten, but he was nagged that something could go wrong. Their laybrinths had met and started to blend, a messy and embarrassing process which set off a twinge of alarm as if, when two such forces collided, control would be lost and all power extinguished.

He enjoyed walking about the empty house knowing that no one might come back into it at any second. And nobody would. Even so, blessed isolation was little help to his thoughts. A man in a house alone was incomplete because he was more at the mercy of himself. He couldn't tell who or what brought such irrelevancies to mind, but perhaps the world of the house was too small, only seemed big when other people were in it with him. He didn't like the sensation of being so far off his normally firm centre.

A car sounded along the unmade track. Maybe Amanda had got tired of sulking at her girlfriend's, and was coming back to more comfortable accommodation. She wasn't the sort who would be happy to share the living space of a small flat – if she was ever happy, that is. He had treated her well, but was aware of never having done his proper duty as a husband, such as being there to hear her thoughts and wishes every minute of the day and night.

He liked to think there was nothing wrong with her in wanting such constant attention, that it was mainly due to him that she disliked being herself, which led her to dislike him even more. On the other hand there were times when she made an effort to love him, or at least endure him without rancour, though perhaps only as a way towards thinking better of herself.

Whatever it was, it had been too much for him, and now that she had gone he could only think they had been in no way made for each other, which he had said from time to time and which she hated to hear, as if it might be true. Yet if two people weren't made for each other they weren't made for anybody else, especially when they ought to feel made for each other, which they did at the best of times, however rare those times were. In any case with him she had a house, and a car, and enough to live on, so what more was needed except patience and tolerance, and a certain regard when they didn't exactly feel made for each other?

Going to the window he saw a magpie fly from the trees and skim the top of Laura's Peugeot, a black and white warning of a hard time as she turned by the derelict barn and parked on the open space of grass before the garden gate. She manoeuvred to face outwards, as if a quick getaway might become necessary, though maybe it was her normal habit. He went to meet her at the door.

On the way there she had been wondering how to tell him that Howard wasn't fit to go on a small boat trip out into the Atlantic. He wouldn't be allowed to, she would say, would only go over her dead body, and if that was the ultimate sacrifice she wouldn't hesitate to make it. But if she could win Richard to her side such a sacrifice wouldn't be necessary.

She noted the orderly living room, everything in its place, not much used, now that his wife had gone. He intercepted her gaze, glad that he had, by coincidence, bumped the vacuum cleaner around only that morning, always a man for keeping the old ship tidy.

His wife's departure had obviously not bothered him much, which made her less sure of what she had to say. He had the same caring though distant expression as when they met by the roadside. 'I suppose you know why I'm here?'

'I've been expecting you.' He pointed to an armchair. 'In fact I was going to call you later today. Let me get you a drink.' He was still amazed by her youthful and untouched aspect, though helped by the dull light of the day.

'I shouldn't drink since I'm driving,' she said, 'but I'll have a sherry.'

He found some Tio Pepe in the cupboard, halfway down and hadn't been used for months: shot a whisky in for himself. 'Pity you had to come all this way,' for nothing, was his meaning.

'Oh, I don't mind the drive. The countryside's so pretty around here.'

The fixed smile showed the force of her worry, then was crossed out by a flash of uncertainty. 'I'm glad you caught me in.' He was, had been about to drive to the pub, anything to escape the weight of the house for an hour.

'You know what I've come about, I'm sure.'

He sat in the other armchair. Amanda had spent over a thousand pounds having them reupholstered – totally redone – and she had scarpered a week after he had written the cheque. But they were damned comfortable, and the one Laura sat in suited her wonderfully. 'About Howard, of course. You must be worried. I know I would be. It's a funny situation, and I don't know how I got into it.' He wasn't going to tell her point blank that Howard had to come, or even admit in any way that he was on Howard's side, unwilling at the moment to fight another man's battle, at least directly. 'How either of us got into the situation I'll never know.'

They had talked it up like a pair of schoolboys, probably suggested by something in one of those ridiculous morse letters. 'Well, you did, it seems. Howard's deadly serious. He's all ready. I have to stop him, and you must help me.' In the excitement of feeling her task would be easier than imagined she drank her sherry – and a good sized measure he had given her.

The idea of getting her half seas over made him smile, and as if in encouragement he swallowed the last finger of his whisky. 'I'd like to, but I don't think anybody can.' She indicated no, but he refilled her glass. 'Sorry, leave it, then. A stray tomcat comes around and I'm sure that if I pour it into a saucer it'll lap it up.'

She was supposed to laugh, but felt no reason to: 'You're the only one I can turn to. I've no one else,' forgetting the other arguments in her mind before coming down to this.

He put on what Amanda called his 'irrecoverable silence', knowing they were only at the beginning. Was she trying to beat him at his favourite game of saying nothing for as long as possible? He refilled his glass and she, unaccountably, took a swig at the sherry. So far from the road, the tomb-like quiet of the house was broken only by the tapping of raindrops.

'I never thought Howard was serious,' he said, 'but when I knew he was, I put out feelers, to see if someone would let him come with us.

Maybe I was too persuasive, though it's hard to believe, but the skipper thought it a benevolent act, to take him. I think that was because he had a brother who was blinded in a flying accident with the Fleet Air Arm in Korea, and he'd often taken him on boat trips. He enjoyed them no end. The men looked after him. They took exceptional care, though he rarely needed it. The various crews thought it lucky to have a blind man on board. A bit of a novelty. Took their minds off the harsh reality of separation from land, you might say. I went on a couple of their trips, and there was never any instance of danger or inconvenience. In fact Old Blind Harry, as we referred to him, always looked – and felt, I'm sure – in absolutely top form when he stepped back on dry land, saying he'd never had a better time in his life. He gained no end of confidence. Movement, coordination – that sort of thing, which can't be bad for a disabled man, if you'll forgive me using the term. He even volunteered for the washing up, and always gave a hand with the sails – though Howard's trip will be on a motor job. He was almost as useful as the rest of us in the end. Mind you, we joshed him around a bit, teased him, but that seemed to please him as much as anything. He took it in good part when one of the men put a sextant into his hand at midday and told him to take a sight on the sun. Made him feel more like one of us, when he was teased. There was the time when we went cruising around the Shetlands and Orkneys, and ended up in Iceland for a week. We had a brilliant time at the hot springs. He particularly took to Iceland because the people were so interested to meet a blind sailor. They were really kind to him.' Especially the girls, they were all over him, he was going to say, but thought better than to add such a touch to his fantasy. 'He was singing pop songs on the way back. We all were. Getting into Aberdeen was hilarious.'

He went across to a carriage clock on the shelf and wound it as if to bring the tightness of its spring to the same tension as her heart. Tension was good for her, even necessary if she was to have some kind of release. It would do her good. He came back to his chair. 'Then again, I can put myself in your place, and see how the idea disturbs you. If you and Howard have never been apart, as I understand you haven't, the prospect can't be very appealing. I don't suppose Howard should be allowed to go scot free on such a trip if it's going to distress you. That's the last thing I would like to be responsible for. I've too high a regard for you – and for Howard, come to that – to help him make you in anyway unhappy.'

Surprised by such an easy win, she wished he would stop talking. Another swallow of her drink could do no harm. 'You're very kind and understanding about it.'

It was wonderful what breathing did to a woman's bosom, at least to hers. Her breasts, even at the faintest movement under her thin blue sweater, were as well shaped as those on a girl of twenty. They positively invited him to touch them. A one-second glance took everything in, and he wondered if she was aware of it. 'Thank you for saying that, because I know how important it is for you.'

'Of course it is.' She was a skinful of emotion, and he would have said anything she wanted merely for the pleasure of being close. If Howard envied him being able to see whatever went on in the damned and for the most part dismal world he envied Howard for being married to a woman like her. 'I'll do whatever you like,' he said. 'If you say he ought not to go, then he won't.'

'It's true that I don't want him to, but you've taken trouble, and made arrangements.'

'Well, yes, I have. They're expecting him, looking forward to it, you might say. I gave my word even. But I'll willingly throw all that to the winds. I simply thought I was doing a favour for a friend in getting him out into the world, on a voyage he would remember with pleasure for the rest of his life. But it's off now. Say no more about it. I'll phone and tell them as soon as you've gone. I'd do it now if I didn't want to break off the pleasure of your company.'

Every word was making her more uncertain, but did he know it? She didn't think so. He was open and honest, and what did it matter to him, after all, whether or not Howard went? During the car ride from home she had intended saying that if he thought the only way to stop Howard going was not to go himself she would meet his salary for the aborted trip with whatever amount he would be paid. Even as far as that, but the notion shamed her now that he had relented like a gentleman, made it possible for her to tell Howard that Richard wasn't going to take him, that the trip was called off.

249

'I'll never forget our first meeting,' he said. 'Such a memorable encounter for me, being able to help a lady in distress. I suppose it sounds very corny, to put it that way, but I have such admiration for you at having got Howard through so many difficult years. He's a terrific person, and it's been quite an experience knowing him.'

Did he mean that after this he wouldn't be knowing Howard anymore? Yes, my dear, he said to himself, and I'm letting you know it. Nobody fucks around with Richard in the way you're doing. Howard is coming with me whether you like it or not. He smiled, drank a little. 'I'm prepared to help all I can. I'll call Howard this evening, and tell him the score myself.'

The picture of Howard at sea, bare-headed in the sun, as if looking into the distance from his stance at the front of the boat, going through the supreme enjoyment of his life, cared for and cosseted by a group of men who never let him out of their sight, as if he was their sacred charge, wouldn't leave her alone. He would love it, be absolutely in his element.

Richard walked to the telephone, by her glass on the table, even if only to be closer while lifting the receiver, and to show how sincere he could be, to get the side draught of the emotional reasoning he supposed was going through her. 'I'll call the skipper now. No point keeping him on the hot plate,' and he pressed the first three numbers.

'No,' she called.

'Sorry?'

'I want to think some more.' Two creases across her brow, a third trying to get born, complexion showing her turmoil. She finished the drink, and he poured another. Three had to be her limit. He was already hoping she wouldn't crash on the road back, and pull Howard out of the trip that way. Besides, he'd like to see her again. And yet even if she had an accident Howard might not see it as a reason to remain. People were funny that way. He'd stay just long enough to see her buried, though what thoughts are these? It was love he wanted, not death, but at least they brought mind and therefore body back to life. All in all the day was going nicely, and he lifted his glass for a toast. 'I wish the two of us a good few years yet.'

'Thank you.' She drank, needing to break the shock, because the last time she had heard such words for a toast came from her uncle, after he had forced her (she still found it hard to use the word rape) to have sex with him. The tremor stayed, till she went on: 'You know I can't stop him, don't you?'

'You can, with my help, willingly given, I might say.'

'No, I don't want it.' Uncertainty had given way to pride, which conquered her fear of letting Howard go. 'It wouldn't be fair, but thank you, all the same.'

'I feel very brotherly towards him' – might as well put that to some use.

'I know. And it's wonderful you do. But from what you've told me I know I must let him go. I'd have no future if I didn't. Never forgive myself. And I couldn't go on living with someone who wasn't able to forgive *me*. Oh, I'm sure he would, and yet how could he, really? If I was in his place I don't think I would. But he'll be all right?'

She had been charmingly disarmed by him giving in so easily to her concern for Howard, and now he had the pleasure, far from malicious (though not too far) of hearing her accept his plan. He felt the self-satisfying warmth of altruism. Whether she would go back on it he couldn't say, though it was unlikely, being a woman of her word. Besides, there was more to her giving in than his persuasive eloquence, and he wondered whether he would ever know the extent of it. No one was as simple as they seemed. At least he had learned that much from Amanda. 'I promise to guard him with my life.'

What tosh. If she believed that she'd believe anything. Nevertheless the words seemed ominous, though meaningless for coming out too easily. The notion that a promise was a promise to be kept and honoured came starkly to mind, but all he conceded for the moment was that Howard would go, and Howard would come back, and that would be the end of the matter. What more could anybody want? Though he needed Howard on the trip, more than he cared to admit, he had never thought himself cut out to be anybody's keeper, not even his own, come to that, having always lived happily enough within the unity of one. Why he should take on such a load at this late stage puzzled him, though if it had something to do with this oh so morally upright woman sitting oh so primly and self controlled before him he could have no regrets.

'I can't,' he added with a laugh, 'see any such sacrifice being called for. It's not that kind of issue.'

'I'm sure not,' she said, 'but he'll be in your hands.' She wanted to make sure, though there was no need. Trust was the essence of the affair, and she would suppress all anxieties, settle herself down to the everyday worry of waiting for a loved one to come back from an extended vacation. Her last remark called for no reply. Everything had been said, and it was time to leave. But she couldn't make up her mind to stand up, as if the last half hour had passed in the hardest kind of work. Drinking the rest of her sherry was no help, but she had to get up, even so.

'Maybe you'd like some coffee?' he said when she did and, without an answer, added: 'Let's go into the kitchen, and I'll make a pot strong enough to put you on the right road. I could do with some as well.'

She accepted, as he had known she would, taking his lack of an answer as a kindness, for she hadn't thought of coffee. He flicked the kettle on and poured beans into the grinder. 'I'm looking forward so much to getting to sea. I know Howard will like it.'

She didn't want any more talk about what had been settled, but supposed it would be normal parlance for him now. He was no longer trying to reassure her, so no response was necessary. She liked his forthrightness, and indeed kindness, and thought she might even have fallen in love with such a man if she had never met Howard. It could easily have been, though she tried not to smile at the idea.

Perched on their stools to sip the scalding black coffee, both enjoyed a friendly and it seemed to him intimate silence as if, he thought, we've been man and wife for a long time. She was older but it didn't seem by much, especially with that figure, a little fuller since they had first met, which improved the breasts he so wanted to touch. Her stockinged legs hung from the stool, as if on getting down she would run joyfully to her lover. The impulse to take her in his arms and kiss her was almost overpowering, and if she did not resist they would go upstairs. He imagined them lying naked together on the bed. He was aroused but well controlled, as he knew he had to be, at such an infamous and unlikely picture, though in previous situations with a woman he'd had to tell himself it would be impossible to get her to bed before he could devise the means to do so.

'Good coffee,' she smiled. 'You knew exactly what I needed.'

'I made a guess.'

'I'm happy it was the right one.'

'Not all my guesses are, as you can imagine.'

She was sorry for him, with his wife gone, and being alone in the house. Hard to know how many people in the world were happy, whatever happy meant. It was easier to say when you weren't happy, which was the most one could expect. Any happiness you experienced was gone in a mere flicker of time, as when he must have been guessing what she wanted, while a state of not being unhappy was only good for helping the years along, in a situation you had been engineered into by events more powerful than yourself. He had said Howard would be happy from setting foot on the boat to getting off at the end, a matter of two or three weeks, so she had him to thank for that. Such tangible happiness for so long ought not to be denied anybody. Between them they had made such a thing possible for another human being, and one so near to her, which brought her close to happiness: 'I have much to thank you for.'

He wanted to say: Save it for when we get back from the Azores – but didn't care to alarm her, though couldn't think why, because he expected they would turn up at the house all sound in wind and limb on their return. 'Not really. But I have to tell you that I would do anything for Howard. And also for you.'

The last sentence turned him into the enigma all men were, because there was no reason why he should do anything for her. 'Thank you again. I don't see why you should, for me, though.'

His passion declined, and thank God for that, he said to himself. Lust it may have been (it most certainly was) but there was so much depth to the feeling he could hardly believe it wasn't love. At the moment he thought that making love to her would put the final meaning to his life, and that he would tell her so, if the opportunity came. The faintest sign, and he would see no distance between them. He would edge across the space, on his best behaviour, and draw her in as she would by then have been drawn to him.

She was pleased to know that he would do something for her alone should the occasion arise, but she didn't trust herself to relax in the way he seemed to think was appropriate. She had done so once, but never again, even though to stand by the rule now would be no more than to punish herself. Resolution was losing all meaning, however, as his blue eyes looked so intensely at her. 'I think I had better be going. You've been very good about everything.'

He stood, though she didn't. 'Yes' – I think you should.

She felt weak, finally enlivened by the coffee, drowsy now, happy and relaxed as he came and held her hands. She knew at last what sort of thing he was going to come out with, but he drew back a step. 'I just wanted you to know it,' he said.

There was no surprise, finally. He hadn't put anything in the coffee, or the sherry, so maybe she had come specially to hear him say such things as much as to talk about the other matter, now so unimportant. After all, she was her own woman, and had known he was alone in the house. 'To know what?'

'That ever since I first saw you,' he said. 'You must forgive me. I shouldn't have said it. But I couldn't bear you not knowing how I felt.'

She smiled, and put out her hands to be warmed and comforted, the pressure telling that she had done right to come to him. 'I think I knew.'

He could do nothing but kiss her warm lips. Her stupefaction was washed aside as he drew her from the stool into an embrace, her bosom against her shirt. 'I love you, is what I've been trying to say.'

When her arms came around him, some form of agreement in her action, he let a hand roam under her sweater, and pressed it against the warm flesh of her back. Any moment he would relax, leave her, step aside, and they could amicably part as if nothing had taken place. They would say their polite goodbyes, and he'd give a last heartfelt promise to take good care of Howard – she assumed. But the move was postponed, scorned in fact, ignored because such kisses would never allow it. With other women he always wondered what the hell am I getting into? – but the question didn't come now, as if he had been waiting for such a woman all his life. Her forehead was wet with kisses, everything happening without words but with more surety.

She was a woman who for some reason hadn't evolved to the age she was supposed to be, and he couldn't tell what she was thinking, as he might with anyone else – crude assumptions as they had always been. It didn't matter. She acted out of her body, all reflection gone, otherwise why with him who, though feeling love, was never to be loved or trusted?

She only knew she was letting herself go, be carried wonderfully away, as if she had waited for it even before Howard turned up at the station dance, even before the encounter with her uncle, feelings from so far back there was no resisting or holding off. I love him, she told herself, hardly knowing she loved her freedom more.

He knew nothing more piquant, more profoundly erotic, than hunger in a woman for what (never mind who) was strange and morally forbidden. What magic button had he touched? He'd give a lot to know. At this stage there was nothing you could do with them, because they were hungry beyond what you could provide, yet hoped you might satisfy. He felt it, and knew he wasn't wrong. 'I love you, I love you,' she muttered, bringing such a tight response from his arms that, if it increased, she would break as she deserved.

'We can't stay down here.' He loosened his hold. 'You know that, don't you?'

'Oh, I know.'

He licked her tears away, and led her by the hand, nothing else for it, all the signs there of her wanting to be with him and no one else. He brought her to the double bed in Amanda's room, a happy thought that Amanda wouldn't be needing it anymore. They kissed by the window and he thought let the cows on the hillside see, as he lifted the sweater up and off, and unlatched the vital clip at the back, lips to her warm breasts. He broke away, the drill to get out of his shoes first, unclasp his watch, while she unzipped the skirt and let it fall, as if she had done it many times before though he knew she hadn't.

Naked on the bed, she said with a young woman's smile from oh, so long ago: 'I'm sending my husband and my lover out to sea!'

I'll be back, at any rate, thinking how hopelessly naive to mention her husband, whom he had no difficulty in blotting from his mind. 'This is like being in love for the first time in my life' – something they always liked to hear.

'And I want you both safe and back, though I shouldn't be thinking about that now, should I? Because I love you more than I can say.'

Her nipples were almost flat on the surface of her breasts, till his caresses brought them out. 'I want to see you again and again.'

No hurry, he said, let's have no hurry, none of that. Kiss her in every place – she deserves as much – until she doesn't know whether she's coming or going, and then make her come.

She gasped and bucked, then mostly lay unmoving, so he halted halfway through his travels, kissed her closed eyes and ecstatic lips, and went slowly in.

TWENTY-THREE

Howard fixed himself at his desk to tap out a letter to the police, as satisfying a task as he had ever been set. They would find someone to transcribe it, or they wouldn't. If they didn't, or thought it was a hoax, or a joke, or a mysterious nothing to be thrown aside, the expedition would be a success for what he knew to be the criminal fraternity. But if it was interpreted properly and passed to Interpol, or whatever agency was mobilised to take action, his adventure would enter even further into the unpredictable.

He polished the brass parts of the key with a square of yellow cloth, the metal angles and edges sharp or smooth under his fingers, a solid piece of the best British mechanism, with its springs and narrow gaps to spark the longs and shorts of intelligent incrimination, a telegram to stiffen the lips and set the heart to bump, if it got to where he hoped, and if they knew what to do with it.

Hot breath went like the best polish onto the slate base and across the maker's mark, sliding and smoothing to bring out a shine for anyone but himself to admire. A sighted man might see his face in the glow: mirror, mirror on the wall, who is going to play the most dazzling morse key of all? He saw it, even more glistening than buttons on parade, so the time was for feeling good, because all things bright and beautiful were coming his way. Laura had unaccountably fallen in with his going to the Azores, because Richard had converted her by a matter of fact account of a safe and happy life on the boat. How Richard had done it he would never know, though his was not to reason why, only to be glad he had somehow managed to talk her round, though more than one visit had been needed to convince her.

When the winged steeds of retribution descended from the sky onto the open sea – a mountainous island in the background – or when the police surrounded them on getting back to a lonely estuary in England (the crew thinking themselves safe, and about to cook an evening meal of celebration) the customs officers would not be able to include him among the guilty, because how could a blind man be one of the smugglers, and who but he, having appended his name and address, could have sent the morse-warning which had put them on the alert?

A foolproof coup was the order of the day, and if Judy happened to be caught up in it, as well she might, and was taken with the rest of the crew, at least there was a chance of his getting close and proving her innocence, though he hoped, and had good reason to suppose, that the boats would be far apart when the crisis came. While no plan drawn up before battle could be expected to look tidy after victory or defeat, one had to be made nonetheless.

The first requisite for good sending was to be comfortable, so he drew up the chair and adjusted the cushion behind him. A spoken message on the tape recorder would be easier to make, and more facile for those to understand who received it, but sending in morse was a more difficult medium, thus more memorable, more intriguing, giving the message a patina of importance which other methods couldn't have. That which was more difficult was more believable – or so he hoped. They would need a few days to find the appropriate person to transcribe it, though little would be lost, because the boat would be just out of the Channel.

Long experience told him that in sending morse the upper arm should be vertical, the elbow resting against his side, and the forearm going horizontally towards the key. He adjusted the contact gap a tenth of a turn and, putting his fingers on the key, sent a few flourishes, like the soloist tuning his instrument before the orchestra can begin. His elbow remained stationary, movement a mere up-and-down flexing of the wrist, and never more than an inch or two. Thus he could send for half an hour at twenty words a minute in near perfect morse without making a mistake, so that whoever read it, if he knew his job, would find it simple to transcribe. The last thing necessary was to set the tape recorder going, and hope for as little outside noise as possible.

What he proposed saying, and went on the express, had been rehearsed for days. He had played and replayed his recorded logs to extrapolate dates and positions, names of boats and people, movements from day to day, and whatever was gleaned on future intentions to fit into the collage based on evidence picked up from correspondence with Richard and whatever he knew about him, whose tapes he ran through over and over so as to mull on them and miss nothing. The satisfying acuity of his intuition allowed him to put such evidence together as would convince anyone. If his element was darkness, where conventional vision was of no use, the advantage to him was multiplied in that he saw what no one else could when it came to creating a shapely web from a scattering of loose ends, threads drawn so neatly to the centre that the picture would be plain for all to see.

Two boats were setting out on a certain date and on a certain course, and at a certain speed, for an island of the Azores, where a significant transfer of drugs would take place. He gave the radio frequencies his messages had come from, in case they had also been picked up by the authorities, but who hadn't been able to make the same interpretation.

He would have been a detective if his life had taken a different course. Joining the police on leaving the Air Force would, he thought, have been a more acceptable move, and fighting against those who profited from selling hard drugs a good enough cause. Whoever fecklessly used such psychic dynamite to blast away any vestiges of sense would be helped in spite of themselves. Reducing physical pain was one thing, but imbibing drugs so as to extend the limits of perception, or reach a state of mind thought to be otherwise unreachable, which the mind would in any case reveal in its own good time, was an admission of inferiority, a denial of hope. Young people might take them out of curiosity or, because they were mentally ill and not yet medically diagnosed, in an effort to forestall the onset.

The use of drugs to calm or stimulate was bound to lose its power, but people went on taking them in the hope that more would work this time, or next time, or the time after. And after a while it seemed to – easy to think such help was needed forever. He supposed many indulged out of bravado, or for the experience, imagining themselves strong enough not to be damaged by what even the worst could do, and assuming they could stop when they liked because sufficient willpower would always be available. Perhaps that was so, but many suffered torments which called for more and larger doses, so that what began as self indulgence ended in despair and maybe death.

However much he suffered mentally there would never have been any such drugs for him, not even if they had been offered free. The mind anguished for a reason, and was not to be tampered with, all wounds being curable by time and endurance, and respect for its processes.

Great wealth was made by those evil-doers who transported and sold drugs, people who had no moral or human feelings because they considered life to be cheap, and were convinced that those who bought drugs, often with what they stole or mugged – thus lengthening the chain of distress – were the lowest of the earth. The more drug distributors who went to jail therefore the better. Argument was useless, and if action meant that Richard was put away for a long time then he, Howard, would see himself as the instrument for saving his soul. And perhaps even Richard would then so regard it when he'd had time to reflect and repent.

He knew his views could be thought of as reactionary, yet they reinforced his purpose. The message's melodic chatter eased his soul, oscillations concatenating into the microphone of the recorder, a text distilling into morse the computerised manifestations of his intuition. Speed and rhythm were as perfectly matched as he could make them, but when he had finished, and signed himself off, he wondered whether his story hadn't after all been assembled from a farrago of false assumptions, that he was no more than a madman enslaved by the talk of two lovers, infatuated by one of their voices.

He pushed back the chair and searched the table for a miniature tape recorder often used as a standby. He put the larger one close, wound back the tape, and set the mini going to make a copy of the letter, so that in the future, if nothing came of his denunciation, he would know that he had made it.

The tape to be sent slotted into a case, and fitted the shape of his pocket, to lie there till stage two went into operation – thinking in nostalgic service terms as if to bolster himself for doing what he had no option of carrying out. Fat chance, he smiled, of me not dropping it in the postal box.

When Laura called from the front door he went to help, but she bundled the plastic bags into the kitchen, unable to pretend he could be useful anymore. 'Don't bother.'

Maybe it was part of her willingness for him to go away and enjoy himself. If so he thought it a fair bargain, change being good in anybody's life. She was touching him again, kissed him more often, laughed at the slightest thing, resentment unaccountably gone. He wanted to ask a question, but since there had never been any need for answers in their life he didn't, knowing the answer to be that it was Richard who had changed her mind, set her at rest regarding all fears, though without giving away the real reason for the trip, as indeed how could he? Richard also knew how to be devious, though Howard had much to thank him for, because who didn't want peace of mind at home? The left hand rarely knew what the right hand did, so that no one could see behind your eyes, or guess what you were thinking, or know that whatever you did express could be the basest lies. As for body language, tell me another, for who better than a blind man could disguise it, muffle the signs, or make so many that no single one could be picked out?

'I've bought you a new duffel bag.' When she took off her coat he caught the ravishing odour of her body mixed with the new perfume, glad she had bought something expensive for herself. 'I got it from the camping place in town. It's in the plastic bag. You'll get most of what you have to carry in it. The rest can go in the hold-all you took to Boston.'

Even the name of the place could now come out in normal parlance, without vindictive overtones. She hadn't told him what Richard had said, but it would be ungentlemanly to question her surrender to him. He was more than satisfied that she had. 'That should just about take care of my luggage allowance,' he said. 'I can't see us being away all that long.'

She shot the coffee grinder into action. 'Yes, but you'll need clean shirts.'

'Only three: one on my back, one in the wash, and one to spare. We managed that way in the Air Force.'

261

'What about sweaters?'

'Two, I would think. It's not a sailing boat, where you have to work at the mercy of all weathers. A spare anorak, and that should be it, apart from the usual socks and underwear.'

She kissed him. 'Well, darling, we'll lay it out tomorrow, then go over the list.' You could cut the unreality with a knife but he seemed not to feel it. For her also the rarified air of release took some getting used to. Hard to tell whether she was in love with him anymore, though he was certainly a factor in her life. But she loved Richard carnally and therefore, she thought, more truly.

'I'll take the morse key and oscillator,' he said. 'They can be stuffed between clothes to keep them safe. I'll need a couple of spare batteries as well.'

'Will you have time to play with that?'

'Who knows? But Richard and I might want to have a secret exchange of views while on board. Or I could do some sending to keep my nerves in trim. It'll be a pastime, if I get bored.'

She imagined them a thousand miles from land, sitting on the deck in the warmth of the evening, Richard tapping out a long message saying he had made love to her, and giving all details. She had encouraged him (and she felt that she had) and when such a text sank in Howard in his despair would tumble into the depthless water and drown. Her flash of nightmare had Richard laughing at the ease of how it had happened. That's all she would need to release her, and a new life would be hers. She saw no need for such pessimism.

In any case Richard would do no such thing as tell Howard. It was in his interest not to. He would guard Howard well, because he would rather have his friend's wife for a mistress than some bewildered disconsolate widow who might become a millstone of responsibility. 'What do you mean? Why should you and Richard want to keep anything secret?'

Shouldn't have said that. He had waited for her query. Subtle though you be, liar that you are, silly words escape. Judging by those who would be on board there might be every need to communicate secretly with Richard. 'No one, of course. It was only a silly schoolboy remark.'

She couldn't believe him or anyone, though must give the impression that she did, and laugh at his funny ways, at how like a child he must have toys to take away with him. She was sufficiently relaxed to say this. Nothing threatened to blight her frankness anymore.

'I don't mind that you find me so silly,' he said lightly. They embraced, and she felt him wondering why she had changed her perfume from the common scent she had used before. 'I'm strong enough to let you go without any worry, though I shall miss you terribly.'

He was flattered. It was good to feel cared for. At least she wasn't tearful in her assertion that she would be bereft. 'Everything will be fine. I know it will.'

'There's a change in my life,' she said. 'It's a step forward, and I have to think it's for the good.'

'So it must be. It can only make me happy for you.'

'It's taken me long enough.'

'Seems to me,' he said, 'that it's happened since Richard came into our lives.'

She was glad he couldn't see the wash of crimson that must have gone over her. 'You could say that. If not him, then something else. Or someone else. I like to think it would have happened anyway. A change is a way of absorbing the shock of your going. That's what I think it is.'

Such uninhibited talk was more interesting than otherwise, worth it for whatever reason. He wanted to say that Richard isn't all you think he is, but that would let a very sprightly cat out of the bag, and the old argument about him not being let off the leash might be resumed. 'He's a good old friend, that's all I know.'

'Very true,' she said, 'which is why I don't mind you going. He explained everything.' She put the cup before him. 'I have no qualms. All we have to do is decide what you're taking. Another thing is I called at the library, and found a couple of books about the Azores.' She wanted to know what Richard would be seeing as well. 'I'll go through them. There might be something interesting.'

After lunch he said he would go for another stroll into town. 'Twice a day now, to get my legs into shape. I shan't be able to walk much once I'm on board, but I'll need to be halfway fit.'

He wanted to go faster than usual, but speed could be dangerous. He counted the steps, tapping the cassette in his pocket every moment or two to make sure it hadn't gone walkabout, the most important thing in his life at the moment. He must go with care to avoid falling smack on his face; worse if he rolled and damaged the tape. He went with purpose nevertheless, the gulls crying about their hardships in the world. God would look after his own, but even they howled enviously, as if aware of his purpose.

The tap-tap of his stick lost its usual rhythm, and he didn't wait the normal time before getting over the road. Brakes failed to disturb him, as did shouts and hooters disputing his passage. 'You silly old bastard! Are you blind or summingk?' a skinhead crowed, half out of his van door.

Two young lads were shouting, but why bother cursing back? – though the impulse was there. When the end came, however it did (and it came for everyone) there'd be only blackness, nothing, a clean finish, neither them nor anyone to be met again.

He walked along the High Street without smiling, counted the shops till he came to the post office and stationers. Back at the wireless he would write the weather from Portishead, build a picture of what sea and sky would be like when they set out from Plymouth.

He stood at the counter and pulled the tape from his pocket. 'I'd like a Jiffy bag for this, please.'

She knew him, as who didn't in town? 'Not your usual time, is it, Howard?'

'I fancied a walk.'

She fitted the tape in. 'Is it your favourite pop group?'

He tried to smile. 'A little thing I found on the beach this morning. I expect somebody dropped it, so I'll post it on to lost property. Some poor young person might be pining for it. So will you write for me – Chief Superintendent, Police Station, Sharbrooke Road? Honesty is the best policy I always think.' He was surprised at how little it cost when the scales had registered, a mere few pence for such a time bomb, if anyone was able to diffuse it.

'You're right there. It's good of you.' She stapled the envelope, and he joined the queue at the stamps counter. Slow and cautious on the way back, he felt nevertheless as if he didn't belong anywhere, wasn't part of the world, more in tune now with the squeals of the gulls, whose noise told him they were waiting to be taken to a land of peace and plenty where they would shriek and manoeuvre no more. On the boat he would know where he belonged. Waiting would have been a torment whether blind or not. Too late to pull the packet back.

Part Three

A Hero of the Code

TWENTY-FOUR

No imagining ever came close to the real thing. You could pitch yourself into the future from the comfort of a room on shore and just about size up what it would be like. Past experience, combined with a sympathetic push of cognition through the limits of understanding into half-known situations – that was more or less it. He should have realised that on the scoreboard of such a business you'd be lucky to manage two out of ten.

Penlee Point was behind, Eddystone somewhere ahead, or would be soon enough. This much he knew. In the meantime everything superfluous to his guts was going over the side. At least he had made allowances for that, though the weakness depressed him.

He'd come aboard with Richard from near Plymouth. 'We'll hide the fact that you can't see for as long as we can. Just keep your eyes down and act drunk.' And now he was half seas over, and the sea seemed half over him, head against the wood, discouraged by the smell of a savoury meal from Ted Killisick's galley, the same gulls mocking that might have followed the car from home.

An hour before departure, Laura was stuffing sweaters and books on tape into his bag. How would he find time to be bored? Unless some unforeseen event turned his holiday into forever, or he never came home and they'd become useful in the next world, or they would form the basis for beginning civilisation from scratch. She was still ironing a white shirt – as if he might be required to dress for dinner at the invitation of some local consul – when Richard came to the door.

You were never so close to earth as when taking in the salt smell of the sea, droplets hitting hands and face like grits of sand. Even the continual earthquake of his stomach afforded a smile, proof at

269

least that he was on his way; and by the time they found out he was blind there would be no turning back. Equilibrium was doubly precious to a blind man stricken with *mal de mer*. He didn't need eyes to see the turmoil of the sky, or the stern old God who may well have been looking down on him. Richard had called it a squall, the last time passing, a bit of nothing, but up the boat went, and down the boat came, all hundred and fifty feet of her, yet bashing powerfully along.

Pushing him up the gangway, Richard had called to George Cleaver one side of the rail and Paul Cinnakle the other: 'I got him out of the pub. Been soaking his bloody self all day. Blind drunk isn't the term for it.'

'It's a good thing Waistcoat ain't here yet,' Cleaver said. 'He don't like lushes.'

Richard helped him to a bunk, came back later with a sandwich and tin of Coke, telling him to stay wide of the bridge till they were well at sea, and even then not to push his way in. 'They'll probably sling us both over the side when they know.'

Howard was in no state to bother. Richard watched him from the stern. He hadn't banked on having a helpless twelve-stone baby on board. On shore he'd been chipper enough, so assumed he'd be getting about the boat on his own by now. No use trying to shame or bully him, and he was best in his hideaway in any case, Waistcoat being nervy and jumping at everyone, as always at the start of a trip. It would be better if he didn't find out till calmer times, though he'd still do his little spectacular, probably bigger than they'd ever seen. He touched Howard on the shoulder. 'You'll be all right in a while, shipmate.'

'Oh, I know I shall.' His face was serene, a smile in spite of the dark waters of ages past trying to engulf him. He rejected the picture absolutely, knowing he must. 'I'll try a walk soon.'

'Hold on tight when you do. We don't want to lose you. Or I don't anyway.'

He could even laugh. 'You won't.'

'Scoff these, in the meantime.' He took a packet of biscuits from his pocket. 'They're the best things out.'

A dying man feels better after eating, Howard supposed, though he still dies. 'I'll give it a try.'

'I'll get you to your bunk. You'll be OK tomorrow.'

But would he, so soon? He might. He had to be. The radio had given a low synopsis, though not so bad, with wind variable, northwest, two to three in strength, and visibility fair, outside the squalls. 'I'm sure I shall,' though his putty face didn't suggest as much to Richard. 'You won't hold me soon. I'll be all over the boat.'

'That's the stuff.' Richard made his way to the bridge, where Cleaver was at the wheel. 'We're doing well. Dead on two-o-five at twelve knots. As long as that light don't go out in front. God swept it away once, didn't He? But it won't crack up in this I think.'

'Where's the chief?'

He turned. 'How should I know? In his cabin sewing a button on his waistcoat, I expect. The less I see of him the better. He's in his usual bad mood.'

Richard hoped he would stay out of the way for the first few days. 'A lot of lows lurking about.'

'I'm ploughing on, that's all I know. We'll lose 'em later. I can't wait to see the dolphins.'

He played with the idea that maybe it would be wise to tell Waistcoat about Howard's disadvantage as a sailor before he discovered it himself. His usual feeling would have been to leave well alone, but for the first time in his life he wasn't sure. 'You don't advise disturbing the chief?'

'Not a good idea. Wait for him to disturb you. He will, soon enough. He'll find something to go off his head about. He always does. There's the light. We're spot on. By the time we pass it'll be your turn to take over.'

'I'll have a stroll beforehand.'

'How's that pie-eyed chap you brought on board?'

'He's getting over it,' Richard said.

'He looked as if he'd been swimming in it. Never seen such eyes. Fluttering like a butterfly just out of the pickle jar.'

'He'll be all right soon. You'd better watch that tanker coming up the Channel.'

The lighted flank of a building slid towards them on the other side of the light. 'I've seen him,' he snapped, as if his competence was being queried. 'I'll pass behind.'

Howard stood, as if he too wanted to see the light blinking in the dusk, and the tanker going by. He might swim to it and get a lift home, certainly felt the backwash. If Laura was on the beach she would see it in the morning, but she was a minuscule figure, no longer real. Richard put a hand on his shoulder. A zone of murky orange flooded from the west: fires being stoked, moiling and fusing northwards, metal blue between the clouds. 'I'm not sure the weather's going to be all that much improved tomorrow.'

'It doesn't matter. I'm feeling better,' not so much in his stomach but from the shock of leaving everything behind. He'd left even himself out there in the darkening east, tapping his way, day in and day out, around the dull town. 'I'll have a go at the radio in the morning.'

'It's early days,' Richard said. 'There'll be a meal later, if you can take it.'

He turned towards the sunset as if he too could see the closing of the day. 'I'll stick to biscuits for a while. Then I can look forward to breakfast. I suppose the boat will be pretty loaded on the way back.'

Richard saw no point not being open. 'We'll keep the deck above water, though what won't go in this boat can be put in another.'

'The one Judy's on?'

'That I don't know. If they're still there. They could be going in another direction altogether.'

'Where might that be?'

'We don't know yet. At least I don't. It may be irrelevant to us where they're going.'

Howard guessed that he did know, but wasn't saying. 'Maybe I can pick them up on the radio later.'

'I hope not. Everybody's supposed to keep to radio silence. Anyone breaks that, and they're dead – a bullet in the brain, and tipped overboard.' No doubt about that, whoever it might be. The silly bitch had done enough damage already. 'You won't hear her any-more.'

'Unless we meet her?'

'There's always that. Maybe she'll come on board when we get to the beach. Everything's in the air, except where we're concerned.'

His stomach was no longer a needle floating in alcohol, the man from home having joined him now, back together in one body on the bouncing boat, forging towards the end point of his search. All those nights of talking to her girlfriend had built up a picture in his planetarium of a mind, and in a few days he might stand close, hearing nuances in her voice not possible or apparent over the radio.

Richard took his arm. 'You're wet and cold. Be a shame to go down with hypothermia. Better get to your bunk.'

He would fall asleep by thinking of Judy, then dreaming about her. 'Maybe you're right.'

'Laura said I was to take care of you, but it might not be possible every minute of the day.'

'That's all right.'

'I'll do my best, but we ought to stay close.' Should Howard go overboard, for whatever reason, expedient or otherwise, Richard knew he could have Laura to himself for as long as he wanted, or as long as she could go on caring for him. 'I'm so easy to seduce, aren't I?' she said, after the first time. 'Only when you want to be,' he told her. Recalling the three occasions they had been together, he knew he must see her again, and it would make no difference whether Howard got back or not, though because of his promise he would have to make sure he did. The responsibility bothered him, a bond he didn't know how to unravel.

Having no right to be on board didn't worry Howard. He was at last where he wanted to be, and this was his life for as far as he could see ahead – now they were so far from land. He was alone, in spite of the crew around him, and whatever happened he was indestructible, because the boat was going exactly where he wanted it to go.

Following Richard, he registered every plank of the architecture, feeling his way so that he would sooner be able to move on his own, a small world to master. Obstacles were noted, he counted steps, the height of a door latch. They met Scuddilaw coming on deck. 'Still out of action, is he?'

'He won't be in the morning.'

Scud's laugh had a touch of envy. 'I'd be lucky to get over a bender like that, at least without getting a string of ulcers.'

Howard tried a suitable growl. 'It ain't the first I've had. Nor the last, I expect.'

Scud looked close. 'Can't you see at all, though?'

'I'm waiting for the light o' the sun to come back.'

'He'll stand watch for me at the radio,' Richard said. 'You don't need eyes for that.'

Scud whistled his way up the steps, leaving Howard to fumble a twisting path into a lower bunk, which smelled of mildew and sweat. Richard drew off his boots, unpeeled him from the anorak. 'There's a bowl, if you have to throw up again.'

'Thanks, a lot.'

'There'll be time for thanks when we get back. I'll wake you in the morning, and sit you down to a Killisick fry-up. I expect real life will start then, but we'll be fifty miles off Brittany, so it won't much matter.'

Howard pulled the blanket close, though needed no covering to keep out the light, of which it seemed there couldn't be much. He felt harrowed and helpless with exhaustion, as if he hadn't fallen asleep for months. Flashes of light dominated his human sphere, tail ends of phrases stabbing like toothpicks sticking out of delectable titbits, the sort Laura had put between his fingers at a party they'd given for the neighbours when first moving into the house.

He was happier for being away, gammy stomach or not, though Richard would be on the carpet for bringing someone like him on board. Hard to think why he had, even though I know so much. He could have told me to get lost or do my worst, but supposed I would give the game away, which I have in any case. Stolen a march on them there. Having me on board was safer, but they didn't imagine someone so far at the end of his tether, who could do nothing more to stay alive than get mixed up in a stunt that would either push me into another world, or get off the world altogether.

He gripped the boards, hung on for fear of being thrown out. Neither sea hands nor sea legs were with him yet, and at such bumping around he couldn't see how they ever would be. A scene of Richard talking to Laura played, and to get the picture right he put an age on Laura and gave Richard a more distinctive face, though the one from the first meeting stayed clear enough. He heard him denying there was any option but to give permission for the trip. Out of darkness came enlightenment, for what it was worth, at this late stage. He knew Richard's arguments but couldn't place his tone of voice, or the persuasive phrases he must have used, and sensed a mystery in what had been exchanged between them, something finally powerful enough on Richard's part to win her agreement. From the day she had returned with an altered view of the matter he picked up a connection between her and Richard which no longer existed between the two of them.

He was now in the mind to think about it, with the crunching bump of water against the bunk, and a low whistle of wind carrying down the companionway, feeling emptiness and fatigue, alone in the narrow space, shouts and laughter from the others who seemed all over the boat. Happy to be on their way, they were light headed, relieved that the die had been cast. So was he. When Laura returned from her call on Richard, and said he could go to the Azores after all, he had finally made his decision to send the letter in morse to the police. Searching the labyrinth as to why, he lost consciousness into sleep.

Not a light anywhere, no land between them and the northern hump of Spain, five hundred miles away. On the bridge Richard almost disdained to look at the murk. As always on the first day aboard he wanted to sleep, so much that he felt a pain at the ribs, as if months would be necessary to get him back to normal, though by the second day his alertness was always as sharp as ever.

Slight swell, sea moderate, as they termed it, but one bash after another sent them all over the place. A sunshot tomorrow would show how much they had strayed. Satellite navigation was on its way in, but this trip (probably the last without it) they would go by sextant and radio, which had never failed them before.

George Cleaver was hot stuff with sextant and almanacks, taught to him as a youth by one of the trawler skippers going back and forth to Iceland. He'd practised and studied all his life, and Richard admired his professional stance as he stood on deck like a ramrod to clean and adjust the mirrors, as if he were Captain Cook himself, but with a swinish temper when the midday sun didn't show, as if it stayed hidden to spite him alone. He never took a drink to smooth the creases out of his frown. Richard could work sunsights but preferred to let Cleaver do it so that he would never stop assuming he was top of the class, as indeed he was. The log was also his to keep, and he measured the distance run like a fussy old hen at times, though never cursing when it wouldn't come right. Nothing to do but keep a straight course, he was as reliable as any man could be.

Richard saw Laura, but would she have shot so clearly to mind if Howard hadn't been on board? The answer had to be yes, for such a magnificent woman who had given herself so completely. How he had come to be lumbered with her husband was a puzzle, and he recalled his impulse while driving by Plymouth to stop the car and push him out, leaving him to wander like a blind beggar until – till what? The police would pick him up and he would tell them his story as they drove him home. An intriguing scene, that of shooting off at top speed while Howard fumbled his way around a lay-by looking for a place to piss. The rest was nightmare material. Waistcoat would have so many guts for garters they'd think they were at the Moulin Rouge. So here Howard was, dead to the wide and crippled by seasickness, like an anchor waiting to go overboard.

He shook the vision away, to mull on their present expedition. At this stage it seemed that getting back to England with such a huge pick-up would need a miracle to bring it off, though the collective intention was there and the fires of greed burned in them like the best of true Britons.

Steadying the wheel, he couldn't stop dwelling on Laura's resplendent body, while the enveloping green drek tumbled around the boat slapping its way on a steady two-o-five for land at the end of the world. He would like to spend some of his money on living with her, rent a house in the farthest north of Scotland (as far as they could get away from Howard) where they would fuck themselves out for as long as it took. A mad plan to dote on, yet the prospect wouldn't go away. Better to steer through dangerous shoals with lots to think about, or be anxious at the boat getting lost in empty watery space, the mind only fixed on survival.

More was unknown about the journey than any set out on before. Yet he was relaxed, intrigued on getting at part of himself which damped both hope or anxiety, and brought a peace of mind he entirely trusted, heading into such thoughts as easily as the boat was chopping a way through the drizzle and darkness.

Sometime after breakfast Ted Killisick shook Richard out of his dreams. He had gone to sleep wanting to piss and, unwilling to get up and go to the heads, had experienced a different intensity of dream than when he'd had a little to drink before going to bed and didn't need to do so. Dreams induced by a full and irritated bladder were deeper and more turgid on the pictorial front, yet harder to grasp and impossible to recollect on waking. When not aware of needing to piss he hardly dreamed, or the dreams were so shallow there was more chance of recalling the tail end of one, though being so close to the surface there was little enough worth noting. He saw Ted's grinning face. 'What the hell is it?'

'Waistcoat wants to see you.'

'What for?'

'He's raving about old Blind Pugh. I think he's going mad.'

Back from the heads, he knocked at the door and went into Waistcoat's cabin. The chintzy bed had been made, a button-eyed teddy bear wearing a sailor's hat lying across the fluffed-up pillows. Waistcoat held onto the side rail of his desk. He seemed about to jump up and down, not only hit the ceiling but crash through the superstructure and up into the inclement sky. The hard features of a drug boat master had taken away that superficial resemblance to an eminent Harley Street surgeon. A line of blood showed from the shaving cut on his cheek. He was halfway into his blue and white padded anorak. 'That fucking radio wizard you brought on board is stone blind.'

'He looks it, I know, but he had a few over the odds yesterday. Once he hits the bottle it's hard to get him off.'

'He must have drunk the fucking Thames, then.'

'Should be all right soon.'

'Listen, don't fuck with me. You're lying. He's been blind since birth, you stupid bog-nosed swivel-eyed get. Blinder than the blindest fucking bat, the way he wiggled his eyelids at me. How did you put him onto us? I mean, it's a nightmare. He'll do for us. We'll get three hundred fucking years apiece.'

Richard, split between amusement and wrath, let the force-nine gale wash over him, pulled back his years as a ship's officer so as to stay cool, no twitch or smile or alteration to his face, a stance that never failed. This, however, was a hard one. He had never seen Waistcoat's hand tremble, which did as he lit his usual slim cigar. Maybe something other than Howard's blindness had boiled him up, though impossible to guess what it might be. 'I told you in London why he had to come with us, and you agreed.'

'But you didn't tell me he was fucking blind.'

'I didn't think it mattered.'

'Mattered? On a boat like this? I can't believe it. Do you think it's a floating St Dunstan's?'

'We brought him because of what he knows. We did the only sensible thing. Apart from that he's an ace radio man, the best I've known, and we're lucky to get him. His ears are sharper than those of anybody who can see. He'll be a godsend when we get close. Blind operators aren't rare in full employment. Half those on the coast stations were blind at one time. Another thing is that from our point of view he'll see nothing of what goes on. In that respect we couldn't have a better man. He can take my place at the radio, so that I'll be more use on board. Another thing is you won't have to pay him like the rest of us, maybe just a bit of bonus for a handout when we get back. You'll have a lot to thank me for when it's over. And when it comes to getting back, with the danger of us being intercepted, he'll be very useful indeed.'

Waistcoat must have been a neat man in a cell. He tapped his ash carefully into the silver tray, its handle the debonair figure of Sir Walter Raleigh wearing cap and sword. 'You're either the cleverest man on my books, or you've got more than one fucking screw loose. I can only hope for your sake that you're clever.'

Richard sensed a little cooling down. 'You had a crew of six, and now we have seven. Could prove lucky.'

'Well, I'm not superstitious. I got rid of that crap long ago' – though

Richard noticed his glance at the teddy bear. 'Just make sure he don't fall overboard, that's all I say.'

'I'll see to it.'

'A fucking blind man!'

'Is that all you wanted to see me for?'

'Yes, piss off.'

Glad to go, but Waistcoat called him back. 'Did you hear that Nimrod this morning?'

'I was getting some shut-eye.'

'He buzzed us.'

'They always do. They like to know what's going on.'

'Let's hope that's all it is.'

'They buzz everybody. He took some pretty pictures, I expect. We didn't sign out with the coastguards?'

'None of your fucking business.'

He was sure they hadn't. 'Everything's as normal, then. It's the last they'll see of us, dead on course for Spain they'll think, to stock up on fags and brandy.'

Waistcoat looked troubled. 'The French'll be looking at our number plate next.'

'They'll be none the wiser.'

Waistcoat came as near to a compliment as he could get. 'Not a bad manoeuvre of yours though, to alter course before Finisterre. As long as we don't run out of fuel fifty miles off land. We'd look a right lot of charlies paddling into harbour with our passports. It might have been possible at one time, when they were stiffbacked, but now they're like fucking laundry books.'

Richard arranged a chuckle. 'Yeh, a real come down. But don't worry about that, Chief. It's part of my business, to think,' he said before going out.

Eleven at night, when all lights were off and they were halfway across Biscay, they'd change direction and go due west until eight in the morning, well out of Spanish surveillance. From then on it would be a straight course for the Azores. It had been Cleaver's plan as much as his, but compliments from Waistcoat never came amiss.

TWENTY-FIVE

The sea was losing its bumps, and his lack of sleep led him to think the air was warmer. He scrounged a coffee from the galley, and found Howard looking – if that could be the word – astern, as if to see the last of England, and wonder what Laura was up to. I should know. She'd be mooning about us both, Richard supposed. Take her off to Scotland I will, and when we've done all there is to be done and I can't stand the sight of her stern and lovely face I'll kick her out. Meanwhile I'll cherish the memory and, damn, love her as well.

'I hear you had a hard time with the chief?'

'He gave me hell, but I think it's going to be all right.' Howard's head went back as he laughed. 'I heard a croak or two, and lots of swearing. His face was right up to mine. I thought he was going to punch me, so I got ready to give him a bigger one back. But he pulled off, and I heard a door slam. I can't think why he should be so upset, except maybe he should have been told already.'

'Did you eat a good breakfast?'

'Eggs, sausages, tomatoes and fried bread. Luckily, just before the chief came in.'

'Killisick's good at that sort of thing. But if I'd told Waistcoat before, you might not have been here.'

'And that wouldn't have done at all.'

Not difficult to know what he meant. 'Did you hear the plane go over?'

'Couldn't miss. Four Rolls-Royce engines. A very healthy sound. Nostalgic, as well. It brought back the old flying days with a vengeance. RAF on reconnaissance. I can never forget the sound of the Lancaster's engines, either. They were a bit cruder then, had quite a roar when

280

taking us off down the runway with a full bomb load. Merlins they were.' He turned his face towards Richard. 'Do you think the Nimrod was following us?'

'No, just routine. They usually like to keep an eye on people like us. Think we're a bloody U-Boat, I suppose.'

Howard wondered whether they were being tracked because of his morse letter. 'I gave them a wave.'

'You must have made their day.'

'Maybe they sent our position back to base, wherever that can be. They have air signallers on board, as I recall. Unless they just store it in their computers.'

Such talk brought back what Richard regarded as a normal edginess, after his calm spell on the bridge. Real life, and none the worse for it. 'If you're feeling fit I'll show you the chart room where we keep the communications gear. It's never too early for a spot of listening. See what you can get. There's a portable typewriter to take down the weather from Portishead. You'll be just in time.'

Space was cramped, and he sat side on to the table to find room for his knees. Richard explained the mechanics of the equipment, and Howard's fingers went over the various facias to get an identikit picture of each, almost as if they were human features, hoping his particular languishing at the transmitters wasn't too obvious. Richard tuned in to Portishead. 'I'll go over it with you this afternoon, to make sure you've got it. And once more tomorrow, if you like.'

Howard unlocked the manual typewriter, easy enough to use because of the standard keyboard. The pitch of the boat made it more difficult than on shore, though he hadn't expected to work on a millpond. He turned out a creditable text nevertheless. 'I'll be word perfect in a day or two.'

'You can get this afternoon's weather as well, and between times see what else you can pick up. Best to show your face as little as possible. Keep out of the chief's way, unless you hear something good on the air, though if you do, call me first. I shan't be far away.'

Nothing except mush on most bands, the loudest reception from coastguards on the Biscay shore, or odd-bods on medium wave wanting berths at various ports. He took a break, to breathe the ozone, sensing more than four thousand metres of water under the keel, the sea slightly rougher but no longer bothering him. Back inside, the cramped space reminded him of the wireless position in the Lancaster, when times had been good. The German Numbers Woman, an old friend from far away, came through with the same schoolteacher tone, though he wasn't able to make out every individual cypher. She was concerned for him, warning him that he must look out for his wellbeing. Though her support was only spiritual, he liked it nasalling into his earphones.

He cut her off, clicked back to long wave, and got a bearing from LEC at Stavanger. 'Not much use, though it shows we're more or less on course,' Richard said. Consol was a German wartime direction-finding system, called *Sonne*, to give U-Boats their position in mid-Atlantic, and the Allies kept it on after the war, though it could be far from accurate near coasts and at night. On the other hand it was simple to use, and useful at times. Picking up Lugo or Seville as well would give cross-bearings for a reasonable fix. George Cleaver did more than all right with his sextant, unless cloud cover foxed him, then Howard would get the azimuth of a beacon, fingers already making out numbers on the direction finder. Navigation, with variable conditions, could be a bit of a mix: dead reckoning, radio, astro, which between them tied things up more or less satisfactorily.

He was starting to feel at home, doing what his temperament might have kept him at had it not been for the cannon shell over Essen. This time a similar missile was already lodged on board, embedded in himself, waiting for a different sort of explosion, a tension not too difficult to live with.

Cleaver put down his cucumber sandwich, and took the Consol bearing for plotting. 'Whatever you get, I'll have. Never turned up my nose at anything, except a Chinese breakfast.'

Howard edged away so that he could write up the log. 'Have you ever had one?'

'Not so far, but you never know.' He tapped the chart with his finger. 'The bearing tallies. You're earning your keep. It's all the same to me whether you're blind or not. I don't suppose the rest of us can see very far, anyway. It might turn out just as well if we can't. Richard told me you were a wizard at the radio.'

'I do my best.'

'The more boffins on board the better.' He climbed back on deck. 'Never say die, that's what I say.'

Afloat as a member of the crew was like being one of eight, as in the good old days in an aeroplane, all gung-ho for the target a few nights ahead. He wanted the pleasure of a stroll on deck, enjoying his new found medium, but knew he must show willing and keep the earphones clamped. He searched eleven megacycles for news from aeroplanes in either morse or voice but found nothing, the same on other wavelengths that had been so promising at home. Like a superfluous cabin boy, he had been given something to do, to keep him out of the way, whatever was said or thought, while Waistcoat regarded him as a hostage because he knew too much. The shade of fear was wiped away by Lisbon coming in loud and clear on charlie whisky – which a cabin boy certainly wouldn't be able to copy. 'I'm disappointed at not getting a squeak out of the Azores.'

'You will.' Richard led him to the stern for a rush of clean air from the west. 'You'll pick up stuff soon enough. Best to savour the cruise while you can.' Birds pursued the boat, hoping for snacks. One was wounded, or weak, and slid into a stall over the mast, followed with head swinging side to side as if trying to talk. 'We'll have one on board soon. We usually do about this time.'

'That'll make nine of us,' Howard said, 'instead of eight.' He leaned as if to put a hand in the water but the green line slid down again.

'Don't get too close.' Richard drew him back. The temptation to do evil needed wrestling with. Or was the frisson merely out of concern for his safety? Hard to know, too lazy to work it out. A man must be given a chance. 'Even an old deckhand goes overboard now and again.'

'I'm firmer on my feet than you might think. I've got my sea legs already.'

'Glad to hear it. But don't frighten me or you'll have to wear a life vest whenever you come on deck. We all should, by rights, but it's a big boat, as boats go, and it's not really rough yet, believe it or not. They'll be handing out lunch any minute, so follow in my wake. Ted promised hamburger steaks with all the trimmings, which means spuds and carrots, and apple charlotte to follow. Better than hard tack and a bit of old raincoat. He's a dab hand as a cook.'

The domestic provision satisfied him, everything found and a bunk to get his head down, he and the blankets slowly drying. He stood in line as if others were also blind, recalling a framed print in his father's study of men made sightless by poison gas in the Great War. Richard shuffled from behind, Scud and Cinnakle in front, no queue at all, though Richard's hand on his shoulder steadied him as the deck came up and space opened under his feet. The side wind sent them swinging, gave a spiteful push, force four weather though sea and sky were blue.

He had thought that once on board, and with sea-sickness gone, the joy of being alive would come back, and so it had but eating with such appetite made him afraid to ask for more in case he mistakenly overstuffed. He found a seat on deck, head clear, praying his stomach would take care of him, gazing at space between boat and horizon, little enough to lock onto even if he'd been able to see. The wind, and an occasional warm sun on his cheeks, and maybe a gull now and again resting on the undulations, told him all that was visible.

Richard came from the bridge and put a flask of brandy into his hand. 'I feel the same. It takes three days for the system to settle down, unless there's some action, when it has to right away. Take a suck at this. It'll work wonders. Three-star Napoleon. Only the best is good enough.'

'I couldn't disagree with that.' He controlled his shaking hand, clamped the glass spout to his mouth, and took a flame-like swig. 'You're well equipped.'

'A tot or two of this brew's saved my bacon more than once.'

'Is there plenty on board?'

'Never fear,' he laughed. 'Enough to take us to Doomsday City and three times back. Just ask Ted Killisick, if you feel the need. He keeps it under lock and key, but hands it out to whoever puts a good case, which is to say you don't need a lawyer to blab it out. All duty-free. He's got everything from mineral water to Warrington moonshine. When we get back to Blighty we'll be guzzling champagne by the bucket. Looks like you've got a visitor.'

A weight tapped his forearm, bare below the line of his short-sleeved sweatshirt. 'It must be a bird.'

'A racing pigeon,' Richard said. 'It's dull and dirty grey, but it's looking at you as if you're his saviour. Half starved, it seems. It was just about to hit the water and go under when it spotted this plump white arm at the rail and thought it would take a chance on sanctuary. They do that now and again. There must be something halfway human in them to come to the likes of us for help. Unless they want a bit of company before going into the pigeon version of the great unknown.'

Howard stilled himself so as not to frighten it away. 'It seems fit enough to me. I can almost feel it breathing. Hear it as well.' He fumbled in his pocket and pulled out half a biscuit. 'There you are, Jehu. See what you can make of that.'

'You'll have a friend for life.'

'I think it's eating.'

'Scoffed the lot. On its last legs.'

He shook the rest of the packet on the deck and felt the bird leave him to sort it out, webbed feet padding on wood. 'What a privilege, to save a life, even a bird's.'

Richard resisted telling him it wouldn't live. They never did, always too far gone when they came aboard. 'It knew where to come, which is more than most people know, especially the ladies of the world.'

Disturbed by Howard's laugh, the bird hesitated as to whether it should stay on the comfortable platform of his hand or try its luck again over the water. 'It's up to the men to know that.'

'Ah, well, there's no pattern in that one.'

'Aren't we born knowing it?' He stroked the pigeon's neck, a finger drifting along the warm pulsating feathers that felt like silk, and brought forth a warble of gratitude. 'If we aren't, we should be.'

'There's a ring on its leg,' said Richard, 'with a name, I expect. I'll read it.'

'A message as well?' Laura had set a pigeon to race after them, with words of encouragement for their travels on the briny. She had called at a coop behind the town and urged the man to send his best and strongest. 'Don't keep me waiting.'

'No message. It just says Terry, and gives a number.'

'I'll call it Jehu. Won't I, Jehu? Is it looking at me? I feel it is.'

'Lovingly,' Richard said, as it flew up to the mast. 'It'll come back. We often pick one up, miles off its course, utterly knackered and lost. Maybe it'll stay till we reach land, glad of a lift, and spend the rest of its life in the Azores. Plenty of lovely lady pigeons there. Why call it Jehu? What kind of a name is that?'

'Just shot into my head. As I remember, it's from the Bible. Jehu murdered all and sundry so as to set himself on the throne. Must have heard it at Sunday school. No connection, really, is there, Jehu, my old bird?' – looking to where he thought it had gone.

'Do I feel a spot of rain?' Richard said. 'Or is it a bit of spit? Anyway, I'm due on the bridge for a stint at steering this de luxe waterbus. Floating gin palace, if you like. I'd better get Jehu entered in the log as another mouth to feed. Boiled rice usually goes down well. Ask Ted for a handful. The poor bloody specimen looks as if it needs building up. Then back to the wavelengths. If you happen to chit chat with God ask him to let us know how this little run is going to turn out.'

A build up of the sea and wave pattern made the boat roll, but Howard knew where hands and feet should go to stop him getting too bashed about. One foolish miss left a scrape along the arm, useful in teaching what not to do.

Jehu had a quick flight around the boat, as if to keep its wings in trim, not much to its liking, so it came back, found a way to Howard on the radio, either drawn by the warm billet of his arm, or pulled by the birdlike rhythmical whistle of the weather forecast in morse, and the steady clack of the typewriter.

The head of the bird went from left to right as he moved the space bar. Maybe somewhere in Jehu was the spirit of a dead radio officer from the war, faint echoes of an old life coming back. He couldn't think so, because when you were dead you were dead, a meltdown into the eternal blackout. He took the paper from the machine and tapped, felt, trod his way to the bridge. 'Here's the latest weather, if you want a look-see.'

Richard noted the pigeon resting on Howard's shoulder as if he was Long John Silver, and they'd been friends since the bird left the egg. 'He's looking livelier.'

'He was warbling back there, short-long-short in morse. Same letter over and over again. Maybe R for Richard.'

'If you teach it the rest of the alphabet it might tell us what it's like to be a pigeon.' Richard glanced at the forecast. 'You'll need ten million years, that's all.'

Another person was on the bridge, but he wasn't sure who, until: 'Let's have that fucking weather, then' – unmistakably Waistcoat. 'That pigeon will crap all over the boat, though I suppose it'd be the right sort of camouflage for this shower of a crew.'

'The weather's on the mend,' Richard said. 'Those north-east will have the worst of it.'

Waistcoat took the paper, read, and folded it into his pocket. 'Stay at the wheel. I'm going in for some shut-eye. And I don't want anybody banging on the door to ask any stupid questions. I'll be out.'

Cleaver came in, put his sextant carefully into the box. 'He gets jumpier and jumpier. We'd be a lot better on our own, except he doesn't trust us to run the show.'

'That's how he's got as far as he has,' Richard said.

'Pity they've done away with hanging. I'd love to see him swinging in the evening breeze. He thinks we'll take the stuff to the Bahamas rather than head back for Blighty. There's got to be honour among thieves, though. If we can't trust each other who can we trust? I don't like these big jobs. Never did. I'd rather do two or three smaller ones. You can't help but get jumpy on such jaunts.' He sat down to work out his sights. 'Still, it's better than shovelling cod around on a trawler.'

'We're all doing better than otherwise, or we wouldn't be here.' Richard glanced at the compass, and flicked on the wipers to clear a light drizzle shooting across. Or was it spume from a wave? He turned them off. We're going after the great white whale, and no mistake, packed tight with dope. Half of Europe will be out of its thought box when the stuff gets on the streets and boulevards.

'What's up ahead?' Howard stood to one side, as if his blind eyes were looking at trouble.

'Nothing,' Richard told him. 'So we can feel happy without popping pills or shooting up. The sea's lumpy and in a bit of a twist, as I'm sure you can tell. There's a cumulo stratus about six octers over the grey sea, but it'll better itself during the night.'

Ted Killisick came from the galley with biscuits and tea, and a plate of paper thin cucumber sandwiches for Cleaver. He put a mug into Howard's hand. 'There's a plastic bag of cooked rice left over, so you can feed your pigeon. We usually give 'em a bite. They're English birds, after all, so we have to look after 'em. Anybody else's wouldn't get a crumb, Common Market or no Common Market.'

'You wouldn't starve a French pigeon,' Howard said. 'Would you?'

Ted handed the tea around, scalding and sweet. 'Compliments of the galley, which is so posh I have to call it a kitchen. I might not begrudge a French pigeon, but if I got one that was Spanish I'd wring its neck. I suppose they've got more sense though than to land on us. As soon as they see the flag they hop it.'

'You can't blame the pigeons.' Cleaver stowed his box as if there was a top hat inside. 'They're innocent enough creatures.'

'You wouldn't say that if it landed a streak o' white on your mirror while you was taking a sunsight, would you, Mr Cleaver?'

He sat down as if to think about it, one cucumber sandwich after another going into his mouth. 'Well, it hasn't happened yet.'

Ted put a hand on Howard's shoulder. 'I hope your pigeon don't bring us bad luck.'

'What, my Jehu?'

'I've always thought pigeons were lucky,' Cleaver said. 'Not like seagulls. They're the only things in life I can't stand. If it was a seagull that landed we might be heading for shit's creek at a fair rate o' knots. We had a seagull once, all the way from Aberdeen to near Iceland. It stuck to us like shit to a blanket. Couldn't get rid of it any how. The old skipper had a two-two rifle, and took a few pot shots, but it was so darned clever he could never hit the mark. He wouldn't let any of us have a go in case we took it in mind to shoot *him*. Talk about bad luck. We caught practically nothing that trip. The weather was so bad we all but capsized. We thought it was the end a time or two. When we got out of it and straightened everything up the seagull had gone. They're dead unlucky, but pigeons are all right.'

Howard felt the pressure of Jehu on the palm of his hand, head pecking at rice grains in the other, a gentle scratch against his skin. On deck the wind made him an island, clean air surrounding each searching gust fresher than the last as it washed against him. He wondered why he was here, but the only answer was that he was here because he was here, as in the old song, but also that he was here yet not here, here because he could be nowhere else, and not here because as another person he was able to look on himself vividly from the dark, an entity in control and separate from the self looking on. The soft touch of the pigeon's beak joined the two parts, its throaty warbling a pleasure to hear, so easy was it to make a creature content.

Maybe all on board feel they're not absolutely here either, conscripted by Fate into the same somnambulist trap – until the action starts, when they can be themselves again. To know the truth of it he would have to be able to see like them, and he couldn't. He was the lodestone, the man beyond them and on the outside, the pigeon feeder, the blind wireless operator who could listen but not communicate with any agency beyond the boat. He was among thieves, out of reach, had tricked his way on board hoping to find Judy of the alluring voice, no other reason.

Jehu left his hand, wings whirring into the wind. He would be back. If the radio and all else failed, or the boat sank under them in a storm, Jehu would be the survivor. 'He's off for his constitutional,' Paul Cinnakle said. 'They have charmed lives sometimes.'

'How are the engines?'

'They've got a charmed life as well. Time for a roll-up.' Howard heard the slip of paper rustle out of the packet, the quick manufacture of a cigarette, and the scrape of a match. Paul handed the wherewithall to Howard. 'Make one, if you like.'

'Not so easy for me.' He spoiled the attempt, and put the barely crumpled paper into his shirt pocket, not wanting to untidy the boat, but made a shapely enough fag the second time round. 'Thanks.'

'It's easy enough at the moment,' Cinnakle said. 'We have to take advantage of it. Be daft if we didn't. But I prefer things when all hell breaks loose. That way, I know I'm living.'

Howard felt the pigeon shooting him up, waft of wings across his forehead. 'I'm only living at the radio. Always think I might hear something good.'

'What would be good, though?'

'I wouldn't know till I heard it.'

'Something interesting, or surprising, you mean?'

'If you like. I'm sure you can guess the sort of stuff. The more I glue myself to the wireless the more chance there is, that's all I know.'

'Better you than me. I never did know why blokes like you didn't go off your chump with all those dots and dashes.'

'It's because we were bonkers to start with.' He stood, and Jehu perched again on his shoulder as he made a slow trek to the radio space, thinking he could hear the crumpling of the rejected cigarette paper, so thin and delicate that, if need be, it would fit perfectly into the tube on Jehu's leg, with any message he cared to write. Jehu would be a winged chariot in the sky, braving the underbelly of the worst dank cloud, navigating by the sharpest gusts but careful to stay clear of the spume tops. He would backtrack the course of the boat, bounding against the odds for Blighty and, once over the Devon or Dorset cliffs, would sink for sustenance at some friendly door, so that whoever picked up such a pliant bird to feed would find the clip and read a message written in the tiniest of letters on the cigarette paper.

He was long practised at writing. Often in previous years he would ask Laura to read what she could, and after a while the skill increased, till by strict control on his fingers and a grid of imaginary lines he wrote at least half way intelligibly. At first it was four out of ten for the test, and stayed there for a long while, but by inner tears at his cackhandedness, the five mark was passed, then six and seven. The most Laura gave was eight, which was enough, because even with eyes nothing could be a hundred percent.

He typed half a dozen navigation warnings, none relevant, but it was something to earn his and Jehu's bread. They concerned the North Sea coastal waters, telling of a wreck shifting position by a few feet, or a fog signal not working, or something in the oil fields to be given a wide berth, or a light gone out, vital information for ships and boats in the vicinities.

They were steering southerly, and back on deck Jehu took it easy at the rail as if waiting for a message to be attached to its leg, the antithesis of an albatross hanging around the neck, a friend, if only the unfeeling brain pan of a bird could know it. The warbling was outpaced by the radio teletype of a weather station, a sound beyond the interpretation of either, but soothing nonetheless as the well motored morris dancer of a boat clogged its way into the dusk.

TWENTY-SIX

The German Numbers Woman in her forest cabin parroted her wares, but he was too far off to hear, a thousand miles south-west, threads pulling ever tauter. In any case she was involved with her children, and the lover Howard had generously given her.

The Moscow station had also gone off the air, too far over the horizon to impinge. Vanya was so assiduous at his secret bottle of vodka he would only bother with planes on the east-west run across Siberia. Well into the zone of radio silence, Howard no longer hoped to hear Judy on the *Daedalus*. She had already left by plane to prepare the ground in the Azores, or she was on the boat which would set aside lethal stores which the good yacht Waistcoat was on its way to collect, material Howard knew would never reach the streets. For all its calm moments the adventure was becoming warmer by the hour, more heated than anyone else on board could know. He smoothed under the poll: 'Eh, Jehu, my little darling?'

Richard came down from his stint on the bridge. 'You must be crackers, talking to that bird.'

'I've been barmy all my life. It's a sad world if you can't go through a good half of it off your trolley. Makes existence tolerable. Keeps me sane.'

'For somebody like you, I suppose it does.' He took a packet of rolling tobacco from his anorak pocket. 'I'm out of cigarette papers. Do you have any on you?'

'Wish I had. Can't oblige, I'm afraid.'

'What about the one you took from Paul?'

'I don't have it anymore. I held it up, and Jehu scoffed it. He loves rice paper.'

'On your own head be it.'

Hard for a blind man to realise he was spied on, even to know when someone looked in his direction. Such a boat was a small world, though it still seemed big enough in the complications of getting around. Not to know that he was being watched at all times was a failure of the imagination. If he lost the rice paper Jehu would be out of a job. 'After tomorrow I should be picking up the weather direct from the Azores.'

Richard had cigarette papers after all, must have, because Howard sniffed the smoke. 'That could be useful. We'll need to know. Especially about visibility and wind. It's a small beach we're going to.'

'Where, exactly?'

'Waistcoat only said what I've told you. He keeps things close till the last minute, though I don't see why. Cleaver knows, of course. In any case it wouldn't mean anything to you.'

No more questions. Let them tell him, or not. Or let him overhear, or let the gen leak, as gen had a way of doing. 'Oh, I know it's none of my business. I won't see the place anyway.'

Richard leaned against the table. 'No, but I hope I do, though I won't want to set eyes on it again after we've high-tailed our way north, believe you me.'

'I'm looking forward to that.'

'But for what reason?'

Howard knew something he didn't know, what none of them could, and Richard seemed to think it would be worth his while, and everybody's, and even Howard's perhaps, if he could find out what it was. 'Oh, I don't have a reason. I don't much care how long the trip goes on. If it lasts months I won't be unhappy. I've forgotten everything about the past, a state more than enjoyable to me. It's a blank. Don't even know if I had one most of the time. I just fit myself into the spirit of the ship and feel happy. What's good for you and the others is more than good enough for me.'

'I'm glad you think that way.' Richard stroked the pigeon. 'You've reassured me.' He pressed a finger around the bird's neck, and Howard sensed he wanted to put out the feeble light of its life. So did Jehu, fluttered from his shoulder, up to the ceiling and out of the door. 'Doesn't like me. Only you.'

'He's off for a breath of the old sky.'

'I expect he'll be back.'

'I hope so,' Howard said, the bird his only friend on board.

All hands were called to the chief's quarters. Dinner had gone by, and the sea was calm. 'We're making progress, so we're earning our keep,' Waistcoat said, which Richard considered a fair way of putting it, though only to be expected from someone who'd never earned anything honestly in his life, and who saw those mirrored walls and pastel shades as the height of glamour. More a tarted up penthouse flat near the Elephant than an honest boat made for the ocean and the job in hand, though things would look different after the stowage from the beach. 'Except for that fucking pigeon,' Waistcoat added, glaring at Howard.

Paul Cinnakle sipped his vodka, ice rattling back from his lips. 'I heard it had gone.'

'It has,' Howard hoping it was pressing on regardless along the reciprocal.

'We could have put it on the treadmill and got another half knot.' Scuddilaw sat on one of the leather pouffs scattered around, too low for his legs to be easy, so he stood up as if he had hinges instead of muscles. 'Unless Ted decided to let us have it on toast for breakfast.'

'Slit its gizzard,' Paul said, 'and gravel pours out.'

'It's not a London pigeon.' Waistcoat stirred his little silver swivel stick around the bowl of his purple stemmed fluted glass. 'I know the difference. They taste fucking awful. I once ate one as a nipper. Knocked it down with a catapult, and made a fire on some wasteground. We all nearly puked. Garbage it was, tasted like the back end of a twenty-four bus.'

Howard sat on the sofa, only Richard left standing: 'Maybe it would have been better cooked in a stove.'

Ted cackled. 'With olive oil and garlic, and a couple of bay leaves. You'd think it was grouse then. Wouldn't know the difference.'

'They didn't show us how to do that sort of thing at school,' Waistcoat said. 'I wasn't very good at domestic science.' At which remark they had a good laugh, a booze party in the offing. Unusually gallant, Waistcoat took the vodka bottle from the freezer compartment below the table and poured a good wallop into Howard's glass. 'Knock it back, old son. You might be able to see in the morning, eh?'

'Unlikely,' Richard said.

'Don't fucking tell me. We'll need every eye we've got in a couple o' days. Even a fucking glass eye would be better than nothing.'

Richard wondered whether AIDS, syphilis or cancer would finish Waistcoat off, and hoped for a powerful dose of all three. He wants us to believe he's deteriorating, but we all know he's only dangerous when he stops effing and blinding. 'We'll cope,' he said.

'You don't need to say so. I know we will.'

Jack Cannister wobbled Jamaica rum to the top of his glass. 'I'll be a month in the Bahamas after we've done. I'll need to wind down. I always do. Trouble is, when I've done winding down I've got no money left.'

'They taught us fuck-all at the school I went to.' Waistcoat followed the submarine cables through his own mind, which could put anyone in despair who thought to try and find out how his mind worked. 'I learned to read and write, that was all.'

'Same for the rest of us,' Scud said. 'Except I suppose for Richard and Mr Cleaver, who learned trigonometry at their posh schools.'

'I taught myself,' Cleaver said.

Richard laughed with them. 'I learned to tell the time, as well. It was a grammar school.'

Waistcoat stood, as a sudden thought occurred. 'If you're in here, Mr Cleaver, pardon me for asking, but who's running the fucking boat?'

'It's on auto at the moment. Better be on my way back though.' He finished the cucumber sandwiches, and what was in his glass, and went.

'I'm fucking well self made,' Waistcoat said, fingers stuck in his pockets. 'Every bit of me.'

'Our mums and dads must have had a hand in it somewhere,' Scuddilaw said with a giggle.

'Yeh, but none of you's as fucking self made as I am. Some are more self made than others, let me tell you.' He turned to Howard. 'How about you, blind man?'

Howard held his glass towards their voices. 'Pure grammar school, Higher School Certificate, then into the Air Force. Trained as wireless operator, aircrew, Bomber Command. I've been blind over thirty-five years. Caught a packet over Germany.' The floor to himself, he stopped all talk. 'It wasn't long after the bombs had gone and we turned for home. I'd done a dozen raids, and we knew the war would soon be over, and thought maybe we'd get out of it all right, though we didn't talk about it, just hoped against hope. The chances were a lot higher than what they'd been a year or two before. We had two selves, the other one gung-ho and wanting to bomb Nazi Germany back into the stone age.'

Waistcoat broke in. 'How much did it weigh?'

Howard seemed to stare him out. 'What weigh?'

'The bomb load, fuckhead.'

'Oh, anything up to six tons. More, in some cases.'

'You dropped six tons at one go!' Waistcoat sat down to enjoy the picture, envious of a man in their midst who had been involved in such mass destruction, and wondering if you could ever trust a chap who'd been part of something he'd have given both arms to have been party to.

'Mind you,' Howard went on, 'if you think about it, it was wrong to carpet-bomb women and children, but that's how it had been at the time, no feeling for what you were doing, or you couldn't have done it. Or maybe some of them could. Not that I feel guilty. They sowed the wind and reaped the whirlwind. But the best part of a raid was always when the bombs were away and you felt the kite lift, so much lighter to get you home.' He was shooting a line, had drunk too much, stuck in his maudlin planisphere and seeing comets passing each other for the second (and in some cases the third) time.

Waistcoat fell silent, as did they all, awed by Howard's experience of violence, that they could never hope to match. And he had got away with it – almost.

Waistcoat was the first to break silence. 'Hey, how old are you?'

'A big flash,' Howard said, 'when a cannon shell from a JU 88 ripped through the fuselage. Sight gone forever.'

'So that's how it was?' Scud said.

'I'm pushing sixty.' Howard dropped a year or two so as not to alarm them about his ability to manage on the boat.

Waistcoat poured another drink. Maybe he too had lost count, if ever he had kept one. 'I'd never have thought it. You look about forty-five.' He came close again. 'So how was it you rumbled this trip to the Azores, as Richard conned me into thinking you had? And then getting us to bring you along?'

'He's a radio wizard,' Richard said. 'He found out.'

'I want it from the horse's mouth.'

'There isn't much to tell,' was all Howard could say. 'Anyway, it's in the past, and almost forgotten.' The boat rocked, half across Biscay by now. They wanted more from him. 'I heard two yachts in the Mediterranean talking to each other. They gave nothing concrete away but I put two and two together. Guesswork and intuition, you might call it. I can't prove what I heard, or say exactly how I did it, because I burned the log books before I left, in case somebody found them. You don't keep things like that.'

'I'd give a fucking million to know who it was who gave us away.'

He knew but for some reason was trying to trap him. 'No names were mentioned. I told no one else. Not even my wife. Only Richard.'

'And you thought you would come with us, just like that?'

'I won't say I didn't want to.' He laughed. 'I blackmailed Richard, didn't I? But if he had refused I couldn't have done anything. Nor did I want to. What would be in it for me? Who would believe a blind man?'

'We could take no chances,' Richard said. 'I told you, and you said bring him. So we did. He's in it up to the neck like the rest of us, obliged to keep mum forever to save his skin.'

'That's right,' Howard said quietly.

Waistcoat put his glass down, came across to Howard, and pulled him upright. He looked into his sightless eyes. 'Listen, Howard, we're the "Matter-of-Life-and-Death" brigade, and the slightest sign of fucking around on your part, and you go over the side. No messing. Ask 'em. They'll all tell you. You won't be the first, and you wouldn't be the last. Nobody stamped your passport, and they won't be waiting for you to come back. And if they start to look for you they won't know where to begin.'

Howard wasn't unhappy at this moment to be blind. 'You don't have anything to fear from me,' he said with guiltless calm.

'So let's enjoy ourselves,' Waistcoat said, topping up Howard's glass. 'We'll drink to a good haul and a safe return to our loved ones. Come on, let's see you swill it down.'

They needed no second telling.

Howard fell into his bunk, though not before whatever was in his stomach had gone over the wake, which he hoped would make sleep more willing. For a while nothing could, the glare of incomprehensible lamp signals from shore to shore, from one corner of his brainbox to another. Hard to tell whether he was in sleep or not. From just under the surface a snorkel-periscope cut through to air above, like a wartime Atlantic submarine keeping an ear cocked for a communication from base. There was no base, and an unstable place it was, as the boat indulged in more motion than he thought the sea warranted. Not to have drunk much would have made them think he wasn't one of them, that he had something to hide, was biding his time.

An hour may have passed, no way to tell whether he was going into sleep or being wrenched from a few minutes of it, but the boat turned ninety degrees to starboard, done by a skilled hand at the wheel, calm, inexorable, well planned, onto a westerly heading. Either planned, or the sharp eyes of the helmsman had noted something on the radar screen, or he had seen a glow in the spray ahead, a light, some obstacle to avoid at all cost, though he had time for a deliberate manoeuvre to avoid it. Impossible to decide, unless he put on his trousers and went up to find out.

They were still drinking, voices sometimes angry, occasionally merely rabid. Then came laughter, maybe complicity at past activities, certain remarks rising to hysteria. The change of course stopped his sleep, and because no other occurred it was obvious that the boat had altered direction by prearrangement. He wondered about the reason, but would have to wait to find out, uncertainty drawing him at last into unconsciousness.

Ted Killisick in the galley stirred a large cast-iron pan of bacon and scrambled eggs. 'You're an early bird.'

'I slept well,' Howard said, 'after we changed course.'

He filled a plate, put knife and fork into his hands. 'You noticed it?'

'Couldn't not do. Heading for Florida, are we?'

Which brought a laugh. 'No, it's a scheme of Richard's. We were set for Spain, to throw anybody off our back who might be interested. In an hour we get in line for the Azores again. We'll be going south-west. Cunning, eh?'

He ate from the plate on his knees. 'No business of mine. I'm just here for the trip.'

'We all are, in a manner of speaking.' He adjusted the upper set of his teeth. 'Best to think so, anyway.'

Scud picked a piece of overcooked bacon from the pan. 'The others were up till four last night, so they won't be wanting their scoff yet, which is all the more for them as does.'

At eight o'clock Richard took the wheel from Cleaver, and altered course to two-three-five, dead set for the eastern coast of São Miguel island. The wind shifted, warm from the south-west, a clear sky, prom-ising for sunsights. The sea was still lumpy, but the boat cut through at a dutiful twelve knots.

He saw Howard at the stern, feeding Jehu, who had come back out of nowhere (a streak of crap down the windscreen on its flightpath) left-overs from the galley under its discriminating beak. With less than three days to the longest night all was going well. Complicated manoeuvres of navigation would be called for when they got close, and the slightest whiff of change from any unexpected quarter could make an abortion of the trip, though he had no misgivings. Success lay on his and George Cleaver's shoulders. They had sweated blood over the charts, fuel and range, tides and winds, and presented the package to Waistcoat who was leery at putting himself in the hands of mere chance, and who could fault that?

Richard had said that to make sure of success they should enrol George Cleaver, a navigator who knew his worth, and was worth all he knew. When the amount for hiring was named Waistcoat did a going out of his mind performance. Richard said that Cleaver in the smuggling trade was as priceless an expert as a safe cracker in the burgling game, and

299

though never guaranteeing success knew they might have difficulties without his expertise. A wizard with the sextant, his dead reckoning was second to none.

'We either go without him,' he went on, 'with the prospect of a balls-up, or we take him and have more than an even chance. With millions involved, what's the point arguing about a few extra thousand? If we hit that beach on the nose at just past midnight of day six without him we'll be lucky, but with him it'll be no problem. If we don't get clear days and nights as we get further south we'll still ding along because he'll give us latitudes and longitudes to the split second. I'm not even sure we can get him. He may be tied up. But I'll call as soon as I can and, if he's free, put him on standby. He'll ask for half the money to be put into his account by banker's order, and the other part when we get back. He'll have it no other way. Any day now we'll be getting satellite navigation, but until that time Cleaver is our man. Luckily he wants to make all the cash he can rake in, because when we do fit ourselves up with satellite like everybody else he'll be well and truly superannuated, and his easy days will be over.'

'Yeh, I'll see to it. Paying a navigator that much'll ruin me, though.'

Richard smiled. 'There's one more thing. George Cleaver's mad about cucumber sandwiches. He has to have a constant supply. Don't ask me why. Maybe he likes to think he's still master of his own big ship. I'll tell Killisick to keep it in mind when he's getting the stores.'

Howard talked to Jehu, but in silence. Waves had ears. Beggars can't be choosers, as he had often heard. He registered the second alteration of course, at eight o'clock precisely, over thirty degrees to port, an increase of sound as the creaming foam objected to an arrogant push into another direction.

'Everything going well,' he said, on the third day out, 'but if they knew what we knew – eh, Jehu, my pretty little pigeon – they would be running about like ants in a jam jar.'

TWENTY-SEVEN

By the fifth day Howard felt he had been born and bred on the water, at one with the wind and the sky that had turned blue. Everyone was seemingly content with work and prospects, not a snappish word any-where. From his bunk after midnight he noticed the increase in speed. 'I would guess we're doing fifteen knots instead of twelve.'

Richard came outside with his breakfast plate. 'I'm surprised you could tell.'

The extra noise and lurching power of the engines, as if one of the shafts led through him, had been unmistakable. 'Things seemed different.'

'By midnight we'll be there, or pretty close, all being well. I haven't seen that pigeon lately. What did you call it?'

'Jehu. He took off again. Maybe he smelt land and, as you say, had a plump little Portuguese sweetheart in São Miguel' – unless, as he hoped, it was flying on a Darwinian beam back to a plumper girlfriend in England, with the neat piece of cigarette paper folded into its container, on which he had written their course and ETA at the island. Trouble was, even if it was picked up, their boat would get there sooner, and be away before anyone could intercept them.

He had done his best, a long shot, stupid to think a pigeon could fly all that way. If, too exhausted for the journey, it landed in France, there might be a chance of someone finding the clue and following it up. A telephone call to the Azores needed only the time it took to dial.

Weather prospects came in morse from CUG, Punta Delgada, louder by the hour, pleasing Richard and everyone because conditions were good: light winds, calm seas, almost clear sky. 'In one way, better than we might want.'

301

Howard lifted his hand, and typed out that Tempo promised a slight deterioration around midnight, maybe somewhat worse for tomorrow.

'Stick at it.' Richard took the paper. 'See what else you can get.'

'I'll try VHF soon.'

Radio silence meant not even breathing near the microphone, hands away from switches. But he listened, lulled by static, took a traffic list from Chatham, Massachusetts, then swung onto Judy's old frequency but heard nothing, as expected, since she would be already waiting for their boat to arrive at the Azores. After loading, supposing it took place (despite his efforts, however futile, to put the authorities on the alert) she would get back onto the *Daedalus*, and out of the danger zone by following a track to the Straits of Gibraltar.

If the powers that be – bigger than any of them – were clever, they would allow Waistcoat's boat to be loaded, and apprehend it with the incriminating material on board before they were beyond the exclusion zone. By then the *Daedalus* would be safely away, and Judy out of peril. He didn't want her to be in trouble with customs or police, only to hear the sound of her voice while the stuff was being put on board. Perhaps in the future, at a less risky meeting, they would reminisce about past adventures.

She was the reason for him being on a trip that would have been unimaginable a few months ago. But the second purpose which had entered the equation filled him with anxiety, had come in without him being aware, a mistake demanded as payment for the luxury of becoming himself again. One or the other purpose should have been kept in mind, and rigidly followed, because passion and the laws of morality could never join to advantage. Both were now in train, and he had a glimmer as to how it would end, though afraid and full of doubt.

In his weakness – as he saw it – he thought of Laura, and the picture was wistful, even tragic, a face left behind in another world. Her features were indistinct, hard to recollect, as if under the sea and corroded by salt spray. Even when together the memory of her face had been an effort of the imagination. And now the face was wiped clean and replaced by the supposed one of Judy's, longish and competent features belonging to someone who was easily hurt and vulnerable, making her liable to sudden actions which overwhelmed her before she could try to control them, or take account of the consequences.

Woe betide anyone who gets close to her, he thought, yet whoever did wouldn't find life dull, and once out of her orbit would have plenty to remember her by. He was sure that her relationship with Carla couldn't go on forever. He had picked up nuances in both voices indicating that the affair was coming to an end, the passion diminishing beyond what such natures were able to accept. Their final parting made him both sad and happy, unsure which was uppermost, only aware that they, like he, were controlled by a force impossible to resist.

The boat chopped into the swell, ever forward with lift and crash, as if to eat all water in its way. A strong northeasterly encouraged them along, no other vessel seen for days, Waistcoat saying it was a good thing too.

His stomach none too settled, he went on deck for air, feeling every good reason for tumbling overboard. In like a bomb, and down he would go, pressure building up to burst his lungs, suddenly warmer, and then dead.

A hand gripped his elbow. 'Put this on,' Richard shouted.

'What for?'

'You'd know why, if you went over.' The life jacket was pulled tight. 'We won't want to lose you, though even with this it would be touch and go if you went in.'

'I never think about it.'

'You wouldn't have climbed aboard one of your trundling old aeroplanes without a parachute, would you?'

He looked, as he supposed, along the wake, his favourite stance. 'What clouds do we have?'

'Fair-weather cumulus, or some such stuff.'

He saw the photographic plates clearly, from the folders given out at training sessions: archipelagoes of vari-sized fluffballs, others coming up behind like slow-moving cavalry across the sky, elongated and flat, plenty of blue for them to float in. What else might be coming up was hard to say, which may have been why Richard added: 'You never know what to make of clouds like that.'

Two sheerwaters, battered by heady showers, took refuge on the

303

upper deck. Richard was sorry Howard couldn't see them. 'We pick up passengers all the time,' he told him. 'Tens of thousands of square miles of water around us, and these pathetic bits of living flotsam cling to anything that promises a bit of rest. They feel the closeness of our warm blood, I suppose, as if they can pick up directional beams from it, so subtle only they can detect it. We probably send a Loran grid of rays in all directions, which they know how to use, and home in on us. They find it a comfort before they fly off and die, their last touch of life. By getting close I expect they renew the ability to live, pick up a few scraps from the wake as well. That sort of rest can bring enough survivor's strength to reach land, or another boat halfway to it. Sea birds are a perfect balance of fragility and endurance. We've picked up some who feed and strut about as if they've taken command and will live forever, but a day or two later we find them dead under the davits. That body we thought so nice and plump and full of life turned out to be hollow, its skin like a drum, so that when you press it there's nothing in between. Then again, you get a scraggly pathetic specimen half dead on the boards, looking at you with its button eyes as if to say goodbye, and a few days later it'll go winging away towards land hundreds of miles off. I think they use such an intricate navigation system that they can always get to the exact point aimed for. I don't suppose that pigeon called Jehu had any difficulty finding a place it wanted to go to.'

Howard appreciated the lecture. 'You think not?'

'The chief wondered if you hadn't sent it off on its travels for some reason or other. He mentioned it to me on the bridge last night when he was wandering around in his dressing gown because he couldn't sleep. At such times he's crippled with a persecution mania. I said I thought it a funny idea. I told him you kept the pigeon as a mascot, for good luck. But he's got a bee in his bonnet that you wanted to use it for communication. Well, I thought, at such a barmy idea, how are the mighty – and not so mighty – fallen. I laughed, and said if so you'd only wanted to send a loving message to your wife, though you'd be more sure of one reaching her if you put it in a hooch bottle and dropped it overboard. It might even get there in ten years. And you could get more writing in it than on those micro-dot pieces you'd have to use in a pigeon leg capsule. In any case, I said to him, how can a blind man write, especially on a bit of sparrow's arse paper?'

'It just flew away.' Howard aimed a look at him. 'I was sorry to lose it.'

'I expect it only went fly-around. It'll be back.'

'I'd like to think so. What does the sheerwater look like?'

'It's a Manx, I suppose. Slate-black, with a mottled neck, bit white underneath. There are two, man and wife maybe. I always like a bit of bird life on board. The place doesn't seem so desolate.' He lit a cigarette, cupping the match flame from the wind, and passed it across before making one for himself. 'It's no good hoping they'll take your thoughts or longings away. They've got business of their own, and can't consider us at all. The best thing for you is to get below, out of the rain. Stick to the radio. Try to hear something that'll stop us from sliding into the big hole we might be digging for ourselves.'

Richard had come as close as possible to warning him, without knowing for certain there was anything to warn him about. What better friend could a man have? Friendship was a priceless bond, yet everyone on board was already betrayed, though perhaps more in thought than reality. So much hung in the balance, but who in the scales of villainy would weigh more precious than anyone else? 'You can be sure I'll do my best.'

'You're one of us,' Richard said, as if to cauterise Howard's wound, 'and don't forget it.'

'I won't.'

'There'll be a bit of ready cash when this is over, maybe even more than you expect. Waistcoat can be generous when the pressure's off, and he coughs up the gratitude.'

'I'm not in it for the money.'

'That could be why he doesn't trust you. Try seeing it as if you are for a change. Or at least let him think so.'

'I thought it best not to appear mercenary, being as I'm such a useless lump on the boat.'

'Never a good policy.' Richard let his cigarette go into the scuppers. 'Everybody has a value, and that includes you, so when the sea chops up be sure to wear your Mae West. The low's still moving north, and it'll take a while yet – though we should be clear in a few hours, according to the gen you got from Punto Delgado. Nice bit of interception, that. Waistcoat was pleased to know we'd have a calm sea when we got there.'

So he was one of the crew, no matter how he had set up the machinery of getting caught. He was in it for the money, and there was no reason for them not to succeed if his warning hadn't taken. In gloomier moments, he felt there was little chance that it had, and if all went well, and he landed back in England with more money in his pocket than had ever been there before (how would he explain it to Laura?) there would be little he could do to compromise them.

Crossing the Azores Current meant they were only a hundred and fifty miles from the island, and no regular watches were set or, rather, everyone was on watch. Waistcoat put himself beside Richard at the wheel, Cleaver stood upright like a soldier, and fiddled with his sextant, while Howard kept out of their way at the radio, and Ted Killisick in the galley provided nonstop food and drink. Paul Cinnakle tended his precious engines, and Cannister and Scuddilaw were posted on deck as lookouts fore and aft. The booze had been locked up by Waistcoat, and he would keep the key in his pocket for forty-eight hours.

The sheerwaters did a graceful flyover – part of their ceremonial before departure – and headed south as if the boat was too slow, outlined against the clearing sky. Far to starboard, an escarpment of cloud, like the long trunk of a giant tree, stretched as far north and south as could be seen, stationary, waiting for a wind to rush it towards them.

Richard didn't like the look of it, but it was fruitless to worry about what might never happen. If it did happen no amount of worry would have stopped it, and if it didn't happen you had worried for nothing. Such phenomenon often melted before it got to you, so what the hell? If everything goes all right tonight, he thought, I'll be too happy to worry from then on.

Howard could get nothing intelligible from the waveband he needed to hear from, as if the world roundabout was drawing them into radio emptiness, or to extinction in the earth's biggest hole. Higher up the frequency there were weather reports, and a few ships working messages from the coast, tankers mostly.

On one frequency he heard a forlorn low-note squawking, like the sound Jehu made after an excursion around the boat before flopping hungry and exhausted back on deck. It was as if he was tuned into its body moving north under the menacing cloud base, picking up the faltering rhythm of its wing beats straining to keep up the rate and stay airborne, but losing heart at the distance still to go. Its throat was making the noise, and by some technological quirk the bird had assumed the properties of a radio, so that he could hear its discouragement and the valiant beating of its wings not many feet above the clawing wave tops, hoping for a boat or plank of wood to rest and maybe feed on.

He flipped the needle away from a breaking heart, feeling more blighted by his state of blindness than at any other time. Why now was impossible to say, but the depression had to be climbed out of, so he turned back to the radio, into his all-enveloping home, no different now – except for the motion of the boat – to when he had been in his room on land. Locked in the darkwarm cloth of the ionosphere and all its noises, he was himself wherever he might be. No need to seek a reason for existence, even though too far off to hear Moscow or the German Numbers Woman since, more than anything, he had become part of the *Flying Dutchman*, that ever-travelling phantom hulk of the marine void forging along to who knew where.

Ted put a mug of coffee and a saucer of biscuits in front of him, clicks and rattles of comfort, almost the way Laura had so often done when he had been numbing his mind with too many wasted hours at the radio. Care for each other stopped people sliding uselessly into a state of living death. Talk and action bound them, and a blind man must find a role for himself, so he called thanks as Ted walked out, marvelling that he was again part of a crew whose survival depended on their concern for each other, but this time the mission was to pick up something deadly. The effect would be little better than unloading bombs onto cities, a high explosive powder to destroy the minds instead of bodies.

His hand was close to the VHF transmitter switch. The range was short, not much further than the horizon, so if he sent a mayday call who would pick it up? If he began to talk into the microphone and no other boat was apparent, he would be killed for nothing. He couldn't do it. In any case, it was foolhardy, too stupid even to contemplate.

To die in such a cause needed courage, like going on and on regardless into a wall of flak. He couldn't imagine it anymore, too old except for the imagination – a pathetic substitute for action. He would never do it, had no wish to, was afraid to, was at one with them in their game, hoping all would go well, a wish he hadn't imagined on setting out. The boat had a set purpose and he had become part of it. Blindness wouldn't save the state of his soul if they were caught. After taking in the truth, up to now impossible to acknowledge, he felt exhilarated at knowing that the height of a blind man's existence was in being accepted as a villain by the rest of the crew. He drew his fingers back from the transmitter switch.

He stared into the froth of the wake as if to let the air cleanse him, but he had calmly accepted whatever was coming, no greater bliss to be got from the world. Whatever he had been on starting out, he was now in their thrall, and would not be the same person when he got back to Laura, though the picture of such a reunion wouldn't come, no matter how hard he tried to see it.

Cannister was by his side when he went to the bows. 'I'm keeping a lookout, see?' Jack explained. 'With a pair of old rusty binoculars. They've got a purple haze at the top of the right-hand circle, but they're good enough. They work. I bought 'em for a tenner at a junkshop in Pompey. They make me look like a real bloody captain on the bridge, like in "The Cruel Sea", or something. But you seem full of thoughts, Howard. Are you getting tired? You never say much. You're waiting for that pigeon to come back, I suppose.'

Spray curled up and caught his face, cool out of the afternoon humidity. The splash across his eyes, as if to make him see again, sent vision after vision, each crowding the other out, showing the sky and the pale receding beam of the wake he would have preferred to be looking at. None of them opened onto the detail of everyday life on the boat which he wanted to see, as if he'd been blinded for his sins, but even more sins would not let him see again. God was oblivious to your sighs, and whoever did not hear could not exist. You were left to argue with yourself. He laughed, in his new guise of buccaneer, hoping it sounded hearty enough. 'I was wondering how far we are from Blighty.'

'No good in that. Never look back,' Cannister said. 'When I change watch and go to the stern I'll have to look back, until we hit the coast. Orders is orders. See that blob to port? It's a bloody great tanker, right on the horizon.' He laughed. 'No, of course you don't see it. The funny thing is you look as if you see everything. Even the chief thought you might be putting it on, though I don't think he does anymore. Best not to think about Blighty till it's under your feet, then you don't need to.'

'I wish I was putting it on,' Howard said.

'I'll bet you do. But you should go on top sometime for a change, and make it seem as if you're taking a shufti from there. You might feel a bit better. You'd get a different bump under your feet at least, with everything all around you. It's a long day, though. The last day always is. I'd rather be back in Hartlepool with the family, but on the other hand I've got to be here to earn enough money to keep 'em. They'd never forgive me if I didn't. Four kids eat a lot o' popcorn. How many you got, Howard?'

'I don't have any.'

'Don't you want some?'

'I never thought so.'

'My buggers just came, so I had to shake their hot little hands when they did. I wouldn't be without 'em now.'

Howard was curious. 'Do the others have big families?'

'I wouldn't say big 'uns, but they all have kids. Except Richard, he don't mention any, but he don't mention much anyway. People who go on jobs like this are often good family men. Not much else you can do these days. I've got a nice bungalow to keep up, and a wife who likes to be taken out now and again. I like to go out a bit as well when I'm on shore. I did seven years in the Navy, but there wasn't much money in that, so I fell into this trade. Waistcoat likes to employ men with a bit of service behind them. Makes him feel good. He knows he can trust 'em in a tight corner. He's even glad to have a bloke like you from the RAF, blind or not, though you'll never get him to say so. I think in some ways he regards you as lucky, a bit of a mascot, if you don't mind me saying so. Up in Geordie land where I come from it used to be thought lucky, for instance, if a black man knocked on your door on

New Year's Eve. Or was it Christmas Eve? When we was kids we used to black our faces with a bit of Cherry Blossom and go knock-a-door. If we didn't get a penny or so we got a bun or a piece of lardy cake. They was happy days, Howard!'

'Has Waistcoat been in any of the services?'

Cannister's laugh almost drowned the sound of the engines. 'Him? I wouldn't like to say what kind of service he's been in. Whatever it was, though, it's made him as hard as nails. Mind you, as long as you do as you're told, and do your work, he's all right. He'll stand by you, as much as he can stand by anybody. I sometimes think he's a bit off his trolley when he gets to yammering his filthy language, but that's only a cover. He's a peculiar bloke, that's all. I know he nearly cut your windpipe when you came on board and he found out you was blind, but he's the sort now who might even ask you to come on the next trip because he's got some notion he'll need you – or for some reason he's even taken a shine to you. He's a funny bugger, I tell you. That tanker's gone now, right off the radar screen. Let's go and see if old Ted's got his urn on the boil. I've never known him not to. Chuck the old sod overboard if he didn't. Just follow me, then you'll be all right from the soupy sea. Seems you've seen the last of that pigeon. I expect a shite hawk's had it for its elevenses.'

Balancing his tea mug and a large bun Howard made his way to where Scuddilaw was looking ahead. 'How much longer before we see land?'

Scud took him by the shoulders, turned him for orientation. 'Not long. It'll be over there, but you won't see it, I'm sorry to say. A sight for sore eyes for the rest of us, when we do. Not that I'll see it properly, either, because it'll be dusk already, if not dark. We'll see the light winking at the end of the island, and it'll be welcome after coming all this way. We shan't get too close, because we don't want anybody to see us. It'll be black-out, like in the war, even cigarettes doused, and because I smoke sixty a day that's a rule that gives me the willies.'

Judy was somewhere in the distance, waiting for them to draw near. What would she be doing? She would be peeling an orange, putting it segment by segment into her mouth while gazing north to penetrate

310

the darkness, hoping to see a vision of Carla. She would only find a blind man who had fallen in love with her voice. 'I'm looking forward to meeting this girl Judy, who works on the other boat.'

'You know her, do you?'

'No, I've only heard her mentioned. What's she like?'

He laughed. 'She's her own woman, Judy is. Mad as they come. You can never tell what she'll do next. One minute moody, and the next all lit up. A good sort, though. She likes a bit of fun. The trouble is, you never know where you are with her. She likes blokes one day and women the next. You can't take liberties, and that's a fact. She knows how to put you down if you try anything.'

'What does she look like?'

'Look like?'

'I'm asking because I shan't be able to see her.'

'Oh well, you won't miss all that much. She's tall and gawky. A bit of a tomboy, like a lot of women who've worked a few years on boats. She's got a nice enough face, though. Once you've seen it you'll never forget it. Grey eyes and a beaky nose.'

'Is she blonde or brunette?'

'A shade mousey, though she's been known to dye it a few times. Normally more blonde than brown. You seem quite taken by her.'

'Just curious. I wanted to put a picture to what I'd heard.'

An evening breeze cooled against his cheek, a slightly heavier chop on the sea. He gripped the rail. 'How long before we see the light?'

'Here comes Sextant Blake, our shit-hot navigator. I'll ask him.' Howard heard the definite tread of someone approaching, and a respectful tone in Scud's voice: 'How long before we see the light, Mr Cleaver?'

'In this visibility, I should think' – was he looking at his chronograph watch? – 'at twenty-five minutes past nine. Landfall's always a great moment, Mr Scuddilaw, as regards seeing the light. That's when you begin to feel God might be looking after you again. He presents you with the evidence of his wonders, after you've been lost at sea, which is another of his wonders in that all knowledge comes from Him.'

He sounded like a preacher in a crematorium chapel, though not, Howard thought, at the grave side, for his self assurance seemed rather

311

friable. All the same, since he was talking, you had to listen to someone who had no trouble cranking himself up for a mini sermon.

'He gave man the wit to devise a sextant and a chronometer – bless Mr Harrison for the latter – and make charts – hats off to Captain Cook – and He made the stars on which we can take angles and get our position to one nautical mile or even much less – with sufficient care. So it's down on our knees to Him now and again.'

'No thanks,' Howard heard Scud say. 'I'm on watch.'

'Well, never mind, He'll look after us anyway, but we have to do our bit as well. After all, what more do we want when the sun and the stars are all laid on? I must say, though, I'd give a lot right now for a nice fresh cucumber!'

Howard heard him walking away, the deliberate tread of highly polished boots, he imagined. 'I have to get back to my charts,' Cleaver called. 'It's been good talking to you both.'

'Sanctimonious streak of piss,' Scud said. 'I'd like to slit his fucking windpipe.'

'He knows his business.'

'I suppose so, but you know why? He was master of his own ship once, a real tartar, because I once met somebody as served under him. He worked the River Plate trip, ferrying beef from Buenos Aires to Blighty.'

'Sounds like a good job.'

'The best. Ship's master, and he thought nobody could touch him. Well, like a lot of them toffee-nosed tight-arsed high-and-mighty scumbags he came a cropper, didn't he? Overreached himself. He was fiddling the company something rotten. Off-loaded only half the stuff, and the rest went elsewhere. The manifest was a masterpiece of the forger's art. He was at it for years. Got his fingers in the till all right. He had bandages on both wrists though by the time he'd finished. Spent a few years inside, but he'd been stashing it away for long enough, so he had plenty to live on when he came out. I suppose he could have retired for life, but a bloke like that's got scorpions in his boots, and greed knows no bounds. Instead of setting himself up in a pub, which he thought was beneath him, I suppose – but which I might have a go at one day – he got took on for jobs like this. Richard swears by him, but I don't like him, so I don't trust him. There's just something in the way his grey eyes look at you and don't care whether they see anything or not. It makes you wonder what he's found out about you that even you don't know about. Not that I believe there's much to see when he looks at me, buggered if I do. He's the one I'd say was blind, not you, Howard, though Waistcoat would never agree. All George Cleaver sees is the stars and the sun through that priceless sextant of his, and then he jabbers to the likes of us about God, as if he knew him personally. God! God would turn in his grave if he saw him in church. I don't know what he thinks we carry on these trips, though it ain't jelly babies, and that's a fact. I know what I'd do to him if I had a nice fresh cucumber!' He spat side on to the wind. 'Which reminds me, I'm getting a bit peckish in the old locker box. I wonder what Ted's got cooking in the galley? Bloody chilly, as well.'

'Red sky at night.' Richard put a plate down for Howard. 'So it ought to be good for us.'

'What have we got?' He smelled meat, and rich gravy, not caring that he had put weight on these last few days from sitting too much and eating whatever Ted dished out.

'Stew.'

Waistcoat was passing through. 'And it's too good for all of you.'

'He sounds happy,' Cannister said. 'No turdburgers on this outfit. Must be the red sky. We'll be seeing the happy coastline soon. Better than a bit o' magic lantern, any road up. I shan't be sorry to get away from it, either.'

'Some work to do before that,' Richard said.

'I don't mind. Takes my mind off things.'

Ted laid out the tray, to be taken to Waistcoat's saloon: shrimp cocktail to start, chilled white wine, with immaculate linen and silver cutlery. He looked at his watch. 'I'd better hump the first course in. The chief don't like to be kept waiting.'

'And I'll get back to my perch,' Scud said. 'We don't want to argue with any old tanker coming up ahead.'

'Bang would go my pretty engines.' Paul Cinnakle spread a white napkin over the knees of his pale Rohan trousers, consulted his Rolex.

'Waiting is always the worst. Even with full steam ahead we never seem to get there.'

The boat made almost a full turn to starboard. Howard felt it, vibrations to the feet, a positive increase of tension all round.

'That means we can see the light.' Richard hurried to the bridge. 'Spot on, Mr Cleaver.'

His eyes seemed brighter in the dim light. 'Well, it would be, wouldn't it? But we can't rest on our laurels. Not yet, anyway. I'll be doing the fixes till it's time to turn south. Take over, will you? Keep on at two-seventy, neat as you can.'

'Neat it will be.' He fancied he could make out the hump of the island, but went by the oscultating light.

'How are we going?' Howard asked.

'We're onto it. No lights on board, but that shouldn't bother you. We turn south at eleven, and hit the beach at midnight, as soon as we see the signal. All being well, we'll be away by two, and out of trouble by daylight.'

'I'll get back to the radio, then. Work the push buttons on VHF. See what I can pick up.'

TWENTY-EIGHT

Nothing to help or hinder, so half a minute on BBC Overseas was restful – before serious listening began. The die was cast, the Rubicon boated over, everyone into the venture, out of themselves and agog for what it seemed they were born to do. A turn of ninety degrees into the welcoming sunset would bring them onto the pinhead of light saying all was well for their predatory swoop. Until then the tension of not knowing for sure put them into an ideal state for work.

Shortwave was calm and orderly. Howard caught a message to a departing ship concerning cargo and some dispute over the crew's pay. No weather or navigation warnings of any interest came, and the distress frequency on five hundred kilocycles was quiet except for a sunspot blemish playing its little tune. Half an hour went easily by. He would be a hindrance on deck, was only of use in his corner, earphones close to his head for as long as he could resist being away from the world outside. He momentarily wished to be back in the old shore billet, imagined the cat warming his knees and Laura about to come in with a hot drink or to say supper was ready. Then he was hearing Judy, saw her walking along a palm-lined street. She waved, smiled, and waited for him to come close. By which time he wouldn't care what had pulled him into such an adventure.

A distress call startled him, in voice on VHF, from the north-east, according to a given position. A three-man sailing yacht radioed that the skipper had fallen ill and was thought to be dying. Of what, they couldn't be sure, but he had collapsed at the wheel and was in great pain. A search and rescue plane was looking for them. Howard sensed the alarm behind their talk. Benighted, they grieved for the sick man, lost in a dark world, wind in their sails the only sound.

315

He wondered if those on deck heard the plane, and what it would bode should their escape route lay that way in the morning. A further signal said the skipper had died, date and time given with sailor-like coolness. He typed both exchanges, pulled the paper free, and took it to the bridge.

Waistcoat, standing behind Richard and to the left of Cleaver, read the messages by the light of a pocket torch. He repeated it to the others. 'Anybody hear a plane?'

'It'd be too far west,' Cleaver said.

'Just our luck, to have a fucking kite around.'

'They won't see us,' Richard told him.

'What makes you think so?' Waistcoat's tone was venomous, but Howard detected fear.

'Because they're not looking for us.'

'Let's hope not. That's all we need. The whole Portuguese air force shooting us up. Why did that fucking skipper have to pop his clogs tonight?'

'Are they British?' Cleaver demanded.

Howard told him they were.

'The other blokes on board will have the body in port by morning, or near enough. They'll lose no time, then the search will be off. It probably is already. The plane will identify and get back. It won't come out again. God looks after his own.'

'He'd better,' Waistcoat grumbled.

Howard turned away. 'I'll see what else I can find.'

A call from plane to yacht acknowledged their signal. The yacht said they needed no assistance, and would reach Punta Delgado next day with the body.

'Thank God for that,' Waistcoat said. 'You'll get a medal for this, you blind old bastard.'

Back at his listening post he heard nothing more that was relevant, silence mostly. He drifted towards sleep, which he had been short of since embarking. A dream came, of walking the lanes in spring around the Malverns, Laura's commentary sounding through: 'A splash of sun on the ivy brings out the sheen and shape of every leaf, Howard. There's a patch of primroses, a lovely fresh mustard yellow, about a score of them, a bluish one in the middle that the others are cherishing. It's really beautiful. Ah, now there's a cheeky celandine! We're coming to a dead elm, dead twigs dried by a week of dry wind. They rattle like bones, dry bones, dead bones. It's all dead.'

'I can hear them,' he thought he had said on waking up.

The boat was turning south, and it was quiet on deck, eleven o'clock, lightning flashes towards the north-west, wind shifting, an almost silent chop. Richard was called to the stateroom, leaving Cleaver at the wheel.

Waistcoat was going at a large whisky, though at such a time it would have no more effect than water. Probably cold tea. Better if it was. He stared at the chart. 'This is the time I get nervous.'

'I know how you feel.'

'You don't.' He laughed. 'But I've got the stomach for it, that's all I know. Will they be there, is what I'm concerned about. You never know till it happens. I shouldn't like to come this far for fuck-nothing. Will we get there at all, though?'

'No doubt about that.'

Richard preferred a chief whose nervousness bubbled on the outside, found him easier to trust and more reliable than some of the tight lipped masters he had known. 'We're on our way. Nothing can stop us.'

'But are we tracked? Will that fucking plane pick us up?'

'I wouldn't worry about that. We were lucky it didn't happen under our noses. They've done their work for today. It's good for us.'

'You think so?'

'They won't be out looking tomorrow. It's all happened today.'

'I hope you're right. Let's get back on the bridge.'

The turn shook Howard from his green and pleasant lanes, and the sound of Laura's voice from the time when his eyes were working, in the days when he saw as clear as she did. On deck in the uttermost blackout of the night he was in total darkness anyway. Nor would anyone else see much, hear only the hum of engines and a softened rush of water as the bows cut towards the mountainous island. They relied on Cleaver's skill as a navigator, without which, or a warning light, they would hit the shore at fifteen knots and the end would be quick: a line of surf and a tangle of black razor rocks smashing the boat to pieces.

'How much now?' Waistcoat said.

'Half an hour,' Cleaver's cool voice told him. 'Another seven miles.'

'But where's the fucking light?'

'We'll see it, when we get down to four.'

Howard came and went unnoticed, wasn't part of their fixed unity. Each time inside he reconnoitred the relevant wavelengths, heard a few ships asking if any messages had been left for them at the various coast stations. A gabble of voices from Porto Delgado was killed by static, but seemed nothing to concern them. Unable to sit still, he walked to where Scud was keeping watch. 'Anything?'

'No. But I'd like to suck on a fag. Senior Service for preference. Black as pitch, ain't they? I can see the water, but knock all else. I'll be glad when this part's over. I told my wife that when I got back we'd jump in the car and go off to France. Find a nice three-star hotel to relax in. I'll need cosseting by then.'

'Sounds like a good way to get it.'

'You bet it is. Eh, what's that?'

'Is it lightning?'

'No, it's steady. Now it's gone. I must be seeing things. That's the danger. You expect something, then you think you see it, when you don't at all. Got to be careful, because if I tell the chief I see it, who don't because it ain't there for him, he'll have a fit – and that's not a pretty sight. He can't stand somebody who isn't a hundred per cent sure of what he sees.'

'It's not good for his confidence, I suppose.'

'It don't matter all that much. He can pay for them as knows how to see and how to do. He's better than good at that.'

'You can see the light now, though, can't you?'

'I've just caught it. How did you know? You saw it before I did. Are you blind, or aren't you?'

Howard's head went forward, as if to smell the light. 'I felt it, can't tell why. A light in my darkness, and I'll never know where it came from.' I shouldn't have spoken, he thought, but hadn't been able to resist showing off the powers of instinct. 'It must be my sixth sense. Sometimes jumps into action. Is it still there?'

'It is, for sure this time.' He pushed by. 'They'll want to know on the bridge.'

Richard called Waistcoat from his pacing up and down the state room. 'I knew they would do it. More than their legs are worth not to. Straight on, Mr Cleaver. You found it, anyway. Spot on. Right out of the night, and dead on the snout. Send one short flick on the lamp to say we've got 'em.'

Cleaver grunted himself into a ramrod straightness, shoulders back. He didn't need praise. No praise could be good enough. It was irrelevant. Navigation was an art as well as a craft, dependent on confidence and occasional luck, the ability to move in darkness with no points of reference except those last seen in daylight, or sights on stars and planets when the curtains or night were about to come down. You couldn't be praised for what you did, praise not being praise from those who knew nothing about the profession. 'Just stay on course, I'll tell you when to reduce speed.'

'It's flickering,' Waistcoat said. 'What's it saying?'

'The letter A,' Richard told him.

'Alpha,' Cleaver added. 'Aleph, if I'm not mistaken.'

'Exactly what it should be.' Waistcoat rubbed his hands. 'All's well for the right letter. Anything else and we'd about turn for twelve hundred miles.'

'No need,' Cleaver said. 'Keep straight on. On and on, Richard.' Other lights jewelled faintly up the hills behind. 'Ignore those. Hold the correct one in your mind's eye. He'll send the A now and again, so there'll be no mistaking.'

'I see it,' Richard said. 'No problem.'

'Twenty minutes yet,' Cleaver uttered. 'A piece o' cake, now we've got their signal.'

Killisick came in with a tray of mugs, and each took one silently. 'Cocoa,' Ted said, 'with plenty o' milk and sugar.' He put one in Howard's hand. 'You'll need it as well.'

'Fuck off,' Waistcoat hissed. 'You'll wake the dead. It's lights out and silence till we hit the beach. And the same then.'

Ted whistled a tune as he went.

'Cocoa,' Waistcoat snarled, but he drank it. 'Reminds me of that time when I . . .'

Richard broke in. 'Me too.' Neither he nor anyone else needed to say where. 'It's good stuff.'

'Dead slow, no lights, and not a squeak, that's what I said, wasn't it, Mr Cleaver?'

'It was, sir, and we heard you.'

'Give 'em another glow on the flasher to say we're still on our way. If theirs changes from an A to an N it means we can't land.'

'It's still on A,' Richard said.

'I know, cunt. Even I can recognise it now.'

Richard, as always on such trips, had one of his handguns snug and loaded in the pocket of his naval jacket. He carried it, as a guarantee against what contingency he didn't care to think about. He saw no situation in which he might use it, not in a normal state of mind anyway, which he had no intention of ever abandoning. But a cutting weal flashed over him at Waistcoat's rebuke, and to take out the gun now and squeeze the trigger at the back of his head seemed a short journey towards teaching him a lesson, except there would be no improvement in his behaviour because he'd be dead. Waistcoat had made worse ripostes before, but in less tense circumstances, and wrapped them up in his usual fluent abuse at which you could only smile. Silence as always was good for dignity, and the temptation passed, though he worried that it had come, not liking to have the moods that shot over him influenced by any man.

Waistcoat swayed, as if seeing double from the whisky. 'It's the best sight in the world.'

'A beautiful letter,' Cleaver agreed. 'The first in the alphabet.' Howard thought if he had been a detective trying to work out what recognition light they would choose for the landing he would decide it had to be an A. People like them would naturally pick the first out of twenty-six. It was simple because easy to remember, and they wouldn't have to think further, and be less liable to detection because it was so obvious. They might even imagine it to be safer. They could persuade themselves it was an inspired choice. Having selected it they wouldn't then have to sit around a table sweating for hours about what letter to use.

Yet maybe a detective would never imagine they'd use an A, that they couldn't resist trying to choose something else. In the contest of wits, however (as he looked at the identikit picture of a drug runner pasted up on the wall) he would conclude that to choose A as an identifying letter might be the most subtle move of all.

'You can't go wrong with it,' Waistcoat said. 'Number one. Always go for number one. It's the only thing that makes sense.'

Richard, joined to him by hope if nothing else, saw no reason not to. Yet he was beyond caring, as usual at this stage. The black emptiness of the sea had entered him, a void rarely if ever to be filled, but giving energy for the job in hand. They would refuel, get the bags on board at the double and after the delivery had been seen to he would do no more such trips. No one can be lucky forever. The time had come to enjoy the money in the bank, and find ways for his life to change.

The light twinkled every few seconds, short-long, short-long, like an eyelid trying to shake off an insect that insisted on settling. He took the wheel, going directly towards it, the boat closing with each beat of the engines. Every pull of the water, and he waited for an announcement from the lookout that the shadow of land was close. 'Won't be long,' Howard said. 'I smell it, feel it for sure. Trees and dry soil.'

'Like a canary down a coalmine for the first whiff of gas,' Waistcoat said. 'We're lucky to have you on board. How far, though.'

'Two miles?' he suggested.

'Nautical or statute?' Cleaver must have smiled.

'Oh, statute. They're the ones I'm used to.'

'He's right. I see it, dead ahead.' A trace of excitement came into Cleaver's tone. 'It'll be rocks to starboard for a mile. Then starboard again, and we're right in.'

Scud came to say he had also seen it. 'Even the fucking blind man got it before you did,' Waistcoat said. 'Get back and keep a sharper butcher's. Tell Paul it's half speed. Hear me, Richard?'

'Half speed.'

Black palisades of rock to the right cut them off from the west. 'I'm keeping well clear.' He would need all the tricks of the trade to get in, foam at the base of the rocks as if magnetised to pull the boat onto them, positive touches at the wheel to fight it.

'I see the point up ahead where we turn,' Cleaver said. 'Plain as a pikestaff. We'll make it now.'

'Dead slow when we go to starboard,' Waistcoat said.

'Less than a mile to the beach. We'll see the gravel soon. Let the anchor go half a cable from shore. Head for their light.'

Howard listened again on VHF. Maybe those who normally used the channels were as intent on radio silence as themselves, but if so, why? A clear and empty spectrum seemed strange, as if a trap was laid, unless it was a coincidence. Someone was usually gabbling, yet he'd heard no one since the skipper's demise on the sailing yacht. Perhaps the missive in morse, posted before leaving, had reached its destination, and even Jehu had made land to provide more gen. Unable to sit, he went back on deck as the anchor rattled down. 'I smell a lot of land now.'

'And well you might,' Richard said. 'If you could see the slit we've got into you'd say it was a miracle we found it. Just a touch of beach, no more than a few yards, and a track winding down to it, though how they got Land-Rovers here I'll never know.'

'Midnight,' said Waistcoat, 'as near as damn it, so let's shift our arses.'

Howard heard the oars of a dinghy coming from shore. Time to lean against the rail and guess what was going on. He wanted to smoke but didn't care to hear Waistcoat's screams of rebuke. The earth seemed all around, even behind them, the way they had come. A strange yet homely smell of warm but cooling vegetation mixed with that of the sea. A rattle of the gangplank, and a heavily built man was careful to put one step before the other as he came on board. 'Have you got it?'

The English voice sounded more genuine in its class than Waistcoat's, cool and uppercrust. 'We have our lot, if you have yours.'

'There's no problem, then.'

'None at all, old man. They'll begin loading as soon as I say it's time. Enough juice to get you back as well, though it was no joke hauling it to this godforsaken spot.'

'Come to my cabin, and I'll hand over the wherewithal.'

'Expect no less.' The man laughed. 'But no false-bottomed suit-cases, eh?'

'Not where I come from,' Waistcoat said, as if he had met someone, Howard thought, on an even higher level of villainy, but couldn't openly curse him as he would like.

The crew stood waiting. 'Wouldn't mind going ashore for a drink,' Cannister said. 'I was in Delgado once, and met a girl. Had a wonderful time. Got robbed of every penny!'

'You'll have to come back as a tourist,' Scud said. 'Me, I don't want to see the place. There's plenty better in the world.'

'I'd rather go to Greece,' Ted put in. 'Topless bathing on the islands, and all that. There's one where all the German women are lesbians. I forget what it's called. I hear they rip you to bits if you get close. France is safer. Was that a plane I heard?'

'No,' Cannister said, 'it was a car up the coast. They've got the fuel on the beach, by the look of it.'

'You've got good eyes. We'd better not drop a barrel, or we won't get home.'

Waistcoat and his business partner had done their dealing, and when the door opened Howard heard the man say: 'I'm sending one of my crew back with you – surplus to requirements.'

Waistcoat must have nodded. 'Yeh, all right' – and when the man was settled into his boat he turned to the others: 'Come on, then, get to work. We're loading any minute, diesel one way, dope another.'

Richard, through his night-vision monocular, the latest thing from Russia, watched the boat pulling from the shore. Three people were getting packages and barrels over the rocks. One was a tallish woman, fair hair moving in the breeze, obviously not someone local. The dinghy went ashore with Waistcoat, as if he wanted to know what he was getting. Now was the time for someone to put a knife in his back. Richard waited for the sound of a pig being killed, a squealing to wake the whole island, if not the dead. Music to his ears, he and Cleaver would get the boat home – though not without fuel. But the squeal didn't come, and the signal was given for loading.

Howard heard each piece of cargo bump onto the deck, slide along and be snatched for stowing below, a counterpoint to barrels of diesel for refuelling the engines. Cinnakle dipped a finger in each to sniff the quality (not too much water mixed in so that they would stall within the twelve mile limit and get caught) while Waistcoat fussed and put each bundle to his nostrils, as if any clue of quality could get through the wrapping, gave a pat to one, the rump of a loving girl – or boy, Richard thought, never certain, but he made sure each of the forty packages was checked and counted, and concealed in prepared hidey-holes below.

Howard wanted to know where they were, but was pushed so hard at the doorway, almost a punch, that he fell against the rail, and only the strength of his sending arm stopped him splashing into the drink, where there would be no air-sea rescue service to pick him up. 'Out of the fucking way,' Waistcoat said.

Richard steadied him. 'Are you all right?'

'As far as I can tell.'

'Keep your mouth shut. Nobody likes questions of that sort. Get to the stern, and melt into the night.'

But he stood close enough until everything relevant had been brought on board. The dinghy came for its final call, and Waistcoat said, at someone stepping onto the deck: 'What the fuck do you want?'

A woman answered. 'I'm going back to England with you.'

'Oh no, you're not.'

'I should have gone a couple of weeks ago from Turkey, but I couldn't, so I'm going now.'

'I have all the crew I want.'

'It's all right,' she said, 'I'm only hitching a lift.'

Howard sat, head towards his knees, like a man with perfect sight trying not to look.

'What's in that sack?'

'Pineapples. It's my contribution to the galley. Clarence said I was to come,' she told Waistcoat. 'He promised I'd go back with you. He won't be needing me for a while.'

'And I don't need you, either.'

'Well, you have to take me. It's part of the deal.'

Howard hadn't heard anyone exchange contrary words with Waistcoat, and sensed the explosion on its way. 'Yeh, but he didn't say it was a fucking woman.'

The expletive must have set her off: 'Yes, but I don't suppose he said it was a man, either,' she called, in a tone of fiery sarcasm. 'But I'm as good as any fucking man, you shit-head, so I'm here.' She dropped the bag of pineapples. 'Let some prick take these to the galley. I'm shagged out and pissed off, and I want to get my head down.'

'Ted!' Waistcoat shouted, in a voice of panic and loathing.

'Yes, sir, what is it?'

'Get these fucking things out of the way, then we're shoving off.' He kicked the bag, and sent one of the choice fruits so far it only stopped rolling at Howard's feet. He picked it up, and held the delicious scent to his face.

TWENTY-NINE

Engines bumped into life, a monotonous song that wouldn't stop until the boat was tied up to be unloaded, a song of words that became his own, saying to himself over and over all she had said, fair words and foul, repeated and reiterated, anagrammed and oxymoronned, words that had put Waistcoat in his place and caused fruit to scatter over the deck. The Goddess had boarded the *Flying Dutchman*.

He lay in his bunk and hoped for oblivion, yet too inert to vanish from the world by slipping over the side. Dreams were all he had been given in life, had ever been able to handle. They'd had their uses in lulling him not too painfully through months and years, but one had stepped from his theatre of fantasy, and walked into reality, macerating his ability to play any part.

Anchors up, the boat headed from the cove at a carefully measured rate. Everyone knew what they had to do and how to do it, but he couldn't move. Not a finger would uncurl to get him on deck. Words from the outer world shot clear into his brain, crisp islands of sound, an effort needed to unite one with another in terms of meaning.

Clear the headland, and then it's a course of zero-one-zero, half speed till o-one-thirty. Open up and get as far north as the boat will go before daylight. Lady Moon is still in bed, wind pulling her blankets off and laying them on again. All well because, they said, by morning we'll be beyond the aircraft reporting point at Position Bravo. Let them chew on that. He heard laughter, as if more than a few drinks were being sucked from the leather covered flasks everyone carried, and now thought it all right to use. Forgive them, Lord, they know not what will happen.

He sensed the bumping and sliding of soft packets around him, even under his feet it seemed. If customs officers marched on board they wouldn't find a thing, such was the idea of the others, unless he explained that the only way was to take the boat apart, board by board and strut by strut. 'I saw them bring it on. All of it.'

'What did you see? Don't make us laugh. How could you see anything?'

'It's what I know. I felt it. Heard. Forty or more parcels of hard drugs.'

And they would search the boat, the crew looking on with anger and fear. 'We can't find a thing,' adding when they turned to Howard: 'Don't make stupid jokes. We're busy men. We don't like it.' After their departure he would be allowed off the boat, though not get far before the knife struck or the bullet made a hole in him. The same for Richard.

If someone had taken in the sense of his morse letter the customs would dismantle the boat anyway, and he would stand in panic with the rest, including Judy. The game had been turned upside down, because her skipper had wanted to make up for ordering her to stay behind in Turkey. In the Azores her replacement had appeared, and she was being sent back on their morris-dancing vessel because it saved the price of an airline ticket. Or maybe it was her idea. She liked boats, was at home on them, thought the trip would be more interesting, even adventurous (it certainly would) going back this way. What was the price of an airline ticket to them?

He wanted a helicopter to come down now, didn't want to wait, the game up at the right time. But any time was the right time. They knew exactly what was going on, playing cat and mouse, aware of where the boat was, the direction it was heading. They would strike when the boat reached international waters, the crew lulled by thoughts of a quiet trip. Or they would lurk in ambush at a landing place on the British coast and catch whoever was meeting them as well.

He'd wanted to hear her, to be close, and would now give any-thing to mellow down the banging of a heart unable to manage the sudden gift. He wanted to get up and tell her what was on board (as if she didn't know) and what he had done about it, but they were on their way together, and he could reveal it anytime. She would think him a crazy old man on the *Flying Dutchman* who had been too long at sea. She might even mention his lunacy to Waistcoat.

The door banged open. 'What are you doing?' Richard called, 'at a time like this? I know you're tired. We all are. But pull yourself together. Get on the radio, and find out if anyone's tracking us. Time for shut-eye later.'

People with nothing to worry about slept easily at night, so there was less traffic on the airwaves. His legs ached, knees pressed against the table. Voices on VHF were too distant even to make out the language. Ships or smaller boats were out there. He went on deck with the mobile receiver and its ferrite direction finder, the bearing undoubtedly east, though with so much metal around he couldn't be too specific. Louder chat might indicate a vessel coming towards them, which he mentioned to Waistcoat, on the bridge with Richard and Cleaver.

'You've got to expect it. As long as there isn't a boat coming the other way as well. Still, they might get us on their radar soon, the nosey bastards.'

'Not while we're heading for Polaris.' Cleaver's tone was as close as he would allow to gloating. 'All worry gone when that little sparkler's in sight.' He turned to Howard. 'Listen some more. You're doing well.'

The talk was a shade clearer, therefore closer, timbre and rhythm telling him it wasn't English. After a further report he went on deck, a treacle of cooling blackness all around. Cigarette smoke came against his face.

'I can't sleep. There's too much going on.'

He hadn't heard her approach. 'Well, so it is. Or it might be.'

'I wouldn't mind knowing what.'

'Nothing to worry about.' He fumbled for his cigarettes, and took a step closer. 'Will you light one for me? Keep it down, though. We're still under blackout regulations.'

'I don't care about that.' She gave him hers, without thought. Very matey, but that was the kind of person he'd always known her to be. He tasted the dampness, and a faint flavour of lipstick, a kiss by proxy. She lit one for herself. 'What's your job on this jumblies boat?'

'I'm the wireless hack, listening for any opposition.'

'A sparks, eh? They don't generally carry one.' After a silence she asked: 'How long till we get back?'

He stroked the rail, as if it breathed for them both. 'Are you in a hurry?'

'I've someone to see. The other boat's gone to the Med. I want to see my girlfriend.'

She was so close he touched her when the boat lurched, its course coming into line with the north. 'Can you see anything?'

'No more than you can.' She laughed. 'What a funny question.'

'I can't see, even when I look.'

'How do you mean? You're getting a bit philosophical. I'm not used to that.'

Her voice was so much the same, locked in by darkness, and the rushing of the sea, that he wondered if he wasn't hearing it as in former days, earphones clamped, and she chatting to a male interloper who had wandered onto the wavelength. 'Can you see me smile?'

'If I look close. Your eyes are fixed. I'm not surprised you can't see. How do you do it?'

He jumped the inches, hands going over the features to take in her image. 'Like this.'

'What the hell?' she cried.

'Sorry. I wanted to see you. I wanted to make out what you looked like.'

'Oh, that's all right then. I've never had that excuse before. Very funny.'

'I really am.'

'What are you talking about?'

'It doesn't make any difference being blind if you're a wireless operator.'

'You've got to be joking.'

'You could even say it sharpens the ears wonderfully.'

'I've never met anyone who's blind.'

To say he'd caught her in a rare area was more than right. She'd never been such a way before, and since it was something to his advantage he sensed an element of cheating. 'Not many people have.'

'You aren't kidding?'

'Who would, about that?' He wallowed in the closeness of her voice, and her face as she looked closer for confirmation. 'I only wish I could be.'

'What sort of a boat have I landed on?'

'You may well ask.'

'Was it in a car crash, or have you been like that from birth?'

There was a possibility of her spending a long time in jail, because sitting at his radio night after night he had malignly influenced the turn of events which brought her before him. Back at the radio he might hear voices closing in on them by the minute, a pair of powerful launches crossing searchlights over the bridge, a bellow through megaphones for them to heave-to. The jaunt would be over. She would be handcuffed, and led away with the rest of them.

Better to be with her while he could, time too valuable to waste on such imagining. So many emotions beat at him. He had expected, for all his trickery – sheer bluff – to hear no more than a few casual words, either on the beach or on the boat. She would drift away, and he would be satisfied. Now she was close enough to touch, waiting for him to talk, which was all he wanted, when he should be at the radio, working on a scheme that might save them. 'In an aeroplane. I caught it over Germany, at the end of the war. I was twenty, and haven't seen anything since. I feel I can see you, though.'

'Oh, right! You are a strange bloke.'

'I might not have been, but for this. You're a rare person yourself.'

'How can you know?'

Nights at the radio made her voice as familiar as a friend not seen for a while.

'I suppose it was the way you jumped on board and said you were hitching a lift home. In no uncertain terms, when you didn't seem wanted. You really let rip at the chief.'

She laughed. 'I don't take any nonsense from men like him. He knows who I am. I was on a boat with him on the Med once, for a month's cruise. He treated me like rubbish, until I let him have it. He wasn't so bad after that, though I still think he's a nasty piece of work. I don't often swear, but sometimes you have to.'

'You seem in a hurry to get to England.'

'I suppose so,' she said after a pause. 'I have a girlfriend, and she might be there. She might not be, though. You can never be sure with her. She's got a boyfriend, so maybe she's still in Barcelona.'

He didn't want to hear about Carla. 'Take my hand, and lead me to the wireless place. I can do it on my own, but it'll be easier with you.'

'Why not?' Her fingers closed over his. 'I've done some funny things in my time. Woof-woof! I'm a blind man's dog! Come on, then. The thing is,' she said as they went along, 'I'm not sure about my girlfriend anymore. Everything's getting too difficult for her. I sometimes think I might be wearing her out. And it's hardly ever possible for us to get together. When she's in Spain I can't phone because her boyfriend might answer, so she told me not to. We used to natter over the radio, but the skipper put a stop to it.'

She talked openly because he was blind. He was much older and not involved, so he too could be frank. 'Do you prefer women to men?'

'I don't know. It's just her.'

No more talk. She found him the place, and he tuned in. The voices were no louder, because the boat was pushing along at top speed. A clipped police menace, obvious in any language, was still there. Judy stood by, thinking that if Carla wasn't too far off she would ask to use the VHF, or perhaps even shortwave. 'You could call her, if she's still on the boat,' he said, knowing her mind. 'Except that you would blow our cover. Our lives depend on radio silence.'

'How did you know what I was thinking?'

'I put myself in your place. Everyone has a sixth sense, or whatever number it is, except they don't know how to find it. Being blind, it comes more readily. I developed it over the years.'

'I've often wondered about that. I get a whiff of it when I'm in love, and then it lets me down.'

'If you're blind you have to be in love all the time, with life, just to keep going.'

'Right! I can see that. Do you want another cigarette?'

'Yes, it'll help me stay awake.'

'I'm feeling dead beat.' She drew her chest away from his shoulder. 'But my eyes won't close. Tensed up, I suppose. I always am.'

Waistcoat put his head around the door. 'Any news, Sparks?'

'They're still there, but they aren't gaining on us.'

'Tell us if they do, and we'll dance a few zig-zags.'

'I know what you picked up on the island,' she said when Waistcoat had gone.

'It might be best if you didn't. If we get caught with this lot on board we'll get twenty years each.'

'Probably forty,' she laughed.

The earphones rested on the back of his neck. 'Why did you choose to hitch a ride with us, in that case?'

'It's a free trip. And I have a date. Or might have. The trouble is I'm not sure anymore. Do you think we'll make it?'

'We'll get away from here, but they may be waiting for us up-Channel.'

'Why do you think that?'

'It's a risk we always take.'

'Does Waistcoat know about the odds?'

'I could be wrong.'

'I hope so.'

'I usually am, so don't worry.'

She felt safer with such a man on board, who wasn't the usual hyped-up yuppie or jailbird hysteric. He might be blind, but at least he was more interesting. 'Oh, I never worry.'

'I know how to put you to sleep,' he said. 'I have a technique.'

'You're not a dirty old man, are you?'

He was glad of her laugh. 'Of course I am.' While sleeping she could no longer talk to him, but with four or five days still to go there would be enough time. He followed her to her bunk.

'Lie on your stomach, and I'll massage the back of your neck. I do it for my wife when I'm on shore. You'll be off in no time.'

'I'd like that.'

'I must do another stint at the radio first, but I'll be back.'

'You work hard.'

'Only at times like this.'

The wavelengths were clear, all voices gone, so everyone was happy. Even Cleaver at the wheel was humming a tune. He hurried as safely as he could back to Judy.

His hand, touching her hair, rested gently on her neck, fingers open-ing along the flesh then coming together, firm without pinching. He pondered on the nature of a miracle. No such thing. He made it happen. His mind was beamed onto making her relinquish all connections with her troubled world, threads snapping one by one to let her float into the clear space of nothingness so that he could have peace for a while and take in her apparition.

'I've heard of blind healers,' she murmured. 'There used to be one in Boston.'

'Tell me about it tomorrow. You need sleep.' He wanted oblivion for her even more than she wanted it for herself, needed her to be unconscious so that space for her own thoughts would come back. Kneeling, and leaning forward, both hands worked a rhythm, thumbs coming in from the sides of her neck and pushing a short way upwards, a forceful semicircular motion over and over to the beating of engines carrying them for the moment out of danger.

A changed rate of breathing told him she was asleep, a faint whistle, the slightest snore, but he kept on a few minutes beyond the usual number so that she wouldn't wake at the drawing back of his touch. The insomniac put in such a way to rest either woke up in half an hour, assuming they had been under for days, or they didn't come to until the clock had gone round, thinking they'd slept only a few minutes.

The treatment exhausted him, so he fumbled his way to the bridge, where he sensed people standing around in silence, nothing left to say. The blacked out boat was on one of Cleaver's courses taking them out of trouble, but they might have been dead, turned to stone as the boat drove under its own will, taking the crew on a straight line till there was no more fuel, the timbers went rotten, and it quietly sank. He and Judy, the last people alive, would go under together.

He went back to the comfort of the radio, tuning into morse on shortwave as if to connect himself again to the world beyond this ghostly boat. At the same time as finding Judy it had turned into the *Flying Dutchman*, and he a fully paid-up but soon-to-be-superannuated member of the crew, because everything had its price and there was only one lump sum for that.

A telegram rippled to a Philippines' coastal station, a member of the crew requesting his brother to take two kilos of the best ice-cream to his wife on her birthday. A tanker wanted anchorage at Antwerp in two days' time, giving its position in the eastern Atlantic. Normal life went on, traffic passing to and fro beyond the limbo of their boat speeding God knew where.

Laughter came from the bridge, the touch of glass against glass as he got close. Voices on VHF had faded, leaving them free and beyond range of interception, he said.

'Come in, Howard,' Waistcoat said. 'We're through the worst. The bags are on board, and all's well with the world. Have a drink, and a smoke if you like. We've got enough of it. Or you can have a shoot-up – in the arm though, not the arse!'

'You want it, we have it,' Scud cackled.

'Except it's teetotal with the powdered stuff,' Waistcoat said. 'It's too top quality for the likes o' you lot. Just plain whisky's good enough.'

'Start meddling with the cargo,' Cleaver said, 'and we'll end up chasing skuas in Spitzbergen. It's not the stuff to indulge in at sea. Thank you, Chief, I will have another, but that's my limit. Then I'll go out and get a fix. There are stars about at the moment. You can take her in a tad, Richard. Make it zero-five-zero, and we'll be all set for hearth and home.'

Howard felt the glass at his hand, then a slice of bread and salami from Ted's tray, as half starved as the rest of them, after more excitement for him, he thought, than anybody else.

'You run a good ship,' Cleaver's jaws munched. 'Can't fault the food, Mr Killisick.'

'Cut yer throat if yer did,' Ted said.

'Cucumber's a bit off, though.'

'It's been more than a week, Mr Cleaver,' Scud put in. 'Ted ain't God.'

'No, he's not.'

'More than my life's worth, not to provide a good cook with all the trimmings.' Waistcoat was relaxed and in humour. 'That, and a shit-hot navigator, and we can go anywhere.'

'Thank you,' Cleaver said.

Refills were handed out, the tray passed around. 'How's that tart who came on board?' Waistcoat said.

'She's sleeping,' Howard told him.

'I know her. She bumped in to the big gaffer a long time ago, so he gets her a job now and again. Otherwise she'd be serving in a chippy, or creating hell somewhere. Family man, the gaffer is, though I'd like to sling her overboard. She's got too much lip.'

'I don't think anybody would like that,' Richard said.

'I know they wouldn't. But she was on the radio, the one who flapped her mouth off. She should be taken to task.'

'Better you than me, Chief,' Scud said.

'At least we've got pineapples for a day or two,' Ted remarked. 'Which was thoughtful of her. I can use 'em.' He laughed so merrily that Howard heard his teeth rattle. 'They'll keep scurvy out, and that can't be bad.'

'It's two o'clock, so we'd better get some shut-eye,' Waistcoat said. 'Except for Mr Cleaver, and you, Cannister. Richard and Scud can take over at six. I'm knackered, so nobody wake me. You can sort out the watches among yourselves. I want to see dolphins in the morning. Polish my sea glasses, Ted, when you've got a minute.' He was on his way out. 'There's fog all over 'em.'

THIRTY

Nobody was willing in their work, certainly not with a smile, as if landing and loading, and getting away from the island, had worn them to the bone. Whatever was done had a sullen air about it, no banter, not even grumbling – the worst sign of all. Only Cleaver didn't seem unusual, obsessionally occupied in obtaining astronomical fixes of the highest possible accuracy. Cannister and Scuddilaw, when not on watch, sat behind Howard at the radio and played brag, swearing when on hands and knees to find the rolling ten pee pieces. Ted Killisick's prowess at the stove had gone a step down in dexterity compared to the first week out. On the second day north Waistcoat was seen to lope from his quarters and throw both plate and food into the drink, without even the spirit to berate his cook.

The sea was churlish, grey and uncooperative, so had no say in cheering them up, though the boat drove neatly on. A gull came from no one could guess where, but after an hour or so took off, as if unwilling to stay with such a mournful crew.

Each did his job, as he had to, but whatever joy had been there before had now dissolved. They lived only to reach home, not even that at times, merely to stay alive from one minute to the next.

'We're such a glum lot,' Richard said, 'you'd think the bottom had fallen out of the glass.'

Cleaver grunted, unsympathetic to what he regarded as a drop in morale. 'It's always the same after a big pick-up, though this is a bit worse. I don't like it. You'd think everyone was locked in his own thoughts because they can't decide what they would do with the stuff on board if they had it to themselves. The mood will lift, I've never known it not to.'

336

'What if it doesn't?'

'I'd rather not think about that. But if it doesn't, you and I might have a job on our hands.'

'Who would you be wary of,' – he didn't say afraid – 'if it came down to that?'

'*Everybody*. But whoever tried anything would be very misguided. Nobody could do it on his own, and if we keep a lookout you and I should be able to spot whoever tries to form a combination. It's a small boat. The conversation between those two cardsharpers is pathetic. Worse than the chief's, every word a swear word, though at least they're opening their mouths again. I don't think they have a moral thought between them. They've got lots of immoral notions, but none so strong as would lead them to doing what we fear. Then there's Paul Cinnakle, who's too much in love with his engines to burn his fingers on a stunt like that. Ted's harmless. And Howard is blind, so we can count him out. He's your loyal ex-serviceman type, and in any case he's besotted with that girl. Follows her round like a dog. Or she follows him, I'm not sure which. As for her, she's useful about the boat. She cleaned up my bunk this morning, told me she didn't mind earning her keep on the trip. So neither of them's plotting anything. Wouldn't know how. He's our radio officer, anyway, and he'll be more than useful when we go up Channel.'

'What about me?' Richard said, by way of humour.

Cleaver polished his sextant mirrors one by one with a spotless yellow cloth and slotted them into place. 'We're the backbone of the ship, and you know it. Both of us know Waistcoat would be useless in the face of adversity. Oh, I know he's got a nose like a shit-house rat, but at bottom he's poor stuff. Never had the Nelson touch. So it's up to us to keep the firm afloat. It's always a fraught situation, going back with stuff on board. Too tempting to expect peace. But if you and I understand each other we can make sure peace is kept. The least sign of hanky-panky, and everyone loses, especially any greedy snipe-nosed tyke who imagines he'll get away with the jackpot.' He slotted his beloved sextant into its box. 'No, we won't have any of that.'

'I thought I'd mention it so that we at least could get things straight between us.'

Cleaver leaned over the chart to mark in the position. 'I'm glad you did. I was wondering if you would. Take her five degrees to port. We're getting bumped around a bit this morning. Damned rice pudding flying about.' Spray came over the windscreen, as if an angry housewife was behind it with a cloth. 'You'd better call the lovers inside.'

The aerials got little vision above the tops of the waves, but Portishead came in strong and crisp so that he could take down the weather. Judy looked over his shoulder, and he kept the earphones off for her to hear the singing morse, on top volume so as not to be drowned by the noise of his typing. Waistcoat, bilious and cantankerous, passed on his way to the bridge, telling him to put the earphones back on. 'That noise gives me the fucking heebie-jeebies. How's it going, though?'

'Fine. Not too rough,' Richard said, when he came in, trying levity. 'We'll keep our powder dry.'

Waistcoat laughed. 'That's all we need. But a few smiles on this pig-boat wouldn't come amiss.'

Richard wondered how he passed the time in his state room. Probably played with his little pocket calculator to see how rich he'd be on getting home. Or he gave his teddy bear a good hiding. This morning he was on a high, eyes more button like even than those of the pigeon Howard had looked after. Or maybe Waistcoat had been at the powder. A few doses all round wouldn't do any harm. 'We'll be getting another forecast from Howard soon.'

'If it's bad ask him to shop around and try to get a better one.'

'I'm sure he's doing his best.'

'Funny bloke, though.' Waistcoat looked over the chart to check the latest position. 'I know he's good at the radio, but I just don't have it in my heart to trust him. There's something about him, and I can't throw it off.'

'Is it because he's blind, yet manages so well?'

'I'm not that fucking stupid.'

'He's all right. I'll vouch for him.'

'I'm sure he is, since you say so. You're like a parrot, though. You say it over and over again. Still, I'll be more than happy when the trip's over.'

'Won't we all?'

He went to his quarters, walking as if the boat was on the smoothest of seas, and Richard at least admired his slick sense of balance, glad all the same to see the back of him. The unstable weather was enough to deal with, though there was no sense not trusting a bloke just because you didn't like him. He handed the wheel to Scud and Cannister. Let them earn their keep. On the way to his bunk he met Howard zig-zagging along with the weather forecast.

'A low in south Finnisterre. We might just clip it. Rougher in Biscay, but we'll cut across that. It's south-east four to five in Sole as well.'

'Doesn't sound too bad,' Richard said. 'I expect we'll hit Blighty in one piece.'

He felt the sea in him, dark layers overlapping, folding into his night space, neutral and causing no fear. 'What does the sky look like?'

'Almost clear, a few whiffs of cirrus, though we're bound to hit the arse end of the front sooner or later. I'll pop this into the chief. He won't be happy, but at least he'll know.'

Howard asked what was being chopped.

'Pineapples,' Judy said.

'I could smell it.'

'I'm doing it on a plate so that I can pour all the juice off for you.'

Ted slid a tray of scones in the oven. 'What about the rest of us?'

'Get lost,' she said, but with a smile. 'He's my man on this voyage. Anyway, you'll still have some fruit. There'll be a share for everybody.'

'Howard's a lucky man, to have someone like you so sweet on him.'

'Of course I am. He put me to sleep first night on board with his magic touch, and I didn't wake for twelve hours. Brought me back to life.' She touched Howard's arm. 'No more insomnia, right?'

He wasn't only hearing her voice from nearby, or coming into the box of his earphones, but the affectionate squeeze meant they were closer than any dream had promised. For some reason she liked him, and his heart was like a drum about to burst at the same rich tone, as rich for him as when she had talked to Carla. He caught hold of the table, fearing he was about to fall.

339

She held him again. 'Don't get too close to the stove.'

Ted laughed. 'Yeh, we don't need you for dinner.'

She passed a glass of the juice. 'A reward, for putting me to sleep.'

'It wasn't so much to do. I'd rather wake you up though, so that you would see the world twice as plainly as you do now.'

Ted put the slices onto a platter, and took it to the bridge. She stopped in her work. 'That sounds like something I need, so I want it, but I can't see it happening. I mean, how could it?'

'For a start, I'd tell you not to bother with your lover anymore. She's not waiting for you.'

'How do you know she's my lover?'

'The tone of your voice. Whoever she is, she's not good enough. You deserve someone who would go to the end of the earth and over the edge for you.'

Each word was followed by regret that he had been stupid enough to say it. He'd even known he was going to before he had. The words spilled, they were in him and always had been, and wouldn't be wished back. No stopping had been possible because only in that way could he get directly to how he felt, though it had been plain on first hearing her voice. Words that came were his alone. 'I'm the only person who can make you see. Even though my eyes went bang a long time ago, you'd be a lot better off using what's left so as to sharpen yours. I could show you how to get the best of what's in you.' He couldn't see her, whatever claims were made, had to shape a picture, his skin burning with the effort.

He talked as if they had been close for years, yet she had been on board little more than a day. 'What are you saying? I wonder if you know.'

She was playing at surprise, though her tone was regretful because she wasn't able to take on his mood. She closed her eyes, as if to find out what it was like being blind, and on opening them he had gone.

The radio was tuned to the frequency on which he had first heard her, as if part of her former self might come back and talk to him, an exercise to dull the pain of having spoken so brashly. Yet he couldn't feel ashamed, having nothing to lose. I can say what I like. Happiness was never out of place when you spoke with the honesty of youth.

She stood behind him. 'You're a funny bloke. I was frightened

340

you might walk overboard. Well, not really. I only hoped I hadn't offended you in some way. You're special. Here, you forgot to finish your pineapple juice.'

He drank, the elixir of love whatever happened. 'This is my first long boat trip, so maybe it's going to my head. I function best at the radio, keeping my mouth shut, letting it do the talking for me.'

'I don't mind it, when you talk to me. Not many people have, not properly. It doesn't matter what you say. I love to hear you taking morse, though. It's like magic. Maybe I'll go to college and become a radio officer. They have women doing it on ships now. I could send a message.'

'I wouldn't even need to type it,' he said. 'Your voice would come through with the dots and dashes, and I'd know your "fist". The message would have to be a short one, not more than a few words, because it isn't allowed, to send private telegrams.'

'A short one would be all I'd need. I'd be happy, tapping to you.' She held his hand, bent down and kissed him on the cheek. 'If I did become a radio officer I'd keep myself to myself. I'd be mysterious and quiet, and wouldn't get off with any of the other officers. I'd look very nice in my uniform. But I'd have a peaceful life, which is all I've ever wanted. I can't tell you how tired I am.' She laughed: 'And I don't mean sleepy!'

The exhaustion was similar to his own. 'I knew it the other night.'

'Only you could. Not that I ever show it. I'm paid not to.'

The boat was small enough, but even the largest ship would be seen as small from the moon. 'It's turning rougher.'

'Does it bother you?'

'It's no surprise. I took the forecast.' He didn't care how aggressive the sea became now that she was on board, but stopped himself saying so. Gusts exploded around them, one bang after another as the boat cut over and through the waves. 'All hatches battened, though it shouldn't last long.'

'I'll see if Ted needs help in the galley.' She kissed him again. 'Have a nap. You look done in as well.'

'I'll get my head down for half an hour.'

The sweaty pillow felt like the purest down, his blanket a linen sheet, but sleep wouldn't draw him in. The boat was duck-and-draking on its homeward bound, a caged animal trying to break free, but from what and to where? Sleep in any case was a waste of life. Thoughts were pointlessly tormenting. However mocking wind and buffeting water were produced, the intertial dynamo behind them couldn't drive out Judy's presence. Poignant visions of the boat subsiding into the salty waste didn't alarm him, since they would go down together, though he couldn't say why she should pay the final price for his schemings. He only knew it was hard to imagine reaching land again, because what would he do when he got there? A curtain fell on every scene magicked up by his fevered mind.

Richard took the wheel. The boat seemed alive as it rode one sliding wave after another, up the green silk of a slope then over and through the horizon of white-green foam. Waistcoat came close: 'I can't think I was born for this.'

'We've been in worse.' Cloud was low and ragged but: 'Visibility's not too bad. A tanker over there.' He passed the binoculars. 'North-north-west. Take a look.'

'Where's he going?'

'Coming from Venezuela, I should think. He'll be up Channel before us. I don't suppose he even sees us.'

The glasses were handed back. 'We can hardly hitch a lift, with what we've got on board.'

'We're not exactly lagging behind.'

'I've made enough in this game to get into the airline business. I'm fed up, messing in boats, up to my neck in this shit every time. I'll get myself a Boeing, then we can jet the stuff in in crates. Three hours in the air instead of a week in a motorised bucket. There must be plenty of pilots out of a job.'

'Sounds a good idea,' glad to see him quietened by thinking on something positive. But he came close again: 'I'm still worried about that blind bastard.'

'How come?'

'You brought him on board so that he would keep his mouth shut, right?'

'If I remember. You told me to.'

'It don't much matter now. But what's he going to say when he gets ashore? I mean, is he safe?'

'As safe as any of us. Safer, maybe, if that's possible.' He was far in front of Waistcoat's drift, as maybe he was meant to be. 'He's been useful, and still can be. A bob or two at paying-off time, and he's in it as deep as the rest of us.'

'I expect he will be. But I'm worried, and I don't like to be worried. When I'm worried I feel nagged at, so I want to do something about what's worrying me. Even when I was a kid I didn't like to be worried. I worried a lot when I was a kid. Would the old man come in and try to break my arm again? Would there be anything on the table when I got back home and hadn't been able to half-inch a thing? Had anybody seen me when I snatched the wallet? Every minute of the day and night I worried, so I said that when I grew up I wouldn't let anything worry me.'

'What is it, then, Chief?' Scud said, in from the rain and drek.

Waistcoat pushed by on his way back to the cabin. 'Mind your own fucking business.'

'Bad tempered,' Scud said, 'but who can blame him?'

'He's worried about Howard.'

'He would be, wouldn't he? If it wasn't Howard it'd be one of us. He does worry when he's got nothing on his plate. That's when you've got to be careful, because it means "watch out". He always picks on somebody, and it seems it's poor bloody Howard this time. It's too dangerous to get onto any of us. If he did he might wake up one morning and find he'd got no ear to put an earring in when he goes on the town with his boyfriend. Or he might trip himself up when he goes on deck, and fall into the drink, and nobody'll give him a helping hand back on board because he's been misbehaving. They'd kick his face in and push him back under, like he'd do with any of us if we gave him half a chance.' He rolled a perfect cigarette, in spite of the rocking. 'What's he got against Howard, anyway?'

Richard took the boat over another glassy escarpment. 'He thinks he might blab when he gets ashore.'

'He's off his trolley.'

'He doesn't trust him.'

'Howard mystifies him, that's why. Howard's the sort he likes to hate. You've got to be careful.'

'What would you do?' Richard asked.

'Watch the blind chap every minute you've got.'

'I can't. Will you keep an eye on him as well?'

Scud thought about it. 'Put it like this. If I saw he was about to come to harm I'd do what I could. But it don't look like he'll be needing either of us, not with that Judy around. She's stuck on him, seems to think he's got something. It's just as well.'

'That should take care of it, then.'

'I expect so. But you never know with Waistcoat,' Scud said. 'I'll have a word with the others. Mr Cleaver's only interested in number one, but I expect Jack will understand.'

'The thing was, I promised Howard's wife I'd get him back safe. If he goes overboard we'll all be for the high jump. I can only suppose the chief knows as much.'

'You never can tell. He'd just say he fell, and get us to say the same. We'd have to fall into line to save our necks. But he'd only do such a thing to Howard if he really went off his head, and I don't think he'd do that because there'd be too much to lose. Just tell Howard to give him a wide berth, though it's not easy on a pea green boat like this.'

Richard felt relieved at having put the notion around. Everyone's future depended on the safety of a blind man who – and in many ways it was strange – bound them together as a crew. But if Waistcoat was worried then so was he. Unlike the others Waistcoat never worried without good reason. He's got something on Howard that I don't know about, Richard thought, or he has proof of what some would only suspect. He thinks Howard's jeopardised the trip.

Richard had been uneasy since Howard first proposed coming with them – more like a stipulation. The idea that he was a mole from Interpol, however, was laughable, yet one he couldn't stop popping into his head. Howard had known from the start who they were and what they were going to do, so it was inconceivable that he would do anything to short circuit the trip, especially as a paid up member of the crew unless – a revelation to ice the blood – he had guessed about his fling with Laura.

Perhaps from some stupid notion of marital openness she had told him. There was so much about her he would never fathom that it was easy to imagine her spilling out details of their meetings, with that glassy stare of unreality lighting her up after they had made love. Such a confession would give a little more life to the deadness that was in her, and so Howard, having no other way to get his own back, either on his wife for unnecessarily tormenting him, or on someone who was supposed to be his friend, decided to let it come down, and had found a way to inform on the pick-up before they set out, had arranged a neat little ambush at wherever they landed up-Channel.

Fantasy was running him off. If Laura had talked, Howard would have shown by now that he knew. No man could keep that kind of blow to himself. But if suspicion of treachery goes through my mind, Richard's thoughts went, why should it not lodge in Waistcoat's as well, at least sufficiently to make him wonder. Neither he nor anyone on the boat needed a real reason for distrust – if it was felt strongly enough. When intuition pointed to a rat, motives followed, and among so few people, quartered in a space of wood that became smaller the longer they were on it, and in so large an ocean, a darker cloud was generated than any swirling across the sky.

'I'll take over.' Cleaver, wrapped in a hood and oilskins, came in from his turn about the deck. Pipe smoke spread smells of burning kipper over the bridge. 'You look all in.'

'Nothing one of Ted's fry-ups won't cure.'

'Ah,' he exclaimed, 'it's good to be on a happy ship, even though the chief is off his head again. He's going like a demon at the bottle, pacing up and down the state room. I saw him through the window.'

'Maybe he'll wear a hole in the carpet, if he walks for long enough, and slide down into the briny.'

'Perfect,' Cleaver said. 'But it'd take all of us down as well. I wouldn't like to share hell with the likes of him.'

'I was going to have a chat with him, but maybe I'll leave it till he calms down.'

'Take longer than that, I should think,' he puffed. 'Give him a day or two. Wait till he's all fair and square in that little pink paradise he's got fixed up in Harley Street.'

*   *   *

Darkness brought isolation, talk minimal, but Howard was never without human noise, either voice or morse. On upper shortwave he heard navigation warnings from Karachi, good to know life went on beyond their world, and he the only one who had firm evidence of it. Warship and anti-aircraft practice was announced, coordinates given where firing with live ammunition was to happen, all craft told to stay clear of the danger zone.

Judy read over his shoulder, and wished they were sailing near Karachi. 'I'd be on the sun deck getting a tan, and looking forward to a nice hot curry when we landed.'

'Have you been that way?'

'No. One day I hope. Would you like to go?'

With you I would. 'Maybe I will.'

'You have a funny way of speaking, as if you see too much to use words. You jump your phrases a bit. I like it. I never know what you're going to say till you say it, not like everybody else.'

'Do I fascinate you, then?'

'Utterly, you old thing!'

He laughed. 'I suppose I might, being so much older. You've seen more of the world than I have, yet you think I'm wiser in some way. Well, I don't see it like that.' He paused, then went on. 'Did I tell you I was in Boston a few months ago? It's a nice place. I liked it. Went for a holiday. I'd rather be there than near Karachi, to tell the truth.'

He felt a shock run through. 'Eh! I know Boston. I have relations there. I've stayed often.'

'Maybe I was looking for you.'

'There you go again, jumping ahead. I wasn't there, though, was I?'

'You might have been.'

'Oh, right. You make me think it would have been nice if I had.'

'Walking with your girlfriend – and I would have been taken by your voice as you talked to her.' He enjoyed going close enough to be found out, felt excitement in them both. 'We wouldn't have got to know each other, but I'd have felt a thrill as you passed by.'

'I wanted to take my friend to Boston, but we never made it. I'm beginning to think I'm more in love with her than she is with me. It's flippin' amazing how often it's been like that in my life.'

'Great natures make big mistakes – if mistakes they are.'

'I wish I could talk to her. Have you got shortwave in all this gear?'

'There's the transmitter. My fingers have been figuring it out. How close are we, do you think?'

'She might be near Spain. Close to Corunna, perhaps.'

'The day after tomorrow you could try. If she was listening you'd get her loud and clear, but the chief would have us thrown overboard if he caught us using a transmitter.'

She stretched back on the seat, and he wondered, not for the first time, if her kindness was only because she wanted to get at the transmitter. He would be glad enough to help, would at least have the privilege of being remembered by her. 'You can try if you like. It's nothing special.'

'To me it would be.'

She wanted to know why. So did he, the blind leading the unblind, he thought drawing her close. 'I'm satisfied if I can do something for you.'

'I'm not sure I'm worth it.'

'Who is? Yet everyone is. Best not to ask, unless you want me to say I'm in love with you. I hope it doesn't strike you as strange. Imagine I'm not blind.'

She couldn't keep away from him, that much he knew. When there was no work in the galley she would come to find out what he was doing, wanting to talk, and hear what he had to say. 'I do,' she said. 'I've got used to you, even in so short a time. I feel something for you, though I don't know what. I don't want to know. There's just something good about being with you.' She put her arms around him, lips kissing his. He smelled her hair, the fresh trace of perfume, felt her breasts against him, close bodies providing solace for them both.

THIRTY-ONE

Waistcoat shouted for him to come in. Sunshine made a rising and falling line across the state room, as Waistcoat farted what sounded like the first bar and a half of 'The Sorcerer's Apprentice'. Richard couldn't think such peace would last. 'Have a drink,' he was told.

A good start, though a bad one was usually a better omen. When Waistcoat was pushed into liberality it was time to watch out. 'A short one. I like to keep my wits while running the ship.'

'Don't we all.' He lounged on the sofa. 'Best to start that way from the beginning.'

'I can't fault that. Cheers!'

'Too fucking right you can't. But you boobed over bringing that blind man on board. I've known for a few days now that he's sold us up the river. Or he's tried to.'

Richard thought he deserved to sit for the work he had put in, but wouldn't in such company, deciding to save it for when he could get his head down at home, his usual need after a trip. Waistcoat was talking from more than intuition, however. 'What makes you think that?'

'No think about it. You remember that pigeon he was so sweet on? The ship's pet. What a soft heart he's got, everybody said. Superstitious lot, sailors. Not superstitious enough, if you ask me. I was standing on the top deck for a bit of air, and the fucking bird flopped at my feet. Lost its way, I suppose, and came back, after blind man sent it off. It was half dead, so I wrung its neck. Then I noticed the capsule on its leg. Opened it, didn't I? Read the message. Some scribble I couldn't make out, or thought I couldn't. A blind man can't do copperplate, can he? I was about to throw it overboard after the pigeon, but I put it in my pocket. Yesterday I took it out and looked at it through a magnifying glass. There's one over on that table. Give it a butcher's, and tell me what you think. It's no get-well message, I can tell you.'

Hard to shake anything from the maze of hieroglyphic scratches. For a while he thought the only sense must have come out of Waistcoat's disordered brain. The small oblong of cigarette paper had been scored on by a sharpened dark leaded pencil, and the clear result, enlarging as his arm went up and down and held the glass steady on its highest magnification, jumped into focus with a position in latitude and longitude.

'It's taking you long enough.'

'I'm getting there.' And so he was, until everything was framed in the glass circle, and he could pick out the time and date of the position, isolate the name of the boat, and fix the ETA of their reaching the Lizard. If Howard hadn't looked at Cleaver's navigation summary for the trip, which was impossible, he had done some pretty nifty mental arithmetic. Maybe he had heard Cleaver talking to Waistcoat. 'Could be he has a woman pigeon fancier, and wants to let her know when he'd be getting back.'

'Don't fuck with me. If he's tried to do this he's done something else as a back-up. Or before we left. And if it hadn't been for that pigeon going round in circles we'd never have known.'

'At least whoever it was meant for didn't get it, if it was meant for anybody. I don't suppose he thought for a second it would land anywhere.'

'The way you're talking I could almost think you were in on it with him. I don't, though. I just think you've been duped. We all have. He wouldn't have tried sending a message if the ground hadn't been prepared in some way. The only thing is they don't know our ETA now, which could be anytime, though they might keep up a twenty-four-hour watch for a week. And those planes we saw on the way out must have got a lovely clear shot of the boat.'

'You're jumping to conclusions.'

'That's what I'm here for. It's my job. I could cry my eyes out. Do we have to get just outside the twelve-mile limit and scuttle the most valuable boat that ever was? Or wait for the choppers and a couple of customs launches to box us in? If anything like that happens, old blind fuckpig goes overboard with a bullet in each dead eye.'

'You're painting a worst-case scenario.' He might not be, but it didn't hurt to tell him so. Howard had scorched the sensitive skin off his fingers, no mistake, and deserved whatever Waistcoat thought fit to put him through. He had played for something and lost, maybe scuppered all of them, no use thinking otherwise, unless Cleaver could stage a tricky feat of navigation, and get them clear of bother. He had the coolest brain of the lot, but when Richard mentioned such a possibility, he got no response.

'In this game you never give up. I'd like to blind the bastard for what he might have done, but I can't. He's got us there. We'll find out why he wrote that message, though. Go and get him.'

Richard sat, come what may. 'I will by and by. But we ought to talk first.' Talk eye-wash, because Waistcoat, due to the uncertain situation (it always was, at this stage) and the whisky he had put back, was in a classical fit of paranoia, the sort Richard had often witnessed. Not only that: it was powerful enough for him to catch the sickness as well, so he had to work it out of himself as much as Waistcoat: 'You know that whenever I say there's going to be some sense in my head, it turns out that way.' Talk and more talk had to shift a cloud that could gas everybody on the boat. Happily he also knew that Waistcoat, not a man to whom words came readily – except curses – was always amenable to the gift of the gab, and though Richard had never been aware of possessing such a trait, knew he must find it now.

'There'd better be some sense in it.'

'I'll have another shot. It's good whisky.'

'I'm drinking it, aren't I?' He splashed some in. 'Now earn it.'

'It seems fishy to me as well, you finding this message, and the impulse is, as you say, to push him overboard. That's my reaction, but I think it's the wrong one. It would be totally counter-productive. First of all, my opinion is that he was playing a *Boy's Own* game with that pigeon – a stupid one but a game nevertheless. Even in his right mind he couldn't have thought such a scrag end of a bird would get anywhere. It's his first trip to sea, so he had a go at a message to kill the monotony, instead of knitting socks or making a ship in a bottle. As batty as they come, you might say, but he's one of us, and looking forward to a successful end to the trip, even hoping for a bonus so that he can update his wireless equipment at home. You might think about it. But I know you won't forget him at the handout. You're good at that.'

He liked to hear it, but said: 'Cut the shit, and get on with it,' wanting a bit of entertainment at this uncertain stage, something to divert him, and pass the time.

'The help he's given us on the radio since we set off must be taken into account. None of it's been false. And if he'd been intending to give us away he could have done it when we were taking the stuff on board, but he didn't. He's as keen as the rest of us. You say push him into the drink, but if we do, a bullet in him or no, we're going to be in the drek – and no mistake. His wife at home would leave no stone unturned to find out what happened.'

Waistcoat broke in: 'She'd start with you, wouldn't she? and you'd never talk, would you?'

'No, you know me.'

'Nobody knows anybody.'

'That's another matter. Let me go on.'

'Hang your fucking self, then.'

'I've no intention of doing that.' He surely hadn't, because he knew something Waistcoat couldn't, who neither saw nor suspected the compact and loaded Luger deep in the pocket of Richard's thick coat. 'I stay alive and kicking to the end.'

'And so say all of us, but it wouldn't be such a bad way out if things went wrong.'

'They haven't, and won't. If he disappeared that would be the start of our troubles. It's unnecessary, to top him. He's with us. He might have been playing a foolish game but he's a hundred per cent loyal. Loyalty's all he's ever known in life. He's that sort of person. You know as well as I do, better, I suppose, that you've got to be cunning in this game. I've nothing against violence. When it's the only solution I'm all for it, but my idea is to leave him be, to watch him, keep him in view. I'll find out what he knows, what his game is, or was – if there was or is any game.

'In my view,' he went on, 'we could just as easily mistrust any other member of the crew, though I don't at the moment see why. Anybody else could have written on that bit of paper, and done it so that it would

351

look as if a blind man had scribbled it. Or some of them are so subliterate it's the best they could manage. Or they could have done it as a joke, or out of boredom, or to put a bit of excitement into the trip, but for themselves alone. I'm not convinced Howard did it. I only know for sure I didn't, and you didn't. It could have been anybody. But if you think there might be something in what I say about the others for God's sake don't question them, or mayhem will break loose, and we can't afford that. We're a crew, and a good one, not a group of bloody ballet dancers. Just let's carry on as if we're united, and hope that there isn't an idiot in our midst.'

'You make my blood run cold on all counts.'

'So would mine if I thought the matter was serious. Let me pump Howard, and find out whether he did tamper with that bird. I can't think he did, and if he didn't I might find a way of getting a word from the others, though I don't guarantee it. I wouldn't like to upset 'em.'

They stood at the same time, and Waistcoat looked unblinking into his eyes. 'You've earned your whisky. But he'd better find something on the radio with his magic ears that will get us home and save the ship. Any dust in our eyes, and he's dead flesh, whatever the consequences. And so is anybody else. I'm telling you, the first sign of us getting into trouble, and he'll go, whether he's dropped a bollock or not. I'm leaving it to you, but I shan't rest easy till I'm back in London.'

Richard was sweating when he got outside, shoulderblades as wet as the Straits of Gibraltar. Settled as Waistcoat might seem after such a talking to, he was in a dangerous and friable state, though not likely to do anything to put the priceless contents of the boat at risk. He wasn't born yesterday, but needed watching nonetheless.

Howard at the stern was indulging in deep talk with Judy. It made a pretty picture, though Richard couldn't imagine what she saw in him. He couldn't see much good in her, though the scene gave hope, because Howard must realise that if he sold them up the creek she would be in trouble as an accessory, be seen as guilty as the rest – a very unsmart plot on his part. 'Sorry to have to break up your lovers' chat, but I'd like a word with Howard.'

She turned. 'Can't I be in on it?' – eyes saying she had a right to be, didn't care if she did die, as long as she went to hell and back in her own way, though preferably with Howard.

Richard had always been mystified at how most women latched onto totally unsuitable men, as he had known from Amanda staying so long, and at Laura giving herself to him with such blind confidence. Laura had been perfect for him as he had thought she was for Howard, and he could understand how that was, but he had imagined Judy to be very much her own girl on hearing her put Waistcoat in his place. 'We've a bit of private business to discuss.'

'We can finish our talk later,' Howard said to her.

'Oh, right! I'll see how Ted's getting on.'

Their conversation had seemed the sort that could never finish, and Richard felt a shade of envy. 'You could bring us a mug of tea.' He watched her balance against the ups and downs of the deck. 'What were you talking about?'

'This and that,' Howard said.

'Have you told her about the pigeon you looked after?'

'Yesterday I did.'

'And did you mention the message you put into the capsule?'

'What capsule?'

'Giving our position, and the wildly inaccurate ETA back in Blighty.'

'I wouldn't know how to do such a thing. Nor would I if I could. I'm not that stupid.'

He told him something of what Waistcoat had said.

'It could have been a different pigeon he found.'

That was as maybe.

Theirs wasn't the only boat on the ocean, Howard added.

'It didn't seem like that to me. Only a blind man could have made such a dog's dinner of the writing.'

'Or someone who wanted to incriminate me.'

'The chief's convinced it was you.'

Howard was no longer surprised at his ability to lie so calmly and, he hoped, believably, feeling nothing unpleasant about the subterfuge anymore, in view of the situation, all weapons valid in such a fight. Necessity brought the reward of self discovery, however seemingly unethical the means. 'He would, wouldn't he? I'm the most vulnerable man on the boat, that's for sure. It wasn't me, that's all I know. I have no motive.'

'Maybe not. But the chief isn't the man to mess with. I'm being straight with you.'

'Maybe he isn't, but what can I do?'

'The position on the message had the date and time as well, so it's bound to be somebody who knew a bit about navigation.'

'Everybody on the boat does.'

'Well, I got you on board, and I hope you haven't landed me in the shit. You know that if anything happens to us, Judy will be for the high jump as well, not only you and the rest of us? I can't make your game out. Waistcoat was for tipping you in the drink, but I talked him out of it. If you did it, and I don't see who else, you'd better glue yourself to the radio and see if you can get us out of the hole we might be in – whatever happened.'

Judy steadied the large mugs of tea, Richard's slopping over the brim. 'Compliments of Mr Killisick. Can I have lover boy back now?'

'As long as you don't keep him too long from the radio. He has work to do. And so have I.'

'What was all that for?' she asked.

'He was warning me about the chief.'

'Yeh, he's a nasty piece of work.'

He told her about Jehu.

'He's off his crust.' She looked close. 'Did you do it, though?'

He felt the warm breath. Rain had splashed her cheeks, in spite of the hood, beads on her smooth skin. The roughness of the skin on his hand was the same as that on his face, he assumed, an old man and a young woman. 'Nothing came of it.'

'Why do it? I don't understand.'

'I'm not sure. A bit of excitement. A blind man's gamble.'

'You denied it just now?'

'Not much use. But I did.'

She didn't know what to think. The mind spun. She couldn't adjust to what went on behind the sight he didn't have. There was an all-or-nothing aspect about him, wild and unpredictable, amoral you might say – which she found appealing. 'Luckily, the bloody bird snuffed it.

354

Unluckily though, Waistcoat got in on the act. But as long as nothing happens and we get safely ashore everything will be all right.'

He held her hand. 'What if we did get pulled in?'

'Oh, I'll be OK. I hitched a lift. I just hope they'll believe me. I don't have a clue what they've got on board, do I? And you don't know what they've been up to because you're blind.'

'We'll try and swing it that way.'

'I expect we'll land the stuff with no problem. I've been on many boats that have been as lucky. The pigeon didn't make it with the message, after all. I mean, how could it? You are funny! But if the worst happens and I get arrested, maybe the court will award me ten thousand hours community service, looking after a blind man!'

French and English morse stations were bouncing messages up and down the Channel, the best music in the world. Homeward bound, he would like to know whereabouts the stuff on board was to be off loaded, though from now on it had to be none of his business. Any enquiry would lead to ructions that might be fatal. Not that he was afraid. Such threats made life worthwhile, you might say, though he didn't want unnecessary danger, having no intention of vacating the world willingly now that he had found Judy. He could, on the other hand, see the reverse side of the matter, that being with Judy he couldn't care less what happened, having dispensed with the German Numbers Woman, said a last goodbye to Vanya in Moscow, and found out that you could be more than happy on the *Flying Dutchman*.

THIRTY-TWO

The feeling on the boat was of being almost home and, though far from true, at least they had done most of the journey back from the Azores. The Ouessant light flickered forty miles to starboard, Cleaver keeping well clear of the reporting point before heading into the Channel.

'A sight for sore eyes.' Killisick lounged at the galley door. 'I've been longing for this like a woman waiting to get a kid out of her. From now on it's full speed for the off-loading.'

'But where will that be?' Judy said.

'You'll have to ask the chief, only don't. He's no man for questions. He gets the screaming ab-dabs. Wait and see is the only rule. No use riling him when things are going good, except you don't know whether things are going good till you're sitting in a bed and breakfast making sure the Queen's head on your money is the right side up.'

'It doesn't matter to me,' she said. 'I'm only here for the ride.'

'It might be bumpier the next few days.'

'All that time?'

'If we drop it off on the east coast it will be.'

'As long as I can get a train to London.'

'Somebody might give you a lift. Or we'll dump the stuff and then backtrack, all lily-white to Dover. Only a couple of hours then to London.'

'It seems tailor made for me.' They went inside. 'I'll take Howard his supper.'

'And yours as well, while you're about it.' He ladled potatoes, stew, baked beans and bread onto two plates.

She nudged Howard, and kissed the top of his head before he could turn. 'I like my man to eat.'

'Hardly time.' He scooped it with the spoon.

'What's on Radio Four tonight?'

'Can't say. But there's something interesting on VHF.' He plugged in the spare jacks and passed the phones, undecided before she came in as to whether or not he would let her know.

'Can't hear anything.'

'You will.' The bad dream voice was unmistakable, he had heard it scores of times, and now they listened to the clear transmission, the demanding tone of a woman who knew that persistence furthered. Howard couldn't say how long she had been trying, but the voice put him into despair. Once more it came: '*Pontifex* calling *Daedalus*, can you read me, over. *Pontifex* calling *Daedalus*,' again and again, sometimes with hardly a pause. He wanted the sea to open its green mouth and swallow the woman, which was as much of a miracle as him being here with Judy should it do so.

He had anticipated, was ready, but Judy flicked at the VHF transmitter switch as if she had been looking over the equipment during his absence from the cabin, and only waiting for the moment. '*Daedalus* calling *Pontifex*,' she cried, 'I hear you, darling.'

He gripped her wrist and dragged her away, turned the set off. 'If the chief hears you you're dead. And so am I. It's radio silence – until he says so.'

'They can't stop me.'

'Well, I have. You can listen, but not send.' Tears fell onto his wrist, and he wondered how long he could hold her. Hysterical, she pushed and dragged. He had no will to fight, though strength and an instinct for survival overrode him. 'Let's not argue. Leave her alone. Maybe tomorrow you can talk, or the day after.'

He caught the rush, and her body pressed hard, as if she had come at him out of irresistible passion instead of loathing. 'She'll be gone by then.'

So he hoped. She'd be out of range. There was nothing more to say, and he again exerted all his strength to stop her reaching the switch, till hearing Waistcoat: 'What's going on in here. Is it a lovers' tiff, or what?'

'You might say so.'

'I heard the bloody racket on the bridge. You can sort your arses out later. Just listen in and get some good news.' He poked Judy. 'Piss off to the galley, and earn your keep.'

She walked away, and Howard stayed round-shouldered at his dials, moving onto shortwave to rid himself of Carla's voice. Let her yammer into nothingness, pleas bouncing back and meeting no one's ears but her own – the ultimate in futility. She must have heard Judy's exalted words, so would go on till her windpipe withered and she stopped for lack of air. Judy was his whatever happened.

The north Atlantic forecast played its music, a stream of morse not impinging as it should. Misery forced him out of his stillness to go on deck and look, as if he had eyes, seeing grey and tattered cloud pushing them into the hundred mile mouth of the Channel.

Judy came back, as he had known she would. 'I won't do anything you don't want me to do. I'll only listen. Promise.'

He felt her shirt wet from tears, unless driving spray had caught her coming along the deck, or she had leaned too far over with the idea of throwing herself in. Sea salt tasted like tears. 'My boat and its hero is going up-Channel,' she sang, Ted having given her a glass of icy vodka. 'I finished it before leaving the galley.'

'I'm not your hero,' he told her. 'You wanted me, from the moment you came on board, because I had my hands on the transmitters. I wondered why you were so set on me.'

'That's not true. Honestly. I never thought she'd be close enough to hear on VHF. In any case it was you who told me about her. I wouldn't have known for sure, would I? She might be my lover, but you're my hero for telling me. You're the odd man out on this damned boat. Just let me listen, and I'll be happy.'

Her voice came as if from across the aether, except that now he was close enough to breathe against her cheek. She took his hand warmly, the other on his shoulder. She had come from the Azores with a basket of pineapples, and he could hear her talking.

He went back to the VHF channel, but she stayed beside him. Carla had given up. Two southward-bound yachties chatted about having a piss-up when their boats got to La Coruña – last man arriving pays the tally. 'We can try again later,' he said. 'If she's on the same course she may come back around midnight.'

'She'll be going south. I've lost her.'

'She didn't sound as if she wanted to lose you.'

'I'll never hear her again. Or see her.'

He couldn't believe Fate would be so good to him. 'We'll try, anyway. I don't want you to think I haven't given her a fair go.'

'I'm tired of it all. She doesn't want me, anyway. She only wants me because she thinks I'm available at the moment. I know her. She once left me sitting outside a café in Greece, to follow another woman, and came back half an hour later because the woman told her to get lost or she would call the police. She told me as if it was a joke. Loyalty was a funny notion to her, but I believed in it – though maybe that was because I was in love. She told me she was in love with me, but that didn't mean she had to be faithful, she said. I was a fool to think it meant anything. The only time I'm not burning in hell is when I'm talking to you.'

Love, he well knew, is mostly anguish, which either burns itself out, or goes on till no love is left. Or the light may stay constant, shine with enduring affection, but even then it's a dead end, though what better way is there of being alive?

He tried the radio again, but the yachties were still trading backslaps and guffaws. 'At least they're happy,' she said, and he saw her smile.

'How did a nice woman like you come to work on boats such as this?' She didn't suffer while talking. 'Sounds a strange career, though it must be a long story.'

'Not too long. I'm twenty-eight, and it sometimes feels I've been alive forever. My father's a farmer, owns a lot of land in Lincolnshire, and there were five of us, all girls. I wasn't the sort of university or agricultural college type, not like the others, so I did secretarial. I dropped out, and went to some cookery place, believe it or not. I worked in a restaurant, till I got thrown out. I won't say why. Other places took me on, and I did all right. I met this chap who told me he was a sailor. He was rich, and had a yacht as big as this. We lived together. He had a flat in London and a house on the coast in Devon, and we sailed all over the Med. He was a bully though. He saw me talking to another skipper, in a bar in Corfu, and when we got back to the boat he knocked me about. That was only the first time. But one day I gave him a mouthful, and slammed him back. He went down like a skittle, right? Poor bloke! I didn't know my strength, and he didn't know what hit him. I was crying with happiness, but was terrified at the same time. He just lay there, moaning. Must have cracked his head as he went down. I threw a bucket of water over him, and when he began to stir I ran. Never saw him again. I bummed around, and just before my money ran out got work on another yacht, no strings attached this time. After a year or two I met Carla.

'Carry on from there, if you like. I roamed around a bit. Some boats smuggled, some didn't. The last I worked on did, so I got known by this lot, and worked for them. I even learned how to navigate, and switch the radio on and off. All summer I was talking to Carla, whenever I felt like it. It's the only life I know, and I like it, so I suppose I'll go on doing it.'

She talked as if disembodied, nothing happening around her, and almost, he thought, as if no one was listening. 'You'd be better off giving up the sea.'

'You think so?'

'Get back on dry land and stay there.'

'I sometimes wonder. I've done plenty to live on for the rest of my life. I'd like an income, really, and a nice house. I've got a bit saved, but not enough. My father wants me to live in a cottage near the farm. Don't know that I shall. Wouldn't like to be an old maid with a cat.'

Such dreams might be too late, everyone on the boat finished, doomed. 'This is my one and only trip,' he said.

'Seems you're not exactly made for life as a mariner.'

'Is anybody? I came on board to meet you, and hear your voice.'

'It's sometimes hard to believe you can't see.'

'I don't need to. I see you more clearly than you think. I know you're beautiful, for instance.'

'I'm a mess, is all I know, inside and out. But thanks anyway.'

'If I said that much about myself at least I'd know I was alive and could see properly. I'm happy now, though it hasn't always been like that. When you're blind everything on the outside comes into you, but

360

there's no room for all of it, so to avoid chaos you have to chop the detritus clear, meaning there's so much that you don't see, or can't afford to let yourself see. After a while a lot of what's on the outside stops its rush to get in, and from then on you only see what's essential for your wellbeing. You live in the dark, so what you miss you don't need anyway. At least that's what you tell yourself – another piece of survival technique! Strange, me being able to tell you this, because I haven't been able to tell myself up to now. But I feel a different man to what I was six months ago, because I can let everything rush in that will, though what it means I wouldn't like to say. I don't really know, so I expect I'll just have to wait and see.'

'You are a funny chap. I love it when you tell me things about yourself.'

'I like to hear you talk, whatever you say.'

'I wonder if you'd think so if we'd been living together for five years.'

'You're a bit young to ask that. I'd give you loyalty, though.'

'I'm sure you would. And I'd treasure it.'

He thought of Laura – a rare occurrence since leaving her – knowing he couldn't claim to be loyal at all, because he had no intention of going back, the moral ground cut from under his feet. He was too happy to let the idea disturb him. 'There's not much we can do.'

'When I don't think of Carla, it's you I love. It was just the sound of her voice that upset me. I haven't seen her since Malaga, a couple of weeks ago, and it wasn't so good. I don't care if I never see her again. She's given me the run-around ever since I've known her. Maybe I like that, as well, and that's why I love her.'

He smiled. 'You mean that if I give you the run-around you'll begin to love me?'

'Don't try, darling. I don't want to stop liking you.'

The boat was so battered by the waves that he was fearful it would upend any moment and take them on a zig-zag to the bottom, food for the fishes after their brief time. 'I can't believe in that sort of thing.'

'Hold me,' she said. 'I want someone to hold me.'

He stroked the back of her neck. She liked the subtle hands of a blind man. In his disability he didn't see her, so she felt safe. The spark gap between them lit back and forth, blind man's fingers soothing her anguish. Too much in turmoil to be eased by what he was doing, he only knew he should say nothing for a while. Words distanced people. Sometimes they broke bonds.

The spine was distinct through her sweater, which he lifted, touching warm flesh. 'That's good,' she said. 'You're doing the right thing.'

Easy to know what she wanted, as he stroked her loose breasts with their soon prominent nipples. She kissed him while his fingers moved in a gentle massage. The band of her slacks was elasticated, and as his hand went down he felt no need to speak, an expert touch lulling her into an ease that made her lose all sense of where she was, or even who was giving such comfort and pleasure. Half asleep, she willed him to descend her seemingly enlarged body so that only moments after his fingers became wet and entered, she cried out, gripping him with harder kisses while he went on stroking till she had finished.

'Oh, that was wonderful, my love. I needed that, from somebody else, but most of all from you. Let's go to my bunk. I want all of you now.'

During the night through the morning they passed the submarine training areas, their small craft on the inshore traffic lane, the seascape eerie and silent under a half moon, shadows of tankers and container ships ahead and behind. Waistcoat called on Howard every few minutes, to be told there was only chatter on the aether, which had nothing to do with them.

'He'll calm down when it's dark.' Paul Cinnakle took a rest from tending his engines. Howard, relaxed and easy at the stern, wondered what a man like Cinnakle was doing on such a boat, whom he saw as neatly dressed and knew as quietly spoken, hardly one of the others, though who was similar to anyone else on board? They worked for the ongoing motion of the vessel, each his own well camouflaged rock.

'Night's better for the chief's condition,' Cinnakle said. 'Better for us, as well. As long as the other boats have lights, we don't need any. It's better to be on a dark boat, in more ways than one. When I've made my pile with this lot I'll never go near sea-water again, even if it means living in the middle of Australia. Still, I'm not unhappy, belonging where I do at the moment. As long as I don't have to look at the perishin' water. I like engines, and you know why?'

Howard had to say he didn't.

'Because they can't talk. I listen to 'em singing, but when I shout they don't answer back. Engines are my cup of tea. They sing as they work, and don't give any lip. I must get below. See you.'

That's why we're here. Howard fumbled a way to his radio post, but paused by the rail, as if he had lost his way, direction topsy-turvy, bearings gone. He stilled his shaking hands, couldn't think, reason gone overboard. He wanted the reassurance of his radio gear, craved his beloved toys.

Nothing on the air waves, though there would be soon. Radar was tracking them along the Channel, but they were beyond the twelve-mile limit. If the morse letter had not been taken note of Waistcoat would get the stuff unloaded and away without molestation. It had gone astray. Or perhaps not. He couldn't yet know. If it hadn't, a pre-emptive strike was called for, legal or not. Impossible to predict. Hard to care what happened, warm in the arms of Judy whenever they had the chance to be alone. The suppressed anxieties of everyone on board convinced him he was as much a member of the crew as they were, hoping for success with the rest of them. He had once, beyond his own control, gone into an amusement arcade and pushed every coin from his pocket into the one-armed bandit, waiting for the crash and fall of a jackpot – which hadn't happened.

In the night they would pass the town where Laura was sleeping. She wouldn't know, or see them. He was sorry she had suffered such anxiety – if she had, and who could be sure? He wouldn't go back, but can a blind man take to the road like the Wandering Jew? The wash of the sea made a comforting sound.

The German Numbers Woman came back, with her hectoring repetitive tone, coded instructions going to no one knew where or to whom, though most likely to say they would never make landfall.

'NEUN – SECHS – FUNF – ACHT – VIER – EINS – NEUN – NEUN – SIEBEN – DREI – SECHS – VIER – DREI – EINS,' remorselessly on and on.

He passed an earphone to Judy. 'Take a listen.'

'Who is she?'

'I don't know. What do you make of it?'

'Sounds a nasty piece of work.'

He laughed. 'I'm used to her. Heard her for years.'

'You shivered, just then.'

He had, and not from the cold. Landfall blocked. His sins were too great, he had never atoned, not even thought of it, was responsible for all those members of mankind in all countries over the globe who hadn't stopped evil and done good in the ages of the past. Landfall in the mind of the German Numbers Woman was a paradise no one deserved. He silenced her, by flipping the needle, unwilling to take on a burden that would always be there.

Routine weather synopses were typed and handed in, though anyone on board with a ghetto blaster could bring in local stations and hear the forecasts in spoken language. He must be sure that it matched his own, nothing more he could do for them, or wanted to, turned back to the radio nevertheless, invisible switches on which his nervous fingers found a kind of reality. She tapped his shoulder. 'What would your wife say if she knew we were having an affair?'

The question was soothing, from a more human world. 'I don't know.'

'Course you do! I mean, would she be jealous?'

'I think so.'

'You mean she doesn't have lovers as well?'

'Not as far as I know.'

'Well, maybe a man never does know – if she wants to hide it. It's easy to hide it if you want to.'

'I wouldn't want to, though, with you.' Everything was in the open, nothing hidden, on the boat, so it wouldn't be when they got off it either.

'What's she like?'

'It's hard to tell.'

'Flippin' 'ell!'

'Well, not just like that. But why do you want to know?'

She laughed. 'You always do, I suppose.'

'I'll tell you when I can.'

'Maybe I'll see her, one day.'

That, he thought, would be a right meeting and, wanting to alter the topic, said: 'I haven't heard anymore from Carla.'

She leaned over him. 'I don't need her anymore. I've got you now.'

Impossible to know how true it was, but her words were honey nevertheless, though if Carla were to magically appear out of the blue and walk along the deck, he didn't doubt Judy would run to her. He would expect no less. In any case, she might get in touch – who throughout months of listening had become real enough to him – after they had landed, if and when they did.

Hope was in the crucible, the future chaos, as far as plans between him and Judy went. All was fantasy. His mind, the only means of sight, grew darker. Everyone on the boat believed in a future, for morale's sake couldn't afford not to. Cannister had shaved, smartened himself up for a spot of shore leave, as if still a young and careless rating in the Navy. Cleaver had stopped his jibes about the paucity of cucumber sandwiches, and said how much he was looking forward to: 'Going down the gangway, with pouch, pipe, purse and prophylactics in my pocket!'

'I wonder though, what's going to happen to us,' he said.

She lounged on the sofa opposite and, peeling an orange from the cloth bag she carried, leaned forward to pass him a segment. 'I'll tell you, if you like. We'll get ashore, and I'll take you to the nearest decent place for a meal. We'll talk, and hold hands, and the men in the room will envy you, and wonder what you've got that they haven't. I'll moon over you to make them jealous. Then we'll go to a hotel and have a proper sleep together. I'll lead you by the hand.'

'I'll hold you to it.'

She passed another sliver of orange. 'Eat it. We share. You brought me back to life, didn't you? You made me feel like myself again, and I know it took a lot of doing.'

He laughed, drinking in the spirit of her still uncaring youth. 'I didn't even try.'

'So what would happen if you did? Whizz bang! You'd never get rid of me.'

'I'll never want to.'

'Oh, right. I don't even have to think about what I'm going to say when I talk to you. I just say it and know it'll be all right. With Carla it was different. I had to be careful. I could never be easy with her. She thought I was, but she was so selfish she could never know the tension I was under.'

Nor had he, because she'd sounded relaxed enough over the radio on all those nights he'd listened. She hadn't known about his crafty eavesdropping, though perhaps he would be able to tell her, if such a time ever came. 'What a life it's been for you.'

'Flippin' amazing how you can love someone who's not very nice. She didn't even understand me, I'll never know why. It should have been easy enough. But I'm keeping my man from his precious wireless. You're the ears of the boat, and that's more important than eyes. Everybody's got eyes. They're ten a penny. But ears are different. They're special. Not as special as your hands, though. *They're* brilliant. Still, you'd better get back to it, while I go and see what's for our dinner.'

'A kiss before you go.'

'You don't have to ask.' He had to believe she had fallen in love with him, because a blind man had no right to be sceptical. He had kept the secret of his love from Laura, but she had been his nurse rather than that divine love which every member of the human species who had evolved out of the slime ought to experience once in life. He hadn't been the love of her life, either, merely the purpose of her existence, that of keeping a safe house around him, to make a refuge for herself as well. On a walk in Malvern she had said a car had just passed with a logo in the window saying: 'DARWIN WAS RIGHT', and he was appalled that someone should flaunt such a daft statement, though now, the boat whacking its way through a following sea, he had to believe it.

The staccato rhythm of Portishead pumped out the weather forecast. Everyone on board would agree that Darwin was right, that only the fittest would survive, the fittest being those who saw nowhere to go after death but into blackness, and who behaved as instinct required for the ultimate good of self preservation.

A force five wind, in the North Sea, occasionally gale, but it would diminish and grow calm by tomorrow, a better telegram to hand Waistcoat, he thought, on knocking at his door. He took a few steps to where he smelled the steak being eaten for lunch, and gave him the paper, arm full out, as close as he could get without bumping the table. 'The latest weather, Chief.'

Waistcoat snapped it away to read. 'That's good. We'll need it good by then.' His cutlery rattled. 'Any other interesting stuff?'

'Most of the waves are surprisingly quiet.'

'Let's hope it stays that way.' He ate easily, at home in the serpentine mud walled tunnels of his mind. 'What are you waiting for?'

Howard turned. 'I was about to go.'

'No, hang on a bit.' His appetite was good, wine glass and eating irons moving in harmony. 'I've got something to say to you, Howard.'

'What might that be?'

'Don't get huffy with me. All I want to say is, just watch out for that Judy. She's had more boyfriends than you've had hot dinners. Girlfriends, as well. A few things in between, I shouldn't wonder.'

He punctuated Waistcoat's laugh: 'I'll listen out during the night. Maybe I'll hear something. I don't need much sleep. You never can tell what I might pick up.'

'Yeh, slog your guts out at that boffin's gear. Work like the rest of us. I'll tell you this, though: I rely on you as much as any of the others. Maybe even more – if I think about it.'

He shuffled along the deck, knowing he must stay wary in the maritime den he was trapped in, because Waistcoat's remark was unusual, after the era of mistrust, as if he had hoped to lure him into a mistake plain for everyone to witness, even sending a message for unknown listeners to hear.

Scraps of talk from various places on the boat were joined by zones of darkness, but he found a cleanliness in the sea air which encouraged him in his design. Waistcoat's foul remarks about Judy – made out of spite, hatred, and perhaps even envy – didn't disturb him. Everybody on board knew he and Judy were in love, hard to hide it in such a place, and who would care to, in any case? They noted every move he made, and neither he nor Judy cared.

Three ships on the same frequency were calling different stations – Portishead, Gdynia, and Bahrein – and getting no answers. They would soon enough, so he spun the needle and tuned in to something else. Morse tinkled into space and was lost, and thus were the cries of humans likewise unmet. Even when two bodies were face to face the wrong signals could be sent, or none that were vital be transmitted, or the right ones that were misconstrued.

A Russian ship failed to get through, the same for one calling Algiers, as if a fearful ambush of atmospherics hovered over the coast stations, or the operators' ears were for some reason stopped up. Communication could be uncertain at the best of times, and often there was nothing to do but wait for the sunspot to go, or hope for better conditions, or persist in your attempts until the blockage dissolved from whoever's ears.

He copied the Mediterranean weather, to give the impression he still had his uses. Richard tapped him in passing: 'Keep it up.'

'I will.'

As long as he did he would come to no harm, Richard thought as he stood by the wheel. Being on watch took his tiredness away. When not working he craved sleep, for the trip to be over, to wake up in the luxury of isolation at home, but it was a perilous state of mind, looking so far ahead when the job was nowhere finished.

An engine sounded in the obscurity of low cloud. Aircraft could take photographs through any amount of precipitation, or plot them on their radar, but what was a large piston-engined plane doing out of the air traffic control zone? Gone, as eerily as it had come, but would it return?

He hadn't felt a moment's ease on the trip. So unexpectedly summed up, he knew it to be true. On other jobs his mind had been in neutral from start or finish, a couldn't care less attitude which told him that good sense wasn't buried too deeply and would come when needed. Confident and relaxed – but now he wasn't, not anymore – now that he had told himself so. He wondered if he was the only one on board with forebodings, thought he was, because the others seemed normal enough. Normal however, was button-lipped at the best as well as at the worst of times. You couldn't know what they were thinking even when you had sailed with them so often.

In improving visibility he tried to make out the Isle of Wight through binoculars, not sure whether he fixed on a bank of cloud, or a line of hills.

Land played tricks, coy or perilous, scotch mist or fleeting image. Rain splattered the windows. The cloudscape had gaps, a line of sun either to bless or blemish. Cleaver, never one to shun work, recorded its wayward appearances with the sextant, while Killisick slaved to make ends meet in the galley. Food was running short, at least in variety, though nobody much cared since land was so close. Waistcoat paced his state room, aware more than anyone else that the test was coming.

The waves went on forever, they always did, a sight for sore eyes though not just now, each on the bump and slide, one over the other, fist into fist and here comes the next, an ongoing monotony. Cinnakle hoped his engines wouldn't seize up for lack of fuel, lucky to be thinking of nothing else, no sense of threat from any quarter – as far as anyone could tell. Cannister and Scuddilaw kept watch on deck, three pairs of eyes better than one alone on the bridge. 'More reliable,' Waistcoat swore, 'than your effing radar.' So all were occupied in their allotted ways, except Judy who had been in to say she was getting her head down for an hour.

Time that dragged by the minute had to be endured. Luckily there was no such thing as forever. His course was steady, no shake at the compass, a dead-on zero-seven-five towards the narrowing mouth of Dover, old Cape Grey Nose to starboard.

A single engined low wing monoplane made a shadow over the water. Another inquisitive bastard, this time different. Maybe he was a private aviator coming from France, except that he should have been higher. One plane was fortuitous, a second definitely worrying.

Howard came in. 'He was talking on VHF. Nearly popped my eardrums.'

'Who to?'

'Somebody on shore, I suppose. In English. La-di-da voice. Said numbers, which sounded like course and position.'

'What did the others say back?'

'They just acknowledged the signal. It could have been his coordinates, but the course sounded like ours.'

'We'll lose 'em in the night. A bit of zig-zagging ought to do it. It's far from beyond us. I'll tell the chief as soon as Cleaver takes over. No use worrying him too soon.'

'Meanwhile I'll do a stint on the Interpol frequencies.'

He wanted fog, a nice all-hiding cough-dropping fog, but the last way to get anything was to pray for it, though mist around the Foreland would also have its dangers – like bumping into the wall of a container ship or cross-Channel ferry. Even a fishing boat would mean a nasty smack. Bad luck to kill ourselves, or anyone else, come to that. Such blatant aerial shadowing hadn't happened before.

Waistcoat would scream that they had been shopped, and who could deny it? Maybe the people in the Azores had set the trap. He would believe anything, except that Howard had had anything to do with stitching them up. In the drugs game everyone played dirty. The more stuff at the bottom of the sea, or burned behind a customs warehouse, the more the price of powder and weed went up, so all the better for those who found a chair when the music stopped. On the other hand it could mean a grudge was being settled, someone getting his own back on a bit of pique so ancient that he who had done the trickery – hardly thought of as such at the time – had lost all memory of it. The trouble was, half a dozen good men went down with whoever they were after, and none could be sure who had gone shopping with such a big trolley.

When anybody was caught it was always because of a tip-off, which those betrayed could never see the reason for. Yet even the South Americans – savages to a man- wouldn't do anything to Waistcoat. Or so Richard hoped, a ripple of ice going into his blood. Of course they wouldn't. Waistcoat knew too much, was too solidly embedded in the network. Such treachery on that level of the hierarchy was unthinkable, would ricochet too far upstairs, though never far enough if Waistcoat began to tell all he knew – which he surely would – to get a shorter sentence.

Morbid thoughts because he had heard a couple of aeroplanes, but every sign worried when close to the white cliffs. Keep a good lookout, and forget all else. He stood at the stern after Cleaver had taken the wheel. Pale grey cumulus, settled in the west, had decided to come after them, egged on by those behind flamed into orange by the setting sun. The wind diminished but the chase was on. Only a fool would deny it.

The evening was peaceful enough, but a menace from both west and east was about to box them into a situation hard to avoid or get out of. He didn't like it, tapped the pistol under his coat, and resisted the urge to throw it into the water.

THIRTY-THREE

Howard's inner sight was for the time being of a blacker blackness than during the day. He only knew it was night because he was tired, yet the blacker the blackness the more he needed to see. In the sink of exhaustion he forced senses into sharpness, though for what end he found hard to say. Every shape on the boat haunted him: every person was on the hunt to get him. They were invisible in their prowling.

Hearing didn't give enough proof as to whether they knew what was in his mind. He put fists to his ears, pressed at them painfully as if to get into his head and rearrange his brain. Sharper hearing was the only way, and he wondered whether anyone else would know when he achieved it.

He gave his attention to the radio. The crew had eaten their evening slop, and their vigilance seemed relaxed. Voices were tracking a boat which could only be theirs. Perhaps every small craft was likewise noted. He wouldn't know, but in spite of the elliptical maritime lingo he knew they had found the position of the boat, divined its course and speed – a simple matter if they knew what to look for.

The boat was clogging fair and square into a trap, though Waistcoat might yet have a few sly moves in mind. Should they turn out to be too deviously on the way to succeeding, Howard would break radio silence and reveal the position to whoever was listening. His fingers had explored the face of the transmitter for a dummy run every day since leaving port. He knew how to set the frequency and the morse key in his bag would be plugged in to do its work.

The voices were circumspect, brief and self assured. A few clipped numerals, and they were off the air, confident at not being overheard, never imagining that Waistcoat's yacht would be carrying a man whose only job was to listen at the radio. He would not tell Waistcoat what he had heard: no more cooperation, though it might make little difference.

'Are we going to be all right?'

He felt his soul damned in lying to her. 'Yes, I think so. No problem.'

'Anything startling on shortwave?'

'I listen. Not a word from Carla on any wave.'

'Her boat's done turnaround and gone back to the Med. The skipper she works for doesn't lose any time.'

'Nobody does, if they can help it.'

'Not in this game they don't. I've given her up, anyway.'

He switched on the shortwave transmitter, curbing his despondency. 'Give her a call.'

'Do you mean it?'

She failed the test – for which he was risking his life – yet he wanted her to go on knowing Carla, because if something happened to him she wouldn't be without a friend. 'This is the time she would listen.'

She picked up the microphone: '*Daedalus* calling *Pontifex*, how do you read me, over?' No response, she tried once more, then pushed the microphone aside.

He noted the shaking of her hand. 'She's not there.'

'That's it, then,' she said. 'Thanks for letting me try. You know I only love you, don't you?'

He felt for her. 'I'm aware of that.'

She drew him into her arms, her words so close at his lips that he saw them as if written. 'Don't think I love you only because you let me use the radio. If I'd heard her I would have told her to get lost. I really mean it.'

'Let's go on deck.' He would set no more tests. 'You can tell me what stars are out.'

'You want them to see us kissing?'

He felt the twenty-five he had never been. 'Yes, and even more than that.'

She led him to the bows. 'It's cold. Real England weather.'

'I like it. But you need your anorak.'

'I don't mind.' She put an arm through his. 'I see the Plough, so we must be heading east-north-east. When we turn north the fun will start. There's tension on the boat, but I don't care what happens now I have you.' She kissed him, warm in his arms. 'I don't care about anything. I know we'll make out. I don't want to lose you, and I won't.'

'We'll be together.' He could hardly imagine it, but to question her hopes would smash his own. He was more than happy to welcome back the young man in him, only wishing he had new eyes to see. 'Just as long as you like. I don't want to be with anyone else. I should have met you when I was twenty. I don't feel much use to you now.'

'It doesn't matter. I can be every use to you, if you'll let me.'

'I will, for as long as you like,' though he didn't want her to Laura him.

She laughed. 'It's wonderful what we agree on. We're two of a kind. It's like being with a brother, except it's very sexy.' She turned, head up he knew: 'The Plough's covered. Gone to watch another couple, though they won't be as happy as us. Maybe you ought to get back to the radio. I'll see if the chief needs anything from the galley. Be back later.'

Shortwave, lively in fine sunspot conditions, rippled with activity, Warsaw hammering out its messages, call sign before bubbles of sound, harsh yet rhythmical, pleasant, almost hypnotic to hear. Forecasts came from all corners promising good weather tomorrow. The German Numbers Woman strung him along, and all was right beneath the heaviside layer because he was in love with a woman who loved him.

Voices on VHF indicated that someone was in the know about their boat. His morse letter-tape must have been received. Perhaps even poor Jehu had landed with confirmation of their return. He was aware of Waistcoat standing close.

'Any news, Sparks?'

Howard took off his earphones. 'It's quiet tonight.'

'Even on VHF?'

'There's something in the distance. I think it's in German. Can't be anything to do with us.'

'All right. But keep your ears pinned back.'

Such mateyness was disturbing though he imagined that a man of Waistcoat's moods could occasionally crave ease and openness, unable to survive all the time in an unloved state. A friendly word or two, even a smile, sent him to bed happy. Good that he seemed halfway human now and again.

374

Something had happened. Waistcoat was villainous, as everyone found on coming into his employment, lived so much in his own mind he wasn't aware of the attitudes of others, and didn't care however much they knew it. Waistcoat assumed he didn't need to know or care. Cocksure and brutal, he had been operated on a long time ago by the surgeon of circumstance, any trace of human feeling had been cut away leaving a contempt for everybody, which had led him into a labyrinth without exit.

Even so, Waistcoat must suspect that several stages were missing in his ability to deal with people, knew that he lacked the ability to get more out of them than could be paid for by money, which kept his temper on a fractious and violent level, and his body in permanent thrall to the worms. Because everyone put up with his high handedness he believed cunning to be the ultimate protection. The more he thought it true the more he let success deceive and lull him, unable to see the danger because he hadn't gone through normal experiences of development that most people had as a matter of course. He had jumped, so Richard had implied, from being a battered infant to an accomplished and bitter thief who, as they often heard – from the horse's mouth, no less – stood 'no fucking nonsense'. Howard considered that the so-called nonsense such people were unable to tolerate commonly doomed them.

The rest of the crew members would stay loyal to Waistcoat, too much afraid of him not to do as they were told. They may despise and even hate him, but they worked with competent dedication because it was in their own interests that the enterprise succeeded.

Expecting no help from any quarter, the one man on board they should be wary of, Howard left the radio running, earphones on the table emitting faint noises, and went outside as silently as only a blind man could – as if tempted by the clean air of the breeze. The boat vibrated to its steadily humming engines, wind at the back of his head as he moved along, meeting no one because they were on the bridge or in their quarters. Judy had gone to hunt up a gin and tonic, promising one for him later. Waistcoat's one gesture towards concern for his crew was to make sure the booze never ran dry. 'The grub's a bit short,' Killisick had told them, 'so maybe we'll cast out the fishing lines before we get home, but we've got all the fags and bacca we need, so we can't complain.'

Hands going from port hole to port hole, he felt his way along the deck, hardly knowing where he was heading but drawn on by instinct. A piece of wire that came out of an opening made little impression on his fingers. He passed it, but turned back, and followed its direction to the upper deck, a thin strong length of wire, probably copper, ideal for a radio independent of the main aerials.

He shuffled along the steps, as if out for as much of a stroll as could be got on such a vessel, convenient handrails everywhere. Ordinary men needed every assistance in rough weather, so boats were made as if for the blind.

At the top of the steps, and towards the main aerials, he trod over Waistcoat's state room, taking care not to be heard, holding the rail, putting his heel soundlessly down followed by the rest of the foot, paces completed in silence and slow motion. The wire, almost invisibly laid, came from Waistcoat's cabin. Howard stopped. Easy to snap the strand, though not so as to show that the wind had done it. Otherwise Waistcoat's suspicions would become certainty, if they weren't already. A warning disturbed his darkness, that Waistcoat knew he had been distorting his reports. He shivered in the more erratic gusts from one side and the other. The wire from below was attached to the main system, confirming that Waistcoat had a VHF receiver in his stateroom. He could check what Howard said he had heard, or know what items he had claimed not to hear.

'Hey, I've been looking for you,' she called from the stairway.

A finger to his mouth, he moved quickly down – at whatever risk. 'Don't say anything. I'll follow you.'

She looked back. 'What's it all about?'

'The chief doesn't like anybody stepping over his quarters.'

'Oh, right!' she laughed. 'They never do, especially if they've got the DTs. Take this, then. It's the best gin and tonic between here and a pub in Boston. I made it especially for my lover.' She kissed him, and put it into his hand as they stood by the rail. 'I had mine back there. It wasn't easy carrying two.'

He drank it with the speed of water, made tasteless by the peril he was in. 'A kind thought.'

'Is anything worrying you?'

'Why do you say that?'

376

'You look as if you've had a shock. I can feel everything that upsets you. You've got something on your mind, and won't tell me. Is it that you can't?'

He tried for the right uncaring tone. 'It's just the everyday anxiety I've had since birth. I'm wondering if everything will be all right when we reach land. Nothing more.'

Her lips must show disbelief, but she said: 'It always goes better than you think. Maybe the gin will settle you. It works wonders for me.'

'I feel all right, with you being here.' A shade of dependence was coming back, as when he had been with Laura, which he didn't like but knew was inevitable. 'I'm better when you're near me.'

She threw his empty glass into the sea, following it with her own, turning to hold him. 'Same here. We'll be OK, if we stick together.'

'I love you,' he said, 'more than you can know.'

'Love you, too, Sailor! But don't look so serious. We'll be all right. I've been through the worry of landing scores of times.'

Richard took his stance in the glowing pre-light of dawn. A fire in the east, stoked by some agency, seemed unsure it wanted the trouble of warming and illuminating another day. Might even put a damper on it and go back to sleep, except the day was impossible to stop, would get there maybe sooner than anyone wanted. He had been through too many to know that the blissful grey peace ever lasted long.

A series of courses to steer, handed out by Cleaver, and seconded in no uncertain terms by Waistcoat, were to be followed precisely. Clouds had overtaken them during the night, the red sky hovering as if to swallow the boat and everyone on her. Two large ships and a small coaster were safely ahead, both shorelines as dark and solidly outlined as if about to be rained on – a menacing straits to go through.

They had passed where Laura lay asleep, and she couldn't have known how close her wayward husband had been. If she did maybe she also dreamed of me, he thought, though knew he would never see her again. After the trip, and the ceremony of paying off, he would call on his father and make sure he was all right.

From there he would go back to the house and put it on the market, and after it was sold move to where memories of Amanda could no longer cause him misery. As for Howard, he was too enamoured of Judy to find his way home, though Richard assumed it wouldn't be long before she tired of the novelty of having a blind man in tow, and lit off with someone else, leaving Howard to tap his white stick up the steps to Laura after all.

Cleaver, looking over his shoulder, noted that the compass was spot on and steady. 'We're doing well, after that fine bit of speed during the night. I think the chief's pleased. We'll beat 'em yet.'

'We always have. What's the ETA?'

'Tomorrow night, as close as dammit.'

'I assumed so.'

'No harm you knowing.'

Secrecy among thieves was unnecessary, though Waistcoat seemed to think so. 'Nor for the others to know, either. Nothing they can do with the information.'

'It's that blind radio wizard,' Cleaver said in his ear. 'The chief seems to have a grudge against him. He's the nigger in the woodpile.'

'There's always someone.' He shrugged. 'Howard's straight enough.'

'He's got to be. But the chief wasn't ranting when he said it, and that strikes me as being a tad different. Anyway, keep her going, I'm off for my cup of coffee.'

Ted never offered Cleaver tea or coffee in a mug, for fear of a dressing down. 'Ask Judy to bring some for me, Richard, if you can unstick her from Howard's bunk, that is. As long as he stays shacked up with her we should be all right.'

Cleaver grunted in disbelief as he walked away.

Richard didn't know whether his sudden lightness of heart, so agreeable to the system, promised good or ill. A not-unfamiliar state when close to home, he was unable to care, because in spite of Waistcoat's histrionics he had confidence in him as the eternal survivor, sometimes saw in his face the wilfulness of a little boy dead set on getting whatever was good for himself, which at this point meant for the crew as well. Not to pull off all his ventures was against the rules of the people he had come from, and sailing with someone who plotted but didn't think – who put action before thought – guaranteed getting through to a successful unloading. All the same, Richard preferred not to assume that his mood owed more to hope than to reality.

* * *

Howard felt the boat turn north. They were far from land but the end was close. It had to be. He couldn't figure out what the end would be because the darkness as he stood at the stern became so light he almost thought he could see the widening flail of the wake fanning towards the horizon, and the cauliflower-shaped tops of the crimson-tainted cumulonimbus rising behind the boat. The illusion that the invisible skin of a bubble was about to burst and show him the whole wide expanse of the sea was momentary and caused him to smile: he'd had such feelings before, usually at times of extreme tiredness and uncertainty.

The aerial from Waistcoat's cabin, connected to the main mast, came from a spare VHF receiver. Of that he was certain. There were no flies on Waistcoat, as they used to say in the Air Force about some demon of a drill sergeant, invariably adding that marks could no doubt be found where the buggers had previously been. Nothing heard on the radio at the moment in any way concerned their boat, but the earlier exchanges, which he had denied intercepting, had obviously been heard by Waistcoat, who now realised what lies Howard had told, Howard knowing he was therefore marked down for vengeance, even if all went according to expectation, but he felt a placidity in himself, for the moment, that nothing could disturb. The bullet never struck you, always the next man – except that once it had, and if once, then why not twice? Even so, for reasons beyond his understanding, he felt in control of his own dark sphere, knowing he would not be deterred from his final move.

He was soothed even more by taking down the morning forecast, and Waistcoat in his cabin accepted without a thank-you the clutch of navigation warnings. He didn't need eyes to realise the contemptuous expression of dismissal, Waistcoat taking even less care to hide it from someone who couldn't see.

Howard rummaged in his bag for another sweater, as if an extra layer of protection might bring a glimmer of sight back when it was most needed.

'It's not that cold.' Judy approached, as he was taking down the amount of a tanker's oil. 'They stop me getting close to your skin, so I don't like them.'

'Yes, it's warm in here, but it'll soon be a lot hotter all round.'

'Why do you say that? I want you to be my man, not the ancient mariner prophesying doom.'

'We're close to home, that's all.'

She sat by him. 'You aren't trying to frighten me, are you?'

'That's the last thing I want.'

'Just think what we'll do when we're out of all this.'

'I even dream about it during the day.'

'I'll show you around Boston. It's pretty in the middle, lots of nice houses. And the church is fabulous. Beats all those Spanish ones. My aunt who lives there will let us stay a day or two. We'll be given separate rooms, but I'll sneak into your bed at night, you can bet. I'll hire a car and drive us to Woodhall Spa. There's a good hotel there. Then we'll go to Lincoln. I know a pub called The Magna Carta, and they serve meals. It's right by the cathedral. We could put up at The Bull across the way. That's a very old place, and I'm sure they'll have a big-four poster bed with curtains where even the stars can't see us making love. Better than a damp old bunk we keep falling out of all the time!'

Her talk came from a dream. She was happy, open-minded, optimistic – youthful. He would walk like a jester in cap and bells, playing blind to make the dream his. She sometimes seemed more distant than when he had heard her voice loud and clear from the Dodecanese. But he could touch her now, felt the sting of tears about to break free, as if they were looking back on the joys she was proposing. 'It sounds wonderful.'

'It will be, darling. I know it will. I think about it all the time.'

'I'm afraid to be too hopeful.' There were difficulties in hinting that such happiness wouldn't come about, however wrong to think so. 'I can't say why. Maybe it's because I'm so much older.'

'If I wasn't optimistic,' she said. 'I'd stop living. It keeps me going.'

'And so it will.' He turned for a kiss. 'You light up my life like the brightest lamp in the world. I didn't exist before I met you. I really didn't. I don't even feel so blind anymore.'

'I like to hear that. I can't hear it too often. I want you next to me, with nobody else around. I want you in me all the time.'

He listened to himself talking over the airwaves. 'That would be a bit awkward, you daft girl.'

'Well, as often as possible.' She laughed. 'Even if you couldn't do it. I won't be disappointed. I love you too much to let such a thing bother me. I can always tell you what to do if you can't, though you never need telling.'

She was talking the language of the young in love with the old. Or from infatuation. 'I think I've known you forever.'

'You have,' she said, 'but you always feel like that when you're in love.'

'I've never been in love before.'

'Someone like you? I can't believe it. I'll never know why I let you seduce me, but I'm glad you did. I think you only came on this trip to waylay me. I hope so. I suppose I took to you because you made me feel like myself again. I was all in bits when I came on board, didn't care whether I lived or died after that affair. It devastated me. Now I want to live more than I've ever done. Normally I'd think it strange, but I know it isn't.'

Even in the beginning Laura hadn't made so long a speech, nor spoken anything of such importance, either about him or herself. Nor had he. There had been no need. Hard to fix his past into a clear picture. 'They're changing course again. I feel it.'

'It's none of our business. They'll probably go around in circles before shooting in tonight. Or they'll rendezvous with another boat. They sometimes do. This is the time I close myself off from whatever goes on. It'll soon be over.'

'I suppose so,' he said. 'And we'll hope for the best.' Whatever he did there'd be no danger to her. He turned in his seat to stand. 'Let's go outside so you can tell me what the sky looks like,' any ruse to hear the voice he now had to himself.

Life didn't exist beyond the way he felt, no instrument able to sound the depths of his love. It couldn't go on, no matter what he needed to feel, or whatever he said, because behind landfall there was nothing, and he tried not to let her think he could be in any way unhappy.

THIRTY-FOUR

Scraps of paper littered the state room: hard for Richard to say, as he stepped through the door, whether they were discarded notes reminding Waistcoat who to kill, or soiled tissues – though he didn't seem to have a cold. Split capsules were scattered around, a crushed paper cup in a pottery ashtray with CARACAS block lettered along the side, and empty plastic water bottles underfoot. Waistcoat fingered a radio scanner on the table, sat upright and switched the set on, a finger buttoning the various channels.

'You wanted to see me?' Richard said.

'Too right I did. I'm not happy with the way things are going.'

Any fool could see as much. The drink showed in bloodshot eyes, and more than a little breakfast hadn't got beyond his shirt front. He also needed a shave. 'In what way?'

'Nothing serious as far as arrangements go – luckily. But that blind boffin's about as reliable as an egg with a hole in it. I asked him what he'd been hearing on VHF, and he says not a word. He didn't know I was tuned in as well, with this. I heard so much talking you'd think every ear in the Channel was cocked on us, waiting for us to drop a bollock and hit the nearest beach. So he was lying, wasn't he? Is he an Interpol agent, or what? I can't believe they'd put a blind man onto us, but you never know. They've been blind themselves for years. I'll tell you one thing: the first sign of trouble, and he's dead. I'd like to get him in here and crack every bone in his body, but I don't want the others to hear the commotion. They might get nervous, and that would make things worse.'

'So why tell me?'

Coffee steamed from his Thermos. 'Because you're the one I trust most on this tub. If you see any sign of him misbehaving I want you to top him. Get him overboard. No fucking nonsense. I'm relying on you.'

'I'll do as you say. This is my last trip, and nobody's going to spoil it. I'm getting out of the game, and telling you now formally.'

The announcement was not to be disputed. He couldn't care less whether Waistcoat wanted him to go on or not: he was going, and that was that.

'You disappoint me. We'll miss you.' An uncommon smile. 'We've been through a lot together.'

'I know. I'll miss the life as well. I've always had a real buzz out of it – as you know. Not to mention the money. But my father's old and getting doddery. He's going to need looking after.'

'Oh, right, yeh, well, you've got to take care of the family. I accept that. I like a man who looks after his family. Cleaver don't seem to have one. That's why he's such a dark horse. I might not use him again. Won't have to with these navigational gimmicks coming in. My family, though, they've cost me a million or two, but I don't regret a penny. They've all got pubs to run, or a hotel. I like a man who thinks of his family, but it's an amazing thing how big mine got after I came into the money. I shelled out, didn't I? There's a reunion next week, and I've got to show my face. But anytime you want to come back on a job just let me know. Whatever trip you do with me you won't be out of pocket. Just keep tabs on that blind lunatic. I really think he's got a screw loose.'

'Well, if he says he didn't hear anything on the radio, he didn't. But you know why, don't you?'

'You tell *me*.'

'He spends too much time with Judy.'

The excuse seemed halfway convincing. 'So that's it?'

'There aren't any secrets on a boat like this. But I'd better go. It's getting to be all hands on the bridge right now.'

'Fuck off, then,' he said amiably. 'I'll see you after I've cleaned myself up.'

Long hours at the radio had shown how to tune the medium wave transmitter. Fingers feeling their way over the equipment, he read each wheel and switch, interpreting buttons and plugs so as not to mistake anything or need to hurry when the moment came. He would plug the morse key into its appropriate slot, and send on the distress frequency, as promised in his tape letter, the longest fortnight ago in his life. It was obvious that the tape had been received, that a listener would pick up his message and take action. He saw little chance of escape after breaking radio silence but, boxed into his blindness, wouldn't consider consequences – going again through the processed drill.

The engines droned, but otherwise there was a curious silence on the boat, everyone anxious and expectant. The single dot he sent as a test, the sort Vanya in Moscow used to tap in order to assess the alacrity of a listener's response, sprang like the ping of a tuning fork into his ears and went unheard by everyone else into space. He unplugged the morse key and returned it to the hold-all, pushed out of sight under the table.

Course was altered, and he guessed they were steering in darkness towards the Suffolk coast, maybe to nose a way into one of the indentations recalled from low-level training flights, places in which to lay concealed and unload. On deck a light rain drizzled against his face. He would be a normal crew member till as close to the end as he could get. 'Hello, Jack, how are we doing?'

'Not bad,' Cannister said. 'This is just the night we need. We've got Long Sand Light to starboard, and we'll soon have Sunk Light to port. Couldn't be better. I've been in this way before.'

'How far is Long Sand Light from land?'

'Fifteen nautical miles. About an hour and a half, at this rate. Cleaver's worked it out like a real artist. Never puts a foot wrong. I'd go to bed if I was you. Wake up when it's over. I'd like to, but the chief wouldn't approve. Might stop me wages. I saw him just now, all toffed up on the bridge, spick and span in his pea jacket and naval cap. Just like a gent back from a cruise. I'll want to celebrate when this lot's over.'

'You don't sound too cheerful about it.'

'Well, you aren't usually over the moon at this stage. I suppose it's not the same for you as the rest of us. You ought to get more joy out of life, Howard, blind or not. I hope to be with my wife and kids this time tomorrow. You don't have any kids?'

'I've never thought it would do for somebody like me to have a family.'

'Why not? It's best to do it, and not think. Just get on with it.'

'A bit late now.'

'Go on, it never is, not for a man.' He nudged Howard's stomach. 'Not with Judy, you dirty old swine! I'll bet she'd be game.'

He didn't answer. Maybe she was already pregnant. He felt the subterranean contest between him and Cannister, between optimism, come what the hell would come, and a despair stemming out of his weakness, a fight to which there was no resolution, unless he forgot his plan and let chance take him where it would. A possible future came so powerfully to mind that he clutched the rail to steady himself, glad when Jack went to his post.

The beacon of Sunk Light should be close enough to channel them in, and he wandered along the deck feeling like old Blind Pugh with the black spot stigmatised on the flesh of his palm. The mood of indecision left him, his course as fixed and mapped as if prearranged from before birth, and there was no going back, whatever paradise would be lost, though he thought it would be a kindness if amnesia took him or he was absolutely somewhere else, and felt cowardly for wishing it. At the bridge he stood outside, wanting to be as unseen by them as they were by him, though voices told him who was there.

'Hold her on three-two-five,' Cleaver said.

'Three-two-five,' Richard acknowledged.

'Can't see a fucking thing,' Waistcoat complained. 'Are you sure there's a light?'

Cigarette smoke and raw breath thickened the air. 'Howard's nav warnings didn't say otherwise. She'll come up in a bit.'

'She's there now' – from Richard.

'I'll get a running fix, and check our speed.' Cleaver was always busy. 'There was no difference at Long Sand, but I like to be certain.'

Richard saw him at the door, a lost soul, at this stage of the trip. 'I'll ask Howard if there's any squeak out of the coastguards.'

'I think he'll be deaf to that one' – from Waistcoat, who hadn't seen him. 'But we might as well give him something to do.'

'When you thought he wasn't listening on VHF,' Richard said, 'he

385

was searching the Interpol channels. He can't clock onto every wavelength at once, and the trouble is he doesn't like to make excuses. An old Air-Force habit.'

'Is that right?'

'That's what he told me. He wasn't with Judy.'

'I wish I could believe it. But he'd been told especially to listen to VHF, hadn't he? And he didn't, did he? Nobody told him to fanny around for Interpol at that particular time, did they? He's got to learn to obey orders, so tell him here and now from me to check the coastguards or their boats, and to come straight here if he gets anything.'

Howard imagined Richard's hand signalling him out of sight, so went unheard to the radio, sat bemused and unable to act, until he detected voices, adjusted the set to bring them in more clearly, and typed a short text which he took to Cleaver, who passed the signal to Waistcoat: 'They're watching something in the Thames Estuary. Nothing to do with us.'

Nor would it be for a while.

'Listen out some more,' Cleaver told him.

'That's good,' Waistcoat called. 'Let's hope they're busy rounding up some other bastards. Keep listening, Sparks, like Mr Cleaver said.'

The German Numbers Woman, on her interminable countdown to the *Flying Dutchman*, was talking to him alone, having nailed him at last, putting him to the test as he had known she would from the first moment of her discovery on the airwaves.

Reaching for his bag, he plugged the morse key into its socket, switched on the transmitter, imagining the energised parts but without seeing the fascia's glow. Everyone was hard at it on the bridge or keeping a lookout on deck, so there could be no better moment as they closed with the shore.

Earphones firmly on, he ordered the long prepared message from his brain and, after a few dots for tone, and the easing finger exercise of 'best-bent wire' with its ending flourish, he tapped his first message since the war, in the most correct morse, machine morse, precise morse, the finest morse sent since 'what God hath wrought' was clicked by the great man himself, played like an artist at the game, a *pianiste* indeed, cool and exact in manner, perfect in rhythm, with no trace of nervousness:

'DRUG SMUGGLERS BOAT APPROACHING DEBEN ON COURSE THREE-TWO-FIVE/TEN MILES APPROX.'

He was a resistance wireless operator in France winging out his final report before the Gestapo descended. He was a Marconi telegraphist on a sinking ship tapping a methodical and heroic SOS while lifeboats were being lowered. For better or worse, he couldn't say, nor needed to, fixed in his inviolable sphere of living darkness, determination and rectitude of spirit being the order of the day and night.

He repeated the message, neither fast nor slow, a speed at which no mistake could be made by a listener writing onto his pad, words sent as if flying through the worst of flak, as if the rest of the crew's lives depended on his getting the text away.

The code came through that his message was received and understood, his work done. He saw light instead of darkness for such effort as he pulled the key out, wrapped its flex around the earphones, and put them on top of the set, no more work left to do.

'What were you up to?' Waistcoat asked in an appalled tone. The click of his key had been unmistakable, the lit-up transmitter plain to see. 'You were sending morse.'

An idiot smile would be no defence, too late, anyway, yet he put one on – much to his shame. 'It was an exercise. I practise to keep my hand in.'

A light burst from his head, as vivid and wide as from the cannon shell which had blinded him. The blow at his temple and eyes pushed him up and back, all of Waistcoat's body behind it. A homely and welcoming noise of four Merlin engines roared in from the olden days, keeping the kite aloft on a heading for home.

He fell against the bulkhead, pulling the morse key as a lifeline towards him, the last item to leave go of, as a soldier who must never be parted from his rifle for fear of the firing squad. Waistcoat's metal weapon could have been a handgun and, no time to wonder more, grains of light like powder at last found the right chemical mix to settle Howard's sight. He catapulted upwards, as if flying, caught the breathless and aghast body, and sent it back at the shock. A screech told that his boot found Waistcoat's face, as if a beacon had guided him. He drove against the head with a sharp corner of his key, then pushed his way out to the deck.

Every part of the boat was known to his finger tips, but there were few hiding places. Excrescences of wood and metal were like parts of a body, all familiar, yet unable to help. Pain pushed out the boundaries of darkness, but he yearned to become smaller, gripping the rail for as long as he felt safe, hearing small waves chopping around at the slow speed of their blacked-out boat, which encouraged him and made it easy to find the stern. The choking in his lungs diminished, and he felt the approach of feet under him. A breeze turned his flesh into freezing liquid, which he knew to be blood.

'Come away from there, you blind bat!'

He crouched, hoping his enemy was equally confused by the dark.

'You're dead! Where are you?'

Waistcoat's hand was shaking, but pressure on the trigger packed a universe into the explosion. Light passed through Howard's eyes into the beyond of the boat's wake. The burn of the bullet's track had been close, but he grimaced, almost a smile because the noise would be heard for miles, its echo attenuating to where help might be found. Beneath the umbrella of its sound he moved to the starboard quarter like a sleek-footed animal avoiding the hunter.

The explosion seemed to make a hole in Richard's brain, but he stayed at the wheel, knowing that even without the whys and the wherefores something from the blackest night was on its way, a dread stalking them all. Waistcoat was the only other man on the boat who went armed, and the shot hadn't been aimed at seagulls: if Howard had been caught doing mischief, and was to pay for it, no one could help or interfere, because there was a point beyond which treachery couldn't be seen to pay.

Hearing the noise Cleaver stalked onto the bridge. 'Who did that?' The left fist slammed into his right palm. 'Come on, who was it?'

'It was me,' Waistcoat said. 'I've topped the blind bastard. Or hope I have. I couldn't tell, in the dark.'

'Another skipper up the zig-zags,' Cleaver said, almost to himself.

'No, not me,' Waistcoat said. 'Everything'll be all right if you leave him to me. He might try and send again.'

Cleaver turned himself into the Master Mariner, back on his authoritarian stance. 'If we go under it'll be you that's dead. I didn't get us so close to home for you to pull a stunt like this.'

Waistcoat's face was bloody, a crimson streak at one side. Nobody believed him, they had the wrong priorities, the stupidest prats you ever saw. 'I caught him tapping a message out.'

'Pull yourself together.' Cleaver tried to reason, though with little hope in his tone. 'We'll vanish before they get here. Full speed ahead, and we're out of the limit. Richard!' he shouted, a slight tremor of panic nevertheless. 'Let's get this menagerie back to sea.'

'We're too close inshore. What do you think those lights are? Scotch mist?'

'If you shoot again,' Cleaver said, seeing Waistcoat walk from one side of the bridge to the other, the gun pressed against his stomach as if warming it for further action, 'the bullet will land in somebody's parlour.'

Richard refused to change course till his rightful chief said so, the one who paid him and whose boat it was. You obeyed to the end, come what may. His father would endorse such a rule, though maybe not in the present situation. He felt cold steel at his cheek. 'I've a good mind to put one in you. You brought him on board,' was all he got for his assumption of loyalty. 'He's an Interpol stooge, and he's not even fucking blind. His eyes are as good as mine.'

'You told me to bring him. I didn't care one way or the other.'

Cleaver pulled Waistcoat clear, a grimace of disgust at having his face so close. 'Any nonsense, and over the side you go. I've had it up to here on this trip. We get back to sea and dump the stuff.' He pulled a pair of thin leather gloves from his pocket and put them on before taking the wheel, his six foot body braced for the turn from scattered shore lights showing left and right along the coast. 'Steam those engines up, Paul. They won't get me, but they can have the rest of you for a dog's breakfast as far as I'm concerned.'

Lines furrowed Cinnakle's forehead, but whether due to their peril, or because he might have to flog his beloved engines to nuts and bolts, no one could say. 'There's not all that much fuel left.'

'Use what there is. Shake 'em out of their cradles and get the best cracking speed you can. It's twenty years apiece if you don't.' He spoke firmly but quietly to Cannister: 'You and the others, pull the stuff out of the hidey-holes and let the mermaids have a party.'

He wished he could imitate in fast forward the Incredible Shrinking Man, as in a movie Laura once told him about, but smaller he could not get. In making his way back to the stern, after hearing them trying to deal with their problems, he knew that the storm was yet to come. Doubts that his message had been received tormented him, as if sending the signal was part of an old dream; or those who had taken it down were so dilatory that help would only come when they had finished their tea.

Blood wetted his shoulders, but what could not be seen was easy to ignore. The rhythmically pulsing pain was pushed to one side. People walked on fire. Wounds possessed their built-in anodyne. A beleaguered animal weakened from loss of blood. To avoid losing consciousness he listened to a horse clopping down a village street by a public house, saw a Land Army woman riding as if having somewhere to go, the golden brush of the mare's tail swinging at the trot. A collie dog followed, respecting the hooves. Hard to say why such a scene, but he scrubbed it when the pain went. The mind chucked up queer memories. A rope was loose somewhere.

Waistcoat was no crack shot, but the blow-by had been closer than he thought. A man was easy to miss in the dark. Coastguards, customs and police had been put on the *qui vive*. He hadn't been afraid to do it, that's all he knew, wanting no regrets. Training was everything, and though the drilling and instilling of moral fibre into the system happened so many years ago, the strength came through from it more than ever as he pressed a hand to the pain, and tried to recall in detail what had happened after the cannon shell hit the Lancaster.

All he saw were flowers on cigarette cards collected as a boy, celandine and ragwort, thistles and biting stonecrop in every colour of the spectrum, water lilies in harmony with the light he was beginning to see.

The swing of the boat wiped the soothing pictures clear, rolling him to the far side of the deck, his wound scraping against wood. He crushed back a groan, and aligned with fore and aft as the boat turned, gripped the rail to stay upright and look out to sea: no other boat but their own, steady on its track, a surge and chop of water before the new course stabilised.

Pain brought a light into half focus, showing him the darkness and a curling phosphorescence plainer because of the soft hiss. Inside or out, he couldn't be sure but, wanting to tear at the skin and prove it one way or the other, unclamped his free hand to search the deck carefully, knowing it was better to move than box himself into a fortress anybody could pull him out of. Rubbing the wound to clear away blood made yellowy orange lights to dance, a weird picture which, like others of the mind's eye, he wanted to live with.

Cleaver steadied the wheel at the surge of power, and Richard wondered how long before they stalled through lack of fuel. No subterfuge would save them, when the last drop spluttered into the engine. He took the wheel, hiding his fear. The night was too good for them, enough moon coming up to outline the boat like a metal cutout in an amusement arcade. 'Visibility at least twenty-five miles,' Cleaver said. 'But at this rate we'll lose 'em.'

Better to be halfway up river and ready to unload. Richard thought they should have gone straight in and taken a chance. Luck had always been theirs, and fortune favours the brave – as his father, a Meccano man of screws and flimsy girders, had too often said, the old bastard sometimes adding that 'speed was of the essence'. But Cleaver had tested chance once too often, and lost his Master's ticket. As for Howard, he should have waited till they were on shore, and gone to the nearest box where, for a few coins, he could have phoned whoever he thought would listen to his blind man's babbling. Someone could have dealt with him even before he finished dialling.

'Do you know how many millions this is going to cost us?' Waistcoat said, as if at the moment it was more important to save his precious cargo than get at Howard. 'It's not all mine. If we lose it they'll get me as well.'

'I'd rather lose a billion than go inside again. I'll have your guts for garters if we go up the spout. Your number will be well and truly up.' Cleaver turned, put himself face to face. 'It's the luck of the draw, so shut your scabby box.' Cork Light was coming up to starboard, meaning they were still less than three miles from shore. 'Wait till we're in the clear. The blind man won't get away from *me*.'

'Two boats coming up,' Cannister called out. 'They're boxing us in left and right.'

'When they're closer, alter course dead north. We'll get behind. I'll tell you what to do after that.'

Richard knew that all conviction had gone, especially from Cleaver, who would do more than anyone to save himself. As for the rest of us, we might just as well shut ourselves in the state room for a few last drinks. 'Here's to you! It was good while it lasted – happy days! We'll celebrate again when we get out! Oh yes, don't worry, lads, it might not be as long as you think.' No one had yet found the heart to throw the cargo into the water. 'Take over,' he told Cleaver. 'I need some air.'

'You can run like a rat, but they won't get me.'

As he went along the deck Richard glanced at the boats bearing down, streaks of white light more powerful than any their clogging vessel could produce. All he had to do now was keep Waistcoat away from Howard. A promise was a promise, and though Laura might not thank him for it, Howard's girlfriend doubtlessly would.

THIRTY-FIVE

The spin of the boat pulled her out of her dream: hard to remember the point, didn't suppose there had been one: Howard and Carla among palm trees on an esplanade, white boxy houses scattered up a hill, black clouds coming together, a fur-covered round table ringed with bottles, no one willing to drink. All very awkward, right? The landscape was painful to let go of, but it vanished utterly, and going back to search for it would take the rest of the night.

She stood naked to throw a jersey over her chest, pulled on knickers and slacks, tied her shoelaces. Got to see the fun on shore, would coax Howard from his radio to a pew by the rail, and after the unloading they'd pack their bits and pieces, shake goodbye hands at everybody, and make for the nearest bus or train. However long and dark the road they could stop any time for a kiss and cuddle, and think what to do on their first day of freedom.

The boat swung again, no straight run so what last minute change of plan had flooded the skipper's brain? St Vitus' Dance wasn't in it. Banging her shoulder against the bunk, she rubbed at the ache. Howard must be at his perch by the stern, as if watching all past life go by. What else could a blind man do? There'd be no more of that once they were on *terra firma*.

Shouts and more than the usual cursing from the bridge told that their arrangements had gone wrong. The boat was sheering away from the coast. She flashed her pocket torch at the deck, keeping the beam low. 'So here's my lover-boy!'

He whispered. 'Put it out.'

'The light? How did you know?'

Couldn't unravel the microdot to explain the impossible. 'I'm the *Flying Dutchman*, and you're the German Numbers Woman.'

'Oh yes, thank you very much, but what's that supposed to mean?'
The shadow drifted. 'A fantasy. A little joke.'

'You saw something. Hey, are you all right?'

'Yes, I'm in trouble, and I don't want you in on it.'

'I'm mystified. You can't stop me, though. Where you go, I go.'

'Better not. The chief's gone berserk. He's out to kill me. But let's not talk. Somebody'll hear us.'

She knelt, fingers along his cheek before a kiss. 'I don't care. Only stop messing about. Your face is wet.' She pressed the torch button, crying: 'I don't believe this. Who did it? Oh, I shouldn't have gone to sleep, but how could I know?'

'It's nothing. We're changing course again. North, by the feel of it. They won't get away.'

'You must have banged into something, but it's not like you.'

'I got into a fight with the chief. I alerted the coastguards. I'll vouch for you when they come. He caught me sending morse.'

Everything was in her tone, from thinking him the world's fool, to supposing that what he had done was beyond explanation. 'Oh, why? What the hell for?'

'It was the reason I did the trip.' Yes it was and no it wasn't. The truth was impossible to go into, a built-in yes and no to all questions, a cloud of wasps best to avoid. 'I really came to meet you.'

'I just don't understand.' She held him. 'You've got me flummoxed. Has everyone gone crazy? You're not blind after all. What *is* this?'

'I can't say.' A break in the barrier of darkness came from one angle and then another, a shade here and a form there, her shadow for one thing, yet silhouetting by the moment, which had to be mostly in the mind, because why now? 'Bits of my sight are breaking in. I didn't lie about it.'

'He's down there somewhere,' Waistcoat said. 'But he won't be for long. Root him out.'

'Not me.' Scuddilaw walked away. 'Do your dirty work yourself.'

He couldn't see more than anyone else on the blacked-out boat, but Howard smelled aftershave, whisky, and the rancid vegetation of a cigar, saw a flash of him as Judy moved in front.

'Get out of the way, you tart. He's mine.'

'Leave him alone.' She ran forward, but was thrown back. 'I don't care what he's done.'

'He's sold us down the river, you stupid bitch.' Braced against the rail, he was uncertain where to set his aim, a double murder not in the scale of things. 'Fuck off out of the way, or you go with him.'

Paralysis stopped her running, wanted to but didn't know how. 'If you touch him, I'll kill *you*,' was all she could say. Waistcoat wrenched her arm. She cried out at the pain and kicked back – all right to hurt such a man – to gain time. Two shots splattered the air, a brilliant pyrotechnic clearance for his purpose, but under fire Howard saw his chance, as if the old aircrew energy had taken root again – tinsel and confetti though he supposed it might be.

He reached for her hand, pulled her forcefully along the deck. Dimly uprising steps seemed made out of knitted wool, solid enough on climbing, and at the top she said: 'Two boats are heading this way. Do you see them?'

'The lights? Yes, I can.'

'Half a mile off. Less, maybe.'

'So we'll be all right.' Lamps in the blackout were doubted for a moment, then he couldn't deny they were real, two distinct top points of a V, a sight putting him in the spirit of what seemed to have been inexplicably given back. 'Let's have your torch.'

He buttoned out morse at the starboard boat, a steady and unmistakable SOS, the artful dots and dashes wonderfully sharp. Before dowsing the light he saw the cap and white face, a handgun circling the air. Fingers screwed into the injured eye brought clarity out of the moonlight. Waistcoat, taller than he had imagined, glanced at the boats, crying in a tone of hysterical despair: 'See what you've done? The fucking boats have got us.'

Judy ran in front, but Howard elbowed her away. The Luger was steady in Richard's hand: 'Leave him alone, Chief.'

'You can't frighten me with your replica.'

'It's real enough. So step aside.'

She pulled Howard into the darkness, as if the lights of the incoming boats had switched off, or never been there. The flash of the first shot wiped out interior scenes of ragged robin, clover pinkish among the green, hound's tongue, snake's head, deadly nightshade and blood-red poppies. Light was opening, but the flowers went. He grasped at her, all he could do. Another shot, though not for him, and the returned sight wavered as he fell into her arms, ice of water after a long time covering, as if they were going down together, the skin of consciousness bursting under anaesthetic.

'No!' she screamed. 'Love you!'

Richard's reflex had been a wasted effort. He leaned over the rail, a stab in the ribs threatening to bring up vomit. Nothing to do but watch the boats closing, lights again showing the slumped body of a fool who couldn't be saved, his own victim in the stupid game he had played. He pointed to Waistcoat's body. 'Get that over the side.'

'Why did you have to kill him?' Cannister said. 'Wasn't one enough? I take no more orders on this boat. And put that shooter away. You can't frighten me.'

His will went into meltdown at Judy's wailing. 'He's my boyfriend, don't you know?' She would yammer even more when the customs men came on board, babble till somebody (and it might well be me) smacked her in the chops to bring her right mind back. 'He's the one who put you wise,' she would inform them. 'He told me all about it. We planned it together but they shot him instead of me. Look though, he's still breathing.' Easy to know her thoughts, as she leaned against the rail to send a prayer over the water.

Not needing a weapon anymore he threw his Luger overboard, the first and last time he'd fired it. Let them drag the sea if they want evidence. Putting his shoe against Waistcoat's body he rolled it over and, taking the weight with both hands, let the bag of rubbish rest a moment, then heard its satisfying plunge into the water. The fishes would swim in loathing from it.

Blood smeared his shirt. Should have kept the carcass on board, but it was too late to make good. Always too late to make good. It would be scummed up on some holiday beach, already rotting so that a little boy building a sandcastle runs horrified to daddy, and daddy goes pale at the creaming snot of the water hitting the sandcastle's towers to bring them low, Waistcoat's dull eyes at the battlements he finally failed to climb.

Searchlights from the cutters – a crowded wheelhouse bristling with aerials – pinpointed the boat. His binoculars were a pair of the best eight-by-thirty Barr and Stroud, given by the old man before Richard set off for his first job at sea. 'They used to make range-finders as well, Barr and Stroud did, for the Royal Navy. This pair's been with me on all my voyages, but now I'm handing them on to you, so take good care of them.' Tears streaked his left cheek, recalling the death of his wife who hadn't lived to see this solemn moment with their son – otherwise as if the whole fucking merchant marine was stood to attention and looking on.

A bow wave opened like the ill-omened wings of a giant bird, the law-enforcing vessel on its unstoppable track, the air so still he could hear the engines. No need to look at both, he turned away and settled the magnification on a Martello tower squat against the moonlight. Hardness of heart was the order of the day. Let the sky come down and the moon as well. Behind him, in Slaughterhouse Lane, Judy was raving as if to get Howard back to consciousness: 'He isn't dead. I know he isn't. He can't be.'

Another bullet to finish the job would cost little enough in will or treasure, but the gun had been jettisoned and he wouldn't search for Waistcoat's. Nothing to be done or that he wanted to, musing as he walked away that Howard might have a chance if left alone, though if he died he ought to be buried with Waistcoat, a bit of old England in the same posh box. No doubt the blind fool would get a medal, if he pulled through, for giving away the biggest drug haul in history. Promotions all round, and twenty years in a high security jail for the rest of them.

The police and customs launches had heard the shooting, and there must be someone on board who knew first aid. They would rush up the side with dogs and axes, as the boat under his feet slowed on the last pint of fuel.

'I'm just the cook.' Ted Killisick wrapped a red and white woolly scarf around his neck, as if going down to his local for a pint and a sling or two at darts. 'They've got nothing on me. I was hired as a cook, that's all I know.'

And so the shopping and squealing would go on, while he would be too exhausted not to answer everything. The others would tell what lies came, though not for long. Stuck pigs would have nothing on them. 'Where's Mr Cleaver?'

Cinnakle straightened his tie. 'He went starkers over the side, a plastic bag with his precious sextant, and a length of rubber tube in his mouth. He must have more lives than a Siberian tomcat.'

'I don't suppose it's the first time he's made this sort of a getaway,' Richard said. 'But let's say he was never on the boat, right?'

'He kept the log' – Cinnakle's hands shook – 'didn't he?'

'Go to the bridge then, Ted, and get shot of it. I don't care how. One of us might as well go scot free.'

Killisick was glad to do something he was told. 'Yeh, I reckon he was the only real man among the lot of us.'

Judy's face, turned to the light as she cradled Howard, showed the tragic side of the moon. She keened like a banshee: 'He's losing all his blood.'

It had painted much of the deck. 'I can see that,' no help to give her, nor wanted to. Howard would be a hero if he lived, and have a good woman thrown in as a bonus.

'We need a helicopter to get him to a hospital,' she said. 'Send a mayday. You're a wireless man. Oh, please!'

The boats were as close as made little difference. A chopper would get lift off from the nearest base the moment they saw, because hadn't Howard always said that the RAF looked after its own?

He put cigarettes, clean shirt and underwear into his bag. Having shaved an hour ago, the smoothness would take him till midday tomorrow, and experience told him where he would be by then. It was good to look your best – and feel it – when questions came as from a pump-action shotgun. A final polish of his shoes got rid of Waistcoat's blood and, setting his cap at an angle proper to the occasion, he went out to welcome the boarding party. 'Always do everything in style,' was another axiom from the old man.

But what to say? Nothing to do with me. The skipper hired the boat, and took me on as one of the crew. How was I to know what the trip was all about? But such lies as the rest would tell wouldn't wash, though it might give time to think up a better story. Nothing would come of that, either. They tangled you up in no time. No need to say anything, for as long as you had the gall to keep quiet. In any case they would tell you what they wanted to hear. Howard would be the prosecution's witness, blind or not, and the stuff was there to find. It wasn't brown sugar they had picked up in the Azores, though he would leave them to say that, if such was their wit, which it certainly would be, smiles at all corners of their mouths.

No need to look hangdog. Englishmen never did – or so he had heard. He put all lights on, three boats lit up like Guy Fawkes night. They were as caught as caught could be, and the bumping and shouting would start any moment. He went to welcome them aboard: 'What's all this about, then?'

Judy pushed by, making a plain enough statement: 'We have someone wounded here on deck. Please be quick. He needs looking after. It's serious.'

THIRTY-SIX

The stream was set apart from the village, though the map placed the small agglomeration of houses *upon* it. Even so, it wasn't a long walk to the bridge where one could look down from the parapet at weeds on either side of the water divided by a low rock further down, furrowing thereafter on its self chosen route, a rural scene in a rarely visited part of the Wolds that he could look at forever. In its infant meandering from a spring up the hill the stream's hypnotic power calmed whatever spinal shivers might disturb his peace, though there was little enough beyond the minor worries of domestic life.

He'd heard it said that old habits died hard, but those discarded due to altered times only waited to be brought out again when needed. Habits were precious because they defined you, so he carried a wolf-headed walking stick to roam the lanes and fields, sometimes as slowly as during those never forgotten decades in the dark.

He put on his cap at the first touch of rain, drops from heaven making small craters in the water, concentric circles colourless yet visible. When Arnold was a year or so older they would follow the stream as a playful friend to where another brook came sidling in, two arms of silvery water widening until they joined the Witham and flowed through Boston to the Wash.

Arnold would enjoy the stroll on a summer's day, ceaselessly asking questions which Howard answered whether true or not so as to satisfy and not discourage. The miracle of his eye and heart would chase butterflies and beetles, take handbooks from his purple rucksack to identify flowers, adjust binoculars to magnify birds in flight.

No other spot to stand on than this little humpbacked bridge and watch the stream lapping its southerly way, no traffic beyond the

400

leisurely come and go of the village, no better place for a quiet and anonymous life. Judy had fetched him from the hospital and driven around the county saying that somewhere in it there would be a place to live. 'For the rest of our lives, right?' She laughed. 'I sometimes feel I've kidnapped you!'

'Turn left here.'

'Are you sure?'

'At the next fork. I don't know why. It was me who inveigled you, you know that.'

'Yes, but we fell in love, didn't we?' She had driven from Lincoln along lanes between the bare Wolds seemingly remote, and slowed for him to check the map, by a pub and a low wooden meeting hall on a curve of the village street, crows arguing in a winter tree by the churchyard.

He pointed. 'That's a house for us.'

'Oh, you beat me to it.' She stopped the car. 'The garden gate's open. Let's snoop around.'

The plain brick building had a slate roof, neat and square, about a century old, a wooden porch at the front door, tidy round about from whoever had recently left. An acceptable offer was put in the same afternoon, the For Sale sign adjusted to say so. 'Isn't it a bit sudden?' he said on their way back to the hotel in Lincoln.

'We like it, don't we?'

'You sound annoyed. But yes, we do.'

'It's just what we want.'

'When I did something quickly before it usually turned out to be the wrong decision, but it won't anymore, not now I'm with you.'

Such happiness could be worrying, whether deserved or not, yet everyone was worth the blessing when it came out of the blue, or emerged from a darkness so imperceptible that the lucky person hardly noticed. He smiled at his shivering reflection. She would scorn him if he confessed such nuances of unease, but how times had changed! What God hath wrought! Even the morse had all but died on him, such rhythmic discipline no longer necessary, though he occasionally turned on the radio so that Arnold could witness the writing down of a weather forecast from the Isles of Greece, a demonstration of more magic in the world than the boy yet knew about.

The stentorian enunciations of the German Numbers Woman had finally landed the *Flying Dutchman*: the vessel was impounded, rendered crewless and derelict. Now she was superannuated, and had more than enough to do governing her adolescent and rebellious children.

Vanya from his post in Moscow had gone up the hierarchy to administer the communications network of a whole region. Or he had emigrated to America and was halfway to making his first million. Arnold, drawing imaginary maps of the world, would have enjoyed playing 'Spot the Bomber' – but that too had come to an end.

These days embassies and the police used foolproof equipment which made it impossible to monitor their messages. The heroic hand-sent SOS's of former decades were replaced by a global positioning system, and much of the space between earth and the heaviside layer had turned into a cobwebbed graveyard of atmospherics and dusty memorial stones. Even so, Howard didn't doubt that arcane messages and revealing chatter were still there for the assiduous to alight on.

His old Marconi, plugged into the mains, buttressed a row of large print books, in the hidey-hole Judy allowed for his study. He remembered, when they called on Laura to collect his things, how Judy took his arm on getting close to the house where he'd lived for so long. 'You mean to say you walked up and down these steps every day?'

'I know them so well I could do them blindfold! They look so insignificant now.'

'Is that the house?'

'This is the first time I've seen it, but I'm sure it is.' He also felt trepidation, and took her hand. 'It's going to be all right.'

'She cut me dead when she saw me that time in the hospital and realised who I was. Not that it surprised me, but I was shocked at the look on her face.'

'That was three months ago. We're a bit older now.'

'You're always so matter of fact and optimistic.'

'Well, one of us has to be. Anyway, the letter was quite friendly.'

A teatime meal was set out in the living room, of fruit cake, biscuits and scones, sliced ham and boiled eggs, jam and honey, a feast of plenty which promised ease, though the meeting was cold enough at the start. She looked from Howard to Judy, as if failing to see how any man could live with such a despicable lesbian.

Passing the food she told them of going to see Richard in prison, that he was writing to her. He'd asked her to call on his father who, at her first visit, had shouted from the window that he no longer had a son. 'As you know,' she said to Howard, 'I'm never one to be put off, so I went up again, and this time he invited me in, and asked if it would be possible to go and see him.'

Judy wondered how Richard was.

'Well, in my opinion he shouldn't be there. He never complains, but the conditions are absolutely barbaric. That so-called trial was a travesty.' She turned to Howard: 'And you weren't much help to him in court.'

'I told them everything that happened.'

'Not enough, apparently. But I'll do all I can to get him paroled at the soonest possible moment. Fifteen years is a ridiculous sentence.' Her face was flushed, and she spoke with more passion than he'd ever heard, and he wondered why. 'I'll harry MPs and editors, judges and lawyers – everyone I can. I'll pester them till they can't stand the sight of me.'

Ebony jumped onto his knee to be stroked, as if remembering him. He smiled, that Laura had another aim in life. 'I hope you succeed.'

'Oh, I shan't rest till I do.'

He hadn't thought Richard's sentence undeserved, though decided that maybe it wasn't when Judy agreed: 'Yes, you should do all you can. He tried to save Howard, and me as well.'

Laura spoke whatever came to mind, in a way she hadn't in the days when he had been blind. 'I loved Richard,' she went on, 'and still do. Did you know – no, I suppose you couldn't have – that I had an affair with him before you went on the trip?'

'Oh, brilliant!' Judy exclaimed.

The trace of shame in Laura's smile was overridden by a glint of triumph in her eyes. Shock was printed on him, all the same. He hadn't known, and admitted it. His feelings at the time should have told him, but there'd been no chance to sort them out because of his search for someone else. The three of them suddenly seemed together in an inextricable knot, and it didn't seem unpleasant.

'I only tell you,' she laughed, 'because it can't matter any longer. The only thing I cared about, after Richard, was that you would be all right. It's amazing how life has changed, but I suppose it had to, sooner or later,' she went on, without bitterness he was glad to note, a sly aspect to her smile he could never have noticed before. 'Oh yes, I'm as happy as anyone can be. I go out a lot these days. There's always plenty to do.'

Judy followed her into the kitchen: 'I couldn't help it, you know.'

Laura, who had noticed the bulge in front, held her close, and placed a hand on her stomach as if wanting to feel the baby's pulse, tears hot when they fell on her cheeks during the long kiss. 'I'm glad about this.'

'You'll see whatever it is one day.'

She dried her face so as to collect the rest of the tea things, then talked as if wanting to tell whatever came to mind, though felt it too early to go into the story of her uncle. One day she would, because why not? Life was good when you had autonomy. Talking always made you feel better, and you could say what you liked, no need to hide anything anymore.

She helped them carry the radio and his old fold-up table to their big Peugeot Estate at the bottom of the steps. 'If there's anything else you want, take it now. I might not be in next time you call, though you can always give me a ring and I'll have it sent up.' Then she turned to Judy: 'I don't mean that: come and see me whenever you like.'

'She was fantastic!' Judy said on the drive uphill and out of town. 'So natural and easygoing. I almost fell for her myself. But don't worry, it's you I love.'

All in the past, except that nothing was, since it made the present and never went out of mind. Stitching together a timetable of events to show what exactly happened at the various way-change stations along the way told how he had gone into a near-fatal adventure because of being blind. Such a reverence for the past had pushed him so fundamentally out of it as to change his life absolutely. 'Maybe I imagined this sort of a future for us when I caught a packet on the deck of that morris-dancing boat.'

Judy shrugged. 'It's the way of the world. People go through worse.' She demanded that he think so too. 'Right?'

The spring never ran dry, rainy enough in the Wolds to keep the little river going. He wondered how much of Arnold's growing up he would live to see, though he could, on demand, or giving in to a fatherly wish of his own, carry him this far on his shoulders, and let him down to zig-zag along the bank for tadpoles. Once he slipped into the stream and, as Howard told Judy when she was halfway to giving the darling of her life a punch for carelessness, went in up to his thighs and lifted him out, he laughed, with the speed of morse.

Judy now and again called on the midwife at Skegness who had brought Arnold into the world, and sometimes stayed the night because: 'We have a few drinks, and I don't feel it would be safe to drive back,' knowing that Howard was well able to get Arnold on the school bus after a cooked breakfast and produce a hot meal when he came home. She seemed always to need a woman friend older than herself, but was usually in a vitriolic mood on getting back, against the two dogs whose jealousy, fussiness and habits she couldn't stand.

Laura sent a scientific calculator for Arnold's sixth birthday, and Judy had set the table with her old skill as a stewardess on yachts. Six candles for the cake, and Arnold in his place with hair combed and hands decisively at his fork and spoon. He had, as they had often marvelled, Judy's features and his father's mannerisms, Howard astonished at the similar timbre to Judy's in his voice.

He had helped to serve Arnold and his friends from school, and now that he was in bed they collected the debris, Judy scooping up paper from the presents. 'Look at the table. It's a wreck.'

'Just as it should be.'

'I often think,' she said, 'about how we nearly went over the edge of doom on that bloody boat. Just amazing we got through it. No wonder nothing can ever part us.'

'As long as we love each other. And we surely do.'

She dropped the armful of coloured papers to kiss him. 'You talk like a birthday card. Or a Valentine. I love it.'

'There's no other way I know.'

Arnold stood in the doorway, fastening his dressing gown. 'Oh dear, loving and kissing again! Brilliant!'

'Out!' Judy cried. 'Out, out, out!'

'I only wanted my calculator.'

'Now you've got it, so out.'

'Apart from which,' she said, Arnold clumping up the stairs, 'you'll always be my hero, the way you handled that boat business, even though the customs and police had been tracking the crew for months.'

'But the trip to the Azores was something they didn't know about. I gave them all the gen on that. It was priceless information, and they were glad to hand over the reward.'

She took the birthday cards from the shelf, and slid them into a large envelope, to be put away for Arnold's future. 'You only did it for the money.'

He laughed, and unravelled the story of listening to her and Carla on their boats. 'You were a dirty old devil!' she said.

'I know, but I fell in love with your voice, and knew it was our destiny to meet.'

'Oh, that. Let's not talk about destiny.'

'Well, I had no idea it would happen. I was too timid to be optimistic, but something carried me along.'

'That wasn't timid at all – though I don't believe anything you say.' She pulled him down on the sofa, and they sat together. 'Still, I like to hear the story over and over again, even if you did make it all up to amuse me. And if you didn't it's something else to love you for, so let's go to bed. We'll put the light out, and make hot love. I feel like it. As long as that little devil doesn't hear us!'

He gave one more glance at the ribbon of water, before turning to go home.